P9-DOH-383

Every Dog Has His Day

JENN McKINLAY

JOVE
New York

A JOVE BOOK
Published by Berkley
An imprint of Penguin Random House LLC
375 Hudson Street, New York, New York 10014

Copyright © 2018 by Jennifer McKinlay Orf
Excerpt from *Wedding Cake Crumble* by Jenn McKinlay
copyright © 2018 by Jennifer McKinlay Orf
Penguin Random House supports copyright. Copyright fuels creativity, encourages
diverse voices, promotes free speech, and creates a vibrant culture. Thank you for buying
an authorized edition of this book and for complying with copyright laws by not
reproducing, scanning, or distributing any part of it in any form without permission.
You are supporting writers and allowing Penguin Random House to continue to
publish books for every reader.

A JOVE BOOK and BERKLEY are registered trademarks and the B colophon
is a trademark of Penguin Random House LLC.

ISBN: 9780399584763

First Edition: January 2018

Printed in the United States of America
1 3 5 7 9 10 8 6 4 2

Cover photos: Winter landscape © S_Photo / Shutterstock Images; Standard poodle ©
Teemu Tretjakov / Shutterstock Images; Man lifting woman up © Tom Merton /
Gettyimages
Cover design by Katie Anderson
Book design by Kelly Lipovich

For the Hub, Chris Hansen Orf,
and the Hooligans, Beckett and Wyatt.
My love for you three troublemakers is without end.

Acknowledgments

Writing these books, I feel so very fortunate to have my own "Maine crew"—Kate Seaver, Christina Hogrebe, Katherine Pelz, Amelia Kreminski, Ryanne Probst, and all of the fabulous readers who have taken this series to heart. I am ever grateful for all of the effort, time, attention, hand-holding, positive feedback, and encouragement you all have offered me over the course of this book, as well as the others in the Bluff Point series. Truly, you make this the best job in the world, and I can never thank you enough.

Chapter 1

"Yeoooow!"

Ugh. Zachary Caine was pretty sure the seizure-inducing caterwauling that was harshing his mellow was annoying enough to reanimate the dead, of which he was one.

He was lying on his overstuffed blue leather recliner couch, affectionately known as Big Bertha, which he'd had since his college days, while watching Sunday playoff football on mute because the unexpected houseguests he had were still asleep upstairs in all three of his bedrooms.

In what had seemed like a singular act of good manners at the time, he had insisted his company take the beds in his house while he took the couch. Now, having spent a sleepless night on Big Bertha because she had a dip in her middle the size of the Grand Canyon, he was sure his spine had been reconfigured into a serpentine S curve of pain. Clearly, chivalry was overrated.

Generally a cheerful, happy-go-lucky sort, Zach was feeling a tad surly. He glared at his couch mate Rufus, the cinnamon standard poodle he was dog sitting for a friend, who looked at him from beneath the poof of curly hair on his head as if trying to determine whether Zach wanted him to bark or not. Zach met his gaze and watched as Rufus rolled over and fell back asleep.

"Really?" Zach asked the dog, who ignored him. "Isn't it your job to investigate strange noises or at the very least bark at them?"

Rufus yawned and Zach watched as his eyes rolled back into his head.

"Yeoooow!"

Crap! What was making such a racket? Zach rolled onto his side, flinching through the back pain, and pulled a pillow over his head.

"Yeoooow!"

Argh! The wailing cut right through the fluffy pillow and now he could hear the sound of voices outside his front door, too. No, no, no! Go away! Seriously, if it was a door-to-door salesman, he might punch the guy in the throat on principle. His doorbell rang.

That did it! Zach threw the pillow across the room and pushed himself up to his feet. His back muscles protested by clenching into a hot ball of pain. He huffed out a breath and forced himself to shuffle to the door.

It was Sunday. Wasn't it supposed to be a day of rest? Why were people forcing him to be upright? And moving? It was just so wrong!

He unlocked the door and yanked it wide. He opened his mouth to bark at the rude people on his porch, since Rufus clearly wasn't going to do it, but the words never left his lips. Standing in front of him were two little cherubs with pink cheeks and tousled curls poking out from under their woolen hats, looking up at him with big blue imploring eyes. Uh-oh!

"Hey, mister," the littler one said. "We need your help."

Zach squinted at her. If this was a Girl Scout cookie dealer, he was all in. Those little round yummies of caramel coconut chewy goodness were his crack.

"Yeooooooow!"

Zach clapped his hands over his ears. There it was, that hideous noise again, only louder.

"Oh, no, he's getting upset!" The taller girl hurried off his porch and back down his walkway. She stopped a few feet away and stared up at his roof. "It's okay, boy, it's okay. We're getting help."

What the . . . ? Zach shoved his feet into the Timberland boots he'd discarded by his front door and strode across his porch, down the steps, and onto the walk. The icy cold air of January in Maine felt like a closed-fist punch in the face, making him wince, but at least it was a new pain and distracted him from the ache in his back.

He stood beside the girl in the purple coat and glanced up. Peering at him over the lip of the narrow porch roof was a tiny orange tabby not much bigger than his fist.

The smaller girl in a blue coat joined them. She glanced up and looked exasperated. Then she wagged her pointer finger at the feline and said, "You are a naughty kitty."

"Can you get him down for us, sir, please?" the girl in purple asked. "He's just a baby. He might freeze to death."

"Yeoooooow!"

For a little guy, he sure had decent lung capacity. For a wide variety of reasons, not the least of which was to end the cat's howling, Zach knew there was no way he was getting out of this without getting the kitten down.

"What's his name? Kitty?" he asked.

"No." The younger one shook her head. She gave him an exasperated look. "We call him Chaos."

Zach looked at her droll little face and laughed.

"Of course you do," he said. "Good name."

The frigid winter air started to seep into his under-dressed hide and he shivered. Flannel pajama bottoms and a thermal shirt were no match for temperatures in the twenties.

"Wait here and keep an eye on him," he said. "I'm going to get my ladder."

The girls looked so relieved he almost felt heroic. Glancing up at the kitten, who continued yowling, he figured he'd better save the self-congratulations until after he got the little furball down.

As he strode back into the house, Rufus passed him, looking fierce. He barked, low and deep, and Zach shook his head at him.

"Too little too late, my friend," he said.

Rufus ignored him and bounded toward the girls. The older one looked nervous and backed up, but the younger girl opened her arms wide.

"You have a dog?" she cried, as if this were the greatest news ever.

"Sort of," he said. "I'm temporarily dog sitting him. Don't worry, he loves kids."

As if to prove Zach right, Rufus dropped onto his back in the snow at the girls' feet, offering his belly for rubs. Both girls laughed and Zach hurried inside, grabbed a thick chambray shirt off the back of a chair, and drew it on without bothering to button it. He then took the short-cut through the small house to the garage door.

He lifted the ladder off its wall brackets and opened the side door that let him back out into his front yard. He didn't want to raise the garage door for fear he'd scare the kitten into doing something stupid. Although one could argue that climbing onto his roof was pretty dumb to begin with, especially on a day when the high temperature was twenty-seven degrees and the ground still had a few feet of snow on it from the icy dumping they'd gotten yesterday. How had the little scrapper gotten up there anyway?

He set the base of the ladder on the ground and propped the top against the porch roof. It took some adjusting, but when it felt steady he began to climb. Not a fan of heights, Zach wasn't surprised when the world did one swift revolution, forcing him to grip the sides of the ladder. He closed his eyes for a second, allowing the vertigo to pass before he attempted to continue on.

"Hurry, mister, he's stopped crying. I think his voice is frozen," the little one ordered.

"Please hurry," the older one added.

Zach opened his eyes and kept going. He was almost at the roof when a shriek sounded from next door. Dang, this had to be the loudest Sunday in the history of the neighborhood.

"Maddie! Gracie! Where are you?" a woman's voice cried.

"Over here, Momma," the younger one answered. She waved as if her mother needed the visual to notice the man on the ladder just twenty yards from where she stood, looking bug-eyed and frantic.

The woman looked as disheveled as Zach felt as she raced across the two yards to grab her girls close.

"What are you doing over here?" she cried. "Girls, you know the rules. You are never to leave the backyard without me. I went inside for a tissue and when I came out, you were both gone! You scared me to death!"

She kissed one head and then the other, as if to reassure herself that they were fine.

"Yeooooooow!" Clearly put out that he didn't have everyone's attention, Chaos let loose his loudest, most grating yowl yet.

Zach was pretty sure his ears had started to bleed. He gritted his teeth and climbed to the top, determined to get this cat and his people away from his Sunday sanctuary of playoff football, nachos, and naps.

"We found Chaos, Momma, he's on this man's roof," the older one said.

"Oh, hi, Zach," she said. She glanced up and when her gaze met his, her face turned bright red. "I'm sorry. You don't have to do that. I can climb up there."

Jessie Connelly. Zach had met her a few months ago when he'd brought his friend's foul-mouthed parrot into the local veterinary office where Jessie worked. He'd made the mistake of calling her "sweetheart," and she had let him have it. He was pretty sure he still had scars from the tongue-lashing she'd given him.

At the time, he'd had no idea that they were neighbors. Jessie had been all too aware that he lived next door and she had a lot to say about how she assumed he lived his life. Being a live-and-let-live sort, Zach had steered clear of her ever since.

He must have done a heck of a job avoiding her, because up until now he'd had no idea that she had two daughters. He wondered if she was feeling bad about their last meeting now that he was saving her daughters' kitten.

Feeling mischievous, he almost called her "sweetheart" or "honey" or "baby girl" just to see if she'd rip into him again.

"Yeeeooooow!"

Luckily, the kitten was keeping him on task. He turned back to the cat, calling over his shoulder, "Don't worry. I've got this."

He trudged up the ladder. When he was nose to nose with the cat, he paused to figure out the best way to grab it. The orange tabby with pale green eyes looked cold and miserable and Zach realized if anyone was having a worse Sunday than he, it was this cat. He held out his hand, thinking the cat would be grateful to climb aboard. The cat took a swipe at him. Okay, then.

"Really?" he asked it. "I'm trying to help you out here."

The cat hissed and his little back arched. The critter had spunk, Zach would give him that. He'd been out here awhile now and it was bone-achingly cold. How the little guy hadn't turned into a furry ice cube Zach couldn't fathom.

He reached out again, trying to coax the feisty feline with reassuring words.

"It's okay, little fella," he said. "I'm not going to hurt you. I'm just going to get you off the roof so you can go home with your people."

He held his hand still and Chaos cautiously sniffed his cold skin. Zach didn't know how much longer he could stay out here without gloves and not lose his fingers. He silently willed the cat to trust him.

When Chaos put a cautious paw on his hand and Zach reached out with his other hand to grab the kitten, Rufus let out a bark of encouragement. A loud one. The cat jumped and hissed, causing Zach to jump and his ladder to wobble. Still, he managed to grab the cat by the scruff of the neck.

He hauled the little furball into his chest, clutching him close with both hands. When he tried to step down without the use of his hands, he felt the bottom of the ladder shift from all of the movement above. As if in slow motion, the ladder tipped away from the roof of the porch.

"Oh, no, mister, look out!" one of the girls cried.

It was too late. Zach couldn't grab the roof without dropping the cat. He couldn't risk the little guy like that, so he tucked him into his chest and just relaxed his body into the fall. The ladder slid, wobbled, slid again, and the next thing Zach knew he was free-falling toward the ground.

Having no idea what he was going to land on, Zach had to revise his earlier assessment. He was most definitely having a worse Sunday than the cat.

Chapter 2

Thump! Zach felt his body drop into a soft cushion of freezing cold snow. The icy, wet chill engulfed his entire body and snow fell in on top of him, burying him in the large snowdrift. Chilly, but at least his head hadn't split like a big cantaloupe on his paved driveway.

"Oh, my god! Are you all right?" Jessie cried as she hurried forward.

Zach popped his eyes open to find her staring down at him. Her big blue eyes were filled with alarm and she was uselessly flapping her bare hands at her sides as if she were trying to achieve liftoff. Her green puffy coat was unzipped and her woolen hat with the oversized pom-pom, earflaps, and braids was askew, allowing a chunk of two-tone bangs to drape over her forehead, almost covering her eyes.

Before he could answer her, she dropped to her knees beside him and began to brush him off, digging him out of the pile of snow.

"Chaos, see what happens when you wander off?" the

younger girl chastised the cat as her older sister scooped him off Zach's chest and held him close.

Rufus sniffed the kitten, who ignored him and burrowed into the girl's coat.

"Thanks, mister." The younger sister joined her mother in the snowbank and grabbed Zach's hands with one of her icy cold mittens, not that Zach could feel anything, as his fingers were pretty much numb. She tried to pull him up but he was still half buried.

"We need to get you inside," Jessie said. She began to brush the snow off his pajama bottoms. "You're frozen."

"No, no, I'm fine," he protested. With Jessie's hands brushing off *all* of his body, he was suddenly relieved that he was numb from the chest down. His teeth began chattering as he tried to roll to his feet without success. "J-j-just g-glad you have y-your cat back. You should p-probably t-take him home now."

"We'll help you inside first," she insisted.

Jessie braced her feet against the icy part of the snowbank and used her body weight to haul him to his feet. She was stronger than she looked and he fell against her, slipping on the icy ground as he tried to get his balance. He flailed and one hand landed on her shoulder while the other latched onto the front of her coat. It took him a second to realize he was clutching her boob and he jumped back, dropping his hand and skidding on a patch of ice in his effort to get away from her.

"Sorry, sorry," he said. He raised his hands in the air as if trying to prove he hadn't been trying to cop a feel.

Jessie looked startled and then like she was trying not to laugh as his feet scrabbled on the slippery ground and his arms windmilled as he tried to get his balance. She pursed her lips and stepped forward, catching him about the waist and pulling one of his arms over her shoulder.

"Come on," she said. "Before you damage something permanently."

"No worries. My dignity has already been frozen off," he said.

This time she did laugh.

"Maddie, go get the door for us, sweetie," she said.

The younger girl in the blue coat scampered up the steps and pushed open his front door. Jessie half carried, half dragged him up the steps with Rufus and the other girl—whom she had called Gracie—bringing up the rear, still holding Chaos the kitten.

Zach did a quick scan to make sure his sparsely decorated bachelor pad didn't have any stray underwear or socks kicking around or anything else that might damage a young girl's psyche. Other than an empty pizza box on the counter and a newspaper on the coffee table, the place was clear. The game was still on and he glanced at the screen to catch the score. His Cowboys were up. Amen!

Living in Patriot country, he knew his love of the Texas team was blasphemy, so he tried to keep it on the down-low, but he had fallen hard for the team during his childhood in California, playing youth football during Dallas's Troy Aikman and Emmitt Smith reign, and he'd never given them up.

Jessie helped him over to the couch and he resumed his seat. She grabbed the thick black and gray afghan his mother had knitted for him and tucked it around his shoulders.

"Do you want some coffee?" she asked. "Tea? Hot chocolate?"

"Hot chocolate!" Maddie cried.

"I wasn't asking you," Jessie said. "I was asking . . ."

"Mister," Maddie said. "I call him mister."

Zach smiled despite his shivers. "My name is Zachary Caine, but my friends call me Zach."

"Am I your friend?" Maddie asked. She hit him with a steady blue gaze and he noticed that her sister stood motionless behind her, watching their interaction.

"We're neighbors," he said. "I think it's mandatory that we become friends, don't you?"

A blindingly bright smile lit Maddie's face and she nodded. He glanced at Gracie and was pleased to see a small smile tip the corners of her lips.

"You're right," Jessie said. "I know the last time we met, I was not at my best. Please forgive me?"

Zach stared into her big blue eyes full of beguiling warmth and humor and felt her working the same magic on him that her daughters had when they'd pleaded for their cat's rescue. He could no more refuse her than he could her girls. It occurred to him then that these women were dangerous to his peace and tranquility; still, he'd been raised hip deep in women and it was ingrained in him to look after them.

"Of course," he said.

"Thank you," she said. "Please call me Jessie, and these are my daughters, Maddie and Gracie."

"Pleased to meet you," Zach said. He gave the girls his most winning smile. Maddie smiled back while Gracie turned a faint shade of pink and buried her nose in her cat's fur.

"So, do neighbors have hot chocolate together?" Maddie asked. Her look was sly and Zach almost laughed.

"Yes, I think they do," he said. He started to get up but Jessie waved for him to sit.

"Sit. Warm up," she said. "I'll get it."

The bottom floor of Zach's house was an open floor plan, so while he visited with the girls, Jessie crossed the room into his kitchen area. She stood in the center as if trying to figure out where everything would be without having to open every cupboard.

"Mugs are in the cabinet over the coffee maker, hot chocolate is on the top shelf of the pantry to the right of the fridge, milk is in the fridge, and the microwave is on the counter," he called.

"Got it." Jessie gave him a thumbs-up and set to work.

"How's Chaos doing?" Zach asked Gracie. He was a little worried that the cat might have gotten hurt in their fall. He had tried to cushion him as best as he could but the kitten was tiny and had smacked his chest hard when they landed.

Gracie unzipped her jacket and took the kitten out. He

had curled up into a sleepy little ball and when she opened her coat, he mewled in protest.

Maddie reached up and gently stroked his head and the kitten stretched out under the attention, letting them see that he was just fine.

"Chaos is a tough kitty," Maddie said. "We think he's going to grow up to be a real live tiger."

Zach raised his eyebrows. "Really?"

Maddie held up her hands and made claws out of her fingers. "Roar!"

"Impressive," Zach said.

"I've been teaching him," Maddie said with the assurance only a child still in the single digits in age could muster when speaking of the improbable.

"Is that you?" Gracie asked.

Zach turned his head to see her pointing to a series of photographs that hung on the wall in his dining alcove.

"Not just me," he said. "Rufus, too."

Gracie busted out a belly laugh. Zach felt his lips tip up in the corners. As the quieter of the two, he suspected Gracie didn't share her emotions as easily as her younger sister. Making her laugh felt like an achievement.

"What's so funny?" Maddie asked. She crossed the room to join her sister. She glanced from the framed portraits to Zach and Rufus, who was once again sprawled on his portion of the couch, and back to the pictures. Then she, too, started to laugh. It was a good sound.

"Girls, what's the racket?" Jessie asked as she came into the living room with four mugs of cocoa, two handles in each hand.

"Mommy, Zach and Rufus . . ." Gracie couldn't go on. She pressed a hand to her stomach and laughed some more.

Jessie quirked an eyebrow at Zach in question but he just shrugged. She put the mugs down on the newspaper on the coffee table and joined her girls. She pressed her fingers to her mouth, which only forced the laugh out of her nose in a snort.

Her eyes went wide with embarrassment, but the sound made the girls laugh harder, and she dropped her hand and joined them. She ushered the girls back into the living room and passed out the mugs of cocoa.

"Explain, please," she said as she handed Zach his mug.

"Where to begin?" he mused.

"The matching outfits?" Jessie suggested. Her big blue eyes, the same ones her daughters had trained on him, twinkled.

"The Fourth of July," Gracie said.

"No, Thanksgiving," Maddie said.

Zach glanced at Rufus. As if he knew he was the topic of conversation, the dog sat up on the couch and struck a pose, sitting at attention like he was in on the conversation. Zach was only surprised he didn't demand his own mug of cocoa.

"Rufus's mom person used to work for me at the Bluff Point brewery," he began.

"What's a brewery?" Maddie asked.

"It's where they make beer," Gracie said.

"Just so." Zach nodded at her. Then he narrowed his eyes. "How old are you?"

"Seven," Gracie said. "She's five. They don't know as much."

"Do, too," Maddie huffed. She gave her older sister an outraged look and muttered, "I know more than you do."

"Do not," Gracie said.

Before they began the squabble they were winding up for, Jessie said, "Girls, do you want to know about Zach and Rufus and the matching outfits?" They both nodded, and Jessie said, "Then maybe we should let Zach speak."

"Sorry," Gracie said.

"Sorry, mist . . . er . . . Zach," Maddie said. She picked up her mug, imitating her mother's dainty hold on her cup, and gave him her full attention.

Zach had always liked kids; his friends speculated that it was because he was so in touch with his inner child, but he found their honesty and zest for life refreshing. He suppressed a grin and took a sip.

He looked at Jessie in surprise. This was not the cocoa from the box of premeasured pouches in his cupboard. She had clearly done some magical voodoo mojo in his kitchen when he wasn't looking. The cocoa, which when he made it usually had a thick coating of powder floating on top, was rich and creamy and had a tiny kick of heat to it.

"Secret recipe," Jessie said. She winked at him and Zach blinked. Had Jessie Connelly always been this adorable?

She pushed her hat off of her head and he noticed that since he'd last run into her, she'd cut her long blonde hair and now it was a much darker shade, but with a couple of inches of the lighter blonde still on the tips. It was styled in a messy shoulder-length hairdo that framed her heart-shaped face becomingly, making her look as if she were barely out of high school.

"Story, Mister Zach," Maddie said. Her voice was so demanding he was surprised she didn't snap her fingers in his face.

"Maddie," Jessie's voice held a note of censure.

Maddie sighed and said, "Story, please, Mister Zach."

She looked as if she would expire on the spot if he didn't tell the story right *now*. Zach nodded. He got that.

"Here, let me show you," he said. "Rufus, come here, boy."

Rufus bounded across the couch to sit beside Zach. He looped his arm around the dog and put his head next to Rufus's. Despite the difference in their hair color, they had a marked similarity of expression, which had started the whole dressing-as-twins-and-having-pictures-taken thing.

"Look at our faces," Zach said. "We could be twins, am I right?"

All three women stared at them, glancing back and forth as they assessed their features. Gracie nodded and spoke first, saying, "You have the same nose and eyebrows."

"And fuzzy faces," Maddie said. She patted Zach's unshaven chin and then Rufus's.

"It's uncanny," Jessie said. She quickly took a sip of her cocoa so Zach couldn't tell if she was hiding her smile in her mug or not.

"Rufus's person, Amanda Willoughby, was the brewery accountant, and she always brought Rufus to work with her. Since everyone said Rufus and I look alike, I decided to take a picture of the two of us dressed in matching outfits for her birthday. Her birthday is March fifteenth, so I went with togas and laurel wreaths," Zach said.

"The Ides of March." Jessie nodded. "Togas were the natural choice."

"Right?" Zach asked. He grinned. Cute and smart and a helluva cocoa maker, there was clearly more to Jessie Connelly than he had figured. He took a sip of his hot chocolate. He liked the spice. "Anyway, Amanda thought it was hilarious so she sent it to our social media team to use and they blasted it out there and the next thing I knew, Rufus and I had our own following, so now we dress up for laughs and use it to promote the brewery."

"Does Amanda live here?" Gracie asked.

"No," Zach said. "She's in England. Her husband got transferred and she went with him. They couldn't take Rufus so I offered to keep him until they decide if they are staying in England or not."

"You're fostering Rufus like we're fostering Chaos," Maddie said. "Except I don't want to foster him; I want to keep him."

"We've talked about this, Maddie," Jessie said. Her voice was mild but firm. "Pets are a lot of responsibility and Chaos, well, he gets into things."

Judging by the kitten's ability to get onto Zach's roof, he had to figure this was the understatement of the century. He met Jessie's gaze and they shared a look of complete understanding.

"Hey, Zach, sorry to be a pest but do you have an extra toothbrush?"

Zach whipped his head in the direction of the doorway. Standing there, wearing nothing but one of his oversized sweatshirts and a pair of leggings, was Savannah Kelly, one of his field marketers.

Chapter 3

"Uh . . ." he stalled. He'd been so enjoying Jessie and the girls, he'd forgotten he had houseguests. Awkward.

Jessie glanced from Savannah to him and then to the floor like she wasn't sure where she should look. Her face turned a hot shade of pink as if she'd walked in on them naked or doing the horizontal mambo or something.

"It's not what you—" he began but Jessie interrupted him.

"Oh, wow, just wow!" she cried. "Look at the time."

Maddie and Gracie both glanced around the room, looking for a clock. There wasn't one in his living room.

"We have to go, girls, *now*!" she said. Jessie jumped up from her seat and set her mug of cocoa on the table.

"But I haven't finished my cocoa," Maddie protested.

Gracie glanced from her sister to her mother and Zach had a feeling that the contest of wills in their house was usually between Jessie and Maddie with Gracie as observer.

"We have cocoa at home," Jessie said.

Her voice was firm and direct in a very do-not-argue-with-me tone, and Zach felt himself sit up straighter even though she wasn't talking to him.

Maddie met her mother's eyes and took a deliberately slow sip from her mug in blatant defiance of Jessie's orders. Zach had to admire the kid's spunk even though he knew as a grown-up he shouldn't approve.

"Oh, don't leave on my account," Savannah said. "I'm just crashing here because of last night's storm."

She strolled into the room and smiled at everyone. With her hair tumbled about her shoulders and her face free of makeup, she didn't look much older than the girls.

Zach did some quick mental math. At twenty-two, Savannah had fifteen years on the girls and she was twelve years his junior, putting her right in between them in age.

He was about to explain further about his field marketers being stranded after last night's storm buried their cars in snow at the brewery, but he never got the chance.

"Our cat got stuck on Zach's roof," Maddie said. She stood and tugged on her sister's sleeve. "Show her."

Gracie unzipped her coat and Chaos's little head poked out.

"Oh," Savannah cried. "She's precious."

"He," Maddie corrected her.

"He is precious." Savannah smiled.

She rubbed Chaos's little orange head with the tip of one well-manicured finger. Even from all the way over on the couch, Zach could hear him purr. Oh, sure, take a swipe at the guy who saves your behind but purr for the ladies. Wily cat.

"Savannah, does Zach have—oh, hi." Desiree Markowitz appeared at the base of the stairs.

She was tall and leggy like Savannah but where Savannah was all tousled honey hair and big blue eyes, Desiree was deep brown almond eyes, dark skin, and a head of massive black spiral curls that bounced down past her shoulders.

Zach glanced over at Jessie. Her eyes were wide and she looked as if she'd lost her powers of speech.

"Desi, look at this kitten," Savannah said.

"Oh, totes adorbs," Desiree said. She bent over to rub his head and Chaos stretched in Gracie's arms, loving the adoration.

"Yo, bitches, did you get—oh, crap," Marla Bikstrom said as she stepped into the room and took in the sight of the two young girls. "Sorry, I didn't know we had little ears in the house."

With her short spiky red hair and hazel green brown eyes, Marla was the firecracker in the group. She was also the one with the foulest mouth, worst taste in men, and lousy impulse control. Of all of his field marketers, Marla was the one Zach lost the most sleep over.

He refused to acknowledge how much of a mother hen that made him. He was just a responsible business owner, nothing more. He glanced at the six females in front of him. The scales had clearly tipped. Six females to one male; he was way outnumbered even if he counted Rufus and Chaos.

"It's fine," Jessie said. Her voice sounded high and tight, however, and Zach got the feeling things were anything but fine.

"Girls, clearly, Za—er, Mister Zach is busy, so we should leave him to it . . . um . . . them, rather, okay, let's go," Jessie said.

When Maddie looked like she would resist, Jessie bent down and scooped her up into her arms, propping her on one hip as she strode to the door. Gracie tucked Chaos back into her coat and followed.

Zach jumped up from the couch and hurried to open the door for Jessie. She didn't make eye contact with him as she passed; instead she stared behind him out into the yard.

"Thanks again," she said.

"No problem," he said.

Before Jessie could leave, Maddie pitched herself backwards until her little fist caught Zach's chambray shirt, using it like an anchor to keep her mother from leaving. Zach had to scramble to keep from losing his shirt.

When he stepped closer, Maddie looped her little arms around his neck and squeezed him tight. Her cheek was soft against his and the scratchy wool hat she wore rubbed against his temple.

"Thanks for saving Chaos," she said. She pulled back to look him straight in the eye. "You're our hero."

Zach lifted his eyebrows at the high praise. Then he reached up and tweaked her nose. "Thanks, Maddie, that's sweet of you to say. I'm always here if you need me."

Maddie's big blue eyes scrutinized his left eye and then the right as if trying to determine if he was telling her the truth. She puckered her lips and nodded. With a final soft pat on his shoulder, she let her mother carry her out of the house.

Gracie glanced up at him from beneath the edge of her hat as if she wanted to say something or do something but she wasn't sure what. Zach smiled at her.

"Take care of Chaos, okay?" he said.

She nodded her head in tight little jerks, still looking like she wanted to speak but couldn't find the words.

"Here," Zach said. He held up his fist and Gracie's eyes went wide in surprise. "Give me bones."

"W-what?" she stammered.

"Fist bump," he said.

"Oh!" She lifted up a closed fist and tapped it against his.

Zach tipped his head to the side, considering. "That's kind of lame and the exploding-fist thing is so five years ago. Huh. What can we add to it to make this high five just ours?"

"I don't know," she said. She glanced down as if the answer might lie on the floor. "Maybe we could tap elbows after we tap fists?"

"I like it!" Zach said with a grin and a nod. "We'll hit elbows and then bring it home with another fist bump. Let's do this."

He held up his knuckles, Gracie banged fists with him, then they both bent their elbows and tapped them together, and then they knocked their fists together again. When Gracie met his eyes afterwards, hers were shining and the small smile she'd worn before had morphed into a big old grin.

"See ya, Zach," she said. She bounced down the stairs, holding one arm across her middle to keep Chaos steady.

"See ya, Gracie," he said.

Jessie waited at the bottom of the steps and when Gracie fell in beside her, she put her free arm around her and the three of them cut across the side yard and back to their house. Zach felt a small pang of regret in his chest. He had the feeling of a missed opportunity. He doubted he'd be seeing much of Jessie or her girls again and he was surprised to find the thought bothered him.

"Zach, my body hair is growing every moment I linger," Marla said. "Wanna help a girl out with a razor?"

Zach stepped back inside and closed the door. He turned to face his kitchen, where Desiree was brewing a pot of coffee while Savannah toasted a bagel.

"Marls, we've talked about your boundary issues," Zach said. He gave her the hairy eyeball. Since he had five younger sisters there wasn't much that fazed him about girl talk. In fact, his field marketers all seemed to think of him as the big brother they could say anything to. On the one hand, he liked that they trusted him, but on the other, there were some things he could live without knowing—for example, Marla's body hair issues.

"I thought that was when I was working the field," she said. "You know, not to share with customers when I'm feeling a tad crampy."

"Yeah, and now you can add hairy to that list," he said.

"Fine." She rolled her eyes and said, "Now can I have a razor?"

"Look under the sink in the guest bathroom cupboard," he said. "I think my sister left some girl stuff in there."

"Thanks, Zach, you're a peach," Marla said. She spun on her heel and jogged up the staircase.

Zach went back to the coffee table and picked up the leftover cups of cocoa. He noticed that Maddie had finished hers, but Gracie's was only half gone. He passed Savannah on his way to the sink.

"Cute kids," she said. She was giving him a sidelong glance.

"I suppose," he said with a casual shrug.

Such a liar. Those two little sprites were freaking adorable, but he knew better than to gush over a kid in front of a woman. It made them think he was good father material—he wasn't—and then they started to either try and reel him in or hook him up with a friend who was looking for a baby daddy. No thank you.

As the older brother to two households of sisters—Zach's parents had divorced when he was a baby and they each went on to remarry and have all daughters, two for his dad and three for his mom, although she insisted it wasn't a competition—Zach was good on babies and toddlers and kids in general, really, totally good. Besides, the one woman he had thought he'd marry and have kids with had dumped him to marry someone else. So, there was that.

"What's the matter, Zach?" Desiree asked. "Don't you like kids?"

"Nah, I love kids but only if I get to give them back at the end of the visit," he said. "Anything more than an afternoon and I start to get hives."

Savannah shook her head at him but Desiree laughed.

"You'd better watch it, Zach," Desiree said. "The guy who thinks he doesn't want kids usually turns out to be the greatest dad and ends up having a six-pack."

"Six-pack? Of kids?" Zach felt queasy. "Not in this lifetime."

Savanah tipped her head to the side and studied him. "You sure? Because I can totally see that."

"No!" Zach shook his head, sending his shaggy blonde hair in all directions. "No, you can't. Nuh-uh. No way. No how."

"He's adorable when he's panicking." Desiree snickered.

A knock sounded on his front door and Zach all but ran to answer it. Anything to get away from the girls and their teasing, which was not funny.

He didn't bother to check to see who was there. At the

moment, he would have embraced an encyclopedia salesman and invited him in for a beer. He pulled the door open
wide to find Jessie standing there.

She was alone, looking past his shoulder in an obvious
effort not to make eye contact. Zach took advantage of the
moment to appreciate that angle of her cheekbones, the firm
line of her jaw, the fullness of her upper lip, and the length
of her dark eyelashes. She was cute—not like puppy cute,
more like wrap-herself-around-a-guy's-heart-and-hold-
fast-until-he-couldn't-remember-what-life-was-like-
before-she-was-in-it cute. In other words, she was deadly
with a capital "D."

"Hi," he said. His voice came out high and tight. He
cleared his throat and lowered his voice and added, "Everything all right? Are the girls okay? And Chaos?"

"Yes, absolutely, everyone is fine." She nodded and the
pom-pom on her hat bobbed. "But Maddie lost one of her
mittens. We checked outside, but we didn't find it. I
wouldn't have come back and bothered you, but she's a
little obsessive about her mittens matching, which would
make you think she'd be better at keeping track of them,
but we seem to have started a collection of right-hand
mittens. No lefts."

Jessie was babbling. Her discomfort at having to come
back to his house screamingly apparent as she continued
to talk to some far point over his shoulder.

"I know I should get her those clips you can use to at-
tach a kid's mittens to the end of their jacket, but I keep
forgetting. I swear it's like a mental problem. I mean one
pair of those and I could stop buying mittens every other
day—"

"Let's go look," Zach said. "What did the mitten look
like?"

"It was pink, I think," she said.

Zach's lips lifted at her unintentional rhyme.

"Sorry," she said. "I have read entirely too much Dr.
Seuss to the girls."

"Don't be, Seuss is the man," Zach said. He moved

aside and waved her into the house. "Let's check the living room."

As they entered the house, Zach noticed that both Desiree and Savannah had disappeared back upstairs. He wondered if it was a coincidence but suspected not.

Jessica searched the floor around the coffee table while Zach checked the couch. He moved a throw pillow, she lifted up the newspapers, but there was no pink mitten to be found.

Jessie stood and scanned the room. She plopped her hands on her hips and pursed her lips. Zach glanced away, knowing that if he kept staring at her lips he was going to think things he should not be thinking about his neighbor.

"Well, I guess she dropped it in the snow somewhere." Jessie sighed. "I suppose we'll have to wait for spring when the snow melts, which is when we'll likely find the five other missing mittens."

Zach was about to agree with her when he caught a movement in the corner of his eye.

"Rufus!" he scolded. "What do you have there?"

Rufus had not gotten up to greet Jessie, which was suspicious because Rufus took his job as greeter to everyone who came inside the house very seriously. And now he was curled up, facing into the couch with his back to Zach and Jessie, and the poof of his pompadour hairdo was bobbing ever so slightly.

"Rufus, I'm talking to you," Zach said.

Rufus's poof of a tail wagged. Zach glanced at Jessie and put a finger over his lips, then he crept up behind the dog and snatched what Rufus had been gently gnawing on. It was the mangled remains of a pink mitten.

"Rufus, that was incredibly rude of you," Zach said.

Rufus glanced over his shoulder at them and then lowered his nose into the couch as if he was ashamed of himself.

"Oh, no, you don't," Zach said. "You can't soften me up with the sad eyes. I am not going to feel any sympathy for you when you willfully chewed up a perfectly good mitten."

Rufus heaved a sad sigh and his gaze shifted to Jessie as if she might be a more sympathetic person.

"Oh, Rufus," Jessie said.

He wagged his tail and she tipped her head and gave him a close-lipped smile.

"Now don't give in to him or he'll be impossible," Zach said. His words were completely wasted on Jessie as she crouched down in front of the dog.

She held the back of her hand in front of his nose and Rufus gave it a sniff and then a lick. Then he wagged even harder, suspecting that he was being forgiven.

"There's a good boy," she said. "You didn't mean to chew the mitten, did you? No, you didn't. Who's a handsome boy? Is it you? Yes, it is. Good dog, Rufus."

Sensing he'd won her over completely, Rufus rolled onto his back with his legs in the air, giving Jessie his belly for a tummy rub. She obliged, all the while keeping up her chatter.

"Who's a good dog? Who's a handsome fella? There's a good boy."

Zach held the soggy mitten, which was beginning to unravel. Watching Jessie with Rufus, it took everything he had not to throw himself down on the floor beside her with his belly in the air, demanding a rub. Okay, so maybe he was longing for some attention a little farther south than his belly. Feeling a light sweat break out on his body, he slapped himself with the soggy mitten in an effort to get ahold of himself.

Rufus, oblivious to Zach's situation, craned his head so he could lick Jessie's face while she dragged her hands through his thick hair. She laughed and Zach felt the sound punch him right in the chest. He wasn't sure why but he suspected Jessie didn't get to laugh with such abandon very often.

She wiped the slobber off her cheek and kissed the top of Rufus's poofy head.

"All is forgiven, Rufus," she said. Then she wagged a finger at him and said, "But no more mittens."

It occurred to Zach that Maddie had executed the exact same mannerism when she was talking to Chaos on the roof. The resemblance between the two females was ridiculously charming and Zach was utterly disarmed.

"He's going to be incorrigible now," Zach said.

"With that hairdo, how could he not be?" Jessie asked.

She smiled at him and it was the first time she'd looked him right in the eye since she'd come back. Zach felt something shift in his chest. He glanced down at the mitten in his hand.

"Sorry about this," he said. He held it out to her and she took it, tucking it into her pocket.

"It's fine." They stood awkwardly for a moment and she sidled toward the door and said, "I'd better go."

"Sure . . . right," he said.

He walked beside her to the door, reaching it first. He put his hand on the knob and paused. "Listen, about the girls upstairs—"

Jessie held up a hand in a *stop* motion. Her eyes were wide and she shook her head and said, "Not my business."

"But—" He let go of the doorknob as he turned to face her. He wanted her to understand that the girls just worked for him that there was nothing weird about the situation, but Jessie wasn't allowing it.

"No, really, what you do in your own home is your business," she said. "No judgment here. Honest."

She dove for the door and yanked it open. Before Zach could form the words to finish his explanation, she was stepping out into the cold.

"Jessie—" he began again but she was moving so fast he was pretty sure she was trying to outrun his words. When she broke into a light jog, he was sure of it.

"Thanks again for helping with Chaos," she called over her shoulder. As she dashed across the yard, he could see both Maddie and Gracie peering out a window on the upper story of their house.

The two girls waved and Zach waved back, wondering if he'd ever see the two little sprites and their mom again. He told himself that it would be best for all of them if he didn't, good boundaries making good neighbors and all that, and he tried really hard to believe it.

Chapter 4

"Zach, not to alarm you, but I think you have a stalker," Carly DeCusati said. She was sitting at his kitchen counter, drinking a pint of Bluff Point Ale while her fiancé James Sinclair worked his culinary magic in Zach's kitchen.

Rufus sat in the middle of the kitchen, watching James's every move on the off chance a chunk of the dry salami James was slicing for his charcuterie went flying into the air. Zach could practically see Rufus willing the meat to sprout wings and fly into his mouth.

"Stalker?" Zach asked. He took a long sip of his own pint and filched a slice of spicy salami from James's cutting board. "Not possible. You know I never bring anyone I might be romantically involved with back to my house."

"Oh, I don't think it's romance that this one is looking for," Carly said. She was gazing past Zach into his living room.

Zach turned around to follow her line of sight. Just as he glanced at the window there was a flurry of movement. Two knit caps were just visible right before they disappeared beneath the windowsill.

"My mistake," Carly said. "It appears you have two stalkers."

Zach turned back around and glanced at Rufus. The dog's attention was solely on James. He wasn't even blinking.

"Fine watchdog you are," Zach said.

"I think he's boring holes into my back," James said. "Our dogs, Saul and Hot Wheels, do the same thing."

"Yes, but they have our parrot, Ike, trained to help them out," Carly said. "Turn your back for a second and Ike will swoop in and steal food for the dogs. It's ridiculous."

"Does he still drop F-bombs?" Zach asked. He rose from his seat and crossed the room toward the front door.

"Yes," James said.

"Only when provoked," Carly defended her bird.

"Uh-huh," Zach said. "Someone went soft in the animal department."

"I did not go soft," Carly argued. "Besides, you can't say anything. You've got Rufus."

"I'm just fostering him until a better situation comes along or his family comes back from England."

"That's why you have portraits of you and the dog," James said. "Because you're planning to give him away."

"That started when he was just a coworker. Ruf is like a bud who gets thrown out by his wife and needs a place to crash for a while," Zach said. He saw two knit caps pop up just above the windowsill. "It's not a permanent situation."

"Why not?" Carly asked.

Zach held up a finger to indicate he needed a minute. Then he yanked open his front door and jumped outside.

"Gotcha!"

"Ah!" Both girls shrieked and fell back from the window, landing hard on their backsides.

Rufus, hearing the ruckus, came dashing to the door, barking in what sounded like a dog explosion.

"Oh, sure, now you come running," Zach said. He frowned at the dog. "You don't have me fooled. I know you knew who it was. I suppose now you want to go play in the snow with them."

Rufus barked one more time and then bounded out of the house and down the steps to the snow-covered yard. He ran in a crazy circle and the then lowered his chest into the snow. With his butt up in the air and his tail wagging triple time, he barked at the girls in an invitation to play.

"Hi, Zach," Maddie said. "Can we play with Rufus?"

Zach glanced at the two girls. "That depends. Does your mom know where you are?"

"She can see us," Maddie said.

Zach glanced at the house next door. He didn't see Jessie. It occurred to him that Maddie had a great future as a lawyer or a politician given that she had not really answered his question. He glanced at Gracie, who was studying the toes of her thick snow boots.

"Gracie, did you two tell your mom you were coming over here?" he asked.

Maddie swiveled her head in her sister's direction and stared at her as if willing her to answer correctly. Gracie glanced from Zach to Maddie and then back down at her shoes.

"We left a note," she said.

"A note? Where is your mom?" Zach asked. He couldn't believe that Jessie had left the girls on their own. It seemed completely out of character for the woman who had freaked out when her daughters left their backyard without telling her.

Maddie heaved a sigh as if accepting that the short-lived adventure was over. "She was in the shower."

"Maddie and Gracie, trust me when I tell you that not telling your mom when you leave the house never goes well," Carly said. She stood in the open doorway to Zach's house, giving them a sympathetic look.

"Hi, Carly," Maddie said. "You look so pretty in blue."

Carly glanced at Zach. "This kid is solid gold."

He nodded.

"I told you we were going to get into trouble," Gracie said. "Momma is going to be so upset."

"Well, let's get you back home so you can apologize to her before she panics," Zach said. He stepped into his house and grabbed his coat off a hook fastened to the wall inside the doorway. He glanced at Carly. "If the others get here while I'm gone, tell them I'll be right back."

"Will do," Carly said. "But I can't promise we won't start without you."

"Don't worry," James called from the kitchen. "I'll save you some meat."

"You're a true friend, James," Zach called. He gave Carly a pointed look and she laughed.

"Men and their meat." She shook her head.

"Phrasing!" Zach cried and then grinned at her.

He shoved his feet into his boots and zipped his coat before he strode outside to gather the girls, where Maddie was running around the front yard with Rufus while Gracie stood looking guilt ridden and ill.

"Come on, ladies," he said. "Let's go see if we can mitigate the damage."

"What does that mean?" Maddie asked.

"He's going to try and get us out of trouble with Momma," Gracie said.

"Oh, good," Maddie said.

Her confidence in Zach's ability to defuse Jessie's ire was unwarranted and he hoped he didn't let the kid down. Honestly, he wouldn't blame Jessie a bit if she freaked out. One of the many reasons the thought of having kids tripped him out was the reality of how many bad things could happen to them. He was pretty sure if he had a kid, he'd never sleep again.

His boots crunched in the deep snow as they strode across the two yards. It was late afternoon and it was already getting dark. There were no lights on in Jessie's house and he was glad he was with the girls so that he could make sure they arrived safely.

Rufus trotted along beside them, obviously feeling the same protective impulse. They were halfway up the walkway when the front door was yanked open and there stood Jessie in a bathrobe with a towel around her wet hair, clutching what looked like a Post-it note in her hand. She also had boots on, so Zach assumed she'd been on her way out when they arrived.

"Madeline Rose, Grace Josephine, get in here *now*," Jessie ordered. She looked a little wild-eyed and Zach was glad he wasn't on the receiving end of her scary mom face.

Gracie hopped right to it, plowing her way through the snow to get to the house, but Maddie did not feel so moved. She dragged her boots, leaving a wide swath in the snow, clearly not feeling the need to appease her mom.

Zach leaned down and whispered, "You might want to put it in gear, kiddo, your mom is looking a bit miffed."

Maddie shrugged. She blinked at him as if to prove she wasn't worried. Zach shook his head. Neither his mom nor his stepmom would have tolerated such insubordination.

"Pro tip, kid," he said. "You want to lead with an apology."

"We left a note," Maddie insisted.

Zach shook his head at her and Maddie made a huffy noise and began to stride a smidge faster to the house.

They had just reached the steps to the front porch when Gracie reached her mom and threw her arms around Jessie and hugged her.

"I'm sorry, Momma," she said. Her eyes looked watery and she clung like a burr. "We should never have left when you were in the shower."

"No, you shouldn't," Jessie said. She sounded unhappy. She held up the note. "And while this was a good idea, you know you have to ask me directly before you leave to go next door, down the street, or anywhere, don't you?"

"Yes, Momma," Gracie said. She looked crushed under the weight of her mother's disapproving eye and Zach had to resist the urge to pat the kid on the back or hug her.

"Maddie, what do you have to say for yourself?" Jessie turned her unhappy gaze on her youngest.

"We left a note," Maddie said.

She put one hand on Rufus's back as if to draw strength from the dog and then she tipped her chin up in pure defiance. Zach blew out a breath. It did not take a genius to know that this wasn't going to go well.

When he glanced at Jessie, he was pretty sure he saw her nostrils flare when she asked, "Is that all you have to say?"

"Yup," Maddie said. She crossed her arms over her chest and met her mother's gaze without flinching.

She reminded Zach so much of his youngest sister, Addison, known as The Wild Thing, that it was all he could do not to move to stand behind Jessie and wave his arms at the kid like he was signaling that the bridge was out. Although, if Maddie really was like Addison it wasn't going to help one bit.

He glanced at Gracie to see her put her hand to her forehead as if she just couldn't believe that her little sister was going there.

"Madeline, you and your sister are too young to be traipsing about the neighborhood when it's almost dark," Jessie said.

"It was just to Zach's house," Maddie protested. "We wanted to see him and Rufus."

"It's also incredibly rude to show up at someone's house uninvited," she said. "What if Zach had company?"

"He did," Maddie said. "We peeked in the windows and we saw her."

"Oh, my god." Jessie's eyes closed for a moment, as if she was praying for patience, then her gaze darted to Zach's. "I am so sorry. I hope they didn't interrupt your date."

"No worries," Zach said. "It's not a date, just some friends, my Maine crew, are over for a potluck dinner, that's all. No big deal."

A look passed over Jessie's face, one of longing, and it occurred to Zach that being a single mom, she probably didn't get much of an opportunity to hang out with her peers.

"If you want, you're welcome to join us," he said. The words flew out of his mouth before he thought them through.

"Oh, I couldn't," Jessie said. One hand flew to the towel on her head and the other to the front of her robe.

Zach wondered for the briefest second, a nanosecond really, if she was wearing anything under the robe. Then he felt Gracie and Maddie watching him, and he shook the thought off like a boxer throwing off a shot to the temple. Bad, Zach, bad.

"Sure you could, Momma," Maddie said. "And we can come, too."

"Maddie, what did I just say about not inviting yourself over to someone's house," Jessie said. She glanced up at Zach. "They usually have much better manners than this. I don't know what's gotten into them."

Zach smiled. She looked adorably flustered and he couldn't help but be charmed stupid by it.

"We're just having some drinks and dinner," he said. "The girls are more than welcome. They can sack out in my den and watch a movie while the grown-ups chatter, and there have been rumblings of a card game happening."

"Please, Momma, please." Maddie grabbed her mother's hand and pulled on it. Gracie said nothing, just pressed herself into her mother's side with hopeful eyes.

Jessie glanced at the girls and then at Zach. She looked as if she desperately wanted to join the big kids. Then she looked down at the Post-it note in her hand and at her two girls and sighed.

"Thank you, Zach," she said. "It's incredibly nice of you to invite us, but I can't say yes."

"But Mo-o-o-o-om." Maddie turned the word into a ten-syllable protest.

"No, Maddie, I can't reward your poor choice to leave the house without telling me by letting you go to the same place that you went without asking." Maddie opened her mouth to argue, but Jessie shook her head. "No, my mind is made up. If you want to visit Zach or Rufus in the future, I expect you to ask me and him properly first."

Maddie's lips compressed into a thin line and she stomped her foot on the porch in a show of temper. "You never let us have any fun!"

"That's enough," Jessie said. "Go inside, please, and wash up for supper."

Maddie shoved the door open and stormed inside. Jessie leaned down and kissed Gracie's head.

"Why don't you go in, Gracie."

"Okay, Momma." Gracie looked at Zach with regretful eyes. "See you, Zach. Bye, Rufus."

She turned to go inside, her slight shoulders drooping under her coat.

"Hey, ho, wait up," Zach said.

Gracie turned back around and he held up his fist. With a small smile, Gracie bumped knuckles with him, they both leaned in to touch elbows, and then they knuckle bumped again. Then Grace added a little hip-hop shimmy, which Zach imitated.

"You added a little something," he said. Then he grinned. "I like it."

Gracie flushed with pleasure and then patted Rufus and dashed into the house. Jessie watched her daughter disappear and turned back around to face Zach. Rufus had moved to sit beside Jessie and as he leaned against her, Zach wondered if the dog, too, was being lured in by the faint lavender smell coming off her skin.

"I'm sorry," she said. "I'll talk with them about respecting your privacy. I can't imagine what they were thinking."

As she spoke an orange furball bolted out of the open door and attacked the shoelaces dangling off Zach's boot.

"Chaos!" Jessie cried as she bent down and scooped him up. "I swear we are not as ill-mannered as we seem."

Zach laughed. "There's no need. The girls are welcome anytime."

"Shh, don't let them hear you say that," Jessie teased. "You'll never be rid of them. They are quite charmed by you and Rufus."

She cradled the cat with one hand and reached down to pet Rufus with the other. The dog closed his eyes as if in bliss. Lucky dog.

"Are you sure you don't want to join us tonight?" he asked.

He gestured back to his house and noticed that several

cars were now parked in front, meaning the rest of the crew had arrived.

"Gavin and Mac will be there, so unless you have a thing against socializing with your boss . . ." he said. He let his voice trail off.

"I really wish I could," Jessie said. She met his gaze and gave him a rueful smile. "Truly, you have no idea how appealing an evening among adults sounds, but I can't. It would give the girls the wrong idea about consequences."

Zach nodded. He felt his bangs flop over his forehead and he gazed at her from beneath them. "You're a good mom."

Jessie waved a dismissive hand at him but judging by her tiny smile, he could tell she was pleased.

"Zach, are you joining us at your potluck or not?" They both glanced in the direction of Zach's house to see Carly, standing with Emma, Mac, and Jillian. Carly waved her arm and added, "Hi, Jessie!"

Jessie waved back. "Hi!"

Zach didn't miss the lonely note in her voice and he felt a sympathetic pang in his chest. He couldn't imagine what his life would be like without his squad. Heck, he owned the brewery with his best friends, Brad and Sam, and he was pretty sure not a day in the past fifteen years had passed without seeing them, texting them, or talking to them.

"You'd better go before they eat all of the food," Jessie joked.

"Right," he said. "So, I'll see you around."

"Yeah," she agreed.

Zach gave her a small wave and then patted his leg, signaling to Rufus that it was time to go home. He didn't think he was imagining how reluctant Rufus seemed to leave. In fact, he was pretty sure the dog felt the same way he did, like they were abandoning Jessie to her loneliness. It didn't feel good.

Chapter 5

"Are you sure about this?" Carly asked. "Most people like to be warned before nine people show up at their door. In fact, if nine people showed up unexpectedly at my door, I'd hit the lights, flip the deadbolt, and belly crawl out of the room so they couldn't see me through the windows."

"Agreed," Jillian said. "Once the bra is off for the day, I don't want to see anybody."

"About what time of day would that be?" Sam asked.

"Shut it." Jillian smacked his arm but she was laughing.

"Trust me, it'll be fine," Zach said. He glanced over his shoulder at his friends, giving them a wink.

"Uh-oh," Gavin said. He was carrying an enormous tray of lasagna that his girlfriend, Mac, had made.

"What do you mean, 'uh-oh'?" Zach asked. While Brad and Sam were his oldest friends, they were brewery guys like he was. Gav was a veterinarian so if he said "Uh-oh," they all listened.

"The only thing missing from your 'it'll be fine' statement is 'hold my beer and watch this,'" Gavin said.

Mac laughed and then stood up on her tiptoes to kiss her man's cheek. "Don't freak him out. This is Jessie. She'll be happy to see us, I'm pretty sure."

"Pretty sure? That's a ringing endorsement," James said. He was carrying his charcuterie board while Carly walked beside him with a basket full of crackers to go with it.

"We're bringing food," Emma said. "I forgive an awful lot if people bring me food."

"That's because you're eating for two." Brad looked at his wife in wonder. Emma's pregnancy had been the news of the holidays, since they waited to tell everyone until she was a few months along. According to Emma, however, Brad hadn't stopped grinning from the moment the stick turned blue.

"Food always makes everything better," Zach said. "Now hush."

He hefted the slow cooker in his arms as he stepped up onto the porch. Maybe this was crazy. Maybe Jessie would be mad, but he hadn't been able to forget the forlorn look on her face when he'd walked away. After fifteen minutes in his house, he'd corralled his crew to pack up their potluck and bring it to Jessie.

He propped the heavy ceramic dish on his hip so he could lean on the doorbell with his elbow. He heard it chime inside the house and waited. Rufus took the opportunity to wedge himself between Zach and the door, obviously determined not to be denied.

It occurred to Zach just as the door was being opened that Jessie might still be in her bathrobe. He had a spasm of maybe-this-wasn't-such-a-hot-idea. Luckily, when the door opened it was Gracie.

"Zach, you're back!"

"And I brought dinner!"

"Awesome!" She turned around and yelled into the house, "Mom, Zach is back and he brought dinner!"

Zach glanced over Gracie's head through the living room to the kitchen beyond where Jessie stood holding a frying pan. He wasn't sure if she was about to start cooking their dinner or brain him with it, so he smiled, showing as much teeth as possible.

He was relieved to see that she was dressed in jeans and thermal shirt with a brightly colored flannel shirt over that. Her light brown hair with the blonde ends was still damp but it was drying in loose waves that framed her face, softening her usually serious expression.

"Well, are we allowed in or are we supposed to freeze our butts off out here?" Carly asked from the back of the pack.

Zach stomped his feet on the welcome mat and led the way in. Jessie didn't move. Her jaw slowly lowered as she took in all of the people filing into her house.

"We felt bad that you couldn't join us, so we decided to bring the potluck over here," Zach said. He made sure he stayed out of striking range of the frying pan. "Is that all right?"

"We brought lasagna," Mac said.

"And cheesecake," Gina, Carly's younger sister, added.

"Oh, well, in that case, come in," Jessie said.

Zach's friends needed no more encouragement. They hit Jessie's kitchen like they were on a rescue mission, plugging in the slow cooker, preheating the oven, and loading her counter until it groaned under the weight of the food. Zach watched Jessie slowly lower the frying pan. So, no cracked skulls. He took that as a good sign.

"Hi, Jessie," Gavin said. He gave her a one-arm hug. "Zach seemed to think you were in need of adult time. If you're not, just give the word and I'll get everyone out."

"No, no," she said. Zach saw her give a furtive glance toward the staircase. "Some adult time would be really nice; besides, I think it's bad form to throw out your boss."

"On the upside, you don't have to cook dinner," Emma added.

"A serious bonus," Jessie said.

"All right, who is drinking what?" Sam asked. As the brewmaster of their brewery, Sam took his beer and food pairings very seriously.

Zach leaned back and watched his friends swarm Jessie.

He supposed there were boundaries to be considered. Gavin Tolliver, the local veterinarian, was Jessie's boss. She was his office manager and had gotten the position when Mackenzie Harris—Mac—who was Gavin's girlfriend, had convinced him to give Jessie a chance.

This had been no small request given that Mac and Jessie had been longtime enemies. Zach didn't know all of the details, because girls, drama, and who cared, but he knew that whatever had happened to mend their rift, they had become friends over the past few months ever since Emma Tolliver had married his friend Brad Jameson last spring, bringing Gavin and Mac together.

And now Emma and Brad were having a kid. Zach paused to let that sink in. He glanced at the petite blonde and his lantern-jawed buddy. They were so ridiculously good-looking, it was like they'd sprung fully formed out of the pages of a J.Crew catalog.

Jillian bustled by him, carrying a box of whoopie pies and a large bowl of salad. Jillian ran a whoopie pie shop in town called Making Whoopie, because she was clever like that. Tall and thin, with dark skin and long curly hair, Zach figured she must force herself to eat one bite of salad and one bite of whoopie pie to maintain balance and her killer figure. Sam, his longtime buddy, was right behind Jillian. Tall and sporting a close-trimmed four-day beard that Zach was pretty sure he'd had since he sprouted facial hair, Sam followed Jillian wherever she went.

Zach and the rest of the crew had been watching the poor bastard pine for the pretty baker for months. The only one who didn't know that Sam was in love with her was Jillian. Gina DeCusati, Carly's feisty little redheaded sister, hip checked Sam, the big doofus, bringing his attention back to her. Gina managed The Grind, the local coffee shop, and had begun to pal around with their group about the same time Carly had moved home and got tangled up with James Sinclair, a stud of a physical therapist, who lived in a lighthouse and had to be the most patient man Zach had ever met. He'd have to be to put up with Carly.

If there was a female version of Zach, Carly was it.

Always good for a laugh, seriously commitment phobic—
at least she had been until she met James, who had managed to clamp a ring on her finger—and quite possibly the
worst dancer ever, the short curvaceous Italian was his
kindred spirit. A lot of people had thought Carly and Zach
were a perfect pair but there had never been a spark between them, just a deep understanding and affection.

While contemplating spark, Zach's gaze moved back
to Jessie. Now there was spark. He shook his shaggy head.
No, nope, nuh-uh, he was not getting involved with his
neighbor. He didn't do relationships and hooking up with
the woman next door would be beyond stupid, even for
him. Besides, he liked her girls and didn't want to have to
avoid them just because he'd slept with their mother.

The girls. Zach frowned. It occurred to him that he
hadn't seen Maddie. He saw Gracie across the room sitting
on the floor beside Carly and James, who were sitting on
the couch. Rufus had made a beeline for the girl and was
now lying on the floor with his belly in the air, demanding
tummy rubs. Gracie laughed at his antics and happily
obliged.

Zach grabbed the beer Sam handed him as he passed
by and took a long sip before he knelt down next to Gracie.
She grinned up at him and he couldn't help but smile in
return. Gracie had her mother's serious expression but
when she smiled, again like her mother, it was like the sun
bursting out from behind the clouds.

"I noticed Maddie isn't here," he said. "Everything
okay?"

Gracie gave him a look that said it was far from it.
"Maddie is in her room in time-out."

"Oh?" Zach took a sip of his beer.

"After you and Rufus left she was being very sassy,"
Gracie said. "Mom told her she needed to think about her
behavior for a while and that she could come out when she
was ready to apologize."

Zach nodded in understanding. Then he grinned at Gracie. "So, you think you'll ever see her again?"

Gracie looked surprised and then she caught the teasing

twinkle in his eye and she laughed. "I don't know. Maddie can be donkey stubborn. We might not see her till she's a grown-up."

Zach laughed and Gracie gave him a shy smile. He reached down and rubbed Rufus's belly.

"Maybe I can help," he said.

Gracie gave him a look of disbelief.

"Give me ten minutes," he said. "I'll bet I can get her to apologize to your mother."

"What do you need me to do?" she asked.

"Make sure your mother stays busy down here," he said.

Gracie nodded. "I can do that."

"Atta girl." Zach straightened up and strolled back through the room. He tucked his beverage into a corner of the counter, pausing to assess the situation.

Jessie was standing talking with Brad and Emma. He only caught snippets of the conversation but the words "episiotomy" and "epidural" were mentioned, both of which made him a bit woozy. He scooted over to the stairs and slipped up without anyone noticing he had gone.

Jessie's house mirrored his so he knew that the master bedroom was on the left with its own bathroom, while the two remaining bedrooms and a bath filled the rest of the floor. There was only one door that was closed with a sliver of light shining out from under it. Inside he could hear the sound of someone moving about.

He glanced back at the stairs to see if Jessie was on her way. He knew it was none of his business, but he had five little sisters and he'd been there for it all, from teething and puberty to teaching them how to drive a stick shift and how to Ben and Jerry their way through their first heartbreak.

He rapped gently on the door. The sound of movement abruptly stopped. He suspected Maddie was not going to open the door, so he leaned close and said, "Hey, champ, it's Zach."

The door was yanked open and there was Maddie. She was wearing about ten layers of clothing, including a bathing suit over her jeans and sweater. She had three hats on her head: a baseball hat, a knit beanie, and then a sunhat. At her feet was a backpack that looked like it was stuffed to bursting.

"Zach!" she cried. Then she threw herself at his legs and buried her face in his stomach. "I was afraid I wouldn't get a chance to say good-bye."

"Are you going someplace?" he asked.

"Australia," she said.

Her face was a study in conflicted misery. He had to bite the inside of his cheek to keep from laughing.

"Fond of kangaroos, are you?" he asked.

She shrugged. "I don't know. I've never met one."

"So, why go?" he asked.

"I need to be free," she said. Her voice was filled with yearning and she heaved a dramatic sigh.

"Australia is pretty far from here," he said. "How do you figure you'll get there?"

"Stowaway," she said. "I saw it in a movie. A dog hid on a train and a boat. He got all the way across the country like that."

"What about your sister and your mom?" Zach asked. "Don't you think they'll be sad to see you go?"

"Nah, they have each other," she said. "They'll be happier without me."

"Oh, I don't think that's true," Zach said.

"It is," Maddie said. "I'm always in trouble and Gracie never is and I bet they won't even know I'm gone."

Her chest was heaving and, judging by the quivering of her lip, tears were incoming. Zach needed to distract her.

"What about all of your stuffed animals?" he asked. "Won't they miss you?"

Maddie gave a sad little nod.

"Maybe you should have a family meeting with them, so you can explain to them why you have to go," he said.

Maddie glanced at her bed, half covered in stuffed animals, and then at Zach. She gave him slow nod.

Together they arranged all of the animals in a circle. When Maddie went to get her tea set so that the animals wouldn't be thirsty, he had to duck his head to hide his smile.

She handed Zach one of the teeny tiny teacups and pretended to fill it using a plastic pitcher. Under her watchful gaze, Zach dutifully took a sip and declared the tea the best he'd ever had. Maddie beamed at him.

"Hats," Maddie said. "Gracie says that when you have tea, you should be wearing a hat."

"Naturally," Zach agreed. Maddie plopped a purple pirate's hat with a large feathered plume on his head while she distributed the many hats she had onto her stuffies, keeping a bright pink fedora with a dazzling amount of rhinestones on it for herself.

She took a moment to give each of the stuffed animals a sip of tea and then she moved to stand beside Zach. She rested one small hand on his shoulder and leaned close to whisper in his ear.

"I don't know what to say," she said.

"Well, you need to tell them why you're going to Australia," he said. He pretended to take a sip of tea. "They're your best friends, you need to explain so they won't be so sad."

"You're right."

She clasped her hands in front of her and gazed at the assembled creatures: big-eyed baby seals, owls, and piglets, a teddy bear in overalls, a penguin in eyeglasses, and a mama manta ray with a mini manta ray in its pouch, and those were just the ones Zach could see from this angle. She paced back and forth as if searching for just the right words. She fretted her lower lip, opened her mouth to speak and then closed it, then resumed pacing.

While she paced, Zach began to voice the conversation of the animals. He decided that the owl would be encouraging but that the baby manta ray would be a bit sassy.

Maddie watched out of the corner of her eye, while he picked them up and gave them voices.

"This is boring," Baby Manta said.

"Be patient," Owl said.

"You're not the boss of me," Baby Manta said.

"I'm older and wiser," the owl said. "I am here to look out for you."

"But I want what I want when I want it," Baby Manta said.

"Settle down now," Maddie said.

She gave the baby manta a sharp look. Zach was pretty sure Maddie had been on the receiving end of that particular look from Jessie.

Zach pretended to drink his tea, adjusted the hard plastic hat on his head, and waited for her to speak. She paced a bit in smaller and smaller circles. Finally, she threw up her hands in exasperation.

"Baby Manta has me all mixed up," she wailed. "I know he was just being sassy. He didn't mean it."

"Yes, he was. How do you think he can make it better?" he asked.

"He needs to say he's sorry and . . . so do I," she said. Her nostrils flared and her lips pressed together in a hard line. She looked unhappy about the solution but also resolved.

Zach picked up Baby Manta and turned him to face Maddie. "I'm sorry. I didn't mean it. I'll try to be nicer."

"You are forgiven," Maddie said, and she hugged the stuffie to her chest.

"See how easy that was?" Zach asked. "Now, why don't you wait here and I'll send your mom up so you can say the same to her."

"Okay," she said.

He rose from his spot on the floor and handed her back her tiny teacup. Then he squeezed her shoulder and said, "I'm proud of you, kiddo."

Zach slipped out into the dark hallway, softly closing the door behind him. Now how to get Jessie up here to hear what Maddie had to say?

He moved toward the stairs when a voice broke the quiet. "Have a nice tea party, did you?"

Chapter 6

Zach let out a small yelp and spun around. Standing there with her arms crossed over her chest, and looking every bit as stubborn as her five-year-old daughter, was Jessie.

"I can explain," he said.

She gave him a hard stare and Zach felt himself squirm as if he were the one who'd been sassy before.

"I'm listening," Jessie said.

"She just looked so sad," he said.

Jessie rolled her eyes. "So, you thought you'd have a tea party with her? That sort of defeats the purpose of a time-out, doesn't it?"

"But we talked and I think she understands that her behavior was unacceptable," he said. "She wants to apologize, really, she does. And she came to the conclusion all by herself."

Jessie continued to stare at him.

"It is very difficult to take you seriously when you're wearing a purple pirate hat with a plume," she said.

"Really?" Zach asked. He struck his best pirate's pose with his chest out and his hands on his hips. "Avast, me hearty, don't make fun of me pirate's hat or I'll be forced to make you walk the plank."

"That sounds pervy," she said.

Zach leaned close and wiggled his eyebrows at her, letting her know he'd intended it to be, and she laughed. She had a surprisingly robust laugh; it came up from her belly and transformed her face from one that was overly pensive to a sparkly-eyed, openmouthed burst of joy. He liked it. He liked her. And he had the sudden crazy notion that he'd like to kiss her.

"Momma." Maddie appeared in the hallway behind them. She held her fingers clasped in front of her and her head was bowed ever so slightly. Zach got the feeling that apologizing didn't come easily to her. "I am really, really sorry."

Jessie turned away from Zach and crouched down so that she was eye level with Maddie.

"What exactly are you sorry for, Madster?" she asked.

Maddie braced herself with a huff of breath. She lifted her face and met her mother's gaze. "I was very sassy. We were wrong to leave the house and make you worry, and I'll never ever ever do it again."

Jessie opened her arms wide and Maddie fell into them. "Thank you for that. I really appreciate you taking responsibility for your actions. You are forgiven."

Zach felt another pang in his chest as he watched the mother and daughter. Either he had heartburn or these women were beginning to get to him.

Maddie glanced over her mother's shoulder at him and sent him an impish grin with a roguish wink and a thumbs-up. Oh, brother, this one was going to be trouble. He started to wag his finger at her and give her his best scolding face but Jessie broke the hug and leaned back.

"We have company," she said. "Do you want to come and meet everyone?"

"That depends," Maddie said. She looked at Jessie with big eyes. "Do I smell lasagna?"

Jessie laughed and hugged her hard. "Go. Gracie is down there with Rufus."

She didn't have to be told twice. Maddie rushed the stairs, scampering down as if she was afraid Jessie might change her mind.

"I like that kid," Zach said. Jessie turned to look at him, her big blue eyes full of mirth with a dab of exasperation.

"She's my handful," Jessie said. "She's afraid of nothing and no one and has never met a dare she didn't jump to accept." She shoved both hands into her damp hair. "I can feel the gray hair sprouting at the thought of her teen years."

Zach grinned. "She'll be all right."

"What if she isn't?" Jessie asked. A crease formed in between her eyes and Zach got the feeling that this thought kept her up a lot at night. "And even if she is, what if Gracie isn't? I mean, she's so timid, what if she hooks up with some bully who systematically destroys her self-esteem and self-worth and then she ends up on drugs, working on the corner as a hooker to finance her crack habit—"

"Whoa, Jessie, whoa!" Zach grabbed her by the shoulders and stepped close so that they were eyeball to eyeball. "Breathe."

Jessie closed her eyes, took in a shaky breath, and then slowly let it out.

"Again," Zach said. She did it again. "Better?"

"No!" Her eyes popped open. "What if it's Maddie who goes off the rails? How will I stop her if she gets all boy crazy and starts sneaking out of her room at night and then ends up a teen mom with a baby or triplets?"

Zach cupped her face and stared at her. "And what if she doesn't?"

"Huh?"

"Every time you start to freak out and play the what-if-insert-horrible-outcome-here game, stop and ask yourself and what if it doesn't?"

"Does that actually work?" she asked.

"For severe anxiety, no, probably not," he said. "But when my sisters would start spiraling about crazy stuff when they were teenagers, I'd keep asking them 'and what if it doesn't' until they got tired of hearing it. It helped that ninety-nine percent of the time, what they feared happening didn't happen, proving that worrying about it was a waste of time and energy."

Jessie blew out a breath and squinted at him. "And what if it doesn't, huh?"

"Just try it," he said. He moved his hands to her shoulders as if to hold her steady when, really, he just didn't want to let her go.

"Okay." She nodded. "What if Gracie hooks up with a real loser? And what if she doesn't?" Jessie tipped her head to the side as if considering her worry from a new angle. "What if Maddie becomes a career criminal and spends her life in jail? And what if she doesn't?"

She paused to let the words settle around her. Then she gave Zach a closed-lip smile. "You're kind of smart."

He realized he was still holding her shoulders and the urge to kiss her, just the corner of her mouth where her smile always began, hit him low and deep and he felt himself lean in. He dropped his hands and turned away from her.

"Five sisters," he said. He held up his hand and spread his fingers wide. He strode toward the stairs, realizing he needed some space between them before he did something dumb like give in to the urge and plant a kiss on her that made her cling to him while she moaned his name. "Five."

Jessie laughed as she fell in beside him. "You poor thing. Your parents must have been exhausted by that many girl hormones."

"No, they had it easy," he said.

She frowned, not understanding.

"My parents divorced when I was six months old," he said. "They each remarried and Mom had three girls and Dad had two."

"Oh, who did you live with?" she asked.

"Both, half-and-half, fifty-fifty." He shook his head as he started down the stairs. He could feel Jessie watching him as she followed, so he forced his voice to stay light as he added, "The lone boy, the bargaining chip in the divorce, and chief babysitter for both houses—you could say I specialize in mediation and girls."

"Yeah, so I noticed," Jessie said.

Zach turned to see what she meant by that, but they had reached the bottom of the steps and Jessie ducked around him before he could see her face. Over the next two hours he didn't think he was imagining that Jessie was avoiding him.

While Zach spent dinner joking around with the girls and talking shop with Brad and Sam, Jessie flitted around the room, making sure everyone had what they needed. Despite the fact that they had landed at her house with no notice, she seemed pleased to have them there.

She joked with Mac and Carly, praised Jillian's whoopie pies to the sky, asked Gina how she enjoyed managing The Grind, and shared some stories about Gavin as a boss. He was a total pushover for his furry patients, not even minding when they piddled during an exam or occasionally snapped at his fingers. This surprised no one.

When Jessie had the girls say good night at bedtime, Gracie and Zach busted out their special handshake to much applause. Maddie demanded a handshake of her own, so she and Zach worked out a complicated variation on patty-cake that involved a spin and snap that they made their own.

Zach watched Jessie head upstairs with the girls. As soon as they were out of sight, he went to work cleaning up the kitchen. He didn't want her to think they were here to trash her house and then leave. Sam joined him at the sink.

"So, Jessie, huh?" Sam asked.

"Just a neighbor," Zach replied. He knew Sam suspected more but there was no more.

"Right. So, the electrical current running between you two is my imagination?" Sam asked.

"Just a neighbor," Zach repeated.

"Seriously, dude." Brad joined them, picking up a towel and wiping down the salad bowl Zach had just washed. "I'm surprised your hair isn't standing on end."

"Funny." Zach ran a soapy hand over his hair. Droplets of water dripped down his bangs and he shook his head much like Rufus shook off water when it rained. The other guys ducked and Zach laughed.

Gina, all dangerous curves and wild red curls, joined them at the counter. She had an unopened bottle of wine in one hand and a corkscrew in the other. She batted her big brown eyes at Sam, and held the bottle out to him.

"Hey, Triple-Shot, you mind?" she asked.

"Huh?" Sam tore his gaze away from Jillian, where it usually lingered, and turned to Gina. "Sorry, what?"

Gina's eyes flashed and she blew out a breath that puffed out her lower lip and tousled the curls that hung over her forehead. Silently, she held out the bottle to him.

"Oh, sure," he said.

He set to work getting the cork out of the bottle while Gina watched him with her heart in her eyes. Zach glanced at Brad to see if he was getting this.

He winced when his gaze met Zach's. Oh, yeah, he was getting it. Gina wanted Sam who wanted Jillian, who was oblivious to all of it. Zach suspected a mighty train wreck coming in the not-so-distant future.

He shook his head at Brad and said, "And that is why I don't do relationships and all of my shenanigans happen out of town, as in *not* in my neighborhood."

Brad returned his head shake. His gaze drifted to where his wife, Emma, sat with her forever friends, Carly, Mac, and Jillian. Emma was laughing at something Carly said. Her lips were parted in a wide warm smile and her straight pale hair reflected the light from the fire in the fireplace. Zach glanced back at his friend. If he were a cartoon, hearts would have replaced his eyeballs, as he was completely besotted with his wife. It was positively unmanly.

Still, Zach was happy for him. Emma was a great girl, and they were going to make spectacular parents. Brad's own upbringing had been cold and distant and Emma, with her exuberance for life, had brought warmth and light into Brad's life. They were kindred spirits, a perfect pair, but Zach knew from personal experience that their connection was unicorn rare.

His gaze moved over to Gavin, who was sitting beside

James. Gavin was tall and rawboned, good-looking in that salt-of-the-earth, reliable-as-the-sunrise sort of way. He was Emma's younger brother and had been in love with Mac, the pretty brunette of the group, since he was ten years old, or so the story went. When Mac had come back to town for the first time in seven years to stand up for Emma at her wedding to Brad, Gavin had made sure she didn't leave him again. They were disgustingly happy together.

Carly said something that sounded like it had to do with James's stamina. Not to let the comment go unchallenged, James jumped out of his seat next to Gavin and swooped down on his fiancée, planting a kiss on her that was just this side of get-a-room-please. Yeah, Carly had picked up James for a one-night stand months ago and now here they were engaged. Zach was happy for his feisty Italian female equivalent. Except she wasn't like him in his commitment phobia anymore. Carly had found someone, a really cool someone, and moved on into couplehood.

"Is it just me or is everyone suddenly pairing up?" Zach asked Brad.

"It's not you. It's happening."

"But why?" Zach protested. "We're in the prime of our lives. Why are we all rushing off to be in relationships and get married?"

The room had gone quiet as they all turned to look at him and Zach realized he might have been a smidgeon too loud.

"Seriously, why? What is so great about relationships?"

No one said anything for a moment but then Carly looped her arm around James's shoulders and said, "Well, duh, because you can crack some marbles whenever you want."

Zach felt his jaw drop. "Oh, no you didn't."

"Yeah, I did." She grinned.

"Game on, people," Zach said. He rubbed his hands together in anticipation. "Alternate expressions for orgasms. Go."

He pointed to Sam.

"Jet one's juice," he said.

"Ew," the girls all groaned together.

"*La petit mort*," Jillian said. She was obsessed with all things French and said it with a French accent that Zach was pretty sure made Sam's pupils dilate.

"Climax," Gina offered.

"Shoot your wad," James said.

"Come," Emma offered. Brad pulled the collar of his shirt away from his neck and shuddered. Emma laughed and kissed him.

"The Big O," Mac said. Gavin wagged his eyebrows at her and she blushed and then giggled.

"What's The Big O?" Jessie asked as she entered the room. Everyone stared at her. Her eyes went wide and she said, "Oh, oh!"

"Yeah, just like that," Carly teased.

They all laughed, and Zach was pleased to see that Jessie laughed with them.

"Any reason why we're talking about that now?" Jessie asked.

"We're coming up with euphemisms for the word 'orgasm,'" Zach said. "Whatcha got?"

"Oh, that's easy. Rockets and waterfalls," she said.

"Brilliant! And it's the Beyoncé reference for the win!" Zach said.

The girls clapped her on the back and Jillian gave her a one-armed hug and said, "Nicely played, sister."

Jessie's grin was as big as Maddie's and Gracie's when they'd busted out their new high fives with Zach. He wondered how long it had been since Jessie'd had a squad of her own, if ever.

The grown-ups lingered as they packed up the dishes they'd brought, finished their dessert, and bundled up to go back out into the freezing January temperatures.

Zach was the last one to leave, clutching his slow cooker under one arm while he stood awkwardly at Jessie's door. He didn't know what to say. Women fell into very specific categories for him: family, employees, friends, and women he wanted to sleep with.

Jessie wasn't family or an employee, and she could be a friend but, unfortunately, it had become clear to him when they were upstairs and he'd been swamped by the urge to kiss her that she was also someone he wanted to sleep with, and he never felt that way about his female friends. Ever.

The girls in his Maine crew were friends first, which nullified any interest he had to see them naked, but Jessie was different. She was a neighbor. She could become a friend but he had a feeling that even if she became his best friend he was still going to want to see her in her altogether. Worlds were colliding. This would not do.

"So, this was fun," he said.

He patted his thigh, hoping Rufus took the hint to stop sniffing Chaos the kitten, who was curled up into a tiny orange ball in an attempt to ignore the big dog who'd been licking him all evening.

"It was," Jessie agreed. She gave him a rueful look. "I owe you an apology."

"What for?"

She blew out a breath and laced her fingers in front of her in a pose of regret very similar to Maddie's earlier. "The other day, I mistook what all of those women were doing in your house. I didn't realize they were your employees who'd been trapped by the storm." She looked up at the ceiling and a soft pink blush of mortification filled her heart-shaped face. "I thought you were a player."

"Me?" Zach asked. He blinked twice, the picture of innocence.

Jessie burst out laughing, her blue eyes twinkling when they met his. "I know, it's ridiculous, right?"

"Well, it's not that far out of the realm of possibility," he said. He felt a sudden need to defend his masculine charm.

"You're right, of course, you're right." Jessie nodded but she was still laughing and he got the feeling she was just saying this to mollify him. "But I am sorry I thought that about you. It wasn't fair. My ex-husband was a player, a real bad boy. I used to find that an attractive quality, you know, before I realized that 'bad boy' is just a euphemism for a dick."

Zach barked out a laugh at her blunt speaking. Smart, funny, pretty, a loving mom—Jessie had it all going on, and it was making him like her and not in a friendly way either. The feelings Jessie brought out in him felt dangerous and Zach knew better than to ignore the warning. He had gone for the happy ever after once before and had learned the hard way that it wasn't for him. Too much risk.

"What changed your mind about me?" he asked.

"Mac and Emma were talking about how you are a big brother to all of your field marketers," she said. "That you're the one who pushed to have the brewery offer scholarships to employees so they can go to college and how you take care of everyone you meet. That's a pretty great quality to have."

"Nah, it's just doing what's right," he said.

"Well, I still say it's pretty great," she said.

They were standing close together. The house was quiet. Rufus had finally stopped harassing the cat and was sitting beside Zach, waiting to leave. Zach knew it was time to go; he knew it, and yet, he found it very hard to leave Jessie. As if he was being pulled into her orbit, he found himself leaning toward her.

"Momma!" One of the girls cried from upstairs. "I can't sleep."

Both Zach and Jessie jumped as if they'd been caught kissing. She put a hand on the back of her neck and looked away and Zach adjusted the slow cooker under his arm.

"I'd better go," he said.

"Yeah."

"Good night, Jessie."

"Good night, Zach."

Before he did something crazy like toss the slow cooker into a snow bank and drag her up close and kiss her, Zach pushed open the storm door and strode out into the cold, dark night with Rufus by his side.

The bite of the wind pinched his cheeks and blew back his collar as if looking for a way to sneak in under his coat.

He glanced up at the sky and noted it was clear. The stars were brilliant pinpricks of light in the relentless black above.

Rufus bounded in the snow next to him, pausing to track scents every few feet, and Zach gave him an exasperated look.

"I almost kissed her, Ruf," he said. "Like that wouldn't be awkward as hell. You need to up your game and run better interference."

Rufus, who had his snout shoved into a snowbank, pulled up his head and barked at Zach.

"Don't judge me," Zach said. "I am way, way, way out of my comfort zone here."

Rufus shoved his face back into the snow, and Zach trudged on. His own house was dark and empty. He glanced back over his shoulder at Jessie's house, whose windows spilled yellow light across the snow and glowed with warmth against the frigid temperatures outside. Zach felt a pull, a longing to be in the house of light, but he ignored it, pushing it down deep, where all of his sadness and disappointment were kept on lockdown.

He had a job he loved, a squad he hung out with, and plenty of girls to call if he wanted company in the sack. He had a great life, the perfect life. He didn't need or want a relationship, especially with someone like Jessie Connelly with her big blue eyes and adorable kids. Nope. That was not for him.

Chapter 7

Jessie knew what time Zach left for work, seven o'clock sharp. His garage door would roll up and he would drive out, looking cold and hunched in the driver's seat while Rufus sat in the passenger seat beside him, sitting up as if he, too, were ready to clock in for his day at work. The sight of the goofy cinnamon dog with the poofy hairdo and a clip-on tie on his dog collar never ceased to make her laugh.

Because their schedules were similar, she also knew what time Zach came home, five thirty on the nose. He parked at the end of his driveway to grab his mail and while Rufus ran to the house, Zach drove into the garage, meeting Rufus at the front door usually with a bag of take-out in hand.

She knew that he and Rufus played in the snow every morning before they left for work and every evening when they came home. They stayed out there for a half hour with Zach wrestling the big hairy beast to the ground right before Rufus rolled to his feet and chased Zach around the yard. She had learned by observation from her kitchen window that Rufus liked to chase a battered yellow Frisbee and Zach had a strong throwing arm.

She noticed that Zach usually went back out in the evenings, without Rufus, for a couple of hours and she knew that when he did he was hanging out with his Maine crew or his field marketers, spreading the love for his Bluff Point brewery. She felt a pang of loneliness in her chest when she thought of all of the crew at Marty's Pub playing darts, singing karaoke at the Bikini Lounge, or bowling a few frames at the lanes in the next town over.

That life was not for the single mom, however, and mostly she was okay with it. She wouldn't give up her time with her girls for anything, but still, sometimes she was lonely.

She glanced at the phone in her hand. She was sitting under an afghan on her squashy couch, enjoying the few minutes of peace and quiet that she got between getting the girls to bed and passing out herself. She noted on her social media app that Mac and Gavin were tagged in a post by Zach that showed them all having a snowball fight on the town green. The pang of lonely she'd felt morphed into a suffocating submersion of sorry-for-herself, and she shook her head and switched off her phone. Her life was so much better than it had been for so long, she could not indulge in feeling bad.

She was proud of the life she had managed to carve out after the train wreck of her marriage. Being with her girls, without the looming moody cloud of her ex-husband and the managing control of her father-in-law, was like getting a new lease on life and she loved it.

Sure, sometimes she wanted to have a conversation that did not involve nagging someone to finish their supper, brush their teeth, tie their shoes, pick up their toys, or go to sleep. But she would never trade in the exuberant hugs and sloppy kisses she received every day, and even hanging out with a squad of adult friends would be a distant second to that.

She knew what Zach and his friends did, because she was friends with Mac and Gavin on social media, and they were frequently tagged in the photos Zach put up on the brewery's social media page. It had become Jessie's habit to check her phone right before she did lights-out to see what the crew was up to. Always, they were laughing, sometimes making goofy faces, and occasionally one of them, pregnant Emma, had fallen asleep—yes, even while bowling.

If Jessie scanned the group pictures looking for glimpses of Zach, she was sure it was only natural. A woman needed to know what sort of person her next-door neighbor was on the off chance he was a demented killer, a peeper, or some other sort of undesirable ick. This was just normal neighborly attentiveness, Jessie assured herself. She was not lightly stalking him. Really, she wasn't.

She reminded herself that she had no interest in a relationship. Once she'd left her ex, she had promised herself she would never be dependent upon a man again. Ever. She'd only been out of her very bad marriage for six months and she was still getting her bearings. Her ex-husband, Seth Connelly, had done a number on her and she knew she wasn't quite right in the head as yet.

She and the girls had been seeing a therapist, Dr. Hawkins, because not only had Seth been a lousy husband but he was a lousy father, too. He'd disappeared a few months ago, telling her he needed to go find himself. Last she'd heard, he was sipping chi-chis on a beach in Costa Rica with no intention of returning. She supposed he was looking for his soul in the bottom of a coconut bowl. Whatever.

She was not heartbroken about this but she did feel bad for her girls. More because they never asked where he was or when he was coming to see them. It was as if they, too, had had enough of Seth Connelly and his broken promises. Luckily, they did have a close relationship with Seth's mother, Audrey. She loved the girls and Jessie appreciated that she tried to run interference between Jessie and Seth's domineering father, Judge Connelly, who had not truly accepted the divorce.

Jessie glanced at the clock as she rose from the couch.

It was late. The light dusting of snow that had been predicted had already begun. She crossed to the window and glanced out, pressing her fingers against the icy pane of glass. Steamy imprints were left behind when she removed her hand and she used the fluffy sleeve of her bathrobe to wipe them away.

She checked the locks on the doors, switched off the lights and made her way upstairs. She peeked into the girls' room. Although she'd bought the three-bedroom house specifically so the girls could have their own rooms, the two of them refused to be separated. It delighted Jessie that her girls were so close, so she was happy to let them share until the day came when they did want their own space. In the dim light, she could see Gracie asleep with one arm thrown over her head and Maddie buried deep in her covers with just her nose visible. The sound of their soft sighs was the only noise, except the steady purr-snore that Chaos emitted from where he was curled up at Gracie's feet.

Jessie eased out of the room and crossed to her bedroom. She opened the book she'd been reading but decided instead to just sleep. She put her phone on her nightstand, counting on its alarm to wake her in time for work. As she wriggled under her flannel sheets, trying to warm them up, she felt herself began to drift.

The image that flitted through her mind while she laid there was one from tonight. Someone had snapped a picture of Zach with his shaggy blonde hair poking out beneath the hem of his slouchy beanie. He was laughing, a big wide show of teeth with a wicked twinkle in his dark brown eyes, as he lobbed a snowball right at the person taking the picture. The image—the sheer mischievous boyishness of his pose—made Jessie smile as she slid into a deep sleep.

It was cold, bitterly cold. The tips of her ears, the end of her nose, and her cheeks hurt from the chill. Jessie glanced down and realized she was standing naked in her front yard and she was knee deep in the snow. Her teeth were chattering and her skin was covered in goose pimples. She hugged her arms close and ran her hands over her body trying to warm up and cover herself at the same time. Jessie frowned.

She saw Zach next door. He was laughing and Rufus was dancing around him, trying to grab the scarf that was wrapped around Zach's neck. Jessie was so cold. She wanted that scarf. She tried to call Zach but she couldn't make any noise beyond the sound of her teeth clacking together. She tried to wave at him, but her arms felt heavy with the cold and she couldn't lift them.

It occurred to her that she was going to freeze to death, naked in her front yard. The horror of it made her redouble her efforts to be heard. She forced her feet to move in the snow and she walked, dragging her feet until she didn't have the strength to take another step and fell face forward into the snow.

She was going to die. Jessie opened her eyes but the darkness remained. She tried to cry out and this time a soft sound escaped her mouth. She blinked.

It hit her then that she was lying in bed. How did she get here? She lifted the heavy bedcovers and felt her chest. She felt the well-worn thermal beneath her fingertips. She was in her pajamas, thank goodness. It had just been a dream. She blew out a breath and felt it mist into the air.

The frigid air in her bedroom swept in under her blanket, making her shiver and shake. Jessie dropped her covers and snatched her phone from her nightstand. The screen told her that it was three o'clock in the morning. She blinked against the darkness. It was so dark. The night-light that illuminated the hallway so that the girls could find the bathroom or her room if they woke up at night wasn't glowing its usual ambient blue light.

Jessie stuck her arm out of the covers and switched on her bedside lamp. Nothing happened. She tried again. Nothing. A boom sounded outside, making her start, followed by flashes of lightning. She remembered it had been lightly snowing when she went to bed, so this was now a snow thunderstorm? Fantastic. Not.

She shoved aside her covers, and using her phone display for light, she found her thick bathrobe at the foot of her bed and pulled it on. There were no sounds of alarm coming from the girls' room but she hurried across the hallway to check on them anyway.

They were both sound asleep. Chaos was snuggled up with Maddie now, his little face poked out beside hers from her cocoon of covers, but their room was freezing, too. It occurred to Jessie that the power must have gone out shortly after they all went to bed.

She grabbed two extra blankets from the linen cupboard in the hallway and added them to the blankets the girls were already under. She then went into the bathroom and turned on the faucet so that it ran in a tiny steady stream, hoping it would be enough to keep the pipes from freezing. She used the flashlight on her phone to find her way downstairs and did the same in the bathroom and kitchen sinks down there.

Another boom sounded outside, causing Jessie to yelp, followed by several flashes of lightning. She turned on the flashlight app on her phone and aimed it at an angle out the living room window and gasped. This was not good. The snow that should have stopped hours ago was falling fast and furious, adding to the thick blanket that already covered the ground.

The thunder continued to rumble and the lightning flashed. Never in all of her thirty-two years did Jessie ever remember snow that came with thunder and lightning. Mother Nature must be feeling especially bitchy these days.

She left the window and went into survival mode. She checked the log basket by the fireplace. It was fully stocked and she had plenty of firewood out back on the patio. She wasn't sure if she should use the wood inside now or wait until later. She opened up the weather app on her phone. The latest report said the storm was predicted to last for three days. They were going to be buried. The entire shoreline was without power and there was no telling how long it would remain so.

Jessie hurried to the kitchen. She found three big round pillar candles and some matches. She lit the candles, her fingers clumsy with the cold, and shut off her phone to conserve the battery, which was at ninety-five percent. She did a quick assessment of her pantry and her refrigerator. She had plenty of food. Water. If the pipes did freeze, they would need water. She gathered all of the pitchers and water bottles she had in the cupboard and filled them with tap water. When she was out of bottles and the counter was full, she stopped, holding her hands over the flames of the candles to warm them up.

She tried to remember how much gas she had in the car. Not that she could go anywhere in the storm; driving a basic four-door sedan in this blizzard would be stupid at best and suicidal at worst. But if things got crazy cold, she and the girls could always open the garage door to let out the fumes and climb into the car and run it with its heater on while she charged her phone off the car battery. They would be okay. She could get them through this. Really, she could. She nodded, then she started to cry.

Maybe it was because she'd woken up in the middle of the night and she was tired, maybe it was because it was really frigging cold in her house, or maybe it was just that adulting, especially alone with kids, was so damned hard sometimes. If Jessie didn't have the girls then any screwups she made would only impact her life, but Maddie and Gracie needed her. They needed her to problem solve and keep them safe and secure while—

Boom. Another rumble of thunder rocked the house.

She wiped away her tears. If nothing else, the thunder had interrupted her bout of self-pity. During her seven years of marriage it became quickly clear to her that crying was pretty much a waste of time. Not that she didn't indulge now and again, but other than the comfort of letting her upset out, her tears had done little to fix her situation.

She grabbed the afghan off the back of her couch and

wrapped it around her thick bathrobe. She sat on her couch, trying to calculate how much wood she had and how much she would need. And how much wood would a woodchuck chuck . . . She snorted.

The wind howled against the side of her small shingle house as if trying to find a way in. When she'd bought the place a few months ago, she'd had new insulation put in and now she was glad. It had taken a hearty bite out of her earnings at the time but while it was cold in her small house, it wasn't drafty, for which she was very grateful.

Okay. Jessie settled back against the couch cushions. She would wait a little while and then start the fire. It would be all right. She had water. Her car was there in case of an emergency. The soft light of the candles illuminated the room. It was even somewhat cozy with the flickering candlelight. Maybe she and the girls could pretend they were Laura Ingalls Wilder, surviving a blizzard on the prairie.

Bam!

A horrific noise sounded on the front porch. Jessie sat up, her eyes wide, her heart pounding in her chest. Another thud sounded and another. That was not thunder. That was someone trying to break into her house!

Chapter 8

♀

She glanced around the room, looking for a weapon. She had her choice of a designer throw pillow or a women's magazine. This would not do. She ran into the kitchen. The candles illuminated the small space enough so that she could see her bottles of water on the counter.

She could throw water bottles at the person outside. No, she and the girls might need the water. She opened the knife drawer. Could she actually cut someone? What if they wrestled the knife away from her and used it to slash her throat? She slammed the drawer shut.

A light flickered on her porch. Someone was out there. She grabbed the first thing at hand, thinking she would throw it at them if they kicked in her door. With her other hand she used her cell phone to call the police. She pressed nine and one and then waited.

Maybe she could scare them away. Maybe they didn't know she was awake and they thought the house was empty. She stealthily approached the door. The wind was howling and it was still snowing. Whoever was on her porch was protected by the roof from the snow and the wind but it was still falling thick and deep and it was bitterly cold out there. Maybe the person was stranded and had come to her house seeking shelter.

Oh, damn, she didn't want to let a stranger into her home during a storm. That reeked of something that would end up on the Investigation Discovery channel, but she couldn't let them freeze to death either. Her need to protect her girls warred with her compulsion to be a Good Samaritan. She decided to try to scare them away. If they were a bad guy, they would go. If they were good, they'd stay and she could help them or at least let them use her phone.

She peered through her peephole. The lamp on the porch was very bright, the sort you'd use to go camping, and within its glow she could see the accumulation of snow on her front steps as well as the person standing there in a puffy green coat. The hood was up and it closed around their face, leaving a hole just big enough to see through.

Jessie made sure the latch on the storm door was locked as she opened the interior door just a crack and shouted, "Stop right there. I have a gun and I know how to use it."

The person whirled around. With their back to the lamp and the snow swirling in the air it was impossible to see their features, but she heard a muffled shout. She grasped her phone, getting ready to hit the remaining digit.

"I have the police on the phone," she cried. "They'll be here in minutes."

The person reached up and Jessie panicked and shouted, "I'll shoot!"

The person held their gloved hands in the air in a position of surrender. They gestured to their hood, indicating that they were going to remove it.

"Okay, but move slowly," she said.

One of the person's gloved hands ripped the Velcro fastening open on the hood, while the other pushed the hood back. A thick thatch of unruly blonde hair was illuminated in the lamplight and Jessie felt herself sag against the doorjamb.

"Zach! What are you doing here?" she cried.

"The power is out," he said. "I was worried about you and the girls."

"You scared me to death," she said. A boom of thunder sounded and she jumped. "Come in, hurry."

She unlatched the storm door and pushed it wide. Zach stomped his boots before stepping into the house. Rufus came bounding out of a snowbank at the bottom of the steps and scooted inside with him.

Jessie pulled the door shut against the wind and latched it, shutting the thick wooden interior door after it. She turned around to find Zach looking at her with a smile curling his lips.

"What?" she asked.

"A potato?" he asked.

"Huh?"

He gestured to her hand. "You said you had a gun. That's a potato."

Jessie looked down at her hand. She hadn't really thought about what she'd grabbed in the kitchen but seeing the big Idahoan in her hand was a bit startling. A laugh bubbled up before she could stop it. She looked at Zach. He was grinning.

"I threatened you with a potato."

"You were going to mash me," he said.

Jessie laughed harder and waved the potato at him. "No, I wouldn't want you to lose your appeal."

"Ha!" Zach laughed. "Nice one."

Rufus pushed his head against Jessie and she felt his cold, wet fur.

"Oh, poor baby," she said. "You must be freezing. Come in and I'll start a fire. Let me just get a towel for Rufus."

She dashed down the hallway to the guest bathroom where she kept some extra towels. She hurried back to the living room to find that Zach had put his lantern on the coffee table and it lit up the entire room. He was kneeling in front of her fireplace, setting up the logs for a fire. She thought about asking him to wait so she could conserve wood, but Rufus felt awfully cold to the touch and she thought he could use the warmth of a fire before going back out there.

She wrapped Rufus in the large towel and rubbed him down. He was happy to let her do so and even rolled onto his back so she could get all of the clumped snow off of his legs.

Zach took one of the long matches that she kept on the mantel and lit the kindling beneath one big log. He blew on the low flame, making it flare until the log slowly started to burn. The flue was open and small tendrils of smoke started to drift up against the occasional snowflake that fell down into the fireplace.

In just minutes there was a crackling fire in her fireplace and Jessie moved closer, hoping the flames would sear away the chill that had begun to seep into her bones.

"The girls are all right?" Zach asked. He continued to nurture the fire, keeping an eye on it so it didn't just flame out.

Another roll of thunder sounded but they both ignored it, although Jessie noticed that Zach flinched, too.

"I put extra blankets on them," Jessie said. "Last time I checked they were both sound asleep."

"That might be the best way to get through the power outage," he said. "Hopefully the electricity will come back on in a few hours."

"I hope so," she agreed. "I'm not sure I have enough firewood to get through several days of this."

"We'll be all right," he said. "I have a generator. We can always go to my place if the storm doesn't let up."

"Can I get you anything?" she asked. "Coffee . . . er . . . no, I can't make that, can I?"

"Nope," he said. He added another log to the fire.

"For coffee alone, we're going to need your generator," she said.

"Agreed," he said. "I don't think I can face a morning without coffee."

Zach unzipped his coat and shrugged it off. He draped it by the hearth and began to unlace his thick work boots, leaving them by his coat. He was in well-worn jeans and thermal shirt under an unbuttoned flannel shirt. He looked solid and safe, like a human shield against the nasty storm outside, and Jessie was surprised to find how much comfort she took in having him, another grown-up, here with her.

Rufus nudged his way between Zach and the hearth. He sprawled onto his back, letting the fire warm his belly. Zach shook his head and absently gave Rufus a tummy rub. His hands were big and square and Jessie felt a longing to feel those same hands on her body, touching her, making her breath quicken.

She glanced away. She shook her head, sending her bedhead into a tumble around her shoulders. It was not a great plan to have inappropriate thoughts about her neighbor, not if she wanted to keep things casual between them.

"How are you for food and water?" he asked. He switched off the lamp, leaving just the candles and the fire to illuminate the room.

Jessie told him all of the preparations she'd taken so far, and he nodded. He gave her an impressed look and said, "Nice job. Looks like you were on top of it."

"Thank you." Jessie was ridiculously pleased with the praise.

"Your pipes should be okay," he said. "I don't think there's anything we can do tonight at any rate. We should get some sleep. If it keeps snowing, we'll have to do some cleanup tomorrow to stay ahead of it."

He rose to his feet and moved over to the large sectional couch, where he stretched out. He put his head on a throw pillow in the corner and closed his eyes as he burrowed into the sofa as if trying to heat it up. Jessie watched him in alarm.

"You're planning to sleep here?" she asked. She was pleased that her voice didn't sound as panicked as she felt.

Zach opened one eye and regarded her under a narrowed eyelid. "Yes."

"But—" she began but he interrupted.

"No buts," he said. "It's too dangerous for you and the girls to be here alone, heck, it's too dangerous for me and

Rufus to be alone at my place. It's better if we stick together and ride out the storm. This way if anything happens to either of us, the other one is there to help or to go get help."

Jessie glanced at the window. Lightning flashed and the wind howled as fistfuls of snow were pelted against the thin panes of glass. The storm raged on and it didn't feel safe to be alone, and it certainly wasn't safe for Zach to walk back home.

She rose from her seat on the hearth and went down the hall to the linen cupboard. She pulled out the only blankets that remained, two well-worn comforters with matching pillows that her former mother-in-law, Audrey, had given the girls when they were younger. They were bright pink with butterflies on them. She carried them back to the living room and shyly handed one set to Zach who was watching her again with one eye open.

"Thanks," he said. "Ooh, and it's just my color, too."

Jessie laughed. "No problem."

She sat on her side of the sectional, feeling uncomfortable about what she was going to say but knowing it needed to be said anyway. "Listen, I am okay with you staying but I need to be clear that there is to be absolutely no funny business."

Both of Zach's eyes opened wide and he regarded her with a mischievous twinkle in his gaze. "So, whoopie cushions and hand buzzers are out, got it."

"Zach," she said. Her voice was low in warning.

He blinked, the picture of innocence.

"Do I really have to spell it out?"

"Spell what? It? I-T."

A tiny smile was tipping the corner of his mouth. Jessie had a sudden urge to press her lips right there just to see what the smart aleck would do. She didn't. Instead, she quickly averted her gaze to the fire.

"Just stay on your side of the couch," she said. "Or I'll brain you with the potato."

Zach barked out a laugh. "Well, with a threat like that, you don't need to worry."

Jessie glanced over her shoulder at him. Could she trust him? Was he the safe guy he seemed? She didn't have a great track record with men and she really didn't want to get burned again.

Zach leaned up on one elbow. His gaze met hers and it occurred to her it was the first time she'd ever seen him look serious. He reached out a hand and grabbed her fingers with his. His fingers were cold but they held hers gently, his grip firm and strong but measured. His thumb ran over the top of hers in light reassuring strokes that made her heart trip over itself in response.

"Listen," he said. "I know you have no reason to believe me but I promise you are perfectly safe with me. I'm just here to make sure that you and the girls get through the storm okay. When I woke up at my house, I got worried about the three of you here alone without power and when I saw a faint light coming from your windows, I figured I'd better check. Think of me as the big brother you never wanted."

Jessie looked from his warm brown gaze down to where he clasped her fingers in his. Big brother, her foot. Her pulse was beating triple time and she felt a little dizzy from the contact. Yeah, it had been that long since a man had touched her in even a friendly way.

She forced her lips to curve up in a smile even though she was feeling anything but friendly. The truth was Zach was the first guy to get under her skin in a really long time and the urge to push him back on the couch and join him under his pink comforter was almost more than she could stand.

She resisted, knowing that it would make being neighbors or friends with Zach way more complicated than she was ready to deal with. She shook her hand free from his and rolled under her own comforter.

"Sure, okay," she said. "Just so we're clear."

"Oh, we're clear," he said.

Jessie settled back onto her side of the couch, tucking the pink comforter around her. The flickering flames of yellow light and the crackle and hiss coming from the fireplace made the room cozy. She felt her eyelids get heavy even as she was aware of Zach's head just inches away from hers.

Rufus remained on the floor in front of the fire, his reddish brown hair aglow from the flames. His chest rose and fell and his feet twitched. Jessie wondered if he was chasing his yellow Frisbee in his sleep.

"This is weird," Zach said.

"What's weird?"

"Sleeping with a woman without sleeping with a woman," he said. His voice lowered on the second "sleeping," giving it a whole different meaning.

"I wouldn't know," Jessie said. "I've never slept with a woman or slept with a woman." She mimicked the way his voice had dropped and she heard him grunt.

"Fair enough," he said. Then he laughed. "I like you, Jessie Connelly."

"I like you, too, Zachary Caine."

In minutes, he was softly snoring while Jessie stared at the ceiling. She had spoken the truth. She did like Zach, but it was useless to speculate about anything happening between them. She had no interest in a relationship and even if she did, she couldn't get involved with Zach.

For one thing, he was good friends with her boss, Gavin, and it would be a whole lot of awkward if she and Zach got involved and something went wrong. And, of course, something would go wrong because as she had discovered when she was with her ex-husband, Seth, she was completely defective in the sack. As in, her girl parts were broken and there was just no fixing them.

Nope, there could never be anything between her and Zach, because if he ever looked at her the way her ex had, with utter contempt and disdain, she would never recover. No, it was better just to be neighbors, maybe friends, the sort that never ever saw each other naked.

Chapter 9

"Momma," a little voice whispered right before Jessie felt tiny fingers on her face prying her eyes open.

Jessie brushed the fingers away and tried to turn away from the little hands. Her head felt heavy and her body was sore as if the muscles in her back had cramped.

"Momma," the voice whispered again. Little hands shook her shoulder. "Zach is on our couch."

Jessie grunted. Knowing that Maddie would not go away, she blinked up at her daughter's concerned little face.

"It's all right," she said. "There was a blizzard and he came to check on us."

Mercifully, the little hands left her alone and Jessie felt herself drift back to sleep.

"Boo!"

"Ahhhhh!"

Jessie jumped at her daughter's shriek. She snapped her head up just in time to see Zach grab Maddie about the middle and start to tickle her. Maddie's squawk of fright turned into shrieks of laughter and Jessie knew that any opportunity to go back to sleep was gone, baby, gone.

Rufus rose from his warm spot by the fire, which Zach must have stoked in the night as it was still burning brightly and cranking out heat.

"Momma," Gracie appeared in the doorway in her bathrobe, clutching Chaos close. "It's so cold in the house and the lights don't work."

Jessie lifted her covers and Gracie climbed in while Jessie climbed out.

"Do it again," Maddie demanded.

Zach lay down and closed his eyes. She crept up to him and pushed on his brow bone until the upper lids of his eyes lifted and he was looking right at her, then he yelled "Boo!" and she jumped and began to giggle.

"Again!" Maddie demanded.

"No, that's enough," Jessie said. "You know the rule."

"Not before coffee," Gracie and Maddie said together.

"What's not before coffee?" Zach asked.

"Life," Jessie said.

"Oh, gotcha."

Zach rose, hooking Maddie around the middle as he did so. He swung her around as if she weighed no more than a pillow and locked one arm around her legs and one around her shoulders, carrying her like she was a human backpack. She started giggling.

"Hey, has anyone seen Maddie?" Zach asked. "She was right here a second ago."

Gracie lifted her arm from beneath the covers and pointed. "She's right there."

"Where?" Zach asked. He spun around as he looked behind him, twirling Maddie with him. She belly laughed.

"There," Gracie cried.

Zach went the other way. Maddie was laughing hard now as her honey-colored hair streamed out behind her.

"Nope, I still don't see her," Zach said. His brown eyes were wide as he looked at Gracie.

Throwing off her covers, Gracie thrust Chaos at Jessie, who hugged him close and watched as Gracie, her shy girl, gestured for Zach to lean down, so she could cup his face and turn his face toward Maddie's.

"Oh! Hello," Zach said. "What are you doing down there?"

"You picked me up," Maddie said through her laughter.

"I did?" he asked. "Huh, I must have confused you with Rufus."

This made both girls laugh and Rufus barked as if he were pleased to be a part of the conversation.

"Beep. Beep. Beep." Zach made the high-pitched sound of a truck in reverse and when his knees hit the back of the couch, he dropped Maddie onto the cushions, much to her delight.

It occurred to Jessie that having Zach here was a lot like having three children underfoot, but he was keeping the girls entertained and that counted for a lot.

Gracie took Chaos back and climbed under the blanket. Maddie commandeered Zach's blanket and did the same. Rufus jumped up to join her but Zach shook his head at the dog and said, "No."

Rufus glanced away as if he thought that not making eye contact with Zach meant he could disobey him. Jessie didn't really care if the dog got on the couch. With two kids under the age of seven, there wasn't much that hadn't been spilled onto the sectional she'd owned for ten years. A little dog dirt certainly wasn't going to be noticed on top of spit-up, juice, cracker crumbs, and several other way more offensive stinks and stains.

"He can stay," she said. "I don't mind dogs on the furniture."

"Nope, he's coming with me," Zach said.

"Where are you going?" Jessie asked.

"Home."

She glanced at the big picture window. It was an icy shade of gray outside. The sky was so pale with clouds and snow that it was hard to see where the land ended and the sky began. The snow was still pelting down and the wind rattled against the house, as if looking for an entrance.

"You're leaving?" she asked. She hated that she sounded nervous but there was no denying that Zach's solid presence as another adult—okay, adult-like person—had made the blizzard less worrisome.

"We're just going to get my generator," he said. "Don't you worry. We'll be brewing coffee before you know it."

Jessie stared at him for a beat and then asked, "Why are you still here?"

Zach laughed. He paused to poke at the fire and then pulled on his boots. Once he reached for his coat, Rufus bounded off the couch to join him.

Jessie walked them to the foyer, closing the door to the small anteroom to keep the blast of cold that would happen when they opened the front door from entering the house. She was curious to see what awaited them outside. Her front door had two long narrow windows on each side of it; she glanced out but all she could see was white. This did not bode well.

She didn't want Zach to go out there. What if something happened to him? How would she know? She wouldn't be able to leave the girls and help him. And she knew it was selfish but she didn't like the idea of riding out this blizzard by herself. Zach was right—they were safer if they stayed together. When she'd checked her phone for a weather update, the forecasters were predicting this blizzard would sit over their part of Maine for a few days.

Zach pulled his hood up and fastened it over his face; then he pulled on his gloves. He gave Jessie a nod to indicate he was ready for her to open the door. Instead, she moved to stand in front of it, blocking his path.

"Don't go," she said.

"What?" he asked. "But coffee."

"I know, and the caffeine addict in me is losing her mind about this, but it's a blizzard, Zach." Jessie grabbed the lapels of his coat and stared into his velvet-soft brown eyes. "You could freeze to death before you even make it to your house. It's not worth it. Coffee is not worth your life."

Zach stared at her for a moment and Jessie realized she had pulled him close during her protest and now his face was just inches from hers. Her attention wandered to his mouth and she noticed he had full lips that were very provocative. She wondered what it would feel like to be kissed by him.

"If you keep staring at me like that," Zach said, his voice a gruff growl. "I'll have to go out in the snow just to cool off."

"Huh? What?" Jessie forced her gaze back up to his.

He grinned at her and said, "Aw, what the hell? It's not like I haven't been wondering the same thing. And if we freeze to death because of this blizzard, it'll be better to know before I die."

"What are you talking about?" she asked.

"This." He kissed her.

Zach fit his lips to hers, softly at first, and then with increasing pressure. It was the sort of kiss that flirted, teased, and invited more even while keeping its distance. He sipped at her lips, learning their shape and feel but never pressing for more. For the first time since the power went out, Jessie felt hot all over.

It was Zach who broke away first. He pressed his forehead to hers. "Wow. That was better than I imagined and I have a pretty good imagination."

Jessie laughed but it was shaky. Zach made her feel things she wasn't used to feeling.

"Listen, my girl," he said. "I have to go. We need that generator. I promise I'll be back as fast as I can."

Jessie hugged him close. Then she let him go, because if she didn't do it now, she feared she never would.

"Okay," she said. "Be careful."

Zach nodded. He pulled the door open and then pushed open the storm door. The wind shoved hard against it, sending him staggering forward. Snow that had been piled up against the door fell into the house in an explosion of cold and wet.

"Don't worry," Zach said. "We've got this."

Rufus darted out into the snow with him and Zach grabbed the door handle and pushed it shut behind him. She watched the man and the dog as they disappeared in a flurry of white. She tried to tell herself it would be okay but she knew she wouldn't feel better until they returned.

She glanced down at her feet and realized she was standing in a pile of snow in her socks. In seconds her toes were frozen.

She charged into the kitchen and grabbed several gallon-sized plastic bags from the box in the pantry. She scooped the snow up into the bags and then put them in the freezer and the refrigerator, hoping to keep her perishables cold.

She came back into the living room to find both girls on the couch under the blankets watching the fire. She peeled off her soggy frigid socks and put her feet up on the toasty warm hearth.

"Is Zach coming back, Momma?" Maddie asked.

"He said he was."

"Men lie," Gracie said.

Jessie closed her eyes for a moment. Of the two girls, Gracie, being the oldest, had suffered more from her father's reprehensible behavior than Maddie had. The number of times Seth had lied to his daughter about whether he would show up for a soccer game or a robotics competition were too numerous to count. For a long time, Jessie had defended him, but no more. It did no good to raise her daughter's hopes just to watch them be dashed the next time.

"Not all men lie," she said. "It's an individual flaw, not one that belongs to boys or girls."

"I bet he doesn't come back," Gracie persisted.

"I bet he does," Maddie argued.

Jessie glanced between them. "We'll just have to wait and see. In the meantime, let's feed Chaos. He could probably use some fuel in his belly to help him keep warm."

The girls silently rolled off the couch and moved toward the kitchen. Unable to help herself, Jessie glanced out the window toward Zach's house. She knew it was ridiculous but she sent up a silent plea. *Please come back, Zach. Not just for the girls but because I could really use a frigging cup of coffee.*

Fifteen minutes passed, then a half hour, then forty-five

minutes. Jessie had taken to standing at the window to see what was happening next door. Had he forgotten about them? Maybe one of his little field marketers had gotten stranded and he'd rushed to her rescue.

Jessie didn't like how the thought of that made her feel so she gave it a solid push out of her headspace. Zach was a businessman. Probably he'd gotten home to a million details he'd missed at work and was even now ensconced in his office trying to catch up on things.

She thought about calling him under the guise of seeing if he was all right—not a total lie—but they hadn't exchanged phone numbers so she couldn't. She debated calling a mutual friend to get his number but that felt too stalkerish, plus she'd have to explain that he had spent the night and that was definitely crossing a line.

Instead, she ran upstairs and put on a warm, dry pair of socks and then tried to figure out how to cook something on the glowing embers of the fire. Using her cast iron skillet, she whipped up a batch of fried eggs. She let the girls try to toast some bread on marshmallow sticks over the fire but Maddie's bread fell into the embers and Gracie's caught on fire and came out charred.

Gracie made a face and Jessie said, "The charcoal is good for your teeth."

"You always say that when you burn the toast," Maddie said. "It's all bitter and tastes terrible."

Jessie could not argue the point. Her grandmother used to say the same thing to her about burnt toast and she never believed her. She cut up fresh fruit and hoped that it with the eggs could hold the girls until she could plug in her toaster or microwave, assuming that Zach actually did come back.

She refused to look out the window. She did the dishes, grateful that she had a gas hot water heater, and sent the girls upstairs to get dressed. She was about to follow them when there was a knock on the front door.

So relieved that Zach had come back, she raced for the door and yanked it open. Standing there in his heavy wool uniform coat was the Bluff Point chief of police Cooper O'Rourke.

Jessie's first thought was that something awful had happened to Zach but that made no sense since there was no way for Cooper to know that she'd been waiting for him.

"Hi, Jessie," he said.

"Cooper, it's good to see you," she said.

She glanced past him to see if Zach was with him. The wind was blowing and the sky was gray. The snow continued to fall and when she glanced at her front steps, she realized the snow was so deep that even the shape of the steps had disappeared. She needed to get out there and sweep.

"Everything all right?" Cooper asked. Jessie gestured for him to come inside and he did, standing in her foyer with his snow-covered hat and boots.

They had a history, as he had come to Jessie's house a couple of times when she was married, usually when he found Seth at a bar too shnockered to drive himself home. There had only been one time when he arrived to mediate a domestic disturbance. For the longest time, Jessie hadn't been able to look him in the eye—the shame had been more than she could bear—but Cooper was a good guy and eventually they moved past it.

Of course, every time he saw her, he told her that she didn't have to stay with Seth, there were places that could help her. Jessie hadn't listened to him. Still, she valued his friendship. Given that not many people knew the truth of her marriage to Seth, she had always appreciated Cooper O'Rourke keeping an eye on her and the girls.

"Power is still out," she said. "But I have food and water and a fire going."

"Best to stay off the roads if you can," Cooper said. "The storm is supposed to last another twenty-four hours and I have no idea how long it will take for the power to come back on."

"I have nowhere to be," Jessie said.

She had checked her phone earlier and found a text from

Gavin saying that they were keeping the animal clinic closed unless there was a life-threatening emergency. That was fine with her. She did not want to leave the safety of her home.

"Excellent," Cooper said. He opened the door and stepped back outside. "If you need anything, just call me. I'll be driving through the neighborhood regularly, making sure the plows are getting through."

"Thanks, Cooper," she said. She followed him out onto the porch. It hit her then that he was a good man. He cared about his community and he worked hard to ensure the residents' safety. Impulsively, she gave him a quick hug. "Be careful out there."

Cooper hugged her back. If he was surprised by her affection, he didn't let it show. Jessie suspected he was getting a lot of hugs from scared residents who were so very grateful to see him.

The sound of an engine broke the quiet and they turned to glance at the driveway and saw a large truck backing up toward Jessie's house. It stopped just short of the steps and the engine shut off. Zach popped out of the driver's seat and slogged through the knee-deep snow toward them with Rufus at his side.

Zach stepped in the same places Cooper had as he plowed through the drift to get to the porch. The wind blew the ends of his scarf as he unfastened his hood and pushed it back on his head. He glanced at the two of them. He was frowning.

"Coop," he said.

"Zach."

Jessie glanced between the two of them and realized she and Cooper still had an arm about each other. She eased out of his hold and said, "Thanks so much for stopping by, Chief."

Cooper glanced at her and then Zach. His sharp cop's gaze missed nothing and Jessie felt her face grow warm and it was not in an effort to fight off the cold.

"Anytime," Cooper said. "Zach, a word."

Cooper jerked his head in the direction of Zach's truck

and Jessie watched the two men walk back into the storm. She wondered what Coop wanted to talk about but not enough to continue to freeze her tail off. She patted her thigh, signaling to Rufus to come with her as she hurried back inside and shut the door.

Chapter 10

Zach was surly. It wasn't for lack of caffeine, although that probably didn't help. It wasn't the cold, although that certainly wasn't improving his disposition any. No, it was straight-up annoyance he was feeling at seeing Jessie hug Cooper.

Were they a thing? How did he not know this? And if they were, where the hell had Cooper been last night when Jessie and the girls needed him? For that matter, why hadn't her mangy ex been around to check on them? No, it was none of his business. Zach knew that but he didn't care.

"What's going on with you and Jessie?" he asked Cooper as soon as he saw the door close behind her.

"I'm sorry?" Cooper shook his head as if he wasn't registering what Zach was saying. Yeah, if that was the chief's way of shutting down that line of questioning, ha, not gonna happen.

"You heard me," Zach said. "I wasn't aware that you and Jessie—"

"We're not," Cooper said. "As far as I know, Jessie isn't

seeing anyone, unless you have something to share to the contrary?"

"Just neighbors," Zach said. But the explanation didn't seem to fit quite like it did a few days ago.

"Uh-huh."

"When the power blew in the middle of the night, I came over to check on her and the girls," Zach said. He jerked his thumb at the back of his truck. "I brought over my generator so she can cook and stuff."

"That's decent of you," Cooper said.

"I thought so," Zach said. "Didn't get me any hugs."

He didn't mention the kiss that had rocked him to his socks. That was strictly need-to-know information and as far as he was concerned he was the only one who needed to know that Jessie Connelly could kiss a man stupid.

"Yeah, well, Jessie and I go way back," Cooper said.

The wind picked up and he turned his back to it. Zach noticed that Coop's cheeks were ruddy from the cold and he knew from playing on the same town league volleyball team that Coop was built solid without an ounce of fat on him. Annoying.

"How far back?" he asked.

"Not like you're thinking," Cooper said. "I was called a few times to help her out with her ex. He's not a good guy, a situation made worse by the fact that his father, Judge Connelly, always protects him."

Zach had suspected as much, given that Jessie and the girls were stuck in a blizzard and as far as he knew they'd heard nothing from her ex, not even a *how are you doing?* text.

"What are you trying to tell me?" Zach asked.

"Jessie's been through a lot," Cooper said. "Be easy with her."

"I'm not following." The snow began falling faster and harder. Zach could feel it building up on his eyelashes; still he didn't blink it away, keeping his gaze narrowed on Cooper.

"Fine, I'll be blunt. She's not one of your usual one-night-stand party girls," Cooper said. "She's been through a lot. Don't hook up with her unless you can be more."

"Seriously? Cops are giving out relationship advice now?" Zach asked.

Cooper shrugged. "I'm just looking out for someone that I know has been hurt pretty badly. I'd do the same for anyone."

Zach considered him for a few seconds. He was beginning to lose the feeling in his toes, so he nodded. "Don't worry. Like I said, I'm just being neighborly."

"Sure," Cooper agreed. "That's why you looked like you wanted to rip my head off when you saw me hug Jessie."

"Neighbors can be protective, too," Zach said. "Remember, I have five little sisters. Now stop with all of the girly talk. Christ, I can practically feel my balls shrinking. Next thing I know you'll want us to braid each other's hair. Come on, help me set this sucker up."

Cooper laughed, letting Zach know they'd reached an understanding. Together they hauled the generator out of the truck and after much debate set it up on the covered stone patio at the back of the house.

When the diesel motor kicked in, Zach ran an extension in through a kitchen window and Jessie plugged in the coffeepot. Cooper stayed long enough for Jessie to fill his travel mug with fresh hot coffee and then he was off to check on the rest of the neighborhood. Zach was not sad to see him go.

He knew he was being ridiculous. He knew it. And yet, he felt a proprietary protectiveness about Jessie and the girls that he couldn't switch off or ignore. He thought about what Cooper had said about Jessie's ex, that he wasn't a good guy.

This held up to everything he'd heard. Seven years ago, Seth Connelly had been about to marry Mac, as in at the church and wearing a tux, when Jessie had driven up and honked and Seth abandoned Mac at the altar. When Mac had returned last spring after a seven-year absence, she and Jessie had come to understand how Seth had played them both. And it was pretty clear that Jessie had gotten the short straw as she was the one who'd married him.

Seth Connelly had a reputation in town as a drinker and a skirt chaser who couldn't seem to keep a job. Zach hadn't had much to do with him, but since he and his field marketers worked the restaurant and bar scene, he'd seen him around. He'd seen him hit on one of his girls—yes, while he was still married to Jessie—but being a liberated sort of woman, his employee had put Seth in his place without having to call Zach in to help. Now Zach was sort of wishing he'd had the opportunity to throw Seth out of the bar on his ass.

Jessie poured them each a large mug of coffee and she pushed Zach's toward him, along with the sugar bowl and the jug of milk. Zach noted that she drank her coffee black. Now why did he find that intriguing?

"You may have saved lives with this," Jessie said. She raised her mug to him just as Maddie went running by screeching as Rufus chased her through the house.

Zach grinned. He liked these ladies. "How about we go crazy and plug in the toaster? I brought bagels. Then we can rally the troops and go shovel snow."

He reached into a grocery bag and pulled out a sack of bagels. Jessie snatched them up, looking positively perky. When she turned away to get the toaster out of the cupboard, Zach told himself not to take advantage and ogle her behind, but it was so perfectly shaped it made his palms tingle.

When she straightened up, he quickly brought his coffee up to his lips to keep himself from doing something juvenile, like letting out a wolf whistle or begging her to go on a date with him, because wouldn't that be awkward.

He ran a hand through his unruly blonde hair, shoving it off his forehead. He had to get a grip. They were just neighbors. He glanced at the window, willing the sun to come out and chase the blizzard away. The snow seemed to fall harder and faster. Even nature was conspiring against him. Great, just great.

*   *   *

After a hearty meal, they all suited up in their thickest snow gear. The girls were in charge of using brooms to brush off the porch while Zach and Jessie used a snow blower and snow shovels to clear out a path along the front walk to the driveway, which had already been plowed by one of Zach's friends.

It was freezing cold but the exercise felt good and as the girls chased Rufus around the yard, Jessie seemed pleased that at least they were running some of their energy out.

Zach put the snow blower away in Jessie's garage and was walking back to the house when the first shot hit him square in the back. He whipped around just in time to see Maddie's bright blue coat disappear behind a snowdrift.

Zach immediately hunkered down and made a small pile of snowballs. Game on. He waited patiently out of sight until he caught a movement in his peripheral vision. Without hesitation, he picked up a snowball and fired in the direction of the person.

Splat! Too late he realized he'd hit Jessie, who was walking back along the newly cleared path.

"What the—Zach!" she cried.

Before he could form an apology, she had dropped to the ground and looked to be packing the mother of all snowballs.

When she lifted her arm, he looked for Rufus, and shouted, "Run!"

The dog barked at Zach, hoping he'd throw another snowball, but there was no time. Jessie was probably already locked in on him—*kapow!*

She nailed him right in the back of the head and all hell broke loose. For the next half hour, it was a free-for-all of snowballs and turf as Zach, Jessie, and the girls battled it out until Jessie formed an alliance with her daughters and all three of them brought Zach down with a perfectly executed ambush that caught him and Rufus in their fort at the mercy of girl power.

"All right, all right," Zach said. "I surrender!"

He was frozen cold and had long since lost the feeling in his toes. He needed one of Jessie's magical hot chocolates and he needed it right now.

"Woo-hoo!" Maddie cried a victory cheer and rushed Zach's fort from her hiding spot. "Girls rule and boys drool!"

"Oh, yeah?" Zach said. He quickly snatched up the precocious five-year-old and lobbed her into the big fluffy snowdrift beside him.

"Hey!" Gracie protested. "That's no fair. You surrendered."

Zach snatched her up, too, ignoring her delighted squeals, and tossed her into the snowbank as well. Both girls were laughing as they threw half-formed snowballs at him. He planted his hands on his hips and dodged their weakened efforts. The cold was making them all sluggish and slow.

He felt a tug on his jacket but ignored it, thinking it was Rufus nudging him from behind. Then the icy cold hit his spine and he jumped, spinning around to find Jessie there. She had dumped snow down his back and she was laughing.

The sound was delightful. Zach realized he'd never heard her full-on belly laugh before. He found he was grinning like an idiot when he strode forward and snatched her up and tossed her over his shoulder. Three strides and he lobbed her up into the air, letting her join her girls in their wintery seats.

Jessie was still laughing. Rufus, delighted with this new game, dashed from the girls to Zach and back, barking as if trying to get him to do it again.

Zach crossed his arms over his chest, trying to give them his best superhero look, with one eyebrow raised and his jaw jutted out. Gracie took the opportunity to hit him in the face with a snowball.

This sent all three women into more peals of laughter and Zach shook the snow off and then shouted, "That's it!" He took a running dive into the enormous snowdrift as if to grab them and all three of them shrieked and ran.

"Come on," Jessie cried. She grabbed her girls by the

mittens and said, "To the house. The house is a safe base, no snowballs on base."

They dashed across the yard. Zach jumped out of the drift and shook off the extra snow, much like Rufus. He let them get a head start since he was now frozen cold and officially ready to call it quits.

As soon as the girls stepped up onto the porch, he followed them and Maddie held up her snow-encrusted mittens to ward him off.

"Safe," she said.

Zach stopped and bent down so that they were nose to nose, winked, and said, "For now."

Maddie busted out a grin and turned around to exchange a high five with her sister.

"Who is ready for hot chocolate?" Jessie asked as she led the way into the house.

Zach watched the swing of her hips as she stepped through the door and realized it wasn't the hot chocolate luring him in; oh, no, he was pretty sure he'd follow Jessie Connelly anywhere she went.

Chapter 11

The power outage continued through three board games, lunch, and an arts-and-crafts project that was supposed to be making snowflakes out of printer paper but turned into an epic fail when Zach unfolded his and it looked like six knobby penises.

"Oh, wow, I didn't see that happening," he said.

Jessie about choked on her own spit from trying not to laugh as Zach tried to hide his pervy snowflake from the girls. He should have known better. When he hid it behind his back, they attacked. Maddie wrestled it from his hands while Gracie distracted him by saying she heard someone on the front porch.

When Maddie unfolded it, she frowned.

"Why don't you like it, Zach? It looks like p—"

"No—" Zach tried to cut her off to no success.

"—arrots."

"Huh?" He raised one eyebrow at her.

Gracie glanced over her sister's shoulder and nodded. "Yeah, parrots. See? Here's the head—"

"Got it!" Zach cried.

Jessie turned away. The urge to laugh was becoming too much and she had to fake a coughing fit to try and contain it. Parrots! Bless her innocent little girls' hearts.

"Are you all right, Momma?" Gracie asked.

"Fine, I'm fine," Jessie answered. Her voice was strained and she was still facing away from them, because she knew if she looked at Zach or his snowflake, she was going to lose it completely.

She felt him at her back before he spoke. One arm appeared in front of her, and he leaned close, speaking right into her ear, and said, "So, did you want to hang my bird-like snowflake on the window with the others? The girls seem to think it's full of peckers."

The laugh, when it came out of Jessie, was something between and guffaw and a snort. As she looked at Zach's phallic snowflake, she doubled up with laughter. The more she tried to contain it, the worse the giggle fit became.

"Momma, you shouldn't laugh at Zach's snowflake," Gracie said. "You'll hurt his feelings."

Jessie pressed her lips together and nodded, trying her best.

"She's right," Zach said. "My feelings will go positively limp."

A snort erupted and tears sprang from her eyes. Jessie gave Zach a warning look that was likely ruined by the smile that still curved her lips up.

"Here," he said. He reached around her, brushing her side with his arm, and ripped a piece of tape off of the dispenser. "Let's hang it right here, shall we?"

Jessie watched as he taped his snowflake along with the others they had made right in the center of the kitchen window.

"Oh, that looks good there," Maddie said. "Don't you think so, Momma?"

"It would be hard to find a better place for it," Jessie said.

This time it was Zach who hooted with laughter. He didn't even try to contain it.

As he walked past her on his way back to his seat, he leaned in close and said, "I feel compelled to say that the parrots on the snowflake are not the actual size."

His teasing gaze held hers and Jessie felt her face get hot.

"Of course not," Gracie said. "Everyone knows a real parrot is bigger than that."

Zach reclaimed his seat at the table and grinned. "Man, I love these kids."

Both of her daughters beamed up at him as he began to fold his next piece of paper, and Jessie felt something in her chest shift. This. This day of laughter and chatter was what she'd always hoped for with her ex-husband, but he hadn't been one to spend time with his daughters.

Seth liked his daughters to be dressed prettily and to be quiet. On the few occasions that they had been in public as a family, he'd expected Jessie and the girls to make him look good. He'd certainly never thrown them into snowbanks, played board games, or made paper snowflakes with them. It used to hurt her that Seth couldn't see the magical creatures that their daughters were but she'd adjusted, trying to fill the space where a father would usually stand in his daughters' lives.

She watched as Zach threw an M&M in the air and caught it in his mouth. This, of course, turned into a game for the girls to see who could throw it into Zach's mouth. When Maddie tossed up an M&M and tried to catch it, Jessie had to keep herself from telling her not to because she would choke. The M&M bounced off of Maddie's nose and she erupted into laughs.

The happy threesome settled back down and began to work on their snowflakes and Jessie grabbed a pair of scissors and joined them. She folded her paper up and began cutting. When she opened it, the snowflake was a series of hearts. She thought it was pretty appropriate, because despite the power outage and the stress of dealing with the storm that still raged outside, she loved this day. When she taped her snowflake right next to Zach's "parrot" one, she couldn't help but laugh.

*   *   *

Exhausted from their time outside and full of beef stew, which Jessie had made in the Crock-Pot, and bread and butter, the sisters demanded three stories from Zach before they clocked out in their sleeping bags on the floor of the living room. The fireplace was keeping the first floor of the house toasty warm, but the upstairs was too cold and dark for the girls. Rufus and Chaos wedged themselves in between the girls, the four of them sleeping in a pile like all good packs did.

Zach and Jessie moved into the dining area on the other side of the room so as not to wake the girls. A chime sounded and Zach took his phone from his pocket and studied the message.

"It's Cooper," he said. "Mr. and Mrs. Lewis, across the street from me, are having trouble with their generator. He wants me to run over and check on them."

"Can I help?" Jessie asked.

"No, but thanks," he said. He dropped his phone on the table and stealthily went to retrieve his boots from where he'd put them on the hearth to dry out.

Jessie glanced at the phone. Sure enough she saw the name Coop and the name Lewis in the text. She felt bad for checking on him like she used to check on Seth, who would never have left his phone where she could read it and discover his many extramarital affairs.

That alone let her know that Zach was a good guy with nothing to hide. It was ridiculous—she had no need to check his phone—but she couldn't help feeling possessive since Zach had been so helpful in getting them through this storm. She really didn't want to share him, which was ridiculous because they were just neighbors. He wasn't hers to share or not with anyone.

He moved from his boots to his coat, gloves, and hat. When he was fully covered, he started toward the door. Jessie hurried after him with his phone.

"Zach, don't forget your phone," she said. "In case you get into trouble and need to call for help."

"Thanks," he said. "Can you put it inside my coat pocket?"

He patted his chest with a thick glove and Jessie unzipped his jacket and tucked his phone into the inside pocket before she zipped him back up.

"Stay safe," she said.

"I promise."

He fastened the hood, which covered his nose and mouth, and his hat sat low on his brow beneath the hood, making just his eyes visible. She couldn't hear him if he said anything more so she turned and opened the door to let him out.

"Do you want Rufus with you?" she asked.

Zach shook his head, and she got the feeling he wanted Rufus to stay here with her and the girls to keep an eye on them. It was a sweet gesture but she would have felt better if he took the dog with him. It was cold and dark outside and she couldn't help but worry.

An hour passed before he returned. Jessie yanked the door open and he hurried into the house on a gust of bitter cold air. Zach looked frozen, with snow caked on his hat and gloves, and Rufus mobbed him, clearly anxious about his human. Zach yanked off a glove and petted Rufus until the dog was assured that his person was fine; then the dog resumed his post between the girls.

Jessie went into the kitchen and used the extension cord from the generator to plug in the microwave to heat some milk for hot chocolate. She had noticed that Zach enjoyed it and she wanted to do something nice for him.

The fact that he had run out of a warm house to go help a neighbor in one of the worst blizzards in Bluff Point history reinforced what she was coming to believe about Zachary Caine: that he was a good man, whether he wanted to acknowledge it or not.

She wasn't used to having someone share her responsibilities and while she knew she could have managed this storm by herself, it would have been infinitely more stressful. Zach collapsed on a chair at the dining room table, and when the cocoa was done, she pushed his mug in front of him and he glanced up at her.

"Thanks," he said. "It's still snowing but it looks like the worst of the storm has passed. They're giving it another twenty-four hours to move out completely."

"Oh, good," she said. "And the Lewises are okay?"

"Oh, yeah," Zach said. "I brought over some diesel for his generator and made sure he had enough firewood. He and Mrs. Lewis looked like they were planning a romantic rendezvous in front of the fire."

"They did not," Jessie said.

"She came out in a negligee," Zach said. "And those little shoes with the feathers on the toes."

"Kitten heels?" Jessie asked. She tried to wrap her head around the elderly Mrs. Lewis dressed like that.

"Yep, those are the ones," Zach said. Then he laughed. "Mr. Lewis couldn't get rid of me fast enough."

Jessie sank into the chair beside his, holding her cocoa in two hands to keep her fingers warm. She took a sip.

"Well," she said.

"Yep, that's pretty much all I could say, too." Zach laughed. "Who knew Mr. Lewis had it in him."

Jessie grinned. "Here's to Mr. and Mrs. Lewis." She held up her mug in salute and Zach lifted his and tapped it against hers.

They were quiet for a moment and Zach shifted in his seat, clearly restless. Jessie had the feeling he had something on his mind. She was right.

"Jessie, I know it's none of my business, but where is Seth? I mean, maybe he's checked in and I'm unaware, but it seems to me that when your daughters are in a blizzard, you should check on them," he said.

Jessie could tell by the deep frown line in between his eyes that he was perturbed even though his voice was even as if he was actively trying to keep out the judgment and derision.

"Last I heard, he was in Costa Rica," she said.

"Excuse me?"

"Right before the holidays, he announced that he was feeling depressed and needed some 'me' time. That's the last I've heard from him."

"He missed Christmas and New Year's?" Zach asked. This time his voice was higher and his frown line deeper.

"Yes," she said. "Honestly, and I don't mean to be cruel, but I think we had a much better holiday without him. He tends to bring very high expectations and a lot of drama with him. The girls and I had a very nice, very mellow holiday for a change."

Zach didn't say anything but his knuckles were white where he gripped his mug. Without overthinking it, Jessie reached out and put her hand on his.

"It's okay," she said. "We're doing all right."

Zach nodded. His gaze moved from her eyes to her mouth. Before Jessie could track his movement, he was pressing his lips against hers.

She stiffened in surprise and he went still but he didn't pull away. Instead, he put his cocoa down and cupped her face with his hands, holding her gently as if she were something rare and precious that he'd found.

Then he kissed her again. This time Jessie was ready and she didn't jump but she didn't kiss him back either. Truly, she was so out of practice, she didn't know what to do, or where to put her hands, and she was pretty sure she'd forgotten how to breathe and was about to pass out.

Zach pulled away again, just far enough so he could see her face. She had no idea what he saw there but whatever it was, he must have been reassured because he came back in for more. Under his gentle pressure, Jessie actually managed to get her lips to pucker a little in return.

She felt Zach smile against her mouth and she relaxed a tiny bit; maybe she wasn't completely hopeless at kissing. Tentatively, she opened her mouth, inviting Zach to deepen the kiss. He did. He licked across her lips and urged her to kiss him back with the same intensity. He moved one hand to the back of her head and buried his fingers in her hair, holding her steady while he took full possession of her mouth, her wits, and any sense of where she ended and he began.

He tasted of spicy cocoa and smelled of pine trees and freshly fallen snow. His body put off a heat she hadn't felt in a long time and a part of her wanted to melt against that masculine warmth and let it consume her.

Jessie didn't remember putting her mug down or turning into him. She only knew that when she finally came up for air, her hands were on his shoulders, her fingers clutching the fabric of his wool sweater as if she never planned to let go.

His face was inches from hers. They were both breathing hard. Zach's gaze met hers and his brown eyes looked startled as if he hadn't expected what had just happened.

"Well, that escalated quickly," he said. He took her hands in his and laced their fingers together.

"Yeah." She glanced down at the table. Oh, man, he'd probably just meant to give her a quick kiss. A sorry-your-life-is-such-a-train-wreck sort of kiss, but her lack of skill and want for affection had spiraled them into a whole new place.

"Hey." He let go of one of her hands and lifted her chin so that she was looking at him again. "That's not a bad thing."

"Oh," she said.

"I've wanted to kiss you since the last time and, well, pretty much since I was lying flat on my back in a snow-drift, looking up at your pretty blue eyes."

Jessie felt her face get hot.

"But since we're communal living here," he said, gesturing at the girls, who were asleep in front of the fire, "I figured I'd better rein it in."

"Yeah, good plan," she said. "Wouldn't want to get carried away."

As if the universe was looking out for her, Zach's phone chimed. He glanced at it and said, "That's Cooper. I'd better take it."

She nodded. "Tell him I said hi."

As soon as Zach answered his phone, Jessie grabbed her phone from where it sat on the counter and dashed into the bathroom that was built into the space below the stairs. It was snug and tiny and with no power she had to use a candle and the display from her cell phone to be able to see but she didn't care. At the moment she needed to put some space between her and Zach and she needed a girl squad council.

Opening her texting app, she quickly typed: Z kissed me. Twice. What do I do?

In less than thirty seconds, her phone exploded with chimes signaling incoming messages. She scrambled to turn down the volume, worried that Zach might have heard it and guessed what she was doing.

Mac: What?!
Carly: Give us deets! How was it? I bet he uses a lot of tongue, does he?
Emma: Aw!
Jillian: Depends. How do you feel about it?
Gina: Kiss him back. Duh.

Jessie read the flurry of messages which rivaled the snow still falling outside. She was looking for something. She didn't know what. Permission? Approval? Acceptance?

She was only a peripheral part of this group and she desperately did not want to blow it by hooking up with one of their men. If anyone had dibs on Zach, she would walk away, no problem.

Mac: Hello? Jessie?
Jessie: I'm here. I just—does anyone mind that Zach kissed me? Because I will totally shut that down if you do.
Emma: Married.
Carly: I'm already taken.
Jillian: Just a friend.
Gina: What Jilly said.
Mac: I think he's yours if you want him, but . . .

The symbol for Mac still typing came up but no words appeared. Jessie stared at her phone, willing Mac to finish her thought.

Jessie: But what?

She stared at her phone. Had she lost service? Nope. The bars were all good. The battery was good.

Carly: What Mac is trying to figure out how to say is that Zach is, well, he's Zach.
Jessie: What does that mean?
Emma: He's lovable.
Jillian: He's fun.
Mac: He's got a good heart.
Carly: He's a great friend.
Gina: And if you fall for him he will probably break your heart.
Mac: What Gina means is commitment is not really Zach's thing.
Emma: So, you might want to view him as a more casual situation.
Carly: He's a fling.
Gina: Leave your heart out of it.
Jillian: On the upside, he's the sort you can have a fling with and then downshift into friends and he'd be great about it.

Jessie stared at the messages. She wasn't sure how she felt about this. Did she want forever? It hadn't really worked out for her before. Maybe this was exactly what she needed. Yes, she believed it was. She just had one more question.

Chapter 12

Jessie: Do you know this from personal experience? Anyone?
Carly: No.
Jillian: Nope.
Emma: Not me.
Mac: No.
Gina: No, but I mean, come on, it's Zach. He's friends with everyone.

Jessie blew out a breath. That was all she needed to know. Zach was a free agent and so was she. Excellent.

Jessie: Okay. Thanks.
Carly: Thanks? Oh, no, you don't. Tell us what is happening!
Mac: Yeah, or we're coming over.
Jessie: Nothing yet, but the possibility exists.
Jillian: Good for you. Now, everyone, quit badgering her.

The group chat turned into everyone sharing where they were and what they were doing. All agreed to meet up at The Grind, the coffee shop Gina managed, as soon as the roads were clear and the power was back.

One by one, they left the group until it was just Carly and Jessie.

Carly: Zach is one of my most favorite people. Be careful with him—that's all I'm going to say.
Jessie: I promise.
Carly: Okay, then go get busy!

Jessie closed the group messages and sat on the edge of the tub. She bent over and pressed her phone to her forehead. Surely, she must be crazy. So, Zach had kissed her. Big deal. Maybe it had just been a random impulse on his part because they'd been tripping over each other all day.

She pressed her fingers to her lips. It had been a really great kiss. Granted, she was no judge because it had been so long since anyone had kissed her with any feeling. He could have kissed her like she was one of his sisters and she probably would have responded. Jessie thought about the way he'd deepened the kiss. Yeah, he didn't think of her as a sister.

Her life had been in stasis for so long. Maybe Zach was just what she needed to move out of her rut and move forward. It didn't have to be some emotionally heavy big deal. It could just be a fling to help Jessie get her mojo back.

Grinning, she rose to her feet, shoved her phone into her pocket, washed her hands, and patted her face with cool water in an effort to clear out the cobwebs. She was a grown woman of thirty-two with two daughters. If she wanted a fling, she could damn well have one, or so she told her reflection.

She opened the door and blew out the candle, making her way back into the kitchen as quietly as she could. Zach was standing in the kitchen, and Jessie knew in that moment she would never forget the sight of him right there.

His shaggy blonde hair was in its usual unkempt disarray as if he'd just taken off a hat and the static had made it spring up about his head. The candles on the counter in front of him illuminated his crooked nose, his wide jaw, and the slash of white that was his smile. He was leaning on his fists on the counter, as if trying to push whatever emotion he was feeling into the granite beneath his knuckles, but when he saw her, when his soft brown gaze met hers, he dropped his hands and reached for her.

Jessie didn't resist. She let him pull her toward him, knowing full well that if he kissed her again, she was done for.

But he didn't kiss her. Instead, he hugged her close. He rested his cheek on the top of her hair and then he swayed back and forth with her from side to side, humming, like they were two kids at a middle school dance who liked each other but had no idea what to do about it.

Jessie let his warmth engulf her. She leaned her head on his chest and put her arms around his waist with his arms over hers, holding her close. It was lovely and soothing and she was pretty sure she could have stayed with him like this all night—except she really wanted him to kiss her again. She really wanted to know if what she'd felt before, that magical electrical spark, happened again.

He moved one hand up and down her back while the other sifted through her hair from the back of her neck and out to the ends; the gentle tugging gesture was probably supposed to be calming or crazy making. Jessie wasn't sure which but she was definitely leaning toward the crazy side.

Just when she thought she couldn't take it anymore, Zach stilled. He cupped her face and his gaze met hers.

"So, what did the girls have to say?" he asked.

Jessie felt her eyebrows shoot up in surprise. "How did you know?"

"I heard your phone going off," he said. "I figured you freaked out and texted the crew."

"I did." Jessie bit her lip. "Was that bad form? I'm sorry. It's just that I'm on unfamiliar ground here and I haven't had anything to text anyone about—"

Her words trailed off. She really didn't know what to say and she was afraid something inappropriate was going to fly out, like, *Hey, I can't remember what a man looks like so can I see you naked?* Yeah, that wouldn't go over well, so she shut her mouth and remained silent.

"It's fine," Zach whispered and then he kissed her again. *Zap.* The spark was back. In fact, it was even more potent than before. Jessie clung to Zach, encouraging him to wake up the parts of her that she had assumed were dead and gone.

The hands that had been gentle now hauled her up against him, one wrapping around her lower back while the other dug into her hair to hold her still for a kiss that was a thorough possession. He kissed her as if he couldn't get enough of her, the taste of her, the feel of her mouth beneath his, or the way she moaned in the back of her throat. Jessie loved it.

She loved feeling wanted and desired and she wanted to return the feeling. She moved her hands down his sides to his ass and pulled him in hard. Zach grunted and Jessie smiled against his lips.

"Wicked woman," he hissed against her lips in raspy gruff growl, but he looked pleased.

"Momma?" It took a second for the voice to penetrate the sexy fog that surrounded her brain. "Momma?"

Zach and Jessie jumped away from each other. Jessie began to fix her hair and shirt while Zach turned away from her. It was Gracie who'd called to her and Jessie hustled over to the living room to see what her daughter needed.

"What is it, honey?" she asked. Her voice sounded rough and she cleared her throat.

Zach passed her as he approached the living room, checking on the situation, too. He swiftly clasped her hand in his, giving her fingers a quick squeeze before letting her go. Jessie gave him side-eye and he winked at her.

"If everything is okay here, I'll just be outside rolling in the snow," he said. "Come on, Rufus, you need a walk."

The dog pushed up from his spot on the floor and

bounded after Zach. Jessie took Rufus's spot and glanced at her daughter. Gracie's eyes were fuzzy with sleep, and Jessie was reassured that Gracie wasn't aware of what had just transpired between her and Zach.

"What's the matter, love?" she asked. She smoothed Gracie's hair back from her forehead.

"Nothing." Gracie's voice was already groggy with sleep. "I just wanted to be sure of you."

"Always, baby," Jessie said.

She put her head on Gracie's pillow, and continued to rub her daughter's back. Gracie let out a soft sigh and fell back to sleep. Jessie gazed into the fire. The flames were low but the heat that poured out of the grate was exquisite.

After kissing Zach, she was sure she was too keyed up to fall asleep. All she could think about was what might have happened between them if Gracie hadn't woken up. The crew said Zach was perfect fling material. Was she ready for a fling? Did she want to have one with Zach? *Hell yeah!*

Her eyelids felt heavy and she knew she should get up, but it was so warm in this spot, wedged between her girls. She decided to rest her eyes for just a moment. She dreamed of kissing Zach. It was a good dream.

She felt his arms around her and she twined her arms around his neck. The temperature dropped and she shivered. He kissed her head and tucked her into bed. With a kiss on her lips, he pulled her covers up to her chin before he pulled away. Jessie wanted to protest. She wanted to lure him back but sleep beckoned and she couldn't seem to fight it. She felt herself falling, falling, falling into a deep slumber.

When Jessie awoke the next morning, she was on her side of the couch, tucked under her blanket. She glanced over to see a thick thatch of honey blonde hair on the pillow next to hers. Zach was stretched out on the other side of the couch.

She frowned. She didn't remember going to bed the

night before. In fact, the last thing she did recall was comforting Gracie after a bad dream. She distinctly remembered lying down on the floor with her daughter, and that was it.

Oh, wait, she'd had a dream about kissing Zach. Had it been a dream? She didn't think so. She suspected he'd picked her up off the floor and tucked her in on the couch. Darn, she wished she could remember more.

She leaned up on her elbow and noted that her girls were still sound asleep. Zach, too, seemed to have been knocked out by yesterday's events. She wondered if things would be awkward between them now.

Would he feel weird about kissing her? Did she feel weird about it? Should she say anything or just let it lie? In the cold gray light of a winter morning, her instinct to protect herself told her to pretend it never happened. Would he go along with that?

"Good morning, my gorgeous girl," he said. He rubbed a big callused paw over his face, pausing to scratch at the golden stubble on his chin.

So, she figured she could take that as a no. Zach was not going to pretend that they hadn't crossed over the friendship line and kissed yesterday. She would have to do some serious damage control to get them back in the friend zone.

"Good morning, Zach," she said.

"Uh-oh," he said. He pushed up onto his elbows. He glanced at the girls and noted that they were still sleeping and then he whispered, "Are you about to give me 'the talk'?"

"You mean the one outlining the reasons why yesterday shouldn't have happened and how it isn't going to happen again?" she asked hopefully.

"Yep, that's the one," he said. "But I'm confused. I thought you polled your girlfriends on the phone last night and they were thumbs-up about us."

"There is no us," Jessie said. "And they were thumbs-up only because I told them all I wanted was a fling."

"A fling?" Zach asked. He rested his chin in his hand

and regarded her with his warm, velvet brown gaze. "Well, you really are the perfect woman, aren't you?"

A flash of heat hit Jessie low and fast. She wasn't perfect, not even close, but Zach sure made her feel special. For the first time in a long stretch, she had the warm fuzzies and she liked it.

The feeling was rare and special and she cherished it. She decided to hug the words close to her chest and when she was feeling blue, she'd bring the memory out and be warmed by it. In the meantime, she had to shut this down.

"Flattery will not get me to change my mind," she said.

She was pleased that she sounded firm. Unfortunately, Zach looked singularly unimpressed.

"Okay." He shrugged.

He shoved off his covers and rose to standing. He stretched his muscular arms up over his head and the hem of his thermal shirt rode up, giving Jessie a glimpse of his taut abs. Was it wrong that she wanted to lick him right there—okay, maybe a little lower? She knew that it was and yet . . . No! She forced herself to look away.

Zach strode to the kitchen. He plugged the coffeepot into the electrical cord brought to them courtesy of his generator and set about making coffee. Jessie stared after him. He seemed to be taking her refusal to pursue anything more than friendship perfectly in stride. Maybe he didn't get it. Maybe she needed to be clearer with him.

She wrapped herself up in her blanket and followed him into the kitchen. He was using the bottled water to fill the coffeepot and she marveled that in a matter of hours, he'd become so familiar with her house, where she kept things, how she liked things done—honestly, in almost seven years of marriage, Seth had never, not once, brewed a pot of coffee.

She shook her head. That was not the point, so not the point. She needed to focus.

"Thank you," she said.

Zach glanced up from filling the filter. "No problem."

"Not just for the coffee," she said. She slid onto one of the stools at the counter. She pushed passed her embarrassment and said, "Thanks for being cool about us not . . . you know."

Zach closed the lid and hit the switch on the coffeepot. He leaned on his elbows so that his face was level with hers.

"No, I don't know. Us not what?" he asked.

"You know, us not pursuing a fling," she said. She glanced at the coffeepot, willing it to brew faster.

"Oh, that," he said. He nodded but he didn't say anything. Instead, he just smiled at her as if he found her amusing.

Jessie studied him. Why wasn't he saying anything? Was he in agreement? Did he not want a fling either? Why did that thought fill her with disappointment? He had called her gorgeous; huh, maybe that was his way of letting her down easy. She didn't like that at all. Now she felt conflicted. It was unsettling.

"I mean, you knew that's what was happening between us last night, right?" she asked.

"Was it?" he asked. He continued to smile at her.

"Yes, last night I was entertaining the thought of having a fling with you, but—"

"But after a good night's sleep, you changed your mind," he finished her sentence for her.

"Yes," she said.

"Why?"

She looked at him.

He waited.

"Oh, well, I . . ." she stammered.

Zach studied her with infinite patience. This time he didn't try to finish her sentence. Instead, he waited for her to think it out for herself.

She watched as he got two mugs and poured the coffee. He pushed hers across the counter to her, black, just the way she liked it, and then doctored his own with a little sugar and milk. They'd continued putting bags of snow in the refrigerator to keep everything cold; still, he paused to smell the milk before adding it to his mug.

He took a sip and watched her over the rim of his mug.

She got the feeling he could wait all day for her answer. She suddenly felt pressured to make it a very good answer, one that wouldn't be dismissed or questioned.

"I just think that since we're neighbors, we should probably avoid doing anything that might damage our relationship—by relationship, of course, I mean our neighborly association. I wouldn't want it to get uncomfortable and then feel weird if one of us needed to borrow some eggs or sugar or something. Plus, there are the girls. I wouldn't want them to suffer any awkwardness if we discovered we couldn't get on after . . . well, after . . ."

Jessie stopped talking and lifted her mug to her lips. Surely, she did not need to spell it out for him in any greater detail than that.

"A night of triple-orgasm, smoking-hot sex?" Zach offered.

Jessie choked on her coffee. He'd caught her on a swallow and she inhaled coffee into her lungs. She choked it back up, coughing so hard that tears sprang from her eyes and a little snot dribbled out of her nose. Gah!

She hastily grabbed a paper napkin out of the holder and dabbed her nose with one end and her eyes with the other. She frowned at him but he blinked at her in complete innocence. Jessie narrowed her eyes. She was not buying it.

"Very funny," she said. "Let's be serious."

"You're right," he said. He lowered his head and peered at her from beneath his bangs. "Three orgasms would never be enough with you."

Jessie slapped her palm to her forehead. "Stop with the orgasm talk." She glanced across the room at the girls, who were still asleep, and then back at Zach. "You are impossible."

"It's part of my charm, or so I've been told," he said.

Jessie resisted the urge to fan herself with her hand. Seriously, was it hot in here or what? She couldn't even look at Zach. He offered up orgasms as if that was so easy for him. She wouldn't know. She'd never had one. Never. Not one. Not ever.

It was her secret shame. Seth hadn't been a good lover.

She'd thought that once they were married everything would suddenly get better. It didn't. In fact, it got a whole lot worse. Before they were married Seth put a token effort into pleasing her but once he put the ring on her finger, he tapped out. When he rolled on top of her at night it was always a wham-bam-thank-you-ma'am sort of situation and Jessie was relieved because at least she didn't have to fake it anymore.

She'd read all the women's magazines; she knew she could take her situation in hand as it were, but life with two little kids didn't give a mom a lot of "me" time and even if she'd been motivated, she usually passed out before her head hit the pillow.

Orgasms just hadn't been a priority for her. But now here was Zach, standing in her kitchen, making coffee and talking about triples. The mere thought of it made her dizzy and she took a deep scalding sip of her coffee, trying to scorch the lust right out of her soul.

"Well, let's just forget about it," she said. She stared at him. "Okay?"

"Forget what?" he asked.

"You know, about—" She frowned. "Oh, I get it. You've already forgotten. Very clever."

Zach shrugged. She found her gaze wandering to his broad shoulders. He was built strong. She liked that. A wave of indecision hit her. Maybe she shouldn't be so hasty. Maybe they could have a fling. Maybe it wouldn't be awkward or weird. She thought about the morning he'd rescued Chaos off his roof.

Three girls had been in his house and while she understood now that it was completely innocent, it had been awkward at the time and if something like that happened after they slept together—she did a quick self-assessment—no, she didn't think she would handle it very well. It would be weird. With her ex having slept with most of the single women, and some not-so-single women, in town, she had enough awkward encounters to navigate in her life, thank you very much.

"Momma," Maddie appeared at her side. "I'm hungry."

And just like that, Jessie shifted back into mom mode.

"Well, you're in luck. I was digging around in the cupboard and I found my electric skillet. How about some pancakes?"

"With chocolate chips?"

"Of course."

"All right!" Maddie said. She turned her big blue gaze on Zach. "Do you like chocolate chip pancakes?"

"Love 'em," he said.

Maddie grinned, showing the gap in her upper teeth where she was missing a tooth. She clearly found comfort in the fact that Zach liked the same pancakes. It made Jessie's heart hurt a little that the girls hadn't had any of that with their own father. She knew that it was Seth's loss, but still she wished it could have been different for them.

"Come on," Zach said. "Let's get your sister moving and straighten up the room. We're going to have to go outside and sweep the snow away again or we'll never get out of here."

Maddie walked beside him and slipped her tiny hand into his. She glanced up at him with a look of hero worship, and said, "I wouldn't mind."

Zach gave her a thoughtful look and then he grinned and swooped her up into his arms. Maddie let out a shriek, which woke up Gracie, who wanted in on the fun, too. While Jessie made a small mountain of pancakes, Zach and the girls picked up the living room and got dressed before devouring the stack.

As if they were his small army of broom-wielding soldiers, Zach got everyone suited up and outside for another morning of snow removal. Since the wind had died and the snow had stopped falling, they played, too, building a family of snow people, including a dog and cat. Zach pulled the girls on an old sled he had in his garage to a small hill at the end of the street where several kids from the neighborhood were sledding. The girls slid down time and again until their eyes sparkled and their cheeks and noses had bloomed with the cold to a bright berry red.

Once inside, they had soup and sandwiches, and the

girls raced up to their room to gather some new things to play with by the heat of the fire. Maddie brought down literally every stuffed animal she owned while Gracie chose her small pink ukulele. She plucked a few notes, looking very shy, and then handed it to Zach.

"Can you teach me?" she asked.

"Oh, honey, I don't know that Zach—" Jessie began but Zach interrupted by strumming a few chords and humming.

"This baby is pretty out of tune," he said. "Let me see if I can fix it for you."

Gracie nodded. Her eyes shone. Her hero knew what to do.

"How did you know Zach knew how to play?" Jessie asked Gracie.

"The picture," she said.

"What picture?"

"The one in his house of him and Rufus in matching Hawaiian shirts," she said. "Zach was holding a ukulele."

"Very observant," Zach said. He held up his hand and Gracie slapped her palm against his. "I'm impressed."

He fiddled with it, while Gracie hopped impatiently from foot to foot. Finally, Zach was finished and Gracie demanded that he play something. He glanced at Jessie and sang the old ukulele standard "Tonight, You Belong to Me."

He fumbled a note or two as he tried to master the tiny instrument with his big hands, but his singing voice was rich and pure and it made the vertebrae at the base of Jessie's spine hum in response. She tried to ignore him, but Maddie wanted to learn the song, too, so they sang it again and again as Zach patiently taught Gracie where to hold her fingers and how to strum the instrument.

Jessie was pretty sure she'd have to be made of stone not to respond to how great he was with her girls. And the thing was, she knew that this wasn't a ploy to get into her pants. Zach was completely tuned into the kids on his own.

While they worked on the song, he gave both girls his full attention. He hadn't even looked at Jessie in over an hour. It was as if he'd forgotten she was there. On the one hand, she loved how attentive he was to her girls, but on the other, it was making her crazy. At the moment, she was half afraid she was going to jump him. Which would be bad—very, very bad.

Chapter 13

When Gracie had gotten the basics of the song down, the instrument was finally retired and they ate dinner, which consisted of sausage and chopped up vegetables that Zach had lightly seasoned with butter, salt, and pepper, and then wrapped in aluminum foil and tucked into the fire. With bread on the side, it made for a tasty meal and the girls had loved helping Jessie dice up the vegetables.

Zach was the chosen one to read to the girls again. Jessie watched them from the kitchen as she hand-washed the plates and glasses they'd used for dinner. Propped up on a pile of pillows in front of the hearth, with only his camping lantern for light, Zach sat half reclined. Before he was done with the first book, both girls were in his lap, leaning back against his broad chest as he read their book to them. Chaos staked out some turf on the top of the pillow while Rufus stretched his length out along Zach's legs.

The girls' honey blonde hair blended with Zach's slightly lighter shade, and the three of them looked as if they belonged to one another. Zach made funny voices while he read, and Maddie belly laughed, clutching her favorite stuffie, a penguin who wore eyeglasses, to her chest. Gracie was more serious and watched his face with an intensity that showed she was swept up by the story. Zach took in her concentration and he delivered.

When he finished book three, the girls lobbied hard for another story but Jessie held firm. It was late and they needed to sleep. Despite their protests, the girls were unconscious within minutes.

By unspoken agreement, Jessie and Zach took his lantern and moved to the dining room table to keep from making any noise that might disturb the girls.

Zach sank into a chair and checked his phone; he'd spent part of yesterday calling his staff to make sure they stayed out of the storm and he chatted up a few of the bar owners in Portland he was hoping to convince to carry the local brew on tap. Other than that, he hadn't done much work that Jessie could see.

Gavin had told Jessie that she could stay home until the girls were back in school. He knew she had no one to watch them during the day. As it was, she usually picked them up from school and they spent her final two hours of the work day with her at the animal clinic. They had both become expert kitten and puppy snugglers, although that was what had landed them with Chaos, so Jessie wasn't sure it was an activity she should encourage.

She took the chair next to Zach's at the round table and studied him out of the corner of her eye. Despite spending the entire day together, Zach hadn't mentioned their kiss last night, nor had he tried to recreate it; in fact, he hadn't done anything that could be construed as a come-on in any way. Jessie knew that it was mental that she was disappointed. This was what she wanted from him. This was what she'd asked for. She should be ecstatic that he was being respectful of her boundaries, and yet, she wasn't.

She couldn't get their kiss out of her mind. The feel of him under her fingertips, the press of his lips against hers, the sense that being with him was so right. How was she supposed to ignore it when she had spent all day watching him with her kiddos? He was so great with them and such a natural at nurturing them that it made her uterus hurt.

She watched as he scrolled through his phone. He looked like he was checking the basketball scores. She opened her phone. There were no messages. No texts. She hadn't heard from any of the girls since they'd badgered her for a report this morning and she'd ignored them. Social media was a drag. The news was depressing. Even the weather held no information of interest.

The worst of the storm had passed but there was so much damage that power remained out in most of the town, and roads still needed to be plowed, so they suspected it might be another day or two before things got back to normal. Jessie's phone chimed with a request to play an online word game, much like Scrabble, which she accepted, thinking it would keep her from dwelling inappropriately on the man next to her.

She and her opponent were equally matched, so when she saw an opportunity for a triple letter, double word play with a high points tile, she took it. There was no small satisfaction in watching her points soar past her opponent's.

"Buxom?" Zach cried. "That's cheating!"

"Shh!" Jessie glanced passed him at the girls to make certain they were still asleep. Then she looked at his phone and saw that he had the same app open. "Hey, I'm playing *you*!"

"Of course you are," he said. "I was sitting right next to you when I sent the request."

"Well, your game name is Z-Ro," she said. "How was I supposed to know it was you?"

"Fair enough," he said. "Now you know so quit cheating."

"I didn't cheat," she insisted.

"Buxom?"

"It's a word."

"No kidding, and it's got me all distracted," he said. "Which is cheating."

"It is not," she said. "You could use any word you want and it wouldn't distract me."

"You sure about that?" he asked.

"Yes," she said.

"All right, then," he said.

He turned back to his phone and frowned at the screen. He considered it, then shook his head; he plucked his lower lip between his fingers and then tapped his lips with his index finger. Jessie had to force herself to look away from him. Every time he touched his mouth she felt like a plane being directed in for a landing.

"Do we need to set a timer?" she asked.

"Don't rush me," he said.

Jessie leaned close, trying to get a look at his letters. "Do you want some help?"

"No, I got this," he said.

He turned away from her and began to tap on his phone. Sure enough, an update to the game popped up on her phone and she glanced down. His word, using the "U" from "buxom," was "nude."

Jessie glanced up at him and he winked at her.

"Still not distracted," she said.

"No?"

"No."

"Huh." Zach grunted.

He leaned closer to her and took her phone out of her hands and put it on the table next to his. Then he looked at her, really looked at her. His brown gaze was as steady and sure as the sun. She couldn't have looked away if she tried.

"About our talk earlier," he said. "I was wondering if—"

That was as far as he got before Jessie launched herself at him. She pressed her body up against his, plowed her fingers into his thick unruly hair, and then she kissed him.

She didn't mean to jump him. Truly, she didn't. But he was just sitting there looking so ridiculously attractive and he was so great with her girls and she just wanted him. She wanted him so badly. So she kissed him, moving her mouth over his, sliding her tongue across the seam of his lips until he opened his mouth, giving her full access to the taste of him. She nipped his lower lip and he growled in response, making her want to do it again.

When they broke apart, they were both breathing heavily. Zach hauled Jessie onto his lap and held her close while he studied her face as if to figure out what the hell had just happened.

"Sorry," she said.

"No need," he said.

"What were you going to ask me?"

"I was wondering if maybe you'd reconsider giving us a go," he said. "But I think you just answered my question, unless you've changed your mind again, in which case I am preparing for whiplash."

Jessie cupped his face, liking the rough feel of his stubbly chin against her palms.

"Watching you with the girls today hit me in all of the feels," she said. "If I do reconsider and we go forward with a fling, nothing serious, can we be sure that things won't change for them?"

Zach leaned back in the chair. He looked thoughtful and Jessie appreciated that he didn't just tell her what she wanted to hear; he was really thinking about the girls and the impact a fling would have on them.

"I think you and I have become good friends over the past few days," he said. "I don't see that changing except to become even better friends, whether we pursue this thing between us or not. This decision is really up to you, my girl, and I'm cool with whatever you decide."

His velvet brown gaze was steadfast and it made Jessie's heart hammer triple time in her chest. Could she do this? Could she have something, a fling, just for herself? The idea made her positively giddy. She hadn't met anyone like Zach before. He was so calm and centered and fun. His ego wasn't involved in every little thing that happened around him. She liked that. She liked him. She wanted to be with him even if it was just once.

She leaned close and whispered in his ear, "Let's do it."

His hands, which had been resting loosely on her hips,

tightened and his voice when he spoke was rough. "When you say 'it,' uh, do you mean what I think you mean?"

"Yes, please," she said.

Zach stood, setting her on her feet. He studied her face and asked, "Are you sure?"

"Positive." Jessie was pretty sure his pupils dilated.

"Your room is upstairs?" he asked.

"Yes—oh, wait, it's so cold up there—"

"Not for long," he said. He pointed at the counter and said, "Let's take those candles and matches."

Then he strode over to where the girls were sleeping on the floor and moved each of them up onto the couch. Rufus hopped up with Maddie while Chaos nestled in next to Gracie. Zach then tended the fire, making certain it was burning low, secure behind the screen.

In moments, he was striding back toward Jessie. She watched him come toward her with a determined glint in his eye. This was the moment she knew that if she was going to change her mind, it had to be now. Yeah, not a chance.

Transferring the candles and matches to the crook of her left arm, she held out her right hand to Zach and deliberately led him upstairs to her room.

It was freezing up there. Zach took the candles from her while she hurried into the girls' room and took their old battery-operated baby monitor out of the closet. She used the light on her phone to guide the way as she tiptoed downstairs and put the transmitter on the table behind the couch, then she hurried back upstairs and put the receiver on her nightstand.

Then she closed and locked her bedroom door.

She turned back around to find Zach standing in the center of the room, illuminated by the soft yellow glow of the candles on the nightstand. He opened his arms and she stepped into his embrace as if it was as natural as breathing.

They kissed and she felt that same pull from her center, that deep longing, to get lost in him. She wrapped her arms around his neck and pulled him close, melting into his warmth as he reached around her and cupped her behind, pulling her in close and tight.

When they broke apart, she hissed and saw her breath on the air. It really was freezing up here.

"Come on," Zach said. "Under the covers. I'm not getting naked in this frigid air. It does terrible things to man parts."

Jessie laughed as they hustled over to her bed. Zach kissed her and pulled her sweater over her head. She kissed him back and returned the favor. Next he pushed her out of her fuzzy sweatpants and she shivered, her fingers trembling as she reached for the fly on his jeans, but Zach gently brushed her hand away.

"Go," he said. He lifted up the thick covers and gestured for her to climb in before he quickly shucked off his pants and joined her.

"Oh, my god, so cold, so cold," he said. He grabbed her and pulled her close.

Jessie laughed as his hands were everywhere rubbing her freezing skin, from her knees to her neck, as he planted kisses on her. Her lips. Her nose. Her eyes. And finally nestling against the curve of her neck into her shoulder.

Jessie put her arms around his shoulders and hugged him, feeling happy and excited and lusty and desired. It was a potent combination for a woman who had felt mostly sexually dormant for the past seven years.

"You smell amazing," Zach said. He inhaled deeply and Jessie felt a small thrill course through her.

They were lying on their sides facing each other. She was only in her underwear and Zach was down to his boxers. Since Seth had stopped looking to her for sex halfway through their marriage, this was as close as she'd been to a nearly naked man in years. She liked the feel of his skin beneath her fingertips. His chest was defined and sported a little bit of hair but mostly it was bare. He was solid, a wall of masculine muscle, which made her feel powerful and protected and toasty warm.

Zach leaned in and kissed her just below her ear, and then he ran his mouth down the side of her neck. Jessie felt her insides liquefy and she let out a huff of air. Zach took full advantage and followed her down when she rolled onto her back, sinking deeper into the mattress.

He draped an arm over her middle, holding her in place while he continued to move his lips down her body, sliding over the curve of her breasts peeking out of the top of her bra down to her belly. Jessie felt herself begin to shake but it wasn't from the cold.

As if sensing her sudden bout of nerves, Zach slowed it down. He let his hands run over every inch of her skin, massaging, caressing, tickling every curve and crevice with his fingers and his lips, until Jessie was just a throbbing nerve ending desperate for some sort of finale.

She wanted to return the favor, and she dug her fingers into his hair and pulled his face back to hers so she could kiss him senseless. Zach let her.

He moved to lie on top of her, letting his weight settle them both into the soft mattress. Usually Jessie hated feeling pinned down, without an escape, but having Zach on top of her felt more like being draped in a security blanket. And she wanted more, so much more of him.

"Time to lose these," Zach said. He trailed a finger over the edge of her bra and across the waistband of her undies.

"I . . . uh . . ." Jessie stammered. She was ready. She knew she was. She could feel the slippery wet heat between her legs and the throbbing ache that longed to be stretched and filled so it could finally find its release. And yet, a part of her shut down in panic.

"Too soon?" Zach asked.

She could feel the hard part of him, right there, pressing against her thigh. He was more than ready and she desperately wanted to know what it would feel like to have him inside her, stretching and filling what at the moment felt like a howling aching void in between her legs, but performance anxiety was beginning to surge up inside of her.

"No, not too soon," she said. "I'm good. I'm totally ready."

Zach kissed her. She tried to bring her thoughts back to the moment but suddenly all she could think about was,

What if after all of the different women Zach had known in his life, she was the lousy one in bed? What if she made weird noises or wasn't a good fit, what if it became awkward?

What if they did this and it was painful or embarrassing? What if it was so bad Zach never wanted to sleep with her again? Not that she was really looking for more than a one-night sort of thing, but still, she didn't want to be locked forever in his mind as the one who sucked in bed—and not in a good way.

Her self-esteem in the sexual arts was not hot to begin with. For most of her marriage, Seth had told her that her pregnant body was a total turn-off and it was her fault he'd cheated because the sight of her made him physically sick. After the girls were born, it had taken her a while to lose the pregnancy weight and then, of course, she had stretch marks that Seth had found disgusting. The few times she'd tried to initiate sex with him, he'd said she was a lousy lay and he couldn't even get hard from kissing her.

Jessie started to feel her desire slip away from her. She didn't want it to go, but she couldn't seem to get back into the lusty brain space of just a few minutes ago. She blinked away some frustrated tears and then did what she'd always done: She pretended everything was great.

She took the condom from Zach's hand that he'd fished out of his jeans and she helped him lose his underwear while she shimmied out of hers. She went to put the condom on him, but Zach slowed her down.

"Hold up there, Speedy," he said. "You're not even completely undressed yet."

He reached for the front fastening of her bra and Jessie grabbed his hand, stopping him. He pulled back to look at her. She bit her lip.

"I'm not . . . I nursed both of the girls," she said.

He lifted an eyebrow, clearly not understanding that the rigors of nursing had taken a toll on her breasts.

"I'm not perky like I used to be," she explained. Her ex had been very clear that he never wanted to see her without a bra.

"So?" he asked. He unsnapped her bra and it fell open. He let out a hum of male satisfaction as he lowered his head to the nipple of one breast while he expertly thumbed the other.

Jessie had no idea what to make of this. He didn't mind that her breasts sagged a bit? When his teeth bit down on one nipple in a razor-sharp tug, she gasped as she felt a bolt of heat rocket from her breast right into her vagina. Holy wow.

"You are a beautiful woman, Jessie," he said. "So fucking beautiful."

He moved his mouth to the other breast and gave it the same treatment. Jessie grunted and arched her back. She wanted to be consumed by him, wholly and completely.

She ran her hands down his sides, moving them to his front so she could grasp his shaft in her hand. Now it was his turn to grunt and swear. Turnabout was fair play, however, and Zach moved his hand in between her legs and stroked her expertly until Jessie thrashed beneath him.

"I don't think I can wait any longer," Zach said. "How about you?"

"Now, I need you now," Jessie cried. And she meant it.

She'd never felt this scorching want before. It was maddening and she knew there would be no relief until Zach pushed into her.

Zach slid on the condom and moved over her. He laced the fingers of his hand with one of hers and held their clasped hands over her head. Then he used his other hand to guide himself into her.

Jessie opened her legs wide to accommodate him and dug her fingers into the hair at the nape of his neck, pulling him close so she could kiss him as he eased into her. He was large—the parrot snowflake really wasn't actual size—and he stretched her wide and he felt amazing.

"You feel incredible," Zach said—exactly what she was thinking. "So hot, so tight, so perfect."

Jessie sighed as he slid into her. It *was* perfect. It was magical. It was amazing. She let out a groan that sounded like a hippopotamus having a hard bowel movement. She tried to cover it up with a cough, but there was no pretending she hadn't just made a noise that sounded like a blooper from a wild animal documentary.

Seth had hated it when she'd made noises, so much so that he'd frequently kept his hand over her mouth, making it difficult for her to breathe. Abruptly, the surging erotic ride she'd been on with Zach suddenly pitched her off and she had no idea how to get back on.

She was suddenly aware of the light sheen of sweat covering her skin, and was that . . . yes, it was. She felt the back of her thighs jiggle. Horrifying. There was no recovering. She was consumed with self-consciousness and an overwhelming feeling of inadequacy that doused her desire like a direct blast from a fire extinguisher.

Zach seemed oblivious to her sudden bout of nerves. He put his mouth close to her ear and whispered, "So good."

Not wanting to disappoint him, Jessie made a sound of agreement. She closed her eyes, willing him not to notice that she'd lost the mood. She reached around and grabbed his backside, guiding him in and out of her in the way that had always managed to get her ex off, while she muttered encouraging words of feigned passion, hoping to coax him along.

Caught up in her mission, it took Jessie a moment to realize that Zach had stopped moving. When she opened her eyes, it was to find him, resting on his elbows above her, looking at her in consternation.

"Jessica Margaret," he said. That got her attention. She hadn't realized he knew her middle name. "Are you faking an orgasm with me?"

Busted!

Chapter 14

Zach stared down at the woman below him. Her blue eyes were wide, but not with innocence—more like guilt—and her two-tone hair was spread out across the pillow, her lips a deep plum color and swollen from being kissed, thoroughly, and a flush marked her skin. From passion or embarrassment, he wasn't sure. He didn't much care. He did care, however, that she was faking her response with him. And doing it really badly, too.

"Uh . . ."

"Yeah, no," he said. "You are so busted."

"But I . . ." She looked panicked and Zach felt his heart soften. He didn't have it in him to torture her.

"Hey," he said. He eased out of her slowly, wincing a little as he slid free, missing her warmth immediately. "If you changed your mind, you should have told me. We didn't have to do this tonight or at all if you decided you didn't want to."

Tears filled her pretty blue eyes and they wrecked him. He ignored his raging hard-on and pulled her close. He pressed her head against his chest and stroked his fingers up and down her spine in what he hoped was a soothing gesture for her, because the feel of her velvety soft skin certainly wasn't doing him any favors.

"It's not that," she said on a small cry that rent his heart the littlest bit. "I want to be with you, I do, it's just that I don't know how to do this. I don't know how to make love."

Zach rested his chin on her hair. "Jess, you have two daughters, so you must have some idea—"

"I know how to procreate," she said into his chest. "I don't know how to enjoy sex. Oh, god, I'm a freak. You should probably run from me as fast and as far as you can."

She sounded so genuinely distraught that Zach couldn't help but smile. "You're not a freak. Sometimes with a new partner it just takes a little—"

"Zach, I've never had an orgasm," she interrupted. She pushed away from him and rose up on one elbow so she was looking down at him. "Not once, not ever. No rockets. No waterfalls."

Zach blinked at her. This information simply did not compute. Finally, when he could move his mouth, he managed one single word, and asked, "Never?"

"Never."

"Not even by yourself?"

"No."

"Not even in a wet dream? I've heard girls have those, too."

"I did come really close once," she said. "No pun intended, but then one of the girls called for me and I woke up. I get so close but I just can't seem to get there. I get distracted or anxious or worried. I feel like I'm a bird with perfectly functional wings who's afraid to fly."

"Wow."

"See? Total freak. Frigid. Repressed."

"No, you're not," he said. "But I wish you'd told me."

"I'm sorry," she said. "I never should have put you in this position."

"Are you kidding me?" he asked. He rose up on his elbow so that they were eye to eye. "This position is awesome."

She stared at him. She looked equal parts suspicious and hopeful. Zach knew she didn't get it but that was all right; she would eventually.

"How do you figure that?" she asked.

He wagged his eyebrows at her. "Because now we have a project. We're going to teach you how to have a Big O."

She fell back onto the bed and dropped her arm over her eyes. "Oh, god, I'm a project. This is mortifying."

Zach nudged her arm out of the way so that he could see her face. She looked embarrassed, which was actually a pretty cute look on her.

"So, is there any issue in your past that I need to know about?" he asked.

"What do you mean?"

"To be blunt"—he paused, making sure she was looking him in the eye before he said—"if your inability to orgasm is because of a trauma from your past, I don't want to do anything that would make it worse. So, if you were assaulted or—"

"I wasn't," Jessie said. "It would be easier to understand if I had something like that in my past but I don't."

"I'm glad," he said. He squeezed her close. "I would have hated for anything like that to have happened to you. I'd have had to go out and punch somebody or something."

Jessie laughed, which had been his intention, even though if anyone had hurt her, he'd likely do everything he could to hunt them down and pummel them into the dirt. There was something about Jessie that made him feel fiercely protective of her.

The candles continued to burn on the nightstand. The room was still freezing but their combined body heat under the heavy covers made it more than toasty. Zach still wanted her—man, did he ever—but not enough to push her when she obviously had some kind of block. He'd seen how ready she was. She'd been right there with him but somehow he'd lost her.

It was an absolute tragedy that she'd never experienced the best part of sex. Dang, what the hell had that ex-husband of hers been doing? He got her pregnant but without her getting off in the process? That wasn't right. Zach hadn't had anything other than casual relationships in a long time but even so, he made sure his partners enjoyed it as much as he did.

"So, did you want to try again?" Jessie asked.

"Uh . . . no," he said.

She stilled against him; when she spoke her voice was small but held a forced brightness to it as if she was trying to gloss over the hurt.

"Oh, I understand," she said.

"No, you don't. This isn't a rejection."

"Really? Cause it kind of feels that way, not that I blame you."

He shifted her in his arms, turning her so that her back was to him and he curled up around her. This was one of Zach's favorite positions to hold a woman because his hands had full access to all of her oh-so-tempting girl parts, but also because he could kiss the back of her neck, a spot that never failed to get a woman's attention.

"Here's how I see this playing out," he said.

He paused to let his hands roam over her dead sexy curves while he pressed his lips to the sensitive spot just beneath her hair on the back of her neck. She pressed back against him with a moan. He closed his eyes for a second, trying to regroup. Perhaps he should have put his pants back on before he let her push into his throbbing shaft with her bare bottom. Damn it.

"We're going to start over," he said. "We're going to move super slow. We're going to figure out what you do like and what you don't like and while we're doing that, we're going to make sure that you become so crazy an orgasm is an inevitability."

He finished talking with his mouth pressed against the curve of her ear, with his voice little more than a growled whisper. His hands were busy touching her everywhere while he cataloged her responses like a scientist studying a slide under a microscope. Nipples, big time responsive; the rest of her breasts, not so much. Inner thighs, a stroke or two there and her breath stuttered, but a touch to the back of her legs made her clench up. Interesting.

"Oh . . . okay," she said. Her breath was coming in delicious little pants as if she couldn't quite manage a full inhale.

Zach smiled into her skin. He'd moved his hand in between her legs and was drawing small circles with his fingers on her most sensitive parts. Not really touching her core, just sliding along the edge. When she began to move her hips as if trying to shift toward his hand, he knew he was getting to her. Too bad it was going to become so much worse for her.

He figured she had so many years of flirting with satisfaction and then failing that he had to ratchet up the desire in her until she was almost crazed. That was the only way she was going to be able to punch through her own barrier to release.

She shifted against him, the cleft in her ass cupping him so perfectly it was all he could do not to fall on top of her and take her up on her idea to give it another go. He didn't. Instead, he winced as he inched away from her. If she didn't get to orgasm, neither did he. He figured it was only fair, although he was half afraid it might kill him.

When she turned in his arms to face him, her eyes were bright blue, sparking with desire. He gave her one long, thorough, wet kiss and then he tucked her head under his chin and loosely looped his arms about her.

Jessie lay still against him for a moment. Then she cleared her throat. "Is that it then?"

"For now," he said.

"But—"

"No buts," he said. "We're rewriting your sexual history and we're going to go take our time and savor every second."

"But I feel so restless," she said. She pressed her lips to the base of his throat. "Like I just need more of you."

"Good," he said. The huskiness in her voice made his blood run thick while the feel of her lips on his skin made his pulse flutter as if looking to take flight. She was killing him but he stayed resolved. He tucked her head back under his chin and said, "Behave yourself."

He felt her lips curve against his skin and he hid his own smile in her hair.

"I don't think I can sleep like this," she said.

"I'll tell you a bedtime story," he said. "We can use it to determine whether dirty talk gets you hot or not."

Jessie burst out laughing. "What's it called, *Jack and His Beanstalk*?"

Zach laughed. Oh, he liked her quick wit. "I was thinking more along the lines of *Goldilocks and the Three Bartenders*."

"Three?" she cried. "At one time?"

"Dunno, does that work for you?" he asked.

Now she was snort-laughing and Zach found it ridiculously charming. It occurred to him that while he always enjoyed his time with women, he rarely spent time like this, naked and laughing. Usually, there was a mission to be accomplished and then he was out of there.

With Jessie, he didn't feel like there was a job to be done. It felt like he was supposed to be here with her, laughing or loving or whatever else she needed. He liked Jessie, he liked her girls, and while he knew she was thinking of them in terms of a fling, he was beginning to hope for something entirely different.

When Jessie let out a jaw-popping yawn and burrowed against him, Zach felt his own body relax. He was surprised because he'd been so sure that having her close would keep him awake and unsatisfied, but the activity of the day, the hours spent in the snow, had tuckered him out. When he heard a soft snore escape her lips, he leaned back to study her face.

She was a pretty thing with prominent cheekbones and a very stubborn chin. She had no makeup on but he liked that. There was a fresh clean scent about her, like lemon cake, and it made him want to devour her. He shook his head. That was not going to help him keep his libido in check.

He shifted a bit, trying to ease the ache in his crotch.

In a weird way, he welcomed the discomfort. Since the woman he had considered the love of his life had walked out of his life, Zach hadn't gotten attached to anyone he hooked up with, keeping it casual in part out of self-preservation but also because he'd become a bit of a work-aholic.

It was different with Jessie. Maybe it was because they'd become friends first or because of his affection for the girls—he wasn't sure—but he didn't want this to be a satisfaction grab, where they had a good time and then went their separate ways. He wanted to be the guy who taught her how to make the most of her own sexuality and then he wanted to be the guy who enjoyed the discovery with her.

He thought about her friendship with Cooper and realized that it was likely that she could end up dating the handsome chief of police. The idea of Jessie and Cooper together made Zach want to smash something. This was not an urge he'd felt over any woman in a very long time.

He studied the woman in his arms a bit more closely. Did he trust her? Could he trust her? If they moved forward with whatever this was between them, his potential to be hurt was huge. And it wasn't just losing Jessie. The idea of having the girls out of his life made his heart hurt in a way he hadn't expected.

Feisty Maddie who feared nothing and no one needed someone to watch out for her, someone to hold out their arms so that when she took to the air, he could catch her when she came back down. And Gracie, so quiet and restrained—she needed someone to lace their fingers together and give her a boost to help her climb up to the heights he knew she could reach if she had a strong someone at her ground zero. Yes, Jessie could be those things for her daughters no question, but Zach wanted to be there, too.

As he thought about the girls and their mother, he felt a peace slide over him, lulling him to sleep, like the warmest, thickest blanket. It was a comforting feeling of belonging and he welcomed it. Zach felt as if his world had been locked in winter, something he'd never realized, but now he had the potential of spring and he embraced it.

Zach wasn't sure what woke him first, the delicious scent of the woman in his arms, or the feel of her hands running over his chest and then his abs, pausing lower but only for a moment before she ran her hand over the length of him, which had woken up like a good little soldier ready to be deployed.

He shifted, unable to resist pressing against her warmth while he lowered his face into her hair and took a deep inhale. He wanted to wake up like this every day. He ran his hand down her spine and she arched her back, pushing her hips into his and making him hiss from the contact.

He lowered his head and leaned in to kiss her. She met him halfway. The kiss was tentative in the way the sun tiptoes over the horizon, nudging the world into wakefulness. Her lips were soft, they parted for his, his hand moved up into her hair so he could pull her closer and kiss her more thoroughly. It was like a direct blast of sunlight.

When he pulled back to study her, the world was brighter, with a brilliant glow to it. Did she do that? Was just being with her what made the world seem so full of light? It made him smile to see her glancing up at him with an expression of wonder that he knew was on his face, too.

"Momma, guess what!" Maddie called.

They both started. Maddie's voice was coming out of the baby monitor.

"Momma, the lights are on!" Gracie cried.

Zach and Jessie stilled, listening. Sure enough. The sound of little feet pounding their way up the staircase caused them to stare at each other wide-eyed for a nanosecond before they both leapt out of the bed as if it had just been set on fire.

"Oh, my god, get dressed!" Jessie cried.

The footsteps were in the hall now.

"No time," Zach said.

He dropped to the ground and rolled under the bed,

letting the mattress curtain hide him from view. Jessie kicked his clothes in after him and he saw her bare feet dash across the room as she snatched a robe from her closet.

She had her back to the door and he assumed had just belted the robe before the knob on the bedroom door rattled as the girls banged on it. Jessie opened the door, stopping their assault on the wood.

"Momma, did you see?" Maddie asked.

"The lights are on!" Gracie said again.

Lying on the hard wooden floor, buck naked, under the bed while Jessie and the girls spoke just a few feet away from him made Zach want to laugh. It was so ridiculous, like he was a teenager caught in his girlfriend's room after curfew, except he wasn't. He was a grown man caught by two little girls. Two girls who did not need to see him in his altogether.

"Wow! The lights are on!" Jessie cried. "Let's go celebrate with waffles!"

"All right," Maddie cried.

"Momma, where's Zach?" Gracie asked.

"He's not downstairs?" Jessie's voice sound strained.

"No, we didn't see him," Maddie said. "We thought he was up here with you."

"I don't see him," Jessie said. Zach admired her deft maneuver at not really lying. "Maybe he's with Rufus."

"Nah, Rufus is still on the couch," Maddie said. "He slept with me and, boy, does he take up a lot of space."

"He does? Let's go see," Jessie said. "I bet Zach appears as soon as I make some coffee."

Zach waited three seconds after she closed the door behind them to roll out from under the bed. He noticed that the lamp on the nightstand was lit. So that's why everything had seemed brighter after he kissed Jessie. The lights had come on. Well, that was a part of the reason. He still thought the world, at least his portion of it, was brighter just because she was in it.

He hurriedly dressed. The room was still cold but he could feel the heat coming out of the radiators as the house began to recover from the power outage. He realized with the power back, Jessie wouldn't need him and Rufus to help her out anymore.

He should have felt relieved. The storm was over. He was going home. Life would go back to normal, except normal didn't have as much appeal as it used to.

He stopped by the bathroom to make sure he was presentable and then he dashed down the stairs. It felt like the last day of a beach vacation and he was overcome by a sudden need to get in as much time in the water—or in this case with the girls—as he could before it was over.

He skidded into the kitchen, drawing up short when he found the female contingent of his Maine crew sitting there staring at him. Ruh-roh.

Chapter 15

"Morning, Zach," Carly said. "Gosh, you look like you *hardly* slept at all."

Jessie glanced up from the waffle iron to see Zach enter the room. Just the sight of him made her insides flutter. His hair was mussed as usual, but now it had a level of bedhead to it that made her feel her blood pressure spike. She knew exactly how those finger trails had gotten into his thick head of hair and her fingers itched to make more.

He grinned at Mac, Emma, Jillian, Gina, and, yes, even Carly, before his gaze found hers. His brown eyes hit her with a level of heat that vied with the warmth now happily pouring out of her functioning furnace. Oh, man!

She cleared her throat and said, "The girls came by to check on us. They brought mimosa fixings."

"Yes, we wanted to get the *naked* truth," Gina said.

Jessie dropped the fork she was using to pry the waffles out of the iron. She glanced at him with wide eyes and he mimicked her look and asked, "You told them about what just happened?"

Jessie shrugged. "It slipped out."

"That's what she said," Mac said. Emma cracked up as did the rest of the crew.

Zach held up his fist to Mac for a knuckle bump. Clearly, he was man enough to acknowledge a good *that's what she said* when he heard it. It made Jessie like him even more.

"I think I'll take Rufus for a walk over to my place and make sure everything is checking out," he said. "So you ladies can talk amongst yourselves freely."

Carly laughed. "You know we'll talk about you whether you're here or not."

"I know," he said. He grinned. "That's why my ego is demanding I make a run for it."

Jessie dished her daughters' waffles and delivered them to the table where Maddie and Gracie sat, nibbling on the peeled Cuties oranges she'd already given them. Maddie licked her lips when the waffle with a dollop of butter was placed in front of her.

"Thanks, Momma," she said.

Gracie looked past her sister to where Zach was headed to the coatrack with Rufus. Ignoring her waffle, she bolted around the crew sitting at the counter, and ran to Zach.

"You're not leaving, are you?" she asked.

Zach paused while shrugging on his coat. He looked down at her and a tender smile curved his lips as he crouched down so they were eye to eye.

"Don't you worry," he said. "I'm just going to check on my house and make sure my power is back on. I'll be back. I mean we have some ukulele to master, am I right?"

Gracie nodded and then she threw herself at him and hugged him hard. Jessie felt her throat get tight. Gracie was her shy one, her wall hugger, her rather-be-alone-than-get-hurt one. The fact that she initiated a hug with Zach made Jessie's heart hurt. Her little girl so desperately wanted to love and be loved.

Zach didn't hesitate. He wrapped her in a bear hug and lifted her off her feet, making Gracie squeal in delight. Then he put her down and tapped the end of her nose with his finger.

"Later, Gator."

"After a while, Crocodile."

With a grin, Gracie ran back to the table to eat her waffle. Jessie checked that both girls had all that they needed and then moved through the kitchen, picking up the mixing bowl of batter and handing it to Emma.

Emma glanced from her to the bowl and then to the doorway that Zach disappeared through and gave Jessie a gentle nudge with her elbow.

"Go," she said. She jerked her head toward the girls. "I'll monitor the situation."

Jessie smiled her thanks and tried to discreetly dash after Zach. He was just pulling on his hat when she stepped into the small foyer. He glanced up at her and she couldn't think of a single thing to say.

"I . . . uh . . . did you want me to save you some waffles?" she asked. Oh, god, so lame. She resisted the urge to do a facepalm.

Zach didn't answer her. Instead, he reached out and grabbed her by her robe. He pulled her forward, shutting the door to the foyer and pushing her back up against it. Before Jessie could say a word, he kissed her.

He pulled the tie loose on her robe, exposing her naked skin to his touch. Jessie arched into his hands when they cupped her breasts, his thumbs stroking over her nipples, which made her crazy. She made low grunting noises in the back of her throat as she pulled off his hat and dug her fingers into his hair while she ran her tongue over his lips and swept it into his mouth.

Zach's hands stroked down her sides and moved around to cup her backside, pulling her up hard and tight against his crotch. She wondered if even through his jeans, he could feel the heat of her, because she felt as if she was on fire. He gently bumped up against her, making her wish they were still back in her bed under the thick covers completely naked. Oh, how she desperately wanted to try making love to Zach again.

When she reached for him, trying to pull off his clothes, he caught both of her hands in one of his and held them up over her head. She was panting and she looked at him, trying to gauge what he was going to do to her next. She didn't think it was possible for him to make her any crazier than she already was. She was wrong. So wrong.

Zach used his free hand to stroke down her body, letting his fingers trail across her skin from her shoulder between her breasts across her belly until he was cupping the sensitive flesh between her legs. He used his thumb to press against her clit, making her see stars. He stroked her until her legs began to shake and her breath was rasping in and out of her in needy gulps.

Just when she thought she couldn't take it anymore, he removed his hand and pulled her robe closed and fastened the belt tight. Then he leaned forward and kissed her. When he pulled back there was a wicked glimmer in his eyes.

He moved his lips next to her ear and in a gritty growl he said, "Miss me."

Jessie let him move her away from the door so he could open it. Rufus, who was sitting patiently on the other side, leapt to his feet and followed Zach across the foyer. With a roguish wink in her direction, Zach opened the door and the adorable twosome disappeared out the front door into the snow.

Two long narrow windows were on either side of the front door and Jessie moved to the one on the right so she could watch them. The snow was thick and deep but the sun was shining for the first time in days and it glinted off the snow, making everything a brilliant bright white.

She watched, pressing her overheated cheek up against the glass, until the two of them vanished from sight. She stepped back and fanned her face. Mercy, what that man could do to her.

She went back to the kitchen, fervently hoping the squad had not finished off the mimosas. When she stepped into the kitchen all conversation stopped.

Jillian handed her a big glass of orange juice, and Carly held up an empty bottle of champagne, letting her know it was fully loaded.

"Thank you," Jessie said. She slugged back half the glass.

"Easy, lightweight," Carly said. "We don't want you passed out on the floor when Zach returns."

"Momma, can we go up to our room? We haven't played up there in forever!" Gracie asked. She entered the kitchen with her empty plate and put it in the sink.

"Of course," Jessie said.

Maddie was right behind her sister with her juice glass. Jessie looked at her and shook her head. Maddie frowned and stomped her foot, but Jessie shook her head again and Maddie spun around and grabbed her empty plate off the table and put it in the sink. Then the two girls hit the stairs running.

As soon as they disappeared from sight, Carly leaned over the counter and snatched a waffle off of the stack Emma had made. She took a bite, and then swallowed and said, "Okay, girlfriend, dish. How was our boy Zach and are you two a thing now?"

Jessie tipped her glass to her lips, but Mac snagged it out of her hand before she could knock back the fizzy fuzzy juice.

"Hey!" she cried.

"No, not until you catch us up," Mac said. "We haven't heard from you since you asked if it was okay to have a fling. That was like . . ." She glanced at her friends, clearly having lost track of the time.

"Allow me," Gina said. "Speaking on behalf of the few of us"—she paused and gestured between herself and Jillian—"who were not banged stupid for the duration of the blizzard, it's been a day and a half since the news broke that you were thinking of doing the horizontal bop with Zach. So, how was it?"

"It—well, we . . ." Jessie glanced at the front door. She wasn't sure how she felt about talking about what had happened between her and Zach. Then again, it hadn't gone well for her when she pretended with him, and knowing this group, it wouldn't go well for her if she tried to bluff with them either.

"That bad, huh?" Gina asked.

"Hush your mouth," Carly said. "That's my boy Zach you're talking about."

Gina shrugged and Carly looked at Jessie and said, "Say it ain't so."

"The thing is . . ." Jessie began and then stopped.

She felt all of them staring at her and she diverted her gaze to the countertop, feeling like an outsider looking in. She'd never had real girlfriends before. This was her first time being accepted into a group of women who weren't friends with her just because she was rich.

She didn't want to blow it, but trusting other people was hard for her. She hadn't had a lot of experience being accepted for who she was, and during her marriage, she had been cut off from everyone as she tried to keep her humiliation at Seth's drinking and cheating quiet. It had been easier not to have friends.

"Hey, it's all right," Mac said.

"You don't have to tell us anything you don't want to," Emma said. She held up the platter she had filled. "Waffle?"

"What?" Carly protested. "But I want details."

"Get her another mimosa," Gina said. "We can juice it out of her."

"Good thinking, Sis." Carly reached for an unopened bottle of champagne.

"Stop!" Jillian said. She tossed her dark brown curls over her shoulder and said, "Let the poor girl eat something. Then we can continue grilling her."

"Ha!" Carly cheered in approval.

Plates of waffles were passed around, followed by butter and syrup. The women sat around the kitchen table, with Jillian and Mac using two of the counter stools, which had them sitting slightly above everyone else.

Gossip flowed as fast as the mimosas and when Jessie shared Zach's suspicion about how the Lewises spent their time snowed in, glasses were raised to the Lewises's good health and particularly to Mr. Lewis's stamina.

"The thing is," Jessie said, filling the post-laughter quiet, "I've never had an orgasm."

In slow motion, every face at the table swiveled in her

direction. A bit of waffle fell out of Carly's mouth, and Emma blinked at her as if this was beyond her comprehension.

"Never?" Mac asked.

It was a loaded question. Jessie and Mac did have the history of Jessie stealing Mac's groom right out of the church on the day of her wedding; of course, the fact that it had turned out to be the best thing that ever happened to Mac had helped her forgive Jessie and their friendship had begun. Still, to admit that she'd never really enjoyed sex with the man they had in common seemed bad form, but Jessie wasn't going to lie.

"Never," she said.

"Seth was lousy in bed, very selfish," Mac said. "I always thought it would get better after we got married."

"It didn't," Jessie confirmed.

The rest of the women in the room watched the exchange. Jessie knew that they, like her, were wondering how Mac was going to take this revelation.

"Well, it looks like I never can thank you enough," she said. "Especially since Gavin is so—"

"Dut, dut, dut," Emma interrupted. "He's still my baby brother. I can't hear this."

Mac wagged her eyebrows at Jessie and she laughed. It was hard for her to believe she'd spent her teen years resenting Mac for being so well-liked by everyone when now that she knew her, she liked her an awful lot, too.

"Yes, yes, we're all delighted that you're having multiple orgasms with your veterinarian," Carly said.

Emma squawked but Carly ignored her, fixing her gaze on Jessie. Carly had been the most sexually adventurous of their group until she'd settled down with James Sinclair, local physical therapist and all-around great guy, who just happened to live in the old Bluff Point lighthouse.

"When you say 'never,' what does that mean exactly?" Carly asked.

Jessie just stared at her.

"No!" Carly slumped back in her seat. "My god, that's tragic!"

"Is there a reason, you know, other than being married to a selfish prick?" Gina asked.

"No hidden trauma, if that's what you mean," Jessie said. "I just can't ever quite get there, you know?"

"Sometimes the female orgasm is like that," Emma said. "Mythological like a unicorn."

"Or a Yeti," Jillian added.

"True," Gina agreed. "Sometimes you're right there and then it just slips away, because some stupid man you like has his heart set on someone else and even though you adore her, you know they aren't right together, because she doesn't even know he's alive, and you're just watching this train wreck and you can't even get the dumb man-boy to look at you, because he's completely preoccupied by her and yet you can't look at anyone else because you can't get his stupid smile out of your stupid head. Fuck."

Jessie was more than happy to join the others while they stared at Gina. It was a nice change. Gina tossed her red curls and blew one spiral off of her forehead.

"What? I'm just saying it could be like that," she snapped and they all turned back to Jessie.

"So, have you told Zach about your situation?" Emma asked, "Communication is key."

"Yes," Jessie said.

"And?" Mac, Carly, and Jillian asked as one.

Jessie tossed back the last of her mimosa. "And now I'm his project. He is determined to make this happen for me."

Carly clapped her hands together and bounced in her seat. "Atta boy, Zach."

"But what if I can't?" Jessie asked. The fear she'd been holding down like a balloon under water burst through the surface. "What if he puts in all of this effort and time and I still can't? What if I fail?"

Chapter 16

"And what if you don't?" Zach asked.

Jessie's head whipped around at the kitchen behind her, where he stood with his arms folded over his chest, looking as handsome as any man she had ever seen.

"And that's our cue to leave." Jillian popped up from her seat and led the way to the kitchen. The rest of the girls followed.

One by one they paused by Zach, offering him bits of wisdom.

"Lube is your friend," Jillian said.

"The brain is the biggest erogenous zone," Emma offered.

"Dirty talk is hot," Mac said.

Emma spun around and stared at her. "Really? With my baby brother?"

Mac laughed and pushed her forward.

"Don't hold our heads, we hate that," Carly said.

Zach looked outraged. "As if I'd do that."

"A little extra time spent on oral is never a bad thing," Gina said. She patted his cheek as she walked by. "Have fun, kids."

In moments, the women grabbed their things and disappeared out the door.

Zach turned back to Jessie and gave her a rueful smile. "I'm not sure how to feel about that."

"Horrified works," she said. "I am so sorry. I'm not sure how they got all of that out of me. Let's blame the mimosas."

"Not your fault. That crew is relentless and very sneaky. If they hadn't gotten it out of you, they would have gotten it out of me," Zach said. He glanced around the kitchen. "Where are the girls?"

"Reacquainting themselves with the toys in their room," Jessie said.

"So, we're alone?" Zach asked.

His brown eyes scorched and Jessie felt her body start to hum. This was not good. If he kept looking at her like that she'd let him have her here on the kitchen counter. She reached beside her and held up a plate with the stack of waffles she'd put aside for him.

"Waffle?" she asked. She shoved the plate into his chest and he caught it in his hands with a laugh.

"I'll take that as a waffle brush-off," he said.

His eyes crinkled in the corners when he laughed. He didn't have any wrinkles yet, but she knew that when he aged Zach was going to have deep laugh lines. She'd never known anyone who enjoyed life as much as he did. It lifted her spirits just to be around him.

"Not a brush-off," she said. "I need to shower."

"I could help with that," he offered.

Jessie felt her face get hot with embarrassment. "Thanks, but I've got it." Then she tipped her head to the side and considered him. "But if we're going to keep working toward our goal, you might want to fortify."

She strode out of the kitchen with her head high, giving him a firm slap on the ass as she passed him. He jumped under her hand and she heard him laughing, even as he called after her, "Wicked woman!"

Jessie grinned as she climbed the stairs. Oh, she liked playing with Zach, yes, she did.

* * *

After days without electricity, it felt like a luxury to shower with the lights on instead of by candlelight and to use her blow dryer on her hair. Jessie even went so far as to use a little makeup just to make herself feel more put together.

When she arrived back downstairs, the dishes had been done, the bedding the girls had used to sleep on had been folded, and the toys the girls had brought downstairs had been brought back to their room, all without Jessie having to ask, plead, beg, or bribe. In other words, a miracle had obviously taken place while she did her hair.

Even better, the girls were fully occupied in the living room with Zach. They were singing and dancing while he was playing his ukulele and the three of them looked to be having the time of their lives.

"You can't come in here," Maddie said.

"Why not?" Jessie asked.

"We're working on something," Gracie said.

Zach shrugged and then said, "Give us one hour."

"All right," Jessie said. She wasn't sure how she felt about being tossed out of her own living room but the girls looked so excited, and she really needed to catch up on the laundry.

She went back upstairs, thinking how lovely it was to have someone else entertain the girls. She figured she could use the time to call in to work and see if Gavin planned to open the clinic tomorrow. She imagined he would since the latest local reports said the power would be back to everyone by the end of the day and that all of the roads in town had been deemed passable. She tried not to feel bad that her time with Zach as a live-in whatever-he-was was over. She failed.

An hour later on the dot, she reappeared in the living room.

"Okay," she said. "Show me this something you've been working on."

Zach and Gracie were sitting side by side on the hearth; each of them had a ukulele in hand. Zach was very patiently showing Gracie where to put her fingers to make chords and then how to strum the chords. She had her tongue pressed up against her lip as she concentrated.

"Momma, Gracie and I are going to be in the school talent show and Zach, too," Maddie announced.

"Huh?"

"The talent show," Maddie said. She looked at Jessie as if she should know what she was talking about.

Jessie vaguely remembered a flyer coming home for a show at the girls' elementary school but if she remembered right it was a father-daughter talent show. She felt the first tingles of alarm ripple in her belly, sort of like an early warning system for out-and-out panic.

"Oh, honey, that's a father-daughter talent show," she said.

"It doesn't have to be your dad," Maddie said. "Sadie Tyson asked Mrs. Townsend if her uncle could fill in for her dad, since he's a soldier, and Mrs. Townsend said yes."

"Okay, but an uncle is still family," Jessie said.

"Maggie O'Brien is performing with her mom's boyfriend because her dad lives far away," Gracie said. "Like our dad."

Jessie was about to point out that Maggie's mother's boyfriend was still a member of their family, since they were dating, but Zach spoke before she got the chance.

"Why don't you see our show and then let us know what you think?" Zach asked. "I brought my ukulele and everything."

Jessie hesitated and Zach looked at the girls and whispered, "Deploy sad puppy eyes now."

All three of them looked at her with their lower lips out and their eyes all droopy and pitiful. Jessie blew out a breath.

"Oh, all right, fine," she said. "Show me and we'll see."

"Yay!" Maddie clapped her hands and jumped up and down while Gracie gave her a shy smile.

Jessie settled into the couch to watch. She didn't know

what to expect. She wasn't musical and she'd never thought of either of her girls as being particularly musical either. From the first note, it was readily apparent that, no, her girls were not musical.

She felt the smile on her lips wobble when Maddie didn't sing so much as screech the lyrics to "You've Got a Friend in Me," while Gracie furiously strummed her ukulele in an effort to keep up with the chords that were required. Jessie might have thought it was just her, but she saw Chaos bolt upstairs before they were through the first verse and Rufus lie down and put his paws over his ears. By the time they were done, having wound down to a very dramatic finish, Jessie checked her own ears to make sure blood wasn't pouring out of them. Nope. Shocker.

The girls, of course, were beaming at her as if they'd bust with pride. Jessie glanced between them. What to say that wouldn't squash their enthusiasm. It was quite the parent conundrum. She looked at Zach, hoping he had a bright idea. No such luck. If anyone looked even more jazzed than the girls, it was Zach. Oh, boy.

"What did you think?" he asked. "Are they fantastic or what?"

"Or what," Jessie said with a nod. She tried to force her lips into a smile but could only manage one side of her face and wondered if the song from *Toy Story* had just given her a stroke.

"Yes!" Maddie made a fist and pulled it down to her side. "Did you hear that Gracie? We're going to get to perform in the talent show. Come on, let's go pick out our outfits!"

Maddie grabbed her sister's hand and dragged her to her feet. Gracie looked giddy with excitement and Jessie knew she needed to stop this madness immediately.

"Actually, I don't know if it's such a great idea," Jessie said.

All three of them looked at her in shocked dismay as if they couldn't believe what she had just said.

"Why not, Momma?" Gracie asked. "Don't you think we're good enough?"

"Um, well, it . . . you know . . . sounded . . ." Jessie stammered, not wanting to hurt her girls.

"Amazing, right?" Maddie asked.

"Right," Jessie said. Looking at two sets of hopeful blue eyes, there was no way she could crush her girls' dream even if it was going to be a mercy killing.

Gracie sagged with relief and let her sister drag her upstairs so they could raid their closet for costumes.

"Do not make a mess!" Jessie called after them.

The sound of their door slamming was their only response.

Jessie turned to Zach. He was smiling at her and she almost had the same reaction to him that she'd had to the girls in not wanting to hurt his feelings, but she shook it off.

"You have to talk them out of this," she said. "It won't go well and it could scar them for life."

Zach looked at her in surprise. "What? No way, they're going to be great. I know today was a little rough, but—"

"Little rough?" Jessie asked. "Maddie sounds as if she's a cat and someone is pulling her tail and Gracie hit so many sour chords on her uke that I thought she was using a hammer to play it."

"I know. It was an awesome start," Zach said.

"Awesome?" Jessie cried. "I think we have different definitions of awesome."

"No, we don't. I mean did you see them?" he asked. "They were fearless, putting it out there and not giving a hoot what anyone thought. That's art, that's music, that's freedom."

"Oh, my god, you're crazy," she said.

He grinned at her. "Maybe. Listen, we have one week until the talent show, do you trust me to get them ready?"

Jessie felt her insides twist. She had zero capacity to trust people. She knew it was her issue, begun when she arrived as a late surprise into her parents' lives when they clearly didn't want children, reinforced by the people who had befriended her her entire life for her money, and then solidified by her ex when he proved to be the worst of them all, leaving her broke and heartbroken.

Zach asking her to trust him was like asking her to jump from a plane without a parachute. As if he understood how hard it was for her, Zach took her hands in his. He looked into her eyes, and said, "I promise there will be absolutely no psychological trauma involved in their being in this show."

"Zach, we need you . . . please!" Gracie cried from the top of the stairs. "You have to tell Maddie she can't dress like a mermaid."

Jessie raised her eyebrows at Zach and he grinned. "See? They're into it. It's gonna be great."

"All right, but if this goes badly, you're paying for their therapy," she said.

"Yes!" Zach made a fist and drew it down and into his hip just like Maddie had done, letting Jessie know where her daughter had picked up that mannerism. "It's going to be amazeballs. I promise."

He stepped around her to head up the stairs but then spun around, looped an arm around her waist, and pulled her in for one smacking kiss. "And don't worry, I haven't forgotten our project."

He wagged his eyebrows at her, making her blush, and then he disappeared upstairs, leaving Jessie sighing after him. A fling with Zachary Caine was proving to be a lot more than she had bargained for and she was deeply concerned that she wasn't more concerned about it.

Chapter 17

Zach knew he had an ulterior motive for wanting to do the show with the girls. Yes, he wanted to do it for them. Judging by how attached they'd become to him, it was clear they were feeling the lack of a positive male influence in their life. Given that he had five younger sisters, he felt like this was something he could help Jessie out with; plus, those two little sprites had really wormed their way into his heart.

Every time Maddie hit him with a high five or Gracie gifted him with a shy smile, Zach felt like they were giving him so much more than he was giving them. He wanted to be worthy of their affection and so he paid attention to them, helped them out as he could, and while they rehearsed for their show, he made sure it was fun for them and not fraught with anxiety.

But he also knew that he wanted to be close to Jessie. When the power came back on and there was really no need for him to be hovering around her house, Zach and Rufus, who'd gotten rather attached to Chaos and the girls, had packed up and gone home. Except it didn't really feel like home as much as it felt like a place where they ate and slept and kept their stuff.

Working on the show with the girls gave him an opportunity to see Jessie every day after work. He was surprised at how quickly they fell into a routine. Jessie and Zach cooked dinner together and they all ate at the table in the dining room, where they discussed the events of the day. Afterwards, Zach and the girls hid out in their room while they rehearsed for the show.

At some point in the evening, when the girls were otherwise occupied, Zach would manage to get Jessie alone and kiss her with a savage intensity that made them both breathless. With the girls underfoot, however, he didn't dare do much more. Which was how he realized he needed to get Jessie out of the house and out with the crew at the first available opportunity.

The days following the blizzard had been a blur of activity as the residents of Bluff Point got back to normal with power restored and roads dug out and the sun, a rare visitor over the past few weeks, made its presence felt even though it didn't bring much heat with it.

When Zach's phone popped open with a group text, inviting everyone in the crew out for drinks at Marty's Pub, he knew that the storm was officially over. He also knew that he wanted to see his friends but he wanted Jessie there with him, too.

The trouble was, he needed someone to watch the girls while he and Jessie went out. He needed someone who would be firm but kind with the girls, as he knew from observation that Gracie responded best to kindness. Also, they needed to like children but not be a pushover, because he suspected Maddie would test the boundaries of the limits set like all feisty children do.

In a flash the answer came to him: Mac's two septuagenarian aunts, Sarah and Charlotte, assuming their busy social calendar wasn't already full. One problem. He didn't know how the aunts felt about Jessie, because while Mac had forgiven her, thanked her even, for saving her from marriage to Seth Connelly, the aunts might still hold a grudge.

Bribery would likely be needed. Zach was down with that. He texted Mac to ask where the aunts might be and what their current raison d'être was, then he skipped out of his office at the brewery to go and track them down.

Sarah and Charlotte Harris lived in the Harris family home, which was one of the oldest houses in the town of Bluff Point. Halfway down Elizabeth Street, the big old beautiful Victorian, white with a forest green trim and matching shingles on its mansard roof, sat as if poised for visitors at any moment.

Zach drove his truck up the gravel drive and parked in front of the house. He grabbed his bribes from the front seat and trotted up the steps onto the wide front porch.

He rapped three times on the door frame and waited. There was no answer. He glanced around the side of the house to the detached garage. Yup, through the window, he could see the aunts' blue Dodge Challenger with the white racing stripe parked in its spot, so it stood to reason that the aunts were here, too. Yes, they drove a sports car, which was one of the many things Zach loved about them.

Zach rapped on the door again. This time he could hear someone grumbling, which meant it was most likely Aunt Sarah, since she was the sassier of the two, as she came to the door.

"I'm coming, I'm coming, keep your shirt on," Aunt Sarah said. She pulled the wooden door open and pushed the storm door out. "Zachary Caine, it's you! Well, in your case, don't feel you need to keep your shirt on."

Zach busted out a laugh as he stepped inside, leaving the day's bitter cold behind him. "Good to see you, too, Aunt Sarah. Um, nice outfit?"

Sarah glanced down at her paint-splotched coveralls. She wagged a finger at him. "Do not mock the artist. I have a whole Grandma Moses thing happening. Come on back. Charlotte is in the studio."

Zach fell into step behind Sarah as she led him through

the house to a large back room that was presently empty of everything except two easels with canvases propped on them and a short table on which perched a mannequin, a naked male mannequin, posed to look like it was running. Zach couldn't blame it. Playing softly in the background was John Legend's "P.D.A. (We Just Don't Care)."

"Who's the stiff?" he asked.

Charlotte turned away from her canvas. She had a paint-brush clenched between her teeth, another in her right hand, and a cloth in her left.

"Zut wuh ugh ha?" she asked. Both Zach and Sarah looked at her and she took the paintbrush out of her mouth. "Sorry. Zach, it's nice to see you. What are you doing here?"

"I heard from Mac that you two had taken up a new hobby," he said. "So I thought I'd bring by some supplies to encourage you."

"Presents!" Sarah cried. "Gimme, gimme."

"Sarah, honestly, a little decorum," Charlotte chided her twin. Then she smiled at Zach and snatched the bag out of his hands. "Oh, you shouldn't have."

"Wine," Charlotte said as she hefted out a bottle of red and a bottle of white.

"Cheese," Sarah said as she lifted out a platter of different cheeses.

"Oh, two berets," Charlotte cried. She tossed one red beret to Sarah, who immediately put it on her sleek silver bobbed hair while Charlotte donned the other atop her curly chin-length hair of the same shade.

"Adorable," Zach said. "Now you look like professional artists."

The sisters exchanged a look and then Sarah wrinkled her nose. "We need a live model. Mr. Molded Plastic over there isn't doing it for me."

"Carly let us borrow him from Penmans, the department store she is a buyer for, but it's not working out," Charlotte agreed. "His pecs just aren't inspiring."

"Pecs, huh?" Zach asked. "What would you be willing to do for a good pair of pecs?"

Sarah and Charlotte both turned to look at him with mischief in their eyes.

"Do you want trade favors, dear boy?" Sarah asked.

"Maybe," he said. "I need a babysitter for Gracie and Maddie Connelly tonight, so I can invite their mother, Jessie, out with the crew."

"Jessie Peeler?" Sarah said. She had staunchly refused to ever use her married name. "The one who took Mac's groom right out of the church?"

"The one who inadvertently saved Mac years of heart-break and horror," Zach said.

"She and Mac have become friends," Charlotte said. "Mac always did have a forgiving heart."

Zach waited. He knew if he launched a defense of Jessie, it could backfire by getting the aunts to dig their heels in. No, it was best to let them work through it and hope for the best. That didn't mean he couldn't nudge them a bit. He shrugged off his coat, pleased that he was wearing a body-hugging thermal shirt underneath. He flexed ever so slightly.

Sarah and Charlotte glanced at his chest and then at each other.

"Cecilia and Markus Peeler were the worst," Charlotte said. "Cold, selfish, and utterly preoccupied with their social standing."

"Bleh, I loathed having to converse with them," Sarah agreed. "Name-dropping, pretentious, money obsessed, truly, it's no surprise Jessie latched onto the first person to show her some warmth."

"Unfortunate that it was someone else's fiancé," Charlotte said. "But she did do Mac a favor in the end and she certainly suffered being married to that repulsive letch."

"Ugh, that could have been Mac, and then Mac never would have found her Gavin," Sarah agreed.

"We should get to know Jessie and her girls," Charlotte said. "My calendar is clear tonight, you?"

"I have a guitar lesson, but I will reschedule," Sarah said. She looked at Zach. "What time?"

"Seven okay?" he said.

The aunts nodded, then Sarah poked him in the chest and gave him a soft smile. "Nice pecs. You remind me of my Stuart."

Zach had never heard either of the aunts reference a man before. He had to know more. "Stuart who?"

"Captain Stuart Stovall; he was my first love. You remind me of him." She spoke the man's name with a yearning that surprised Zach.

So, Mac's aunt Sarah had once had a true love. He thought it explained quite a lot about her. Perhaps her cantankerous nature was more the result of a broken heart. Zach understood that and he was filled with sympathy for her. As if sensing his concern, she shook her head like she could ditch the memories that easily.

"He was a big, buff blondie like you," Sarah teased. She glanced at her sister. "I think I'm feeling inspired." Then she gestured for Zach to take the mannequin's place. "Up you go."

"Okay," Zach agreed. Then he looked at the sisters with a considering gaze. "But the pants stay on."

Sarah and Charlotte exchanged a look and for a heartbeat he was sure they were going to haggle for full frontal. Then Charlotte laughed. He'd been had. He shook his head at the two of them and dutifully dropped his shirt and took the place of Mr. Molded Plastic.

Zach had just finished rehearsing with the girls when there was a knock on Jessie's front door. He dropped his ukulele and dashed down the stairs, running past Jessie to get to the door first.

"Zach, what are you doing?" she asked as she hugged the door frame that led into the foyer to keep from falling over.

"Sorry, I might have forgotten to mention that I was thinking we could meet up with the crew at Marty's Pub for a beer, and I have two babysitters coming over."

"What?" Jessie looked at him like he was nuts. Not an impossibility.

She had changed from her animal clinic scrubs into jeans and a pretty blue sweater that was reflected in her eyes. She looked lovely and for a second he forgot why he was standing at the door. Until an imperious set of knuckles rapped on the wood again, louder this time.

"Just trust me," he said. He turned and opened the door and Sarah and Charlotte Harris strode into the house.

"It's freezing out there," Sarah said. "Were you waiting until we were popsicles?"

"Sorry, Aunt Sarah," Zach said.

"Oh, quit fussing, it wasn't that bad," Charlotte said.

They shrugged out of their coats and handed them along with their handbags to Zach, who hung them on the coatrack.

"Come on in," he said. "The girls are looking forward to meeting you."

Jessie was staring at the aunts and Zach as if she couldn't believe what she was seeing. He took her hand and gave it a gentle squeeze.

"Hello, Jessica," Charlotte said. "Don't you look lovely."

Jessie's eyes improbably got even wider.

"That's a very flattering blue on you," Sarah said.

"Thank you," Jessie said. "You both look lovely as well."

The sisters nodded in thanks as if they knew they were looking good. Rufus rolled off the couch at the sound of voices and came bounding in the direction of the aunts. Sarah took one look at him and said, "No!"

Rufus immediately sat down. Zach looked from Rufus to Sarah.

"She's a natural alpha," Charlotte explained.

"Zach, can I have a word?" Jessie said. Her voice sounded high-pitched and weird as if she was having a freak-out and trying really hard to keep it all inside.

Sarah looked at Zach with a frown. "You didn't tell her we were coming to babysit?"

"I was going to," he said.

"Never mind, where are the girls?" Charlotte asked. "We'll go introduce ourselves while you two figure it out."

"Up in their room," Zach said. "First door on the right."

Rufus trotted beside the aunts as they made their way upstairs.

"I can see why Mac says she likes her," Charlotte said. "She seems very direct."

"Maturity does change people; well, that and parenthood," Sarah said. "Once we meet the girls we'll have a better sense of her."

At that, Jessie started to follow the two women, but Zach held her back.

"Whoa there, I thought you wanted to talk," he said.

"But the aunts are up there with my girls," she said. "They hate me. What if they say horrible things about me?"

"First, they don't hate you," Zach said. "We're all in agreement that you did Mac a huge favor, sparing her from marrying that dumbass."

Jessie nodded. "Mac and I have agreed that the karmic payback on my taking off with her fiancé was epic."

"Second, the aunts are great with kids; just look at how Aunt Sarah handled Rufus," he said.

"Kids and dogs are not the same," she said.

"No, but the aunts are really good with both. Besides, you never get to go out and there was a group text to meet up at Marty's Pub, and I thought you could use it after being cooped up here for the past few days."

A look of longing passed over Jessie's face that was so intense he felt himself take a step toward her as if in response. He stopped himself before he touched her but only just.

"That sounds really great," she said. "But honestly I'm on a budget here and I don't have the extra cash for a sitter, never mind two."

"Don't worry about it," Zach said. He could feel victory in his grasp. "I got it."

"No, I can't have you paying for my babysitter," she said.

"I didn't pay them," he said. "This was an exchange of goods and services."

"What sort of goods?" she asked.

"Don't worry your pretty little head about it," he said. "But we definitely have the use of them for two hours, so let's say good night to the kids and skedaddle."

"Are you sure?" Jessie asked. Her gaze searched his as if trying to determine his trust level.

"Absolutely," he said.

Whatever Jessie saw in his gaze must have reassured her because she nodded. Then she led the way upstairs to the girls' room.

They were unprepared for what greeted them. Aunt Sarah and Aunt Charlotte were standing in the middle of the room with the girls while listening to some hip-hop song playing off one of their smartphones while they taught the girls some basic dance moves.

Zach and Jessie stood transfixed as the aunts busted out Silentó's "Watch Me (Whip/Nae Nae)." The girls imitated the older ladies as they all sang, "Now watch me whip; now watch me nae nae."

Jessie clapped a hand over her mouth, barely covering the giggle. Zach turned and smiled at her.

"Yeah, they've been going through the hip-hop thing for a while now."

"Mac said they were driving her bonkers with their shenanigans but I had no idea."

They turned back and Jessie smiled when Charlotte helped Gracie with her arm movement and the girl looked up at the older lady with gratitude.

"So, are you two going or what?" Sarah asked.

"On our way," Zach confirmed.

Jessie went forward and hugged both of her girls, reminding them to mind their manners. When she thanked the aunts, they waved her off with big smiles, clearly enjoying the girls.

Zach paused to do his special high-five handshakes with each girl. The routines were becoming more and more complicated every day, but he loved it. Until one of them threw a cartwheel into the mix, he was all good.

He hugged the aunts, and did a little whip and nae nae

of his own, which made the girls, all of them, laugh. Zach was not known for his dancing but he figured what he lacked in skill he made up for in enthusiasm.

In minutes, he'd hustled Jessie out the door and into his truck and they were barreling down the road toward Marty's Pub.

They had to park in the lot behind the bar and hoof it around the building. The night air was bitterly cold, giving Zach the perfect excuse to wrap an arm around Jessie and pull her close as they trudged through the snow to the bar.

Just before they entered, Jessie slowed to a stop and turned to face him.

"In case I forget to say it later," she said, "thanks for this."

Zach leaned in and kissed her. It was just a soft brush of his lips against hers; anything more and they'd never make it into the bar. But as usual, she had the ability to rock his world.

He had no idea what it was about Jessie that made him throw out all of his carefully constructed barriers but he found he didn't care. He wanted her, he wanted to be with her, and not just for a fling. He was playing the long game here and hoping that at the end of it he had Jessie and the girls in his life on a permanent basis.

It occurred to him that the fact that he was even thinking like this should be freaking him out on the level of being chased by a scary-looking clown wielding a knife, but it wasn't. He'd never been more certain of anything in his life and he was going to use everything he had to get Jessie to feel the same way about him.

Marty's Pub was packed. Shots of Fireball whiskey and pints of Bluff Point Ale were being dished out in a feeding frenzy as the Celtics ruled the large screen TV. Zach took Jessie's hand in his as he led her though the crowd to the back, where the Maine crew liked to take over a large booth close to the dartboard.

Zach scanned the group piled into the booth. It was the usual suspects: Gavin and Mac, Carly and James, Jillian, Sam, and Gina—but no Emma and Brad.

"Zach, you're late!" Gavin called. "I had to recruit Jillian to play darts for you."

"Where are the expectant parents?" Zach asked.

"Emma was feeling a bit tired," Mac said. She glanced around Zach at Jessie. She half rose out of her seat to give Jessie a hug. "You made it out. I'm so glad."

"Hold that thought," Jessie said. "Your aunts are babysitting my girls. I'm worried the four of them may start a biker gang."

"Oh, I want in on that," Carly said. She stood and hugged Jessie, too, and Zach realized he had to relinquish Jessie's hand so she could greet everyone properly.

He didn't really like that, which was weird because he was never possessive about women. Then again, he'd never taken the time to woo a woman like he was with Jessie, so he was feeling a bit more caveman than normal, which he supposed was only natural. He watched as she hugged the rest of the crew, including the boys. Nope, he didn't like that. Not at all.

When Sam said something that made her laugh, Zach stepped forward and took her hand in his again. She glanced at him with a smile in her eyes and she squeezed his fingers as if happy to find him there. He was reassured. Then she leaned against him and he could smell the faint lemon scent that was uniquely hers. A vision of her beneath him, the memory of him inside her from their short-lived attempt at lovemaking, flashed through his mind, and he blew out a breath.

"Are you okay?" she asked him.

Zach turned to meet her gaze and then he leaned in close so only she could hear and whispered, "Just wondering why we're here with these idiots when we could be naked at my house, working on our project."

Jessie's mouth formed an O and she fanned herself with her free hand as she flushed a faint shade of pink. Just seeing her reaction to his suggestion made Zach feel better.

"Dude, you're up," Sam said. He thrust a fistful of darts at Zach.

"Excellent, because it's time for girl talk or shots or girl talk *and* shots," Carly said. She kissed her man on the mouth and then looped her arm through Jessie's and dragged her toward the bar, leaving Jillian, Mac, and Gina to follow.

Zach stared after her and Gina paused beside him. "Don't worry. I'll keep an eye on her for you."

"You always were my favorite," Zach said. He caught the direction of Gina's gaze, which was on Sam per usual. He jerked his head in Sam's direction. "I'll keep an eye out for you, too."

"I don't know what you're talking about," Gina said. She blinked at him and followed the girls as fast as her thick-heeled boots could take her.

Chapter 18

Jessie let the girls drag her to the bar. Carly managed to wiggle her way in and ordered only the bartender knew what while the rest of them formed a loose circle.

"All right," Gina said. "Don't keep us in suspense. What's happening with 'the project'?"

"We're working on it," Jessie said.

"And?" Carly prodded.

"And she'll share the results with you if and when she wants to," Jillian said.

"But I want updates," Carly protested. She passed out the shots she'd purchased.

"Maybe there's an app for that," Mac teased. "You know, something that will tell the world you've just enjoyed an orgasm."

"Well, it would be a hell of a lot more interesting than seeing what people ordered for lunch," Gina said.

"No pictures, though," Jessie said. She sniffed the beverage in her hand. It burned her nose hair. "I live in fear of what my orgasm face might look like."

The others laughed and Carly held her glass up high

and said, "Ladies, here's to your genitalia, may it never fail you or jail you!"

They clinked glasses and tossed back the shot. Jessie sputtered as the alcohol burned its way down her throat. She had never been much of a drinker, mostly because with Seth in a constant state of inebriation, she'd felt like she had to remain sober at all times to take care of the girls.

She blinked the tears from her eyes to find Cooper O'Rourke standing beside her, looking at her as if he expected her to fall over. The alcohol seemed to want to punch its way back out of her and Jessie shuddered and shook her head. Maybe it wasn't such a bad thing that she'd never been a drinker.

"You all right?" he asked.

"Yeah," Jessie said. "But I think I'm done."

"Wise choice. Did I hear right?" Cooper asked. "Were you all just drinking a toast to your lady parts?"

"Aw, Coop, you're so cute," Gina said. She tossed her red curls over her shoulder and batted her long eyelashes at him. "It's okay to say the word 'vagina.'"

"No, no," he said. He grinned down at Gina. "I'll blush and lose all of my street cred."

Jessie tipped her head to the side and studied the big, rawboned chief of police. He wasn't in uniform presently and he looked less severe than the other times Jessie had seen him, which unfortunately had usually been in an official capacity at her house to deal with her ex. She'd always thought he was a rules-and-regulations sort of guy and his discomfort with their wordplay proved it.

"Okay, then, how about taffy puller?" Carly asked, pointing both pointer fingers at Cooper. True to his word, he turned a faint shade of pink.

"Catcher's mitt," Mac offered.

"Mount Pleasant," Gina said.

"Oh, my god, you really are blushing," Jillian said. She put her hand on Cooper's arm and gave him a sweet smile. He looked momentarily stunned and then her brown gaze turned wicked and she said, "Or we could call it snake charmer."

Cooper laughed out loud at that one, even as the tips of his ears turned bright red. He glanced over their heads and cried out, "Hey, Zach, a little help over here!"

Jessie whipped her head in the direction of the dartboard. Sure enough, Zach put down his darts and made his way toward them. The others must have suspected some shenanigans because Gavin made a beeline for Mac while James locked in on Carly and Sam brought up the rear, his gaze as always on Jillian. Honestly, how did the woman not know he was in love with her?

"What's the trouble, Chief?" Zach asked. "Are these women causing a problem?"

Jessie noticed that Zach moved so that he was standing right in between her and Cooper. She felt his hand slide smoothly about her waist and she couldn't stop herself from leaning into him just a little bit.

"You're the wordy one," Cooper said with a laugh. "Do me a solid and get me out of this."

Zach raised his eyebrows in intrigue. "All right, what's the wordplay?"

"Euphemisms for girl parts," Jessie said.

Zach turned his head and looked down at her. His brown eyes flashed with heat and Jessie didn't know if it was the way he was looking at her or the alcohol making her feel suddenly overheated. She suspected it was Zach.

"All right, game on," he said. His hand moved down toward Jessie's rear and he gave her a gentle squeeze, making her go cross-eyed for just a second. "The happy valley."

"Birth cannon," Gavin offered.

"Really?" Mac asked, giving him a look.

"Sorry, veterinarian," Gav said with a shrug.

"Velvet glove," Sam said.

"Flaming lips," James said. Carly laughed out loud and slapped him on the back.

"How are we doing?" Zach asked.

"We are tied, with our only non-participants being Coop and Jessie," Gina said. "Come on, Jessie, you can do this."

"Coop, you can't let us down, man," Gavin said.

"I'm not a word guy," Cooper protested. "I'm the strong silent type."

"Same," Jessie said. She gave Zach a side-eye, wondering what he'd think of her if she couldn't keep up with his gang. She found she wanted to be a part of the fun but for the life of her she couldn't think of a thing to say.

"Coop! Coop! Coop!" the men chanted.

The chief raised his hands and said, "I can't believe I am about to say this, do not judge me." He paused and they all waited and he said, "Love muffin."

"Oh, yes!" Sam cried. He raised his hand and said, "I am going to high-five you so hard."

Cooper winced when Sam connected and they all laughed. Then the entire group looked at Jessie. She felt the pressure ratchet up. Oh, man, she wasn't good at this. She had no idea what to say. She didn't want to let the girls down, but the only one she could remember was the one Zach had said to her the other night; the one that had made her snort. She glanced at him and he gave her a little nod of encouragement.

She cleared her throat, and said in a voice just above a whisper, "Cock socket."

"What?!" Carly cried. "That is the best one ever! I declare Jessie the winner."

"You can't declare her the winner," James said. Then he kissed Carly. It started friendly but didn't stay that way and Jessie smiled when it appeared James had to force himself to let go of his woman.

"At best we're into overtime unless we call it a draw," Gavin said.

The group glanced around at each other and Cooper nodded. "No one is going to beat Jessie's. I'm good with that. Agreed?"

While the others turned back to their drinks, Zach pushed Jessie into a dark corner of the bar. He was grinning when he looked at her.

"That was filthy and also funny, you wicked woman," he said. "I'm so proud."

Before Jessie could remind him that he'd taught her the word, he kissed her. It started very sweet as if just to reassure himself about her but it turned as soon as she wrapped her arms around his neck and opened her mouth beneath his. Then it became a claiming, but honestly Jessie wasn't sure who was claiming whom. She just knew that the taste of Zach, the feel of him pressed against her, the scent of him in her senses, made her feel safe and secure while it also lit a fuse of hot longing that licked at her insides as if trying to detonate.

"Jessie, you are driving me crazy," he whispered as he moved his lips down the side of her neck to nestle in the sweet spot at her shoulder.

"Likewise," she said. She brought his mouth back to hers and kissed him with the pent-up desire that had been her constant companion since the morning she'd woken up in his arms.

Never had she wanted anyone like she wanted Zach. She suspected that was exactly why he was taunting her and teasing her every day, making her so befuddled with lust that all he would have to do was look at her and she'd orgasm on the spot. In fact, judging by the throbbing heat at the juncture of her legs, it could happen any second now.

"Yo, Zach, you're up!" Sam called from across the bar.

Zach broke off the kiss, then hauled her up against him for one more indecent press of their bodies before he kissed her again. Jessie began to sweat and pant a little and she wondered if everyone in the bar could tell she was on the brink.

"You are killing me, my girl," he growled in her ear. "In the best possible way."

"Huh." Jessie had lost her powers of speech.

Zach ripped himself away from her and Jessie was vaguely surprised not to hear the sound of Velcro being separated when he did so. Zach kept her hand in his and led her back toward the dartboard, pushing her into the nearby booth with the girls as if he needed to keep her close. It made Jessie feel valued, and she smiled. It was such a nice change to be treated as if she mattered. She knew she needed to be careful and not let it go to her head. Everyone said Zach wasn't that sort of guy, but even knowing she might get hurt, she knew she couldn't walk away from him if she tried.

"Zach, dude, you're destroying us and not in a good way," Sam said. "Where's my guy who owns the bull's-eye?"

"Huh, what?" Zach asked.

He had no idea what Sam had just said. He'd been watching Jessie while she laughed with the girls. Her two-tone hair was a mass of messy waves and it fell about her shoulders, reflecting the blue glow of the neon beer sign that hung in the window behind their booth.

Maybe it was because they hadn't done the deed as yet, but he found that he was hyperaware of her. Where she was, what she was doing, how she was feeling, all of it. It was like he was connected to her and everything she felt, he felt.

Sam moved to stand beside him and waved his hand in front of his face. Zach pushed his hand out of the way. Jessie was leaning in to hear something Carly was saying and she got a glint in her blue eyes, the same one she always got just before she—yep, there she went. She was laughing. A wide openmouthed musical chuckle that came from deep inside her and always made Zach smile when he heard it.

"I may be just an animal doctor, but even I can diagnose this boy as being lovesick," Gavin said.

"Huh, what?" Zach snapped his gaze to Gavin's at the use of the "L" word. "No, I'm not."

"Oh, please," James said. "You can't take your eyes off Jessie. You are consumed by her. We've all been there. There's no judgment here."

"Leave me out," Sam said. "I am single. I am not in love. I am the cheese."

"And the cheese stands alone," Gavin said. "So you've been telling us, but we all know you are in—"

"Hey! We're supposed to be talking about me," Zach said.

Sam, who looked decidedly nervous, slapped Zach on the shoulder and said, "Yeah, let's stay on task here. Zach's the one who is practically nonfunctional."

"Whoa, where'd you get that?" Zach protested.

Sam waved an arm at the dartboard. "You've had more darts hit the wall than the board."

"It's just an off night," Zach grumbled.

James handed Zach his pint of beer and said, "Maybe this will help."

"At the risk of overstepping my boundaries," Gavin said, "I need to ask you not to break my office manager's heart. Good help is hard to find and Jessie has been amazing at the animal clinic. Don't screw that up for me."

"We're not—it's not—oh, crap, it is, isn't it?" Zach asked.

"Let's see," James said. "Do you think about her all the time?"

"Yes," Zach answered.

"Is her happiness more important than your own?" Gavin asked.

"Yes."

"Do you feel better just because she's around?" James asked.

"Yes."

"Does the thought of not having her in your life wreck you?" Gavin asked.

Zach looked at his three friends. He didn't want to answer this question because he knew what it meant. He was done for. Somehow over the past few days, he had fallen ass over teakettle in love with Jessie Connelly. Damn it.

"I'll take that silence to mean you are screwed," Sam said. "If you want my advice . . ."

"No," Zach said. "You're single. I love you like a brother but you are no use to me right now." He looked at Gavin and James. "What do I do?"

"Tell her," they said at the same time.

"Now?" Zach felt a little queasy at the thought of it.

"Soon," Gavin said. He nodded to the booth behind Zach. "Before someone else does."

Zach spun around to see Ryan Stanek, the annoyingly

good-looking manager of Marty's, leaning over the back of the booth. He was talking to Jessie, who was looking up at him with a small smile on her lips. Zach, who had never been jealous a day in his life, suddenly felt an unfamiliar clawing in his gut. Oh, hell no.

"Excuse me, brothers, I've got to go," Zach said. He shoved his near-full beer at Sam and strode over to the table. He clapped his hands together and said, "I hate to cut and run but I promised our babysitters we wouldn't be out too late."

Jessie turned from Ryan to him, and the smile she sent him dazzled him. There it was. The sparkle in her eyes that was just for him. Suddenly, everything was all right in his world again. Ryan would live to see tomorrow.

Zach clapped the manager on the shoulder and said, "Take my place in the dart game."

Ryan looked from Zach to Jessie and back. He shook his head. "Thanks, but I'd better get back to work. Ladies."

He dipped his head toward the girls and they all waved at him, except for Carly, who blew him a kiss. Zach glanced back to see what James made of that. Judging from the way he was striding toward the booth with his stare focused on his woman, Zach had a feeling James was about to stake his claim. Nice to know he wasn't the only one feeling turfy.

He helped Jessie out of the booth and they gathered their things, pulling on their coats, gloves, and hats. Hugs—the girls—and fist bumps—the boys—were exchanged and soon Zach was hustling Jessie out of Marty's to the warmth of his truck, where he planned to kiss her until the engine either in his truck or within himself overheated.

In truth, Zach had meant to wait until he'd seen Charlotte and Sarah safely off before he kissed Jessie, but it didn't work out that way. The close quarters of the truck made the intoxicating lemon scent of her draw him in like warmth on a cold day.

He scooped her close, pulling her up against him. The console between them made it awkward but Zach was willing to work around it. He kissed her, letting his mouth mold to hers before he nudged her lips open with the tip of his tongue, sweeping inside to get the taste of her.

Jessie was right there with him, starting back where they left off in the bar. She pressed up against him as if the feel of his firm chest against her soft one completed her.

Zach dug his fingers into her hair and held her steady while he kissed her. He used his other hand to trace patterns on the skin he could reach between the waistline of her jeans and the hem of her sweater. Her skin was incredibly smooth and he wanted to feel all of it, all of her, wrapped around him, holding him close, pulling him in.

When he noticed the windows were beginning to fog up, he forced himself to let her go, so they could both catch their breath. Man, he hadn't made out with anyone in a car since he was in college.

He was pleased to see that Jessie looked as winded as he felt and her eyes were unfocused and a bit dazed. She looked like a woman who was beginning to understand the depths of her own desire. Excellent progress.

Zach figured a couple more nights like this and she'd be right where he wanted her. An image of Jessie naked with her back arched, responding to him and finding her own pleasure, made Zach shudder from the inside out.

He glanced at the snow still pushed into large drifts around the truck. Snow. Ice. Cold showers. Getting kicked in the junk. He tried to bury the image of Jessie behind the others, hoping to snuff out the lust that had him in a stranglehold.

"Zach, are you all right?" she asked. Her voice was gruff and Zach couldn't look at her.

"Yeah, I'm fine," he croaked. He glanced back out the windshield at the snow. Maybe a quick roll in the snow was in order.

She put her hand on his forearm, a soft gentle touch. Zach glanced from her hand with the neatly trimmed and polished nails up to her face. Her eyes looked concerned.

"Thank you for tonight," she said. "It was fun."

When Zach looked at her, her blue eyes sparkled at him

in that special way they had. He was done for. He lifted her fingers to his lips and kissed her knuckles, wishing he ·could have her tonight but knowing it was too soon.

He reached past her and on the foggy window, he used his finger to draw a heart and put the initials JC + ZC inside of it. It was the closest he could get to telling her how he felt about her.

Jessie looked from the heart to him and smiled. It was a shy smile and she ducked her head and tucked her hair behind her ear. When she spoke her voice was just above a whisper.

"Me, too," she said.

Zach was pretty sure his chest was going to explode. Any coolness he had ever developed in life was gone, and he was suddenly back in middle school crushing on a girl who was so far out of his league, he couldn't even talk to her, except this time she was here with him and she felt the same way. With a grin, he put the truck in drive and drove Jessie home.

Chapter 19

The night of the talent show, Jessie was a hot mess. Zach and the girls hadn't let her see their performance and even though she knew the song and heard them through the door of the girls' room rehearsing, she had no idea what to expect.

She was afraid that they hadn't had enough time to prepare, that the girls would flounder, that irreparable damage would be done to their self-esteem if they failed. Still, Zach had asked her to trust him and the girls had pleaded with their big eyes to be allowed to try.

Jessie knew that failure was critical to a child's development, and that learning to try again and to shake off defeat were crucial life skills. It didn't mean that it was easy to watch as a parent.

She sat through a dance number by a bedazzled seven-year-old and her dad, in matching spangles, that included jazz hands. Next there was a magician and daughter team that riveted—okay not really—but they did have a cute bunny in their act. Then there was a dad and daughter acrobat act. It was cute but with every minute that ticked by Jessie felt her anxiety spike.

"Hey, sorry we're late," a voice whispered in Jessie's ear.

She glanced to her right to see Mac and the entire Maine crew filling the seats beside and behind her.

"Oh, hi, I didn't realize you all were coming," she whispered back.

"Are you kidding? And miss Zach's ukulele debut?" Sam said from behind her. "Never."

Jessie smiled at them all—even Brad and Emma were here—and she felt herself visibly relax. There was something about having friends in attendance that bolstered her spirits. It was a new feeling for her and she liked it.

They sat through two more performances and then Mrs. Abbott, the music teacher, announced the MGZ Trio. Jessie smiled, recognizing that Zach and the girls had used their initials to form the name of the group.

A nervous flutter began in her belly and she felt the smile on her face get tight. As her two girls stepped out on the stage in matching outfits, their favorite bright blue poofy-skirted dresses bought by her mother-in-law, Audrey, for a wedding last year, Jessie felt her heart flip over to see Zach step out with them in a matching blue plaid shirt and a tie. His blonde hair was slicked back, making him look like a grown-up. Jessie felt her heart do a crazy somersault as she took in the sight of him with her girls. She tried not to notice how right they all looked together and it wasn't just the matching outfits.

Zach sat on a stool, while Gracie stood beside him. They each plucked a couple of strings on their ukuleles, checking one more time to make sure they were in tune. Gracie nodded at Zach and he smiled at her. Maddie took the handheld mic from Mrs. Abbott. She stepped out in front of Gracie and Zach and then turned and nodded at them, letting them know she was ready.

Gracie started strumming the familiar tune and Zach joined in. Mac leaned close to Jessie and whispered, "Oh, my god, they are the most precious things I've ever seen and that includes Zach."

Jessie nodded because she had no powers of speech. Watching the girls up there under the lights on the big stage, she felt so very fragile, as if her insides were made of glass and could shatter and at any second. She was thrilled and terrified, proud and petrified.

She watched, not blinking, as Maddie brought the mic up. She looked so tiny on the massive stage. Maddie had her hair up on the top of her head with a blue bow that matched her dress placed precisely in front of it. Gracie's hairdo was the same, making the sisters look impossibly cute. She wondered if Zach had done their hair. It seemed improbable, but then he did have five little sisters; maybe his skills were richer than Jessie knew.

Jessie wanted pictures, video, all of it, but she was incapable of functioning, she was so nervous. She glanced past Mac at Gavin and handed him her phone.

"Can you tape it for me?" she asked.

"Got it," Gavin said. He took her phone and opened up the video app.

"I've got it, too," Carly said from behind her.

"Thanks," Jessie whispered.

She turned back to the stage. She watched as Maddie glanced over her shoulder at Zach and Gracie, nodding her head to their beat, waiting to come in. Then she turned back to the crowd and took a deep breath.

Zach and Gracie exchanged a look while playing their ukuleles. Zach was keeping the time and Gracie was following him. Jessie noticed right away that Zach played the harder chords while Gracie played a lesser version, but she was keeping up with him and her smile was so bright it practically lit up the room. Jessie felt her heart lift out of her chest as if it had sprouted wings.

Gracie glanced at her sister and then at Zach. She didn't stop playing but Jessie knew immediately that something was wrong and then she looked at Maddie's face. Her fearless little warrior girl looked wide-eyed in terror. She wasn't moving, she wasn't singing, she looked frozen in place as if she had forgotten not only the words to the song but everything she had ever learned in her short life.

Jessie leaned forward, trying to catch Maddie's eyes. She wanted to give her a signal to let her know she was there and she would save her. She half rose out of her seat, but just then Gracie looked at Zach and he nodded at her.

As Jessie watched, her older daughter moved to stand beside her little sister. She stopped playing her ukulele, but that was okay because Zach kept playing, and she dropped an arm around her sister's shoulders. In a calm, clear voice that reached all corners of the cafeteria-turned-auditorium, she sang the opening line to the song.

"You've got a friend in me," Gracie sang.

Maddie ripped her gaze from the crowd to her sister. A wobbly smile curved her lips, and she put her arm around her sister's waist and pulled her close.

"You've got a friend in me," they sang together, continuing the song, grinning at each other with every word.

Jessie felt a sob choke her. It was too much. She was feeling too much, love for her girls, pride at how they were there for each other, joy at their achievement, and gratitude for Zach who was giving them this moment in the sun.

At the bridge, Gracie stepped back to play her ukulele, but it was okay because Maddie was over her case of stage fright and continued the song herself. Her voice was clear as she hit every note with confidence and a grin as wide as the sky.

When they finished the song, both girls moved to stand beside Zach and they all sang the last lines together. The crowd went nuts. Jessie jumped to her feet and clapped like a crazy woman as the Maine crew around her did the same. Carly put her fingers in her mouth and let loose a piercing whistle, while Brad yelled, "Bravo! Bravo!"

Gavin handed Jessie her phone and said, "They were awesome."

Mac handed her a tissue out of a small pack and took one for herself. It was then that Jessie realized she was crying happy tears. She dabbed at her cheeks and laughed as the girls joined hands with Zach and the three of them walked to the front of the stage to take a bow. When Zach straightened up, he looked right at Jessie and blew her a kiss. She felt her knees buckle just a little and she grabbed the chair back in front of her to stay upright.

The show continued but Jessie saw none of it. The happy glow inside of her filled her to bursting and all she wanted to do was rush backstage and hug her people hard. Finally, the show was over and Zach and the girls came out onto the stage for one more bow with the rest of the performers. As soon as it was done, Maddie jumped off the stage and ran straight at Jessie.

"Momma, did you see? Did you see?"

Jessie bent down and opened her arms wide. Maddie threw herself into Jessie's arms, hugging her hard.

"I did see!" Jessie said. "You were wonderful! Amazing! Fantastic!"

"I know!" Maddie said. She laughed and wriggled out of Jessie's arms to hug and high-five the rest of the Maine crew.

Gracie, quieter than her sister, came up to Jessie and leaned against her. Jessie wrapped her arms about her and hugged her tight.

"I am so proud of you," Jessie said. "Not just for your brilliant ukulele playing but also because you were there for your sister when she needed you. And, Gracie, you sang, too, and it was beautiful."

"Thank you, Momma," Gracie said. She hugged Jessie back, and hid her face against Jessie's side before she broke away to get her congratulations from the crew.

Jessie watched as Sam pulled two giant bouquets of flowers out from behind his back. He handed one to Maddie and one to Gracie. Both girls turned bright pink and made little O's with their mouths. In a move that charmed the entire crew, they each curtseyed to Sam, who gave them a very gallant bow.

He straightened up and looked at Jessie and said, "They are never allowed to date. There is no man alive worthy of them."

"Agreed," Zach said. "Good luck to any poor boy who thinks he's going to get past all of us."

"Count me in," Gavin said.

"Me, too," Brad added.

As if Jessie's heart wasn't already about to explode, this

just wrecked her. She felt as if she and the girls had been alone for so long and now here they were belonging to all of these wonderful people.

"Hey, my girl, what's this?" Zach leaned close and wiped the tear from her cheek with his thumb.

"I'm just . . . I'm . . . I'm undone," Jessie said. Her throat felt tight as she watched her girls flocked by their school friends, all of whom wanted to see the spectacular flowers they'd been given. She glanced up at Zach, meeting his warm gaze and feeling like she could stare into his velvet brown eyes forever. She pressed a soft kiss to his cheek and said, "Thank you for this, and for being you."

Zach swallowed, looking a bit undone himself. He opened his mouth to speak, but Mrs. Abbott shouted at him from the stage.

"Zach!" she cried. "A word, please."

He waved that he heard her and then turned back to Jessie. He gave her a quick squeeze. "We'll talk more later, okay?"

"Yes, please," she said.

He stared at her for a second and then he scooped her close and planted a kiss on her. "I'll see what Mrs. A wants and take the girls to grab their coats. We'll meet you back here. Don't move."

"I'll be right here," she promised. She hoped by the time he and the girls got back that she had stopped feeling so choked up, although she doubted it. Tonight had been a night she'd never forget.

The crew filed out with hugs and waves. Jessie loved that they'd come to see the girls. She was beginning to see that even though she had no family left and Zach's family lived far away in California, they had a family of sorts here in Bluff Point. She'd never had that before, certainly not while she'd been married, and she desperately didn't want to lose it.

She moved aside to let people exit and found a spot out of the traffic flow up against the back wall, where she waited for Zach and the girls to return. She glanced at her phone and opened the video feature. She hit play and as she watched Zach and the girls perform, her heart puffed up again inside her chest. This. This was what a father was supposed to be. Zach had been more of a father to her girls in the past week than Seth had been in their entire lives.

She didn't know what was going to happen between her and Zach but she knew that he cared for her girls and no matter how it played out for them, he would be a constant in Maddie's and Gracie's lives. Maybe just as a neighbor or a friend, but still a constant. He was, she was coming to understand, a remarkable man.

A shadow crossed over her phone, bringing her attention up to the person standing beside her. The man was tall and mostly bald, with a silver beard that he kept meticulously trimmed, as if it made up for the hair missing on the top of his head. He was dressed in a business suit, always a suit, with his overcoat draped over his arm and his hat, a trilby, clutched loosely in his hand. It was Jessie's former father-in-law, Judge Vincent Connelly. As he stood glaring, it was easy to surmise he was very unhappy with her. Oh, joy.

Chapter 20

"Who was that man?" he asked. His voice was harsh, filled with outrage as he stood there bristling with anger.

Jessie tipped her chin up. She had put up with a lot from the Connelly family and she refused to take it anymore.

"Hello, Judge," she said. "Why, I'm fine, thanks so much for asking, and you?"

"Do not mock me," Judge Connelly said.

Jessie ignored him, continuing her one-sided conversation. "Yes, the girls were particularly good in their show tonight, weren't they? I am so proud of them and you must be, too."

"Who is he, Jessica?" Judge Connelly persisted. "A boyfriend? Some lowlife you picked up online or in a bar? I heard you were out at Marty's Pub the other night making quite a spectacle of yourself."

Jessie felt her temper flare. After all of the nights her ex had gone trolling around Bluff Point, cheating on her by sleeping with any woman who'd have him, his father dared to sit in judgment of Jessie, when she'd never so much as looked at another man while she was married. She sucked in a breath, trying to calm herself.

"Zach is a friend of the family, and he's a good man, a very good man, a much better man than your son," she said. "Not that it's any of your business."

"Those are my granddaughters," Judge Connelly snapped. "It is absolutely my business. This is a father-daughter talent show; how dare you let a stranger take the place of my son?"

"The son who's been missing since before the holidays? Surely you're joking." She felt her voice get louder and she consciously lowered her tone before continuing. "I'm sorry your son skipped out on us. Last I heard, he was enjoying a life of leisure as a beach bum ex-pat in Costa Rica. No one is replacing him. He isn't here to be replaced, is he?"

"I am working on bringing him home," Judge Connelly said. "And when I do, I know you'll do the right thing and give him another chance."

"At marriage?" Jessie stared at him bug-eyed. He could not be serious. "No way in hell."

"He is their father—" Judge Connelly began but Jessie cut him off.

"And as such, he is always welcome in their lives," Jessie said. "But that's it. Our family unit will never consist of the four of us again. After all your son has put me through, I will never ever take him back. Ever."

"Then you leave me no choice," Judge Connelly snapped.

"No choice about what?"

"If you continue to fraternize with unsuitable men, I will be forced to petition the courts for custody of my granddaughters." He glared at her. "In short, I will take them away from you."

Jessie felt her entire body go cold. Could he do that? Would he do that? How could she stop him? Then she shook her head. Seth was a bully and he'd probably learned it from his father.

"No court will take my girls from me," she said. "I'm a good mom and if you try to prove otherwise then every nasty thing your son ever did to me, and the list is quite extensive, will come to light. Do you really want to do that to Audrey?"

Judge Connelly glared at the mention of his wife's name, but Jessie knew that Audrey was his weakness. She had been the only Connelly who had been consistently nice and kind to Jessie but she was no match for her powerful husband and miserable son.

"Audrey will understand that what I do is for the greater good," he said.

The look in his eyes was cold and Jessie realized he wasn't bluffing. He would do this. He would try to take the girls away from her. She refused to let him see her fear.

Seth had never suffered any consequences for his actions growing up. The privileged only child of a very powerful judge, every misdeed he'd ever committed—from cheating on tests to drunk driving—had been made to go away, disappear, by the power and purse of his father. She would never let her girls grow up like that. She'd take them and run if she had to.

"Jessie, how are you?" Audrey joined them, breaking their staring contest. "Thank you so much for letting us know the girls were performing tonight. I would have been crushed to have missed it. I was just telling the girls backstage how wonderful they were. I had no idea that Gracie could play the ukulele and Maddie could sing. What a nice man your neighbor Zach is to fill in for Seth."

Jessie ripped her gaze away from the judge and forced a smile at Audrey. *Fill in?* As if Seth had a bad cold and couldn't make it and had asked Zach to take his place at the last minute. She studied her former mother-in-law with her silver hair bobbed in a stylish cut, the pink pearls she wore at her throat with her navy sweater set. How deep did the denial go about her own son and his lack of fatherly skills? Jessie reminded herself that this was not her problem.

"I'm glad you enjoyed it. I was just telling the judge that the girls are very fond of Zach and he of them."

Audrey glanced from Jessie to her husband and back. "Yes, well, it was a lovely performance."

"Thank you. If you'll excuse me, I should go see what's keeping them."

"Mind what I said," Judge Connelly said. His voice was low with warning. "I meant it."

Jessie suppressed a shiver of dread and nodded at her former in-laws before striding toward the door that would lead backstage. Why had she invited them? She could have said nothing and they never would have known about the show or Zach.

She sighed. She couldn't do that. Like it or not, Audrey loved the girls and she knew that the judge did, too, in his own bossy, manipulative way. She hadn't thought he'd see Zach as a replacement for his son; rather, she'd assumed he'd be happy that the girls had someone to do this sort of thing with. She should have known better.

The Connellys, at least the men, had an inability to experience life without filtering it through their own ego. Everything and everyone was a statement upon them or their existence. Truly, it was exhausting and Jessie didn't know how Audrey put up with the judge. Then again, as far as she knew he wasn't the cheating party boy that his son was so maybe that made it easier.

"Momma, Zach says we can celebrate the show with ice cream. Can we? Please?!" Maddie cried.

She came flying out of the door that led backstage, followed by Gracie and Zach. They all had their coats on but the girls still clutched their big, beautiful bouquets while Zach carried the two ukuleles.

"Of course we can!" Jessie said. "You have all earned enormous ice cream sundaes, and I do believe I have all of the fixings at home."

"Hot fudge and whipped cream, too?" Zach asked.

"Naturally," Jessie said.

"Let's go!" Zach cried and the girls cheered as they all hustled out the door to Zach's truck. He helped both of the girls into the backseat of the crew cab and then offered Jessie his hand as well.

She knew she could have hauled herself up into the cab of the truck but it was so nice to have him help her. Jessie had forgotten what it was like to have a man show her courtesy and kindness. It warmed her heart and made her even more furious with the judge for trying to taint the goodness that was Zach.

"Are you okay?" Zach asked as he handed her the ukuleles. "You look mad."

Jessie widened her eyes. There it was. The Connelly poison, seeping in where it shouldn't be, causing grief. She wouldn't let it. Not anymore.

She reached up and cupped Zach's cheek. In a soft voice, she said, "Sorry. I'm not mad. Quite the opposite."

Then she winked at him and he blinked, once, twice, then he grinned and said, "Well, okay, then."

Hot fudge, whipped cream, three different types of ice cream, chopped up strawberries, and bananas, with a cherry on top. Jessie looked at the sundaes Zach created and noted that they were about the same size as the girls' heads.

Gracie's eyes were huge and Maddie looked like she was going to die of sugar rapture without even taking a bite of the ooey-gooey confection. Jessie snapped a few pictures of the girls with their spoons poised.

"Okay, now!" Jessie cried and the girls dug in with gusto.

"All right, my girl, get over here," Zach said. He had made another huge bowl that she'd assumed was for him, but he pushed it between them and handed her a spoon. "Help a poor guy out."

Jessie took the spoon, figuring if she could manage a quick workout tomorrow on her lunch hour it would totally be worth it. She tucked her spoon into the double chocolate ice cream and lifted it up through the hot fudge, grabbing some bananas and whipped cream on her way.

Maybe it was the hot guy watching her eat, maybe it was the fact that her girls were giggling with the joy of a mountain of ice cream on top of a triumphant performance in front of their classmates, or perhaps it was the knowledge that life moments like this one were rare and magical; whatever it was, Jessie closed her eyes as she took the first bite of her sundae and savored it.

The ice cream was cold and sweet and the hot fudge was warm and gooey, the whipped cream melted away on her tongue and the bananas added the illusion of a healthy quotient, which alleviated her guilt, and gave her something to chew on. She swallowed and opened her eyes. Before she could go for another spoonful, Zach reached forward with his thumb and brushed it across her lower lip.

"You had some, uh, chocolate right there," he said.

Jessie felt her lips part as she watched his thumb disappear behind his full lips. She didn't think he was trying to be sexy, he was just being efficient, and yet as she watched his mouth pucker around his thumb she felt her heart rate kick up and a sheen of sweat cover her skin.

She glanced up and caught his velvet brown gaze watching her with an intensity that almost set her hair on fire. Scratch that earlier thought. He was being sexy on purpose!

He wagged his eyebrows at her as if he knew full well what he was doing. Jessie arched a brow back at him. Two could play this game.

She glanced at the girls, who were preoccupied with their own sundaes. Maddie was humming tonight's song under her breath, and Gracie clutched the kitten, Chaos, on her lap while she tucked into her ice cream. Rufus had spent the evening here while they were out, and he was sacked out on the couch; Jessie was betting the kitten had given him no peace.

Jessie took advantage of the moment. She loaded up her spoon, stared at Zach with her best come-hither look, and then in the most seductive way she could manage she licked the ice cream off of the spoon. She felt utterly ridiculous but she refused to give in to the embarrassment, wanting to make him suffer just like she had. When Zach dropped his spoon, and stared at her mouth with his nostrils flaring, she knew she had him.

Victory was short-lived. Zach jabbed his index finger into the whipped cream and popped it into his mouth. Jessie's breathing became uneven and wicked thoughts about what else he could lick whipped cream off flooded her brain in a flurry of mental porn that left her dizzy.

There was only one way to win this. She reached for the cherry with the long stem sitting on top of their sundae. She bit off the cherry, chewed and swallowed, and then took the stem into her mouth. She wedged one end in between her bottom teeth and used her tongue to tie the stem in a knot. She then delicately removed the knotted stem from her mouth and dropped it onto the table in front of Zach.

He glanced from it to her. Two red spots of color highlighted his cheeks and his gaze was so hot she was surprised it didn't leave burn marks on her skin.

"That's it! Time for bed!" he said.

Jessie started to laugh and glanced at the girls. They both looked droopy in their chairs, their spoons hanging from tired hands, their eyes at half-mast.

She glanced back at Zach and nodded. "You take Gracie and I'll carry Maddie?"

He nodded. Together they circled the table, taking the spoons out of the girls' hands. Zach lifted Gracie, while never dislodging Chaos, up into his arms and Jessie followed with Maddie.

Once in the girls' room, Zach set Gracie down on her bed and lifted up Chaos, moving him to the fuzzy pink pillow that was his sleep spot on her bed. Chaos gave one cranky meow and settled into his pillow to sleep. Zach leaned forward and kissed Gracie's head. She wrapped her arms around his neck and squeezed him tight.

"Good night, Zach," she said. "Thanks for teaching me to play the uke."

"My pleasure, you were awesome," he said. Gracie beamed at him as if his praise meant everything in the world to her.

Jessie went to grab Maddie's pajamas while Zach stepped over to her bed and kissed her on the head.

"G'night, Maddie," he said. "Your singing was brilliant."

"I was so scared," she said. Her little voice was slurred with sleepiness.

"But you did it anyway," Zach said. "I'm so proud of you."

"Me, too," Maddie said. Her eyelids slammed shut and Zach chuckled.

He stood and turned to Jessie. "I'll go clean up the dishes." He paused and then asked, "Should I wait for you or are we done for tonight?"

Jessie studied his face. It was perfectly calm and cool, letting her know that no matter what she decided, he was good with it. There were no words for her to express how much she valued that. Controlling her own destiny, making her own choices and having them be respected—it was an incredibly empowering feeling.

She wanted to hug him, kiss him, squeeze him, and let him know just how much his kindness and patience meant to her, but that was for later; right now she had to get two sleepy girls tucked in. Still, she wanted him to know that she had plans for them.

She leaned close as she brushed past him, letting her free hand trail down his back, where the girls couldn't see, and she gently squeezed his butt. Then in a low, throaty voice, she said, "Stay."

Zach started and then his brown eyes darkened into a deeper shade of almost black. He gave her a close-lipped smile and nodded.

"See you . . . ahem"—he paused to clear his gravelly voice—"downstairs. I'll be downstairs."

He left and Jessie turned back to her daughters. This was going to be the fastest three chapters and lights-out in the history of their nighttime reading.

It only took one and a half chapters and the girls were done. Maddie zonked out first, while Gracie fought it, wanting to hear more about what happened to Ramona and Beezus. Sleep won this round, however, and when her breathing became steady and her eyes stayed shut, Jessie closed the book and waited.

She counted to thirty to see if the girls were good and

truly out. No one moved. She marked their place and put the book on the table between their beds and snapped off the light. She switched on the baby monitor she had moved into the girls' room after the storm, knowing with Zach's "project" happening that an early warning was now needed for children on the move. The girls slumbered on and Chaos snored softly from his perch on the pillow.

Jessie backed slowly out of the room. There was a night-light in the hallway, which glowed in case the girls called out to her, but otherwise their room was a safe dark cocoon against the cold winter outside.

Jessie ran her fingers through her hair and then fluffed it. She straightened out her clothes, smoothing the creases at her hips, because, yeah, Zach was really going to notice those when she jumped his bones. Holy bananas, was she really going to do that?

She started down the stairs on wobbly knees. Yes, yes, she was. Because something had changed tonight. The feelings between them had shifted and twisted and re-formed themselves into something new. And it wasn't just because he had looked so right up there with her girls. Oh, sure, that was a huge part of it; finding a man who understood girls, who knew how to care for them and support them and teach them to be fearless, was an amazing thing.

But it was more than that. When the judge had tried to cast Zach as a bad guy, every instinct in Jessie had risen up to protect him. He was a good man, he deserved respect and kindness and trust. So, she was determined that after all of these days of flirting and playing and making each other crazy, she was going to go for it. She was going to trust Zach with everything she had to give him.

She knew from what the Maine crew had told her that he wasn't a relationship type of guy. She was okay with that. If all she could have with Zach was temporary, she'd take it. She just wanted to be with him. And, hey, maybe if they didn't achieve their project goal of getting her to have an orgasm right away, maybe he'd stay around a little longer. A girl could hope, but right now she really didn't care because in this very moment she just wanted to be with him in the way that only two lovers could be, naked, with nothing between them but total trust and understanding.

She'd never had that before and she wanted it with Zach with everything she had. Now she just had to screw up the courage to go and get it.

Chapter 21

Zach wasn't going to stay. He knew Jessie was feeling overly emotional because of the show tonight. Heck, seeing the girls stand up onstage and singing their hearts out had even him overly emotional. Zach was so damn proud of them, he thought he might bust. Gracie for being there for her sister and then for kicking it on her ukulele, and Maddie for punching back her stage fright and singing with all of the earnestness in her sweet five-year-old heart. Man, he was crazy about those two kids. And he was even more crazy about their momma.

He had seen Jessie watch her daughters onstage. He had watched first her terror, her desire to run to her girls and protect them from failure, and then her even greater love in trusting her girls to figure it out for themselves.

When he'd seen her crying during the girls' performance, he knew it was because the love in her heart was too great to be contained and had to be released through her smiling tears. He'd wanted to kiss her senseless ever since.

In fact, he wanted to kiss her so badly right now that

he knew he should probably leave before he pushed for something she wasn't ready to give. When Jessie came to him, he wanted her to do it because she was ready, because she wanted him the same way he wanted her, not because she was grateful to him for giving her girls a father figure.

The dishes were done, the kitchen wiped down. He went through the downstairs, checking that everything was off and locked. He gave a low whistle to Rufus to wake the lazy dog up. Rufus was sleeping with his belly and legs in the air. He ignored Zach, opening one eye to look at him before he rolled over, away from Zach, as if that would make him go away.

"Come on, boy, we need to go," Zach said. He patted his thigh as he walked toward the foyer, where he'd hung his coat and kicked off his boots.

"You're leaving? You're leaving me?"

Zach turned back around to see Jessie standing at the bottom of the stairs. With the lights mostly off, she stood in the ambient glow of a single low-watt lamp. Her heart-shaped face with its prominent cheekbones looked so fragile. Her lips quivered and her blue eyes shimmered with nerves. Zach felt his heart give a lurch.

"It's been an emotional night," he said. "I don't want you to do something you're not ready for, it would ruin all of our progress."

"Progress?" she asked. She tipped her chin up and began to walk toward him. "Is that what we're calling it? The all-consuming I can't stop thinking about you, naked you, and all of the things I want to do with you twenty-four seven even when I sleep? That progress?"

Zach swallowed. It went down hard. He'd been wrong; the look in her eye hadn't been nerves. It was excitement. She looked like she was on the precipice of taking a huge leap off a very high cliff, throwing herself into the abyss and hoping for the best. Oh, crap, now he was nervous.

What if he couldn't make this good for her? What if he failed? He watched as Jessie grabbed the hem of her sweater and pulled it up over her head, tossing it carelessly aside, leaving her upper body bare except for the bra she wore that pushed her breasts up high and tight. His entire body clenched in response, and he thought, *And what if I don't?*

In three steps, he was on her. His hands skimming around her waist as he pulled her up against him. Then he was kissing her. It wasn't like the kisses of the past few days that wooed and teased, taunted and tormented, oh, no, this one was clearly full of wicked intent.

She tasted of chocolate ice cream and maraschino cherry. He felt himself get even harder as he remembered what she had done to that cherry stem. Jessie had unexplored gifts and it was all Zach could do not to throw her over his shoulder and storm upstairs to her big bed to discover just what other talents lay dormant inside his girl.

He swept his hand up her back, over her silky soft skin and up into her hair where he cradled her head as he pulled back to look her in the eye. He had to be sure. Before they hit the place of no return, he had to be certain she was ready.

"Are you sure?" he asked.

His voice was low and gruff and Jessie shivered, but her gaze met his directly and her hands moved over his shoulders and down his chest to flutter at his waist before she moved one hand lower. She moved her hand over the front of his jeans and Zach hissed a breath.

"Yes," she said. She cupped him and gave him a gentle squeeze. "Please."

It was the please that did it. Zach went from trying to be a nice guy who didn't push for more than she was willing to give to a lust-crazed man who could not get his woman naked fast enough. He stepped back from her and spun her around, then he propelled her toward the stairs with his hands on her hips, nuzzling the back of her neck as they went.

"So beautiful," he said. He trailed kisses up the side of her neck as they walked, making her shiver as her skin rippled with goose bumps. "So soft. God, I just want to be lost in you."

Jessie stopped walking, as if she couldn't remember

how, and she arched her back, thrusting her breasts into his palms. Zach squeezed them as he held her in place, up against him, and let his mouth move over her incredibly soft skin. She gave the quietest, sexiest moan he'd ever heard and it about killed him. Playtime was over.

He turned her around, hoisted her up into his arms, locking her legs around his waist, and then he took the stairs two at a time, pausing on the stairs twice. Once to kiss her mouth so thoroughly he left her lips red and swollen and the other to lower his head and nuzzle her pretty breasts.

"Zach, I really don't think I can take much more," she said.

She was panting and Zach pulled back to look at her. Her hair was a tangle, her chest was heaving, making her breasts bounce in the most delicious way, the heat coming from between her legs rivaled that of any flame, and her eyes were half closed as if her desire for him was weighing them down. She was the sexiest woman he had ever seen and he craved her with every cell in his body.

"Ah, but there is so much more," he said.

He grinned at her and she melted against him, pulling his mouth back down to hers. Her kiss was fierce, as if she was trying to imprint herself upon him. It made Zach's knees buckle, something that had never happened to him before.

Sex for Zach was not usually this intense. It was fun, he made sure everyone had a good time, but he always kept it one and done, no repeat performances, no emotional investment. He was all about fun and frolic, but this, this was so much more. He didn't want to look at it too closely on the chance it would freak him out and send him running out into the night, but there was no question: The stakes were higher with Jessie and he simply did not care. He ended the kiss and pressed his forehead against hers.

"Easy, my girl," he said. "Or I'll end up taking you right against the wall."

Jessie gasped but not in a bad way. The heat in her blue eyes let him know that if he tried it, she'd let him.

"Okay, so the dirty talk is a go," he said.

He tried to tease to keep it light, but it wasn't working. He shook his head to loosen the thought of her against the wall, with her legs wrapped around his waist, letting him plow into her. That would be for another time. Tonight he was determined to do it right.

He hauled her up tighter against him and finished dashing up the stairs two at a time. Jessie was laughing when they entered her room. Her eyes sparkled and her contagious chuckle broke forth. Zach grinned then he kissed her, letting her slide down his body until her feet hit the floor.

He put a finger over his lips and tiptoed out into the hallway. He peeked in on the girls just to be sure they were still asleep. The light from the hallway combined with the light of the moon shining into their bedroom window gave him just enough illumination to see that they were out cold.

Zach was again filled with pride for these two amazing girls. Like their mom, they were something special. He then closed the door so it was open only a few inches and he snuck back across the hall to Jessie.

He closed and locked the door, having already noted that the monitor on Jessie's nightstand was on. When he turned around, he almost tripped over a pile of clothes on the floor. He glanced up and saw Jessie mostly hidden under the covers, peeking out at him. With her hair tumbled about her shoulders and the blanket drawn up to her neck, she was that devastating blend of innocent and sexy that Zach always found so irresistible.

Normally in his dating life this was when a woman waved him in, calling to him in a sexy voice to join her in bed. Not Jessie. She took one look at him and her face turned a hot shade of embarrassed pink. Then she pulled the covers over her head and disappeared from view.

It took everything Zach had not to laugh. Oh, he liked this girl. He figured she was trying to be sexy, trying to be what she thought he wanted, and failing miserably because she was also shy. The ridiculous part of this was that she already was everything he wanted. He figured it was time for him to show her just how much.

He assessed the lump under the covers, where specific body parts were and where he wanted them to be and then he took a flying leap onto the bed, pinning the delicious woman under the covers beneath him.

"Hey!" a laughing voice cried, muffled beneath the thick blanket.

Zach stretched out as if he weren't lying on top of someone. He wriggled, he wiggled, he pressed his hands all along the body beneath his.

"Huh, this mattress sure is lumpy," he said. He moved one hand to the curve of her rear end and the other to her breast. He let his fingers caress the dead sexy curves, mentally cursing the thick blanket between them. "But in the nicest possible way."

A hiss of breath sounded from beneath the blanket and Jessie's head popped up from under the edge. Her gaze was hot when she looked at him.

"You don't play fair," she said. She reached out a delicate hand and grabbed the collar of his shirt as if she'd yank it off of him. "And you're overdressed."

"I can fix that," he said.

He rolled off of her and sat on the edge of the bed. He could feel her gaze on him—man, that was hot—while he shucked off his pants, leaving his boxers on. His shirt came off next and then he was diving under the covers to get to her and her heat.

He pulled her up against him so they were lying on their sides facing each other. He ran his hand up and down her back and she arched into him, pushing her hips into his and making him momentarily see spots. Mercy! He had no idea how he was going to last long enough to get her where she needed to be first.

"Tell me if I do anything you don't like," he said.

Jessie nodded but given that she had been willing to fake an orgasm with him before, he wanted to be very clear that she needed to tell him exactly what she liked and what she didn't.

"And if I do something you do like, be sure to let me know that, too."

Again, she nodded.

He moved his hand to her breast and gently pinched her nipple. She gasped, bit her lip, and arched her back, but she didn't say anything. Zach wanted to hear her, he wanted her to own her pleasure. He removed his hand. She frowned.

He looked at her, his gaze steady on hers, and said, "Tell me."

Jessie huffed out a breath. She nodded again. She swallowed and then wet her lips with the tip of her tongue. Zach pushed his hips into the mattress to relieve some of the pressure. Man, he wanted to be inside her.

"That was good," she said.

"Good?" he asked her.

He put his hand back on her breast, flicked the tip with his thumb, and watched her blue eyes go cloudy with desire.

"Just good?" He caressed her again and added a pinch.

"Really good." She panted out the words.

"Now we're getting somewhere," he said.

He gave her a lascivious grin and moved his mouth to her other nipple. He bit down and then caressed her with his tongue repeatedly, until she began to writhe beneath him. Jessie made several breathy groans that caused his blood to run thick but he pulled away, forcing himself to slow down.

"What's that, my girl?" he asked. He ran one hand down her belly, letting his thumb circle her navel, before dipping lower, in between her legs.

A light sheen of sweat was coating Jessie's skin. He nuzzled her neck, taking in her particular scent of lemon cake, knowing in that moment that the smell of her would haunt him for the rest of his days and probably cause him to have an immediate hard-on. There were worse problems, he supposed.

"I can't . . . it's too much . . ." Jessie was trying to speak but her body was distracting her, making it too hard to think. Excellent.

Zach wanted her to be focused on one thing and one thing only, the pleasure that was building up inside of her as he stroked her clit with the pad of his thumb. She arched her hips into Zach's hand, and he would have done a fist pump, but his hands were full of her. One hand continued to torment her breasts while the other relentlessly stroked the cluster of nerves at her center.

She thrashed her head, she arched her back, she bucked against his hand. She was right there. He could feel it building in her like a rain cloud swelling with moisture before releasing it in a downpour. He wasn't going to let her lose this. Not this time. Not with him.

"I'm close, so close," she said.

She opened her eyes and gazed at him and in that second Zach saw every vulnerability she'd ever had—parents who ignored her and a husband who mistreated her, both convincing her that she wasn't worthy—roar up inside of her as if trying to wrestle her from the pleasure she so richly deserved. Oh, hell, no!

Zach kissed her. It was a hot wet possession of his mouth claiming hers, his tongue mimicking what his body wanted to do to hers. And then he moved his lips down her body, with one direction in mind.

Jessie, as if sensing where he was going, withdrew. He didn't let her. He pushed her thighs wide and settled in between her legs.

"I'm not sure I'm comfortable—" she began but Zach put his mouth on her and sucked hard.

She groaned, she arched, she pressed her flesh against his lips as he worked her over. She started to tremble and he knew she was close. He slid one finger into her and she gasped, then he made it two, while he sucked hard on her clit.

And just like that, Jessie came hard against his mouth, her muscles clenching around his fingers as if they'd keep him in there. Her entire body convulsed and she let out the softest, sexiest cries he had ever heard.

It was done. She was his and he was hers.

Chapter 22

Jessie felt as if everything she'd ever known to be true was a big fat lie. She'd convinced herself over the years that orgasms simply could not be that big of a deal. It had made going without much easier to accept if she believed it was much ado about nothing. Holy bananas, she had been wrong. So wrong!

Her heart was pounding hard in her chest, her breath was coming in little pants, and she was sweaty. It was glorious. She popped her eyes open and looked at Zach. He was leaning up on one elbow, looking incredibly pleased with himself. She tackled him.

"That was amazeballs!" she said. "There are no words."

She kissed his lips, his chin, his nose, his eyes, his ears. His chest started to shake beneath hers as a laugh rumbled out of his mouth. She moved lower to kiss his chest.

She would have kept going, but he caught her, cupping her face and meeting her gaze with his laughing velvet brown eyes. Then he kissed her and it was sweet and tender and lovely and she melted onto him, thinking she would remember this night for the rest of her life and marvel at it, at him, Zachary Caine, the man she now considered her first real lover.

She leaned up on her elbows to study him beneath her and noticed that everything was fuzzy and little off-kilter. Her eyes went round and she looked at him in surprise.

"My ears are ringing, is that normal?"

"Really?" he asked. Then he laughed. "I made your ears ring? Well, that's a first."

Jessie bit her lip. She didn't want to push it, but she had never wanted anyone as much as she wanted Zach right now. She nudged his rigid shaft with her hips.

"Want to see if I can make your ears ring?" she asked.

She didn't mean to sound so sexual when she asked but her voice was gruff from her own passionate cries and it just came out that way.

"Hell yeah," he said.

He rolled over, trapping her beneath him. It was as if he couldn't touch her enough or taste her enough. His mouth and hands were everywhere but Jessie didn't want to be denied. She'd not had a man in her life in a long time and she realized how much she'd missed the male form—well, a male form like Zach's, which was ridiculously fit and firm. He was muscular, solidly built with a dusting of hair on his chest and a thicker thatch down between his legs.

To Zach's credit, he let her explore to her heart's content. When she wrapped her fist around his cock, and stroked him up and down in a firm grip, he looked like he might pass out.

She grinned and asked, "Are your ears ringing yet?"

"That's it," he said. He captured her hands and held them over her head. "I think I might literally die if I don't fuck you right now."

It was the hottest thing Jessie had ever heard. Unable to speak, she nodded and spread her legs wide, letting him know that she was ready.

Zach pulled a condom out of the pants he'd dropped to the floor. He slipped it on and came back to her. He looked her in the eye and asked, "Are you sure?"

"More than I've ever been of anything ever," she said.

She enfolded him in her embrace as he slid into her. He stretched her wide, even as he moved slow, taking his time, easing their joining. Jessie wasn't having it. She hooked her legs around his waist and the next time he went to ease in just a little bit, she used her legs to pull him in all the way.

Mine, she mouthed into his shoulder so that he couldn't hear her. *Mine*.

Zach pulled out a little bit; Jessie hated it and tightened her legs and pulled him back into her. She clung to him and felt another shift in her chest. She realized it was her heart yielding to him. He had a claim on her now, one that she couldn't pretend wasn't there. For as long as this lasted between them, she belonged to him and he to her.

Her grip on him was tight, and he laughed as he reached behind him and unhooked her legs. Jessie resisted, not wanting to have any space between them. She wanted to remain connected, fused together, so she wouldn't feel so alone anymore. She realized that it was needy on her part, still she couldn't help it.

"I'm not leaving you," Zach said.

He cupped her face and kissed her while he rocked against her. The friction made Jessie's insides tighten and she dropped her feet to the mattress so she could push up against him, meeting each thrust with one of her own.

"That's it, my girl," he said. "Just like that."

He moved his hand between them, stroking her again with his thumb, making her brain go fuzzy as she felt herself chasing that cataclysmic pulse of pleasure.

This time when the orgasm hit, she was stretched full of Zach and she clenched so tightly around him that it almost hurt, but then it burst into waves of pleasure that shocked her with their intensity, causing her to call his name as if it was a mantra.

"Zach, oh, Zach, oh, Zach," she cried.

He removed his hand and began to pump into her with a ferocity that made her arch into him again as aftershocks coursed through her, and then he was wrapping his arms about her and pulling her to him as he lost himself inside of her.

"Jessie, damn it, my girl," he growled in her ear. "I was hoping to last longer than this but, oh, what you do to me."

She felt the shudders ripple through him and she pulled him in close and tight, his sweat-slicked skin pressed to hers as they both fought to catch their breath. She could feel his heart pounding in strong sure beats as he dragged in several deep breaths.

He leaned back from her and shook his shaggy blonde hair as if trying to get his wits back. He relaxed down on top of her, pushing her deep into the mattress as he groaned with satisfaction. The sound made Jessie smile.

"You're right," he said. He leaned up to kiss her. "That was amazeballs."

Jessie laughed. He kissed her again. She reached up to caress the face that was becoming so incredibly dear to her.

She traced his lower lip with her thumb and he opened his mouth and gently bit down on the pad. Heat streaked through her and she gasped.

She gazed into his eyes, reveling in the warmth and affection she found there, then she winked at him and said, "Let's do it again."

Zach laughed and then rolled so that she was on top of him. "I thought you'd never ask," he said.

And so they did.

They had kicked the covers to the floor. Jessie lay across Zach, feeling their sweat cool and their heart rates return to normal. She was exhausted and exhilarated at the same time, feeling as if she'd just been invited into some secret society she had never known existed. Nothing would ever be the same for her again and she was thrilled.

She wondered when she would feel sated. She glanced at the handsome man beside her and realized never; she was never ever going to get enough of this man or the way he made her feel. She shivered.

Zach must have thought she was cold, because he

reached over her to pull the blanket up and over them. He tucked her into his chest with her face against his throat and his chin over her head. They were entwined like two vines and she wasn't sure where she ended and he began or vice versa. Instead of feeling stifled, as she had in the past when Seth had clung to her in a drunken stupor, she felt worshipped and protected and adored; amazing what a difference shared pleasure could make.

He was so still she thought he might have drifted off. Her own eyes felt heavy but she didn't want to drift off without saying something, letting him know how much this meant to her. She felt like her own personal curse had been broken. What could she say to him that would make him understand? She didn't know, she just knew she had to say something.

"Thank you," she said. She pressed a kiss against the base of his throat and felt him shift so that he could see her face.

"I'm not sure you should be thanking me," he said. Although he did look pleased. "I think I should be thanking you."

"Really?" she asked. "Was it your first orgasm, too?"

"Uh, no." He laughed but then grew abruptly serious. "But I have to say I've never felt . . . that is . . . it's not always like that."

His tone was light as if he were trying to keep the conversation from becoming too emotional. Jessie understood that. She was feeling vulnerable in a way she never had before and given what they had just shared she suspected he must be feeling it, at least a little bit, too.

"Did you ever wonder about your parents' sex life?" she asked.

"What?! No!" he said. "And why would you be thinking about that *now*?"

"Because what we just did was so very hot and my parents were so very cold," she said. "They were both career-driven professionals and I never saw anything between them other than the barest acknowledgment of the other's existence. Truthfully, I know I was an accident because they didn't even share a bedroom—well, that and they told me."

Zach was running a soothing hand up and down her spine. It stopped at her words and he leaned back again to look at her. "They told you you were an accident. Are you serious?"

"Well, they preferred the term 'unplanned,' not even the word 'surprise' because that might mean a happy event," she said. "I felt like I spent my whole childhood trying not to be noticed to please them and then my teen years trying desperately to be noticed because I was so lonely. I think the strain made me socially defective."

"In what way? You don't seem defective to me." His voice was a rich deep rumble that made her feel as if she were sleeping with a big bear. She liked it. She liked him.

"I didn't trust anyone. I was angry, bitter, and resented anyone who seemed to navigate the world loving and being loved without question," she said. "Honestly, I became what you'd expect, a horrible person raised by horrible people."

"I don't see that," he protested.

"Not now, but then. I did a bad thing going after Mac's fiancé. In my defense, Seth picked me up in a bar when I'd just gotten back to town after being away. He was a smooth talker in his youth, and he didn't mention that he was engaged to Mac. When I found out I went a little crazy, thinking she was going to get the best guy and I would get nothing, again."

"Oh, poor Jessie," Zach said. "That jerk played you."

"It was no better than I deserved for agreeing to pick him up outside the church at his own wedding," she said. She looked grim. "I can't believe I did that. What an awful person I was."

"We all make mistakes when we're young," he said. "And I can testify that you're not awful now. Besides, in the end you did Mac a huge favor, even she says so. What changed you?"

"Motherhood," she said. "The day they put Gracie in my arms, everything changed. I loved her so much, I was *in* love with her, and Maddie, too, when she came along. I still am. I was determined that I would be warm and loving and they would never feel alone or as if they were an inconvenience, and they would never ever doubt my love for them."

"You are an incredible mom," he said. He kissed her head. "Those girls know how much you love them and you've given them a family to belong to, not every kid gets that. It's a rare and beautiful thing."

Jessie met his gaze. There were shadows she hadn't seen before in his eyes that looked like long forgotten pain and confusion.

"Tell me," she said. He looked like he would refuse, so she snuggled close to him and in her softest voice, she said, "Please."

"There's nothing to tell," he said. "Not really."

She said nothing. She just waited.

"I know my parents love me," he said. "But—"

Again, she waited.

"They divorced when I was six months old. They were a bad match. My mother is an attorney and my father an artist. How they ever got together to begin with, I can't imagine. Well, that's not true. They had a first date that ended with them eloping to Vegas. I think they were drunk."

Jessie listened without interrupting, letting Zach share what he would without questions.

"Seven months into the marriage, my mother discovered she was pregnant. They tried to make a go of it for my sake but things were already starting to unravel. I was still a baby when they divorced and divided up custody. Over the next few years, they both remarried and started new families. The custody agreement was fifty-fifty, so I did one week with Mom and one with Dad, no trading, no swapping, no deviation."

"That sounds very reasonable."

"It was and it wasn't," he said. "I was like a part-time member of both families. Stuff happened when I wasn't around with each family, so I was left out of a lot of the inside jokes in both families. If there was a drama with one of the sisters, I usually missed it. I spent my entire childhood feeling like an outsider looking in, never really belonging. No one meant for it to be like that but that's what it became."

He shrugged and Jessie could see the little boy he must have been, forever playing catch-up with both of his families. She knew what it was like to feel like an outsider, and the thought of Zach having to spend his life like that with two families broke her heart a little bit.

"The girls are lucky to have you," he said.

Jessie ducked her head. Being a good mom was everything to her, and his praise meant an awful lot. She had to be honest, however; she didn't want him to believe something that wasn't true.

"I've made a lot of mistakes," she said.

"All parents do. It's how you correct them that matters."

"I should never have stayed with their father as long as I did, but I kept hoping that I could change him, that we could be the family I always dreamed of, but then one day when Seth missed Gracie's science fair at school, I just lost it.

"I tracked him down and walked in on him with a woman. He'd been cheating on me all along, but this time it hit me that he wasn't just cheating on me, he was cheating on his girls, making some bimbo more important than they were, and that was it. I was done."

She felt Zach squeeze her close as if he could absorb her pain. She didn't need him to do it. The truth was that since she had left her lying, cheating, drunken spouse behind, she had never been happier.

"Oh, my girl, I'm sorry he didn't value you like he should have," Zach said. He kissed her head and Jessie felt soothed.

"It's all right," she said. "I learned quite a bit about myself in that relationship. I learned that I can't really forgive a person for cheating or lying. I tried, repeatedly, but I knew I would spend the rest of my life doubting him and that's no way to live. When he let down Gracie, after promising he'd be there, and I watched her cry, there was no going back. It was a good life lesson."

"Agreed," Zach said. "Sometimes it takes a while to realize a person isn't who you thought they were."

Jessie glanced up at him. She sensed there was more behind his words but she didn't want to press. If she was totally honest with herself, she didn't want to find out he'd been in love with another woman who had broken his heart. It would explain why his friends had told her he was a no-commitment sort of guy, but she still didn't want to hear it. She knew she was being a big chicken but she didn't care.

Tonight had been amazing and she didn't want anything to taint it, so she kissed him. She made it a long slow exploration of her mouth on his, tasting, licking, biting his lower lip gently between her teeth until all conversation was forgotten and his hands were on her body, drawing a response from her that left her breathless and weak and belonging to just him, even if it was only for tonight.

Chapter 23

After last night's workout, Zach was sure he'd sleep for a month. But before the sky began to lighten, he awoke to find himself twined around Jessie as if he could hold on to her heat and light and block the winter's cold darkness with it.

He'd never felt as connected to another person as he did to her. It wasn't just the sex, although that had been unlike anything he'd ever experienced before; it was a connection that ran even deeper.

They had both spent their lives on the perimeter, both wanting to belong. Zach had created his own family with his Maine crew. Sam and Brad were like brothers to him, and as their group had expanded so had his heart, to include the ladies, their partners, all of them. Jessie had birthed her own family with the girls. She'd made something bright and beautiful out of a shitty situation and he admired her tremendously for that.

But where did this leave the two of them now? Were they a couple? Would they go back to being just friends? He pressed her close in a reflexive move at the thought of them going their separate ways. He didn't want that. In fact, everything inside of him firmly rejected that idea.

He buried his face in her hair and the lemon scent of her filled his senses. He couldn't imagine not having that in his life every day. And now that he knew what it was like to hold her in his arms, he couldn't fathom not being able to hold her and kiss her whenever he wanted. He glanced down at her face. She looked completely blissed out and a small smile tipped his lips. He'd done that. Surely she wasn't ready for it to end just yet.

His thoughts strayed to the girls and he felt a gut check. Whatever happened between Jessie and him, the girls needed to know that nothing would change between them. Zach was totally gone over those two imps, and he didn't want to lose them any more than he did their mother. He would stay in their life even if only as a neighbor and a friend. He tried to picture what that would be like. Jessie going off on a date with someone else and Zach there to what? Babysit?

He hated it. The thought was worse than skunk spray, soggy shoes, a red wine hangover, or a trifecta of all three combined. There was only one solution. He was going to have to romance Jessie into seeing him in a more permanent light. He'd make sure she fell for him as hard as he was falling for her and then there'd be no silly talk of them going their separate ways or just being friends. Christ, it would kill him if she went there.

Knowing that the girls would be waking up soon, Zach eased himself off of Jessie. He didn't want to put a strain on what was happening between them by having the girls see him in Jessie's bed and then having to explain why he was there. Not yet. There'd be time for that in the future if he managed to achieve what he set out to do.

Jessie let out a soft grunt but she didn't wake up. He'd feel bad about how exhausted she was except there was that whole mission-accomplished aspect to it that made him grin like an idiot. He tucked her in so that she stayed warm before he quietly pulled on his clothes and left the room.

A peek into the girls' room and he saw that they were still asleep. He went down to the kitchen and made a pot of coffee. Jessie would be up in fifteen minutes and it would be waiting for her. He decided to leave a small note beside it, asking her to have dinner with him that night.

Zach stood with the felt tip pen and the sticky note, staring at the paper and debating what to write. Dinner with a question mark and then just his name? Just his first initial? Yeah, that didn't seem douchey.

He ran a hand through his hair. He'd never had to leave a note before. The importance of getting it just right began to feel like a cinderblock pressing on his chest. He desperately did not want to blow this. Maybe he should draw a picture of a heart or a flower. Nah, his art skills weren't that great and the way his brain kept replaying last night it would undoubtedly look like a naughty porno sketch.

He decided to go for honest and wrote: My girl, I will be thinking about you all day and smiling. Have dinner with me tonight? XO, Zach.

He'd debated about the "X" and the "O" but since that was definitely something they had done, it seemed appropriate and was much less alarming than using the letter "L" or the "L" word too soon. Even in his post-coital haze of infatuation, he knew that, although he suspected the "L" word was exactly what he was feeling for both Jessie and the girls.

A rush of fear hit him like a blast of arctic wind. He was falling. He knew it. He knew there was no stopping it. The only thing he could do was surrender and hope that Jessie was feeling the same way. God help him if she wasn't.

He wrapped up in his coat and hat, pulled on his gloves, and signaled to Rufus, who was still asleep on the couch, that they were going home. Rufus stretched with his back legs still on the seat before he ambled after Zach, clearly not appreciating the life-altering events that had taken place the night before.

Zach was halfway home before he realized he had no idea when or how she would get in touch with him. Oh, man, this could easily be the longest day of his life. He soldiered on, determined not to think about it. It didn't work.

What if she says no? The thought dogged his every step. He arrived at home and glanced back over his shoulder at Jessie's. He'd locked the door behind him, leaving only the kitchen light on. He didn't see any movement yet. He resisted the urge to run back over and talk, or beg, her into going out with him tonight.

No, this was better. This would give her the chance to think about it and answer him honestly. He trudged into his house, which felt cold and lonely compared to hers.

What if she says no? He shook his head and blew out a breath. *And what if she doesn't?*

He felt better for a second and then the anxiety crept back in. Damn it, his pop psychology wasn't working at all. He took his cell phone out of his pocket and glared at it.

It buzzed in his hand and a text message appeared. It was from her. Zach held his breath.

Dinner sounds nice. 7?

Zach expelled his breath and pumped his fist at the same time. Yes! She was going to give him a chance. Now he just had to make it the single greatest date anyone had ever gone on ever. Right. No pressure.

Jessie tried not to fuss with her hair. She failed and her hair fell flat. Damn it. She knew better. Just like when she watched the girls do artwork, there was always that moment with a piece of art—or a hairdo—that you dropped your hands and backed away or the piece or the hair went all kinds of wrong.

She'd been going for big bouncy curls, and she'd had them for a minute, but too much product and way too much fussing and now she had a straggly mess. She glanced at her phone on the bathroom counter. Did she have time to cry? No, she did not.

She grabbed a fistful of bobby pins, twisted her hair up in the back and let the one remaining curl frame the side of her face and then she hit it with the hairspray. Not too much, just enough to keep the pins in.

She stepped back from the mirror and studied her expression. The dark circles under her eyes had been erased, mostly, with a light hand at some concealer. Mascara, powder, and a tinted lip gloss and she was ready to go.

With the snow mostly gone from the sidewalks, she decided to wear her favorite calf-hugging black suede boots with a delicate heel paired with her bright blue cashmere sweater dress with the wide black belt. It was simple but it hugged her curves and made her feel prepared for anything.

Anything being Zach saying, *Hey, that was fun, let's be friends.* Or worse, the dreaded, *That was terrible, here's a steak dinner, now lose my number.*

Honestly, she had no idea what to expect. He'd set out on a mission to give her an orgasm, he'd managed to give her three. Were they quits now? Or had last night meant something more to him, like it had to her? She didn't know. She only knew that she had woken up without him beside her and it had been cold and lonely and she'd hated it.

Oh, she knew he'd likely left so that the girls didn't find him in her bed. Awkward. And she really appreciated that he was sensitive to that sort of situation but she still didn't know what was going on in his head and she found she really wanted to know. She wanted to know how he felt about her, about them, if there even was a "them" to be felt about.

There was a knock on the front door a few minutes before seven. Jessie pressed her hand to her middle. No matter how tonight went, she promised herself she would handle it with dignity. Her ex hadn't left much of her self-esteem intact over the years but she was slowly knitting it back into something significant and she wouldn't let a one-night stand, if that's what it proved to be, rend all of her hard work.

"Momma, Zach is here!" Maddie hollered up the stairs. "And he smells really nice."

Jessie smiled and then grinned when she heard Zach

laugh. Her excitement to see him overriding her nerves, she hurried to the stairs to find him standing at the bottom, waiting for her.

She slowed down just so she could savor sight of him, leaning against the banister waiting for her. He was wearing a suit, charcoal gray with a black dress shirt and tie—there was something wicked in that—and she wanted to take the tie in hand and haul him upstairs to her room. She resisted the urge.

When she reached the last step, he took his hand from behind his back and held out a big, beautiful bouquet of blue hydrangea and white alstroemeria, along with crème roses, yellow chrysanthemums, and eucalyptus. It was lovely.

"Thank you," she said. She couldn't remember the last time anyone had given her flowers. "They're beautiful."

"As are you," Zach said. His gaze moved over her, his newfound knowledge about her body in his eyes, and she felt her face get hot.

"Thank you," she said again.

Ugh, she sounded like an idiot. But she couldn't think when he looked at her like that.

Jessie glanced down at the blooms. She didn't know what to say. The man who was known for being a big kid, who could always come up with outrageous euphemisms for body parts, was charming her stupid. She wasn't sure she knew how to handle this or him.

Thankfully, Gracie and Maddie rushed forward, breaking the spell Jessie was in. They were each holding a large heart-shaped box of candy and grinning at her.

"Look what Zach brought us," Gracie said. "Our own boxes of candy!"

"You shouldn't have," Jessie said to Zach.

"What? Of course I had to bring something to my best girls," he said.

Jessie glanced at Maddie and Gracie. They looked like they were going to swoon at his feet. Yeah, she got that.

There was a knock on the door and Zach said, "That will be Emma and Brad, our babysitters for the evening."

"Babysitters?" she asked.

"Yes," Zach said. He looked wary. "I hope that's all right. We have reservations for a very stuffy restaurant in Portland. I thought the girls would be happier to stay here and eat pizza with Emma and Brad."

Jessie nodded. "Oh, yeah, that sounds lovely."

"Cool," Zach said.

He turned and headed for the door while Jessie went to put her flowers in a vase. Her hands were trembling when she unwrapped them from the cellophane. Flowers? What did they mean? Was he trying to soften the blow or did he want more? More what? More sex? Yeah, that'd be okay with her. More relationship? She didn't want to get her hopes up, but he had brought the girls chocolate. Was he trying to soften the blow to them, too?

She took a vase from under the sink and filled it with water. She found her scissors and clipped the stems on the flowers so they stayed fresh longer. She could hear Zach and the girls talking to Emma and Brad in the foyer. She could hear Emma laughing and she had an unreasonable panicked thought that they were laughing at her.

Jessie shook her head. No, that was the old Jessie. The one who thought everyone was loved except for her. The one who believed that everyone else had a happy ever after except for her. She had kicked that miserable version of herself to the curb and she didn't want her back.

This self-doubt was coming from her own vulnerability. She knew that. She knew that what she'd shared with Zach was making her feel at risk emotionally and it would be so easy to fall back into her old patterns of paranoia and bitterness, especially if it turned out that Zach was taking her out to dinner as a *Hey, thanks for last night, and we're done*.

"Oh, wow, those are beautiful," Emma said. She stepped into the kitchen and leaned in close to smell one of the delicate crème roses in the bouquet. "Zach really outdid himself."

Jessie glanced at Emma. She was a petite, pretty blonde with a baby bump and a husband who adored her. The old

Jessie would have said something cruel and mean just because she was so angry at the world. The new Jessie looked at her new friend and saw the dark circles under her eyes—pregnancy was exhausting—and she knew that Emma's life—losing her mother as a teenager—had been far from perfect.

"He did," Jessie said. She gave Emma a side-eye. "In so many ways."

Emma's eyes went wide. "Oh, my god!"

She grabbed Jessie's hand and dragged her toward the half bathroom just off the living room.

"Where are you going?" Brad asked as they flew by him.

"Lipstick emergency!" Emma said.

"Even at home they go to the bathroom in pairs?" Brad asked Zach. "I never knew that."

Emma slammed the door and turned on the faucet. She pushed Jessie to sit on the closed toilet while she perched on the edge of the vanity.

"Okay, rank it on a scale of one to ten," she said. "Ten being the best sex ever."

Jessie felt her face get hot. "One hundred. Infinity!"

Emma clutched her hands in front of her chest. "Atta boy, Zach."

Then she took her phone out of her pocket and began texting. Jessie frowned at her.

"What are you doing?"

Emma waved her hand dismissively even as her phone started to light up. "One more question, how many?"

"How many what?"

"You know, big ones!"

"Orgasms?" Jessie dropped her face into her hands and then peeked at Emma through her fingers. "Seriously?"

"Yes, it's very important," Emma said.

"If you must know, three," Jessie said.

"Ha, ha, ha!" Emma chortled. She was madly texting and then she yelled at her phone. "I win."

"You win?" Jessie asked.

Emma glanced from her phone to Jessie. "I can explain."

"Try," Jessie said. She crossed her arms over her chest and glared.

"The Maine crew might have had a small—very small, miniscule even—betting pool about when Zach would . . . achieve launch, so to speak."

"You bet on my sex life?"

"It sounds so callous when you say it like that," Emma said.

"How much?" Jessie asked.

"How much what?" Emma blinked.

"Yeah, that innocent blinky thing will no longer work on me," Jessie said. "I want half the take."

"What?" Emma protested.

"You said you won," Jessie reminded her. "Well, since I did all the work, I want half the take."

Emma looked put out and then she grinned. "I like you. It's one hundred and fifty bones."

"You mean bon*ers*," Jessie joked.

Emma cracked up and then hugged Jessie tight. "Thanks for not being mad. It was all in good fun."

"Yes, it was," Jessie said.

Emma leaned back and studied her. "I'm so glad. So, are you and Zach a thing now?"

Jessie bit her lip. "I don't know."

"But you're going out on a date," Emma said. "Sam was sure this was the prelim to the two of you getting it on. Needless to say, he lost the bet. I didn't think it was going to take you two that long, especially being neighbors and all."

"Yeah, well, we haven't talked so I don't know what we are or if we're anything at all. This could be Zach's big kiss-off, done in public so I don't cry." Jessie hiccupped on the last word, unintentionally giving Emma a glimpse at her upset.

Emma bit her lip. She looked worried. "Oh, Jessie, I wish I could say that wasn't true."

"But it is, isn't it?"

"No . . . uh . . . maybe," Emma said. "The truth is I don't know. In all the years I've known Zach, he's never had a girlfriend and the few times Brad and I have talked about it, he didn't seem to think that Zach ever would again."

Jessie closed her eyes and blew out a breath. She felt as if her heart were being squeezed by a giant fist.

"Hey, maybe this is Zach trying something new." Emma put her phone back in her pocket and grabbed Jessie's hands in hers. "You know, if you want more with Zach, you should just tell him."

Jessie felt her eyes go wide. "And put myself out there? Oh, I don't know if I'm ready for that. I kind of feel like I've done enough breaking out of my comfort zone for one week. You know what I'm saying?"

Emma laughed. "Agreed. It's been a big week for you. Okay, let's make a plan. How do you want to handle this?"

Jessie pictured Zach in the suit waiting for her. She wanted to be with him. Even if it was a kiss-off dinner, it was still a date, and she hadn't had one in a very long time. What if he dumped her? She swallowed hard and then she heard Zach's voice in her head. *And what if he doesn't?*

"I'm going to go," Jessie said. "No matter what happens, I'm going to go and have fun."

"And order the most expensive thing on the menu," Emma said. "Zach can afford it and if he does break things off with you, he can damn well pay for it."

Jessie looked at her in surprise and said, "You have a dark side."

"We all do," Emma said. "Some of us just hide it better than others."

She stepped back and checked Jessie over. She pushed in one of the hairpins that was coming loose and adjusted the belt that rode on Jessie's hips.

"Go get 'em," she said and she pushed Jessie out the door and into the living room where Zach was waiting.

When Jessie caught sight of her date across the room, she felt her heart do the crazy fluttery thing it always did when she caught sight of Zach. For a second, she debated turning and running upstairs to hide out in her room and avoid whatever was coming. But the braver part of her—okay, the starving part who wanted some dinner—made her keep moving forward toward whatever the night offered, even if it was heartbreak.

Chapter 24

Jessie spent the entire ride to Portland thinking about what she would say when Zach gave her the old heave-ho. In her mind, she pretended to agree completely, as if surprised he even needed to say anything. They were just neighbors, nothing more. Also, in her mind, she chased the lie down with a gin and tonic and a wave of her hand. Yes, that would work.

As soon as they stepped into the restaurant, she'd order a drink, all the better to wash down her bitter disappointment. A tiny little flutter inside of her, that thing with feathers, stubbornly clung to the idea that he would say the opposite, that he would declare this their beginning. Jessie tried to ignore it but it continued to sing, ignoring any common sense or reason.

They listened to music on the drive and they talked about safe subjects like the girls, how their day at work had gone, what the weatherman was forecasting for the next few days. It was pleasant but it didn't help Jessie's nerves at all. She desperately wanted to know what Zach was thinking about them but she was too nervous to ask, so she said nothing.

She caught him glancing at her repeatedly, as if trying to gauge her mood. She felt like a poker player keeping her cards in tight to her chest, not letting him see that she was feeling all the feels for him. She knew it was cowardly but she'd been hurt so badly before, and after last night, she was as vulnerable as a woman could be. This boy owned her and that terrified her.

The restaurant was on the water. Big windows offered them a breathtaking view of the ocean at night. The table was draped in a white cloth with a small candle in a cut crystal candleholder beside a narrow vase filled with brightly colored gerbera daisies. Classy and elegant but in an understated way.

The hostess showed them to a table and Zach held her chair out for her.

"In case I haven't said it yet"—Zach leaned over as he pushed her chair in—"you look beautiful tonight."

"Thank you," she said. She could feel the heat of him at her back and she wanted to turn around and hug him but she didn't.

Instead, she watched as he took the seat across from her, drinking in the sight of him as if she hadn't seen him in weeks rather than a few hours. Candlelight suited Zach. It brightened his pale hair and enhanced his masculine features, making his handsome face appear even more rugged. Jessie felt her heart beat hard in her chest.

The hostess told them that their server would be right with them and she left them with their menus.

Jessie glanced at the words, seeing nothing. The entire menu could be in hieroglyphics for all she could tell. She had to get a handle on this situation. She decided that she would retreat into what she and Zach seemed to do best. She would tease him.

"So, apparently, there was a bet," she said.

"A bet?"

"Between our friends, about us and when you'd deliver, if you know what I mean."

"What?" he asked and then he laughed. "Ha! I should have known they'd do something like that." He gave her a thoughtful glance. "You aren't offended, are you?"

"Are you kidding?" she asked. "Emma won, so I'm making her split it with me since I feel like I facilitated her win."

"You facilitated it?" he asked. "Correct me if I'm wrong but I think I'm the one who made the magic happen."

He wagged his eyebrows and cast her the most delightfully wicked grin she had ever received. Jessie fanned herself with her menu. Was it suddenly hot in here?

Contrary to her own plan and Emma's advice, Jessie did not order a gin and tonic, nor did she get the most expensive thing on the menu. She and Zach shared a bottle of wine, and while he had the steak, she had the baked fish.

The conversation was light and fun; they talked about their favorite movies and television shows, where they'd gone to school, what they had thought they were going to do with their lives as opposed to what they were actually doing.

Jessie hadn't known that Zach had studied engineering. He had been on track to take a job with a company working on Boston's infrastructure when the brewery began to take off. Sam was a chemist, which was how he became the brewmaster, and Brad was a business major. Of the three of them, Zach was the extrovert, so he'd had to cram in a quick master's degree in marketing while they tried to get the brewery up on its feet.

Jessie narrowed her eyes at him and said, "So what you're telling me is that you're a fraud."

He popped open his mouth in surprise and asked, "How do you figure that?"

"You present yourself as this handsome, charming, irresponsible man-child when you're really just cultivating a carefree persona that hides the calculating businessman underneath."

"Wait," he said. He held up one hand in a *stop* gesture. "I deny nothing, but let's go back to the handsome and charming part." He fluttered his eyelashes as her.

Jessie laughed. Oh, he was a charmer for sure.

"What about you?" he asked. "What was your plan before life happened?"

"I was a business major like Brad," she said. "But I didn't really have a plan. At the time, I still had my inheritance, so working wasn't really an issue. I thought I'd invest my money and live off the dividends."

"Did your ex blow through all of your money?" he asked.

"Every dime," she said. "Even the girls' college funds."

Zach's face went dark. Jessie had heard the term "murderous expression" but she'd never really seen it until now. She didn't want their dinner to become consumed by her tale of woe. She shook her head.

"But look at me now," she said. "I manage Gavin's animal clinic and he pays me very well. I have a house and my girls are safe, well cared for, and most importantly loved. I'm actually pretty proud of my life right now."

"You should be," he said. His brown eyes were fierce as they swept over her face. "I think you're—"

"Zach? Zachary Caine, is that you?"

Jessie ripped her gaze away from Zach's intense stare to look at the woman who was standing beside their table. She was strikingly pretty with light brown hair that was stylishly cut in soft waves that framed her delicate features and highlighted her arching eyebrows, upturned nose, and deep dimples. Her lips were parted, showing her slight overbite, and she bit her lower lip as she looked at Zach as if uncertain of his reaction to seeing her.

Dread filled Jessie's middle. She didn't know why but she sensed this woman was not one of Zach's short-lived flings. No, she was somebody important. She glanced at Zach and noticed that he blinked at the woman as if he couldn't believe she was here and then he looked a bit sickly. Uh-oh. These two had a history and whatever it was, it wasn't good.

"Alexa," he said. "Wow, what are you doing here?"

"Dinner date with my husband," she said. She gestured behind her at one of the tables, but Jessie couldn't tell which one held her husband. She looked at Jessie expectantly.

Jessie didn't know what to say so she said nothing. She glanced at Zach, but he was staring at Alexa as if sifting through a million feelings and trying to sort through them. His pain and confusion was a palpable thing, and Jessie wished she could help him with it but it wasn't her place.

Alexa turned away from Jessie and met Zach's gaze, then she jerked her head in Jessie's direction. It was the prodding he needed.

"Oh, sorry, got a little lost there," he said. He reached for his wine and finished it off in a long swallow. "Alexa Bracken, this is Jessie Connelly, my . . . er . . . uh . . . neighbor . . . no, that's not it . . . my . . . um . . ."

"Girlfriend?" Alexa supplied.

Jessie started to shake her head but Zach nodded and said, "Yeah, that."

Jessie might have been okay with it if he didn't look so uncomfortable at the term. She frowned at him and was about to say that they were just friends but Alexa cut her off by clapping her hands and hugging Zach. Jessie didn't like that. Not one bit.

"Oh, Zach, finally," Alexa gushed. "I am so happy for you."

She turned around and took one of Jessie's hands in both of hers and clasped it tight.

"This is just wonderful," she said. "A girlfriend after all this time. I was beginning to think you'd never get over . . . well, never mind. This is just the greatest news ever. I am thrilled, absolutely thrilled."

There was something wrong here. Zach was looking more and more irritated and Jessie had no doubt that the forever bachelor in him was resisting being called anyone's boyfriend. This more than anything else clued Jessie in to what had been on deck for this evening. Zach had been charming her for an easy letdown. Well, now he didn't have to bother.

She pushed down the hurt that was bubbling up inside of her and decided to take back control of the situation.

Jessie didn't like this Alexa person, and she didn't like the woman going on and on about Jessie and Zach, as if their relationship or lack thereof was any of her business. She gently tugged her hand out of the woman's grasp.

"I'm sorry," she said, "but we're not a couple. We're just having a thing, a fun-filled fling, and that's it."

"Oh, sorry." Alexa put her hand to her throat. "My mistake."

"No, apparently, it was mine," Zach said.

Chapter 25

His velvet brown gaze locked on Jessie. His mouth, which always seemed to be tipped in a mischievous grin, was set in a hard straight line. Jessie stared back. She was not going to feel bad for calling their relationship exactly what it was, especially when the word "girlfriend" seemed to make him physically sick. People were betting on her orgasms for Pete's sake!

"Well," Alexa said. Neither Zach nor Jessie turned to look at her but continued staring at each other as if they were entering in a contest of wills, although Jessie would be hard-pressed to explain about what. "I'll leave you to your dinner then."

Jessie saw Alexa leave out of the corner of her eye and said, "Nice to meet you."

It was a lie. It wasn't nice to meet her. The woman had ruined a lovely dinner and forced Zach into labeling their relationship something it wasn't, which pushed Jessie into acknowledging what this whole dinner was really about.

After years of lies from her ex, she was scrupulous about telling the truth even to strangers. And the truth here was obvious. Zach had taken her out to reestablish their boundaries and reset them back to being neighbors. Fine. She was only sorry she hadn't taken Emma's advice and ordered the lobster.

"Good-bye, Alexa," Zach said.

He didn't turn to look at her when he said it and Jessie wondered about that. Then she realized there was a finality in his tone that indicated he was talking to her instead of Alexa. She felt her poor bruised heart lurch at the thought.

Their waitress reappeared and asked if they wanted dessert. It forced them to break eye contact and Jessie took the opportunity to escape to the ladies' room.

"Nothing for me, thank you," she said. She grabbed her handbag and left the table. "Excuse me."

When she returned from the restroom, Zach was ready to go. He had her coat and he helped her into it, but there were no lingering touches, no kiss at the nape of her neck, nothing to signify that he felt about her any different than he did a friend or a sister.

The ride home was excruciating. Heat cranked out of the heater on the floor, but it felt as if the cold winter air was pressing hard on the glass windows, determined to get in. Jessie shivered into her coat.

As if aware of her every move, Zach reached for the heat knob on the console and turned it up, sending even more warmth into the cab of his truck. Jessie was about to thank him but the hard look on his face made her feel as if the words wouldn't be welcome so she kept her silence.

When they arrived at her house, she didn't wait for him. She just hopped down and made her way up the stairs and onto her porch. She had her key out but before she could unlock the door, Zach took the key from her hand and did it for her. First the storm door and then the interior one before he handed the keys back.

"Thank you," she said.

"Sure," he replied.

He wasn't looking at her but staring at the porch floor as if studying the grain of the wood. Jessie wanted to say something that would bring back the old, smiling Zach but she didn't know what to say. The woman at the restaurant, Alexa, had brought out a side of Zach she'd never seen before, namely a deep unhappiness that made her want to hug him.

She resisted the urge, mostly because she had a feeling that hugs, or anything else, between them was at an end. It was bad on her if she was feeling sad or mournful. The Maine crew had warned her that Zach didn't date, didn't do commitments, and was more of a free-range sort of guy. If it bothered her, it was her own fault for not listening.

Of course, she could argue that having never had an orgasm before, she had agreed not to get attached to the orgasm maker before she really knew what she was agreeing to. If she'd known, she would have held on to him for a week, a month, okay, more like a year or two, until she got over this new discovery.

Zach had propped open the storm door with his shoulder, so she moved past him and pushed open the big wooden door that led into the house. Zach followed and together they found Brad sitting on the couch reading a book, wedged between Rufus, who had an alarming number of the girls' mismatched hair bows in his pompadour, and Emma, both of whom were fast asleep.

Brad marked his place in the book with his finger and glanced at Zach and Jessie in surprise. "I didn't figure you'd be here for another hour or two."

"Yeah, well." Zach shrugged and left it at that.

Brad frowned, glancing between them, but neither Jessie nor Zach elaborated. If there was a lower level of miserable and awkward, Jessie was certain she had never felt it.

Zach was unhappy with her. She got that. She supposed he felt embarrassed at her candor with his former whatever Alexa had been to him. But she was equally miffed with him for trying to pretend they were something that they weren't. What last night had been lovely and beautiful and full of promise was now sordid and weird. Ugh.

"Rufus, let's go," Zach said. He glanced at Brad and Jessie. "Early morning tomorrow, so I'll just—"

"Go," Jessie finished for him.

He stared at her for a heartbeat. His brown gaze showed a flash of hurt and then it was gone. He forced a smile that for the first time Jessie could remember didn't meet his eyes.

Rufus, who had rolled off the couch and was now stretching, trotted over to Jessie for a scratch and then once obliged moved on to Zach, whom he leaned against as if claiming him as his person.

"What is in your hair, boy?" Zach asked. There was a hint of his old self in his tone.

"The girls played hairdresser with him," Brad said. "He was very patient with them."

Zach gently removed the bows and put them in a pile on the coffee table. "Come on, boy, you've got to have some self-respect. You'll never find a forever home if you go around looking like that."

Jessie got the feeling he wasn't just talking to the dog, but she didn't ask for clarification. She didn't want to know. Okay, that was also a big fat fib. She did want to know. She wanted to know what caused Zach to withdraw tonight. Was it seeing his ex? Was it being embarrassed by Jessie's honesty about their relationship? What?

He began to walk to the door. With a wave, he said, "Thanks for watching the girls tonight. I'll see you at work tomorrow."

"Anytime," Brad said. "Yeah, tomorrow. Sam wants us in his office at nine, don't forget."

"I'll be there," Zach said. He glanced at her. It was quick, as if he were trying to look at the sun but couldn't bear it. "Night, Jessie."

"Good night," she said.

Rufus trotted after him and Jessie wondered if she'd ever see either Zach or Rufus again. The thought hurt, and not just because she was fond of the dog.

The door shut behind him and Emma popped up on the couch, looked at Jessie, and demanded, "What the hell was that?"

"Oh, my god!" Jessie started and then sank onto the end of the couch. "You were awake? You big faker."

"The vibe was bad," Emma said. "I was pretending to be asleep so I could get a sense of what was wrong."

"She does that," Brad confirmed.

"Nothing is wrong," Jessie said. "Zach and I are just back to normal."

"Normal being?" Brad asked.

"We're just neighbors again," she said.

"Bullshit," Brad said. Both Emma and Jessie looked at him with eyebrows raised and he shrugged and said, "Sorry not sorry, but that's a load of crap. I've known Zach for fifteen years and he's never looked at anyone the way he looks at you."

Jessie crossed her arms over her chest and asked, "Except maybe Alexa?"

"Shut up!" Brad said as if he were a teenage girl. "Did he tell you about her?"

"Who is Alexa?" Emma asked.

"He didn't have to tell me; she came by our table at dinner."

"No way," Brad said.

"Way."

"I am going to have an aneurysm, which would be very bad for the baby, if you people do not tell me who Alexa is," Emma declared.

"Zach's old girlfriend—fiancée," Jessie and Brad answered at the same time but with differing descriptions of Alexa's role in Zach's life.

"Wait. They were engaged?" Jessie asked.

"He didn't tell you?" Brad sighed. "Sorry."

"Zach was engaged," Emma said. She squinted at her husband. "How did I not know this?"

"He doesn't talk about it."

"Clearly," Emma said. She frowned at her husband.

Jessie sat on the other side of the couch. "That at least makes much more sense. Poor Zach."

"Why poor Zach?" Brad asked.

"Well, judging by the way he acted after seeing Alexa, it's obvious he's still very much in love with her."

"Oh, hell no!" Brad barked out a laugh. "Trust me when I tell you that he is completely one hundred percent over her."

"Then why was he so distant after we saw her? I mean, he wasn't Zach at all. He was cold and withdrawn and really unhappy," Jessie said.

"I'm not surprised," Brad said. "He and Alexa were together for seven years."

"Okay, now I am furious that I didn't know about this," Emma said. "Seven years?"

"They met when we were freshmen in college," Brad said. "She was the only woman he dated in school and after school they moved in together. Sam and I were sort of hoping Zach would want to venture out there and date others but he never did. He was steadfast."

"He must have loved her very much," Jessie said.

She hated how this made her feel. She'd been with Seth for the same length of time. She knew it was hypocritical to dislike that Zach had such a significant relationship in his past but she hated it. Absolutely hated it.

"No, he didn't," Brad said. "He stayed with her because Zach is the most loyal person I've ever known. He'd have stayed with her forever if she'd married him whether he was happy or not."

"Why?" Emma asked. "Zach is so great. Why would he stay with someone he wasn't happy with?"

"Because after a lifetime of being shuttled back and forth between part-time homes, Zach desperately wanted to belong. He hated feeling like he was always on the outside of things, and when he proposed to Alexa, Sam and I knew he was just doing it so that he wouldn't ever have to feel shut out again."

That made complete and perfect sense to Jessie. She knew from everything Zach had told her about his life that he hadn't felt as if he belonged anywhere; that's why his Maine crew and the brewery were so important to him. They were his family and home.

"What happened between him and Alexa?" Jessie asked. "I mean, why didn't they get married?"

Brad looked uncomfortable. He looked at Jessie and Emma and then at the front door as if hoping Zach would come back and tell the tale himself.

"If you want me to understand you have to tell me," she said.

Brad nodded. "Zach proposed, pulling out all the stops, Zach style, and Alexa said yes, but she didn't seem super happy about it. Then after a week of being engaged, she ended it. She gave Zach the ring back and moved out of their place. Five months later, she was married to someone else," Brad said. "Now she has a pack of kids and lives in the suburbs of Portland."

Jessie sucked in a breath.

"Wow, just wow," Emma said. "That is stone cold."

"Yeah," Brad confirmed. "It destroyed him. Sam and I had to bird dog him for a few months to make sure he was okay."

"This just proves my point. If Zach was over her, he wouldn't care about seeing her," Jessie said. "Believe me, he cared."

Emma glanced between them. "Tell us exactly what happened."

Jessie recounted the entire conversation word for word.

Brad shrugged. "I have no idea. But you're right. The Zach who walked in here tonight was not the Zach I know. In fact, I don't think I've ever seen him quite so grim."

"Um, maybe it has nothing to do with Alexa. Perhaps it's because he wasn't going to end things with Jessie at dinner," Emma said. She looked at Jessie as if she was as thick as a brick. "Did it never occur to you that he might have considered tonight an actual date with his new girl-friend, and when you told his ex that you were no more than a fling, you were also telling him the same thing?"

"But he called me his neighbor," Jessie said.

"Because he was caught off guard. He also scrambled to come up with what to call you probably because he didn't want to scare you off before the two of you talked about it," Emma said. "But then Alexa called you his girl-friend and you panicked and corrected her and put him firmly in the fling zone. This, my friend, is what they call a clusterfuck."

Had she done that? Had she been so preoccupied with not getting hurt that she'd hurt Zach in a preemptive strike to save herself? "Well, crap."

Chapter 26

"What are you going to do?" Emma asked.

"I don't know," Jessie said.

"Talk to him," Brad said. "This is Zach. He'll listen. I'm not kidding when I say he doesn't look at anyone the way he looks at you."

Jessie felt the hope start to flutter inside of her. Maybe it wasn't over yet. But what was she going to say to him? What could she say when she'd made an absolute disaster out of their first date, if that's what it was, and, oh, she hoped it was.

"I'll think about it," she said. "I mean, this is all speculation. We have no idea what Zach is thinking or feeling."

Emma rose to her feet and crossed the floor to reach down and hug Jessie.

"Remember this isn't just about Zach," she said. "Your feelings matter, too, and if Zach really does care for you then you'll be able to fix this."

Jessie glanced up at Brad, who had his phone out and was texting. She narrowed her eyes at him.

"What are you doing?"

"Nothing," he said. He shoved his phone in his pocket.

Jessie didn't believe him, not for a hot minute. "Did you start another betting pool about us?"

"Look at the time," Brad said. "Come on, Em, let's go!"

Brad grabbed Emma's hand and dragged her to the foyer where their coats were hanging. He held out her coat to her and shoved her hat on her head. Grabbing his own coat, he yanked open the door, pushed open the storm door, and darted outside, pulling Emma behind him.

"I'm betting on you for the win," Emma called out before the night swallowed them up.

Jessie closed and locked the door behind them. She rested her head against the door, dreading going up to her bed, which after last night was likely going to feel entirely too large and too lonely. She sincerely hoped Emma didn't lose her shirt betting on her this time.

Zach sipped his coffee and watched his neighbor's house through the window, knowing full well that staring at a woman's house, hoping for a glimpse of her, was at best marginally creepy and at worst out-and-out stalker-like. But it had been two days.

Two days since he'd seen her smile, smelled her particularly lovely lemony scent, held her hand, or hugged her. And that was just the G-rated stuff he was missing. There was a whole other list of X-rated sights and sounds that he couldn't even let himself remember or he'd be curled up in a fetal position on his living room floor, dripping a steady stream of single-man tears.

Given the way he'd dropped her off at her house after their date, he supposed he couldn't really blame her for not reaching out to him. He'd been distant, aloof, and cold, something so foreign to his natural extroverted personality that even he hadn't recognized himself.

He'd been rocked by seeing his ex. Alexa Bracken or, as he'd known her, Alexa Todd. She'd been his constant for seven years. He'd never realized she was unhappy or that she wanted something different. He'd fallen for her in college and just assumed she was The One and that they'd spend the rest of their lives together. Nope.

He'd run into her a few times over the years, usually when he had a piece of arm candy with him or two, and she'd always seemed disappointed or disgusted or perhaps just full of pity for him. This time was the first time she'd run into him on a genuine date. It had been awesome, right up until Jessie had labeled them a fling. *A fling?!*

Zach had been stung. Whatever was happening between them had ceased to be a fling for him somewhere between her first and second orgasm; okay, that was a lie. In his mind, Jessie had always been different, special, more. She'd always been so much greater to him than something casual and to hear her dismiss them as a hookup, well, it had wrecked him.

He'd been grumpy and out of sorts ever since. Instead of going out last night, he'd stayed in. He'd ignored the texts and calls from the Maine crew, and had let his senior field marketer, Savannah, be in charge of the girls last night. She was ready to start taking over the field promotions and, frankly, his heart just wasn't in it.

Instead he and Rufus had curled up on the couch and watched the animal channel. Rufus had perked up during a show about police dogs, but without the girls, their kitten Chaos, and Jessie, the house had seemed too quiet to Zach. He didn't like it.

The only consolation he felt was that he knew Jessie hadn't gone out either. Her car stayed in the garage and the girls' bedroom light went on in time for stories and went out at their standard bedtime. He missed that.

He missed reading to the girls every evening. Gracie would go quiet as her imagination embroidered every word and Maddie would be furious if the chapter ended on a cliff-hanger. He had learned to pause the books in mid-chapter to avoid the argument she would begin if the characters were left in peril.

He missed the feel of their small hands sliding into his as they walked somewhere or their arms looping around his neck to give him a big hug. He missed the way they romped around with Rufus and Chaos and he missed the sound of their laughter.

The truth was that Zach loved the girls and he'd fallen in love with their mom. There was something about Jessie that hollered back at him, that resonated with him, as if she was the echo to his lonely cry. He wanted to be with her, not just temporarily, but always. But he had no idea how to get her to see him the same way.

Zach looked from Jessie's house into his now empty cup. His excuse for standing here was gone. He turned on the faucet to rinse out his mug. His gaze moved back to Jessie's house while he stalled.

A dark blue luxury sedan pulled into Jessie's driveway. Zach put the cup in the sink and stopped the water. He'd never seen this car before. Was it Seth, her ex, coming for a visit? Zach felt his fists bunch. The guy ditched his kids for the holidays· but shows up now after they perform a father-daughter talent show without him?

No. An overwhelming feeling of possession swept over Zach. He knew it wasn't right or logical. Jessie and the girls were not his. Heck, Jessie had made it clear how not his she was by dismissing what was between them as nothing. Still, he hated the idea of the man who had all but abandoned them strolling back into their lives as if he had a right to just show up when he felt like it or when it was convenient for him.

As Zach watched, a man exited the car. He was wearing a coat and a hat, giving Zach no clue as to what he looked like. He could be a friend of Jessie's, Zach supposed, except they had the same friends and Zach did not recognize this guy as being Gavin, Brad, Sam, James, or even Cooper. It made him feel uneasy.

Without pausing to think it through, Zach whistled to Rufus. He strode to his foyer and shoved his feet into his boots, grabbed his coat, hat, and gloves. Rufus came at a run, assuming they were going for a walk. They were. Next door.

As Zach crossed the snow-crusted yards, he didn't hear any screams coming from Jessie's. He took that as a good sign and yet he didn't slow his pace or reconsider his mission. He could not be at ease until he knew his girls, all three, were all right.

Zach strode up onto the porch and pressed the doorbell. He waited, trying to be polite and not yank open the door and storm the house like a fireman chasing down flames.

He heard someone unlatching the deadbolt and then he saw Gracie's concerned face peer out at him. Once she recognized him, a grin split her features and she pushed the door wide.

"Zach, you're here!" she cried. She threw herself at him and hugged his middle. "And just in time since Grandpa is planning to take us away."

"What?"

Zach stepped inside and shed his coat and boots while Rufus took the opportunity to lick Gracie's face. The empty spot where Zach had kept his boots when he stayed here during the blizzard was still there, as if no one had wanted to fill his space with their shoes. That made him take heart.

"Zach! Rufus!" Maddie reached the doorway and launched herself at him. Zach dropped his gloves and caught her mid-air. "We missed you. Where were you?"

"Oh, you know, around," Zach said. He took it as a good sign that Jessie hadn't told the girls he was dead to them.

"Our grandpa is here," Maddie said. She looped her arm around his neck. "He wants to take custard of us."

"Custody?" Zach asked. He felt his internal early warning system start blaring.

"Yes, that's it," Gracie said. "He and Momma are not happy with each other."

They stepped into the main room, with Maddie perched on Zach's hip and Gracie pressed close to his side. He felt everything in his world right itself now that he had his girls with him. He looked at the living room. It was empty. He swiveled his gaze toward the kitchen. Jessie and the man the girls called Grandpa sat at the dining room table. Jessie held a mug of coffee in her hands while the man had a glass of water. They both looked tense.

"Momma, look who's here!" Gracie cried. "Zach and Rufus."

Zach watched her closely. It was only a flicker but he was certain he saw it all the same. Relief. She was relieved to see him. Zach felt his smile unfurl. Good. Relief he could work with.

"Hi, Jessie," he said. She gave him a small nod and then cast a nervous glance at the man across the table.

Zach studied the man. He had ditched his coat and hat and Zach could see he was tall and angular and mostly bald with just a fringe of tightly trimmed gray hair that circled the back of his head. He had a hook of a nose, and thin lips over a stubborn bearded chin. The same chin as the feisty girl in his arms.

Jessie rose to her feet. "Hi, Zach. This is Judge Connelly, the girls' grandfather."

Interesting. Not "my father-in-law" or "my ex's father," but "the girls' grandfather," and she introduced him as a judge not a mister, which Zach took to mean that the position had shaped Jessie's relationship with the man.

"Zachary Caine," he introduced himself. "I live next door."

Zach held out his hand and noted the man's hesitation in taking it. He gave him a level look and the judge flushed a faint shade of pink before he took Zach's hand in a firm grip and with one up and down pump released him.

Chaos, who'd been asleep on one of the chair cushions, awoke with a yawn and a stretch, which clearly signified to Rufus that it was playtime. He let loose a bark and began to bounce around the chair, clearly wanting the kitten to come and play.

The girls giggled and Zach set Maddie on her feet. He saw the wary look Jessie gave the judge and he noted the judge did not seem pleased with the animals' presence.

"Mr. Caine, Jessie and I were in the middle of a discussion," Judge Connelly said. "Now is not the best time for a visit."

Well, that was blunt. Zach lifted one eyebrow and looked at Jessie. She gave him a small smile that was supposed to reassure him, he guessed. It probably would have helped if she didn't look like she was about to cry.

Whatever was going on, Jessie didn't look very happy about it and Zach was not leaving until he knew that both she and the girls were okay. If what the girls had told him was true and the judge was trying to get custody, Zach would do everything in his power to stop him.

"No problem," Zach said. He raised his hands as if to show he had no intention of interrupting. "Tell you what, I'll just visit with the girls in the living room and keep them occupied so you two can talk."

"That's not—" the judge began but Jessie interrupted.

"That'd be nice, thanks."

"All right, girls, let's work on our next song," Zach said. "How about 'Tonight, You Belong to Me'?"

He didn't mean to stare at Jessie when he said the name of the song, really, he didn't. She put her hand to her throat and turned her head. Zach hoped she got the message. He'd been without her for two days and now that he was here with her, he didn't think he could stand to be away from her again. Not one more night, not ever, and her stodgy former father-in-law was welcome to take note of that.

Gracie grabbed his hand and tugged him toward the living room where both of their ukuleles sat propped up by the cold hearth. Maddie started to sing the tune, doing a little shimmy shake thing as she sang that made Zach laugh. Oh, he had missed these girls.

"We'll just be in the back room," Jessie said. She took her coffee as she led the judge down the hall. He did not bring his water but strode down the hall with the purposeful step of someone who was used to getting his way.

Obviously, they wanted to speak in private. Yeah, not on Zach's watch.

Chapter 27

Zach got the girls started and then excused himself to get a drink in the kitchen. Distraction came when Chaos rolled right into the middle of them with Rufus hot on his orange tabby tail. The girls laughed and then love was given as the dog and kitten stretched out to receive their pets from the kids.

Excellent. Zach used the distraction to beat feet down the hall and listen in on Jessie and the judge. He pondered whether he should feel guilty about it. Nope. He didn't. Then he remembered that people who eavesdropped usually heard bad things about themselves. Zach had a hide like a rhinoceros; he could live with it if it meant the judge wasn't bullying Jessie.

He pressed his ear to the edge of the door. Their voices were muffled but he could hear anger in Jessie's voice and his hand was reaching for the doorknob before he caught himself and forced his fingers into a fist.

It was a better strategy to wait and not storm in there no matter how much he wanted otherwise. He let his breath out slowly and strained to hear.

"It is in the best interest of the girls," Judge Connelly said.

"How do you figure that?" Jessie snapped. Zach was impressed with her tone. She wasn't taking any guff. "They adore Zach and he adores them."

"He is not their father," Judge Connelly barked.

"Yes, well, their father isn't here now, is he?"

"I am working on that—"

"I don't care," Jessie cut him off. "He walked away. He left us and there's nothing you can do to make that right. Denying the girls any other role model in their life is just petty and mean. I won't stand for it."

"You say that as if you have a choice," Judge Connelly said. "I didn't want to resort to this but I need to inform you that I've been having you watched."

"What?" Jessie gasped.

"You've been seen around town with Mr. Caine quite a lot, and I have to tell you that his reputation with women and the fact that he is always out in bars is not one that any judge would be in favor of as a role model to young girls."

Zach felt his temper flare. The urge to go in there and throttle that nasty old man was almost more than he could resist. But he waited. Even knowing it might crush him, he wanted to hear what Jessie had to say.

"He owns a brewery," she snapped. "A very successful one at that, and most of the women he is seen with are the field marketers that work for Bluff Point Ale. There is nothing sordid about being a good businessman whose business happens to boost the economy of our very own town."

The judge made a scoffing sound and said, "I'm sure that's what he's led you to believe."

"No, it isn't," Jessie said. "It's what I've seen with my own two eyes. And you have no right to assassinate his character for working with bars and restaurants when your own son was a notorious barfly."

"Interesting," Judge Connelly said. "Both men you've been involved with in the time I've known you spent a lot of time in establishments that sell liquor. Huh, you seem to have a type, and clearly are not a very good judge of character."

"Don't you dare," Jessie snapped. "Zachary Caine is nothing like your son. Seth was a lecherous, womanizing alcoholic, and Zach is a kind, good-hearted, hardworking man. They are absolutely nothing alike and I won't have you insult Zach by comparing him to your son."

Zach pressed his hand against the door. More than anything in the world, he wanted to go in there, wrap his arms about Jessie, and kiss her senseless and he didn't care if the judge watched him or not.

"Do not disparage my son," the judge said. "He is not a part of this conversation. I warned you the night of the talent show, Jessica, not to engage in a relationship with that man. If you ignore my warning, I will use all of the power of my office to prove that you are an unfit mother and gain full custody of my granddaughters."

Jessie gasped. "You wouldn't."

"Oh, yes, I would," he said. "End your relationship with him or lose your girls, the choice is yours."

Zach felt his stomach turn. The girls were Jessie's life, her everything. How this man could threaten her when she was such a great mom made his vision turn hazy with unreleased rage. What pissed him off even more was that Jessie was alone. She had no parents, no spouse, no siblings, no one to help her fight this guy.

It hit him then. That was their connection. That was why he and Jessie clicked like two cogs in a clockwork. They were both alone and had been for most of their lives. It was also the reason he couldn't let her go.

"I can't imagine Audrey is okay with you threatening me," Jessie said.

"Leave my wife out of it," he said. "I'll be in touch."

Zach knew the judge was coming his way. A decision had to be made. He could dash back to the living room and pretend he hadn't heard this conversation. He could wait until the judge opened the door and punch the crotchety ass in the mouth—definitely the most tempting option—or he could take control of the situation. Zach went for door number three.

He banged through the door, acting as if he had just come down the hallway to find them.

"Hey, there, so sorry to interrupt, but I need to get the girls to their ice-skating lessons," he said. It was a lie. The girls' lesson wasn't until later. He didn't care. He threw a none-too-gentle arm around the judge's shoulders and half pushed, half dragged him to the front door.

"You? You're taking them to lessons?" Judge Connelly gaped at him.

"Sure, we do lots of stuff together, don't we, girls?" Zach asked as he hurried the judge through the living room.

"We bake cookies," Gracie said.

"We go sledding," Maddie added.

"We learn how to box," Gracie said. She put up her dukes and Zach grinned at her.

"And Zach reads the best bedtime stories," Maddie added.

"Bedtime stories?" Judge Connelly whipped his head in Jessie's direction.

She was shaking her head at Zach and the girls, trying to get them to stop, but it was no use. The girls kept listing activities and Zach was busy grabbing the judge's coat and hat off the rack.

As if sensing Zach's need to get rid of the man, Chaos, who'd been playing a game of catch me if you can with Rufus, chose that moment to dart out from under the coffee table and latch onto Judge Connelly's neatly pressed pants. With his razorlike kitten claws he dug into the fleshy part of the judge's leg right above his knee.

"Yeow!" Judge Connelly yelped and kicked his leg, trying to dislodge the kitten.

"Careful, Grandpa, you'll hurt him," Gracie yelled.

"He's just a kitten," Maddie said. "He doesn't know better."

Judge Connelly managed to grab the kitten by the scruff of the neck and rip it off of his pants. He thrust Chaos at

Jessie, who grabbed for him, holding him close to her chest to calm the poor little fellow. Zach had to fight the urge to grab the judge by the back of his collar and toss him out into the snow.

"Feral beasts are an endangerment to small children," he roared. "I will have someone come out here to take that flea-bitten ball of disease and put it down."

"No!" Gracie and Maddie yelled together. "Don't hurt him. He didn't mean it."

"Of course not," Zach said. "Nothing is going to happen to Chaos." He looked at the girls so that they could see he meant it. "And on that note, it is time for you to go, Judge. See ya."

He shoved the judge's coat and hat into his arms and opened the front doors, then he gave him a hearty shove onto the porch and let the storm door swing shut in his face. Zach then slammed the large wooden door with more force than was necessary but, man, that felt good.

He brushed his hands together as if he'd just tossed something rotten out of the house—not completely off base—and then he strode back into the living room. Jessie was staring at him, her eyes wide with horror, as she held Chaos to her. The kitten was rubbing the top of his head against her chin but Jessie looked frozen in place.

"Oh, that's not good," she said. "Not good at all."

She put Chaos down on the ground and turned and bolted up the stairs. Maddie and Gracie hurried to Zach's side and hugged him hard. They looked up at him with worried eyes.

"You promise nothing will happen to Chaos?" Gracie said.

Zach gave them both a fierce squeeze. "I promise."

While he held them close, he made a mental vow. Nothing was going to break up this family. No matter what happened between him and Jessie, he would make damn sure no one took her girls away. Not now. Not ever.

"Thank you, Zach," Maddie said. "Oh, thank you."

"Can you girls play down here?" he asked. "I need to talk to your mom."

The two girls nodded and Zach hurried upstairs to talk to Jessie. She had to be rattled. Having someone threaten to take away the most important people in her life had to have shaken her to her core.

When he got upstairs, he went right to her bedroom but it was empty. He heard a thump and a bang and followed the noise into the girls' room. Jessie was standing on her tiptoes in front of the closet pulling something off of the top shelf. He heard a slide and another bang and a wheeled carry-on hit the ground by her feet.

She hefted it up and plopped it onto Gracie's bed. She unzipped it and then began to dash around the room, throwing in clothes and books and toys. He glanced at the other bed and saw that there was already a half-packed carry-on on Maddie's bed.

"Jessie, what are you doing?"

She didn't answer him but threw in two more items before she hurried across the hall into her own room. A suitcase was on her bed, too, and judging by the contents that were being vomited out of its interior, she was doing the same well-thought packing over there that she was doing in the girls' room.

"Jessie, stop."

He stepped in front of her when she tried to dart to the closet. She dashed around him and began grabbing sweaters off of the top shelf. She looked at the three in her hands as if she couldn't decide which to pack then she threw all three of them onto the floor and ran to her dresser.

This time Zach grabbed her before she could get past him. He wrapped his arms around her and held her tight even as she tried to squirm out of his embrace.

"Zach, you have to let me go," she said. "I need to get us out of here right now."

"Jessie, shh, it's all right," he said.

"No, it's not all right," she said. She was trembling so hard, Zach was surprised her teeth weren't clacking together when she spoke. "Judge Connelly is one of the most powerful men in the state. If he says he's going to take the girls, he will and there'll be nothing I can do to stop him."

"Jessie," he said, "I know he's got you scared—"

"Zach, you have no idea," she said. She pulled back and looked at him and the panic in her blue eyes about broke his heart. "Part of the problem with my ex was that every time he screwed up, the judge bailed him out. He never had to face any consequences for what he did because his father could call in a million favors and get him out of it."

"That doesn't mean he can take your girls," Zach said.

"Yes, it does," Jessie argued. "He's that well connected. I can't fight him. He'll take this whatever-it-is between us and he'll twist it and warp it and make me look like I'm some sort of slut-whore, proving that I'm an unfit mother. Then he'll swoop in and take the only thing that matters to me—my family. The only way I can beat him is to run as fast and as far as I can."

"Jessie, listen to me." Zach shook her gently. "That isn't going to happen. I won't let it."

She gave him a look that said she wanted to believe him but didn't. He understood. After all these years of being under the judge's thumb, she probably had some sort of former in-law post-traumatic stress happening. Being on her own for so long with no backup clearly had her at her breaking point.

He cupped her face. "Listen, I know this is hard for you to believe but you're not alone anymore."

"Oh, Zach, I know you mean well, I do—"

"I don't just mean well," he said. "I plan to do well."

She stared at him, and the look in her eyes was one of such longing, he felt his heart trip over itself.

"I'm sorry about the other night," she said. "I've been wanting to say that for two days."

"Me, too," he said. "But I didn't know how."

"Me either," she said. She pressed her forehead to his. "I know you mean—"

"Jessie, do you trust me?"

He knew she was about to say that she knew he meant well, but he didn't want to hear it. He wanted to convince her that she wasn't alone and he knew just what to do to prove it.

"Yes," she said with no hesitation. Zach grinned.

"Then give me one hour," he said. He kissed her quick on the lips, breaking it off before he got distracted by the soft feel of her mouth beneath his and forgot that he had an errand. Then he pulled her out the door and down the stairs. "Girls, I feel some *Frozen* coming on!"

"Yay!"

Gracie and Maddie dropped the toys they'd been playing with and found their preferred spots on the couch. Zach pushed Jessie down in between them and fired up the television. As the opening credits came on to their favorite Disney film, Zach leaned over the back of the couch and whispered in Jessie's ear.

"One hour," he said. "Just give me one hour and I'll fix everything."

She glanced at him like he was crazy but she looped an arm around each of her daughters and pulled them close. Zach watched as she kissed each of their heads and settled in to watch the movie with her girls.

Rufus and Chaos settled in on the opposite couch, and Zach took a second to appreciate that the beings he cared most about in the world were all safe and sound and he was going to figure out how to make sure they stayed that way.

The movie was at its high point when Zach returned. He took Jessie's hand and pulled her off the couch. The two girls were so entranced by the film they didn't notice Zach's return or their mom's departure from the huddle on the couch.

Zach was stoked. He hadn't been sure when he left that what he'd thought to do as a solution to Jessie's problem was even possible, but not only was it possible, it was brilliant, at least as far as he was concerned. He dragged her upstairs to her bedroom where they could talk in private. Also, there was a bed there and he liked to be prepared.

"Okay, Zach, you look like you're going to explode," Jessie said. She was smiling at him and she seemed calmer than she had when he left. "What's going on?"

"I think the best way to handle this situation is like

this," he said. Then he took out the paper he had tucked into the inside pocket of his coat and handed it to her.

Jessie glanced at it and unfolded it. She stared at it. She didn't move. Zach waited. He was trying to get a read on her face but her features didn't shift in any discernable way. He couldn't tell if she was happy or sad, furious or elated.

Hmm. When he had pictured this moment, it had ended with her jumping into his arms and kissing him, passionately. Then they would fall to the bed and he would make love to her just like he had a few nights ago. This did not seem to be the response he was getting.

"I don't understand," she said.

"It's an application for a marriage license," he said.

"Yeah, that part I got, but I'm not sure why you're handing it to me," she said.

"Because I think the solution to your problem is crystal clear. You should marry me," he said. "There is no blood test or waiting period required in the state of Maine, so I think we should get it done as soon as possible."

Chapter 28

"Oh, Zach," she said. "That is really the sweetest gesture, but I can't—"

"Don't say no," he said. "Hear me out."

Jessie opened her mouth to protest but then pressed her lips together and nodded. She was going to let him have his say.

Okay, then; Zach felt as if he was making the sales pitch of a lifetime.

"If we get married, the judge can't touch you," he said. "We'll be providing the girls with a stable home with two parents and two incomes. I have character references up the wazoo and the girls like me. Really there is no argument he can make that would allow him to try and take your daughters."

Jessie stared at him in wonder. A small smile lifted the corners of her mouth and he felt his heart begin to swell with the rightness of her in his life forever. He was certain this was the best idea he had ever had in his entire life and he'd had some doozies.

She cupped his face in her hands, and pulled him down

so she could brush her lips across his. "Zach, I have to tell you that the two days we were apart were the worst I can remember in a long time. I'm sorry about our date, and I'm sorry I freaked out. I wanted to come and talk to you about Alexa and what I said, but I didn't know how."

"It's okay," he said. "It's ancient history. *She's* ancient history."

She gave him a shaky smile.

"Listen, this idea to get married is the most thoughtful, lovely gesture anyone has ever made to me, but my answer has to be no. If the judge is upset now, he will be furious if I marry you."

"So what?" Zach asked. "Who cares what he thinks?"

"I do. I can't afford to give him any cause to doubt my parenting skills, and a quickie marriage would do just that," she said. She stood on her tiptoes and kissed him again, lingering just a little bit longer this time before she said, "I'm sorry. I can't marry you."

"Why not, Momma?" Gracie asked from the doorway.

"Whoa! Are you two kissing?" Maddie asked.

Jessie dropped her hands and stepped back from Zach. She gave him a wide-eyed look that clearly asked, *How are we supposed to deal with this?*

"I did kiss Zach," Jessie said. "Just like I kiss you when you have a boo-boo."

Maddie, ever the little attorney, looked at Zach with one eyebrow raised and asked, "Do you have a boo-boo on your lips?"

Jessie turned her back to the girls and gave Zach a frantic look. He would have laughed if his heart didn't feel squashed flat. He ran a finger over his lips. He wasn't giving up on his idea. Not yet. So, he had some options here. He could tell the girls that he loved their mom but that might come as a bit of a shock to Jessie since he hadn't even told her yet. No, that needed to be just between them first.

Okay, then he'd keep his feelings on the down-low for now. He nodded at Maddie and said, "I am feeling a bit chapped."

He saw Jessie practically wilt in relief. Well, that really didn't fluff up his ego or anything else for that matter.

"But what about marriage?" Gracie asked. "I heard you say 'marry.'"

Maddie looked from her sister to them and back. Suddenly the room felt very stifling. Zach wasn't sure what to say to this. Since Jessie had said no, maybe he'd let her field this one. To his surprise she was honest with the girls.

"Zach said he would like to marry me someday," she said. "But since we've really just gotten to know each other, we think it's too soon."

"Like Anna and the bad prince in *Frozen*," Maddie said.

"Yeah, you need to take time with these things," Gracie agreed.

Zach would have laughed, really hard, if this was someone else's life. But the truth was he wanted to marry Jessie. He didn't think it was too soon. And he was deeply worried about Judge Connelly coming after her and taking away the girls if he was as vindictive as he seemed.

"Oh, look at the time, you two need to get ready for skate lessons," Jessie said.

"I'll take them," Zach said. Jessie looked at him in surprise. "You could probably use the hour to deal with some stuff. You know, call your lawyer and let them know what happened and ask what you should do about it."

Jessie nodded. Then she gave him a small smile. "Thank you. That would be a huge help. And thanks for understanding."

"Sure, no problem," he said. He shrugged and ran a hand through his hair. "It was a crazy idea."

"But it came from a good place," Jessie said. She put her hand over his heart and Zach shoved his hands in his pockets to keep from grabbing her and pulling her close in front of the girls.

"All right, troops, let's roll out," he said. He stepped away from Jessie and turned toward the door with Gracie and Maddie skipping along beside him.

Maddie tucked her hand into one of his and then Gracie did the same. Dang. They were so small and trusting, they made him feel ten feet tall, and he would gladly slay all of their dragons for them. Even if one of them was their crotchety old grandfather.

The ice rink was freezing. Being a southern California boy, Zach had always been more about surfing and skateboarding than he was about winter sports. Oh, he liked playing in the snow, but he loved the sand and surf of the Maine summer so much more.

He hunkered into his jacket and watched his two favorite girls as they whipped around the ice on blades of steel. Surprisingly, Gracie was the bolder of the two. She hit the ice with some serious speed and threw herself into turns that made Zach's heart clutch. Maddie was more cautious. She stayed closer to the wall, she didn't go as fast, and she clenched up when she lost her balance as if already bracing for impact. Gracie seemed to accept falls as a part of the process but she also had two more years of experience than Maddie.

Zach watched their instructor, who looked like little more than a kid herself, line them up and have them practice their spins. When Maddie nailed hers, she glanced right at Zach and yelled, "Did you see? Did you see?"

He grinned at her, feeling pride leak out of every pore in his body. When Gracie executed a jump and landed on her backside, he had half vaulted over the edge of the rink before she yelled at him "I'm okay!" and popped back up on her feet to try it again. Again, he oozed pride like sweat.

Zach sat back down on a cold hard bench and watched the girls for the rest of their practice. He loved watching them with their friends, how they giggled and smiled, how their brows furrowed when they were concentrating. Several times he saw mannerisms that reminded him of Jessie and it occurred to him that for most of the girls' lives, their mother had been their only role model. They were good kids, with kind hearts, big brains, and wicked senses of humor. He considered himself lucky to be in their lives.

As the lesson ended the girls skated over to where Zach sat. He met them at the rink door, helping them onto the rubber flooring. He untied their skates and slipped on their boots.

"Girls, you were just wonderful!"

Zach glanced behind him to see Judge Connelly and a woman he presumed to be Mrs. Connelly. She was the one who was gushing to the girls.

"Thank you, Grandma," Maddie said and hugged the woman hard around the middle.

"Thank you," Gracie said. She hugged her grandmother, too, but she looked warily at Judge Connelly and Zach figured Gracie was a little bit more aware of what was happening between the grown-ups.

The judge bent down and both girls hugged him. Zach found he didn't like that. He didn't like it at all, as if he was afraid the judge might take the opportunity to snatch them.

"Hi, I'm Audrey," the woman said to Zach. She held out her hand and he shook it. She had curly gray hair and hazel eyes. She was bundled up in a puffy coat with a hat and a scarf and expensive leather gloves.

"Hi, I'm Zach, the girls' neighbor and a friend of Jessie's," he said.

"He's going to marry our mom," Maddie said.

"Hush," Gracie said. As if she understood the complexity of the situation, she added, "These things take time."

Both of the Connellys were looking at Zach as if they wanted him to confirm or deny. He refused. It was none of their business and he took a certain satisfaction in meeting their alarmed stares and saying nothing.

"A word, Caine," Judge Connelly snapped.

"Truffle," Zach said.

The judge frowned and the girls laughed. They got it. They got him and darned if he didn't love them for it.

"You asked for a word, so I gave you one," Zach explained.

The judge glowered. "Follow me. Please."

It was the please that made him follow. Zach stood and

glanced at Audrey. She seemed distressed but not angry like the judge. He decided he would trust her with the girls but only if he could keep an eye on her.

"Stay with your grandmother," he said. "I'll be right back."

Judge Connelly moved out of earshot of his wife and the girls, and Zach moved so that he was able to talk and watch Maddie and Gracie at the same time. Their grandmother seemed to dote on them, so he had to assume that most of the ill will came from the judge. Fine. He was more than capable of giving it back one hundred percent.

"You can't marry Jessica," Judge Connelly declared.

"Not really seeing how it's your concern," Zach said. He wasn't a violent man by nature but, oh, he was really feeling the urge to hit something.

"Those are my granddaughters," Judge Connelly said. "Everything that concerns them concerns me. If you marry Jessica, I will ruin you. I will find a way to revoke your liquor license and drive your brewery right out of Bluff Point."

"We're the largest employer in the town since the local lobster industry dried up, so good luck with that," he said. He crossed his arms over his chest. This self-important blowhard couldn't touch him.

"You think you know so much." Judge Connelly shook his head. "You know nothing and you haven't seen the last of me."

"I hope not," Zach said. He studied the man in front of him, who was turning a mottled shade of purple. "You are my future stepdaughters' grandfather, I would assume you're going to stay in their lives and will, of course, also be in mine."

"Stop!" Judge Connelly barked. "Don't you play with me. I deal with smart-mouthed slackers like you every day in court. You want to keep up the joking, fine, I will do everything in my power to take those girls away from Jessica permanently."

"That's crazy," Zach argued. "Why would you do that? Why are you so angry? What's wrong with you?"

"What's wrong with me?" Judge Connelly looked incensed. "My son is gone. Gone! And why? Because that woman, Jessica, is an unfit wife and mother. She drove him away from his children, his home, his family. Everything I ever tried to give to him, a good life with a loving woman in a happy home, he has rejected, and why? Because she is poison and she drove him away. She drove my only child away from me and I can never forgive her."

Zach gaped at him. He had heard some pretty screwed up revisionist history in his time but this guy took the cake.

He could not let it stand.

"Are you even listening to yourself speak?" he asked. "You know you can repeat a lie a million times but it doesn't make it true."

"I am not—"

"Oh, please, you're spouting so much fiction, you're going to find yourself shelved in a library. You know it, I know it, your wife knows it, hell, everyone knows it. You won't succeed at taking the girls from Jessie, and the only people you are going to hurt are the girls because they won't have their grandparents in their lives and that's just sad."

"You have no idea—"

Zach held up his hand in a *stop* gesture. Maybe it was because he was thirty years younger, six inches taller, forty pounds of solid muscle heavier, but for whatever reason, the judge let him speak. Which was good because Zach knew it was time someone called this jackass on his bullshit and Zach was thrilled to be the guy to do it.

"Let's be real here for a second," Zach said. "Jessie is an amazing mother. Look at those girls. They shine like bright, beautiful diamonds. Why? Because of their mother not their father. Jessie has a big heart and a lot of love to give and I am betting that she gave it all to your son, and being the selfish prick that he is, he didn't appreciate it one bit."

Judge Connelly opened his mouth to argue but Zach shook his head.

"Nope, I'm not done yet. I think Jessie was probably as wonderful of a wife as she is a mother. I am betting that your son spent their seven-year marriage trying to crush her soul with his lying, cheating, and drinking. None of that is Jessie's fault. All of that is your son's fault. If you want to blame someone for the end of their marriage, blame your son. You know, the guy who is MIA, missing holidays, father-daughter talent shows, yeah, all of that."

The judge's nostrils were flaring. He was practically quivering with rage. Zach was giving zero fucks about the judge's fragile feelings.

"Just so we're clear, if you go after Jessie, you're going to have to take on me and most of the town of Bluff Point. She works for Dr. Tolliver at the animal clinic and everyone, and I do mean everyone, loves her. Hurt her or the girls and they will fight you with everything they've got and that's assuming there's anything left of you when I get finished."

"Are you threatening me?" Judge Connelly demanded.

"I thought it was more of a promise," Zach said. He gave the judge a hard stare until the man turned away. Good thing because Zach's more natural tendency to crack a joke in times of tension was bubbling to the surface and he didn't think he could squelch it much longer.

Chapter 29

Judge Connelly spun on his heel and stormed toward his wife and the girls. He muttered a terse good-bye at the girls and grabbed his wife's elbow in his hand. He started to pull her away and she dug in her heels and shook him off.

She bent over and hugged the girls close, promising to see them again soon. The judge stood fuming but he waited. When he took his wife's arm again, Zach noted he was much more gentle.

Audrey Connelly gave him a concerned look, and Zach forced himself to give her as much of a smile as he could muster. He didn't think she was participating in her husband's campaign of terror but he wasn't going to be overly friendly either. If she had any influence with her husband at all, now was the time to use it.

Zach strode over to the girls and picked up their skates. They each latched onto his coat sleeves as he made his way to the front door. He was seized by the overwhelming feeling that he wanted to protect them and keep them safe. They were so precious, so innocent and young. When he glanced down at them, they looked up at him as if he knew what he was doing in this crazy adult world. He was a fraud. He didn't have a clue and, wow, adulting was really hard. So he reached for his old standby, a joke.

"Why kind of key opens a banana?" he asked.

The girls frowned and then shrugged.

"A monkey," he said. He made a funny face. Gracie laughed and Maddie rolled her eyes.

"How about some ice cream?" he asked.

"Yeah!" they answered together.

Zach knew he was doing it to extend his time with the girls. Now that Jessie had rejected him for marriage, he didn't know what role he was going to have in their lives. The thought filled him with an unhappy feeling of panic.

Today had been on the dramatic side and he wanted to make sure they were okay after seeing their grandparents. He also wanted to go eat his feelings. All of this emotion these Connelly women were pulling out of him was straight-up exhausting and yet if he thought about it, he had never felt more alive.

Zach paced around his house, while Rufus watched him from the couch. He had dropped off the girls after ice-skating and ice cream, deciding not to mention his altercation with the judge to Jessie. She had enough to worry about without adding Zach's kerfuffle to it.

Things had been awkward between them. Despite the time apart or maybe because if it, Zach felt as if there were a million things they'd left unsaid. He knew there was for him. He'd asked her to marry him but he hadn't told her the real reason. He'd stuffed the cotton balls of logic and problem solving around his suggestion of marriage as if they could cushion the raw truth, which was that he was in love with her. He wanted to marry her not to help out her and the girls but because he loved her and he wanted to be with her. Always.

But since she'd said no to him, where could they go from here? He couldn't tell her he loved her now because she likely wouldn't believe him. She'd think he was just saying that to pressure her to say yes to marrying him. Damn it.

He had totally messed this up. And what was killing him, what was crushing him all the way down to his soul, was the fact that she was a couple hundred yards away in her house, alone, just like him, when they could be together. He felt as if they'd barely begun exploring what could be between them and it was over.

The snowy front yards between them might as well be a snow-covered Alp for all he knew how to close the gap. He'd been texting the crew and none of their suggestions had helped.

Go knock on the door and ask to borrow something, Sam had texted.

Yes, Sam, the same idiot who'd been pining for Jillian while ignoring Gina, the girl who'd been pining for him for months. This was why nothing happened for Sam. He lived his life on the sidelines.

Send her a naked picture. That was Carly's suggestion.

No, don't! James, Carly's fiancé, responded immediately.

Bring her food, Emma texted.

Whoopie pies! Jillian shamelessly self-promoted.

That only works on pregnant women, Brad wrote.

I disagree, Mac responded.

Just go tell her how you feel, Gavin, usually the voice of reason, texted. This suggestion did not seem at all reasonable to him.

Now that's a bold maneuver, Gina texted, stating, Zach believed, what everyone was thinking. Then she put up an emoji of a knuckle bump.

Zach couldn't do it. Jessie had already shot him down once. He didn't think he would survive it again. And so, he stood in his kitchen, as these windows offered the best view of her house, looking out across the snowy lawn like a sad pitiful clown; he was just missing the bad face paint and the rainbow wig.

He watched the girls' light go out in their room. He glanced at the clock. Bedtime. He missed their hugs. Their soft kisses on his cheek as he pulled the covers up to their chins. The smell of kids' shampoo, drying in their post-bath hair.

And he missed the tingling anticipation he'd feel now that he'd get to be alone with Jessie, to sit by the fire and talk or watch a movie, which really meant him watching her watch a movie.

He liked the way she got lost in the story, with a fur-rowed brow, or a ghost of a smile, or when she belly laughed at a particularly funny part and looked at him to share the laugh. He had laughed but not because he thought the movie was funny—he usually had no idea what was going on—but because she made him happy.

And now that they'd spent the night together and he knew her more intimately, he missed the scent of her, the soft feel of her body against his, the sexy way she moaned when she was lost to the sensation of him fitting inside of her so perfectly.

He missed how she looked deeply into his eyes after they made love, as if looking to see how honest he was being. He knew it came from her past and he didn't mind when she studied him like that because he liked having her full attention. He liked that she might see how he really felt about her without him having to tell her. Gawd, he was such a chickenshit. His friends were right. He needed to tell her.

He continued watching her house, knowing that she was likely upstairs getting ready for bed. That thought made him throb. Damn it.

But then he saw a silhouette move into the window across from his. It was a woman's form and he knew from having loved on those curves that it was Jessie. It occurred to him that she could see him, too. Well, hell.

The lust rose up sharp inside of him, making his cock hard and his brain buzz. He wanted her. He wanted her naked in his arms, coming apart for him while he pumped into her. He wanted to hear her moan, and even more specifically, he wanted her to cry out his name. The vision was sweaty, it was carnal, it was like a fever raging through his body and he knew he wouldn't get any peace until he made love to Jessie again.

He saw her pressing her hand to the window pane. If a silhouette could cry out in longing, hers was. He grabbed his jacket off of a nearby chair, and called out to Rufus, who was asleep on the couch, "Don't wait up."

In seconds, he was across the icy lawn and stepping onto her porch. She met him outside, throwing herself at him, almost knocking them both back into the snow. Zach caught her in his arms and hauled her up against him while his mouth sought hers in a kiss that staked a claim, his lips on hers, his tongue sweeping inside her mouth, tasting her and letting her taste him, too.

In three strides he had her jacked up against the wall, tucked into a dark corner of the porch. His thigh wedged in between her legs, holding her in place as his hands moved up from her hips to her breasts, shoving aside her sweater so he could cup her breasts and gently pinch her nipples between his fingertips.

"Zach, I need—" Jessie's words were cut off with a gasp as she arched against him.

This. This was exactly what he'd needed. Her coming apart for him. Jessie pushed his clothes aside. She reached for the snap on his jeans but he brushed her hands away. He wanted to savor every bit of her. He didn't want to be rushed.

"Tell me, my girl," he said, his voice a gruff growl, his breath steaming out between them on the freezing air. "What do you need?"

He moved his mouth to one nipple and gently bit down. She moaned. She dug her fingers into his hair and rocked her hips on his thigh. His erection got so hard he thought it might break through his pants without assistance. To want someone this much felt amazing. He moved his mouth to her other breast. He licked, then sucked, then nipped. She practically melted right off his leg.

"Tell me," he said. He ran his mouth up the side of her neck and she made a soft grunting noise, as if words were beyond her ability right now. Zach smiled into her hair.

He grabbed her hips, dragging her slowly up and down his thigh, causing the constant rubbing friction against her clitoris to work her into a mild frenzy. The soft cries coming from her throat were making him insane in the best possible way.

Still, he wanted to hear her say what she needed from him, just him, because he wanted to believe he was the only man who could ever make her feel this way.

He stopped dragging her across his thigh. He put her down on her feet and spun her away from him. He took both of her hands and braced them against the side of the house. He pressed his erection into her bottom and she arched back against him.

He moved his hands to the front of her pants and unfastened them, pulling them down just enough for him to slide his hand inside and cup her warmth. Holy fuck, she was wet for him.

Zach sucked in a breath and locked his knees to keep them from buckling. He lazily circled her opening with his fingers, teasing and taunting her. He pressed one finger to her hyper sensitive clit and then he pressed his body the length of hers and whispered in her ear.

"Tell me what you want, Jessie," he demanded.

She was shivering but judging by the heat coming off of her skin, it wasn't from the cold. Her breath was sewing in and out in harsh pants, her entire body was tight. He circled her opening with his fingers again and again. He teased the nub at the center of her, flicking over it again and again. Incoherent moans poured out of her mouth, while she pushed her hips against his hand. She was close, so close, but Zach wanted the words.

"Tell me, my girl, what do you want?" he asked. He removed his hand and she let out a small cry of distress.

"You, Zach, I want you," she said. She turned her head and found his mouth with hers. She kissed him hard then slid her tongue against the seam of his lips until he opened his mouth and she thrust inside, showing him with her lips and tongue exactly what she wanted from him.

It was Zach's turn to groan and he returned his hands

to her pants, pushing them down so he could have access to all of her. With one hand, he worked her over, sliding his fingers inside her, while with his other hand, he unfastened his jeans, letting his cock spring free and press up against the cleft in her backside.

Jessie made a deliciously sexy noise in the back of her throat and pressed against him. Zach was pretty sure he was going to come right there. When she would have turned to face him, he put his hands over hers, still braced against the wall, and held her in place while he continued to kiss her, gently biting her lower lip.

Knowing his strength of will was slipping with his need to be inside her, he swiftly found the condom in his wallet and moved away from her, just for seconds, so he could slip it on. He thought the freezing cold air would hip check his desire to the curb or at the very least bring him back from the brink. Nope. If anything the contrast between her heat and the cold made him even crazier.

"Jessie, I can't wait," he said.

"Then don't," she said.

She had barely uttered the words when he grabbed her hip with one hand and his cock with the other and slid into her with one smooth push. He locked an arm around her hips and held her still, her back to his front, the intoxicating smell of her filling his senses.

He could feel his cock pulsing inside of her. She was hot and wet and he was completely surrounded by her. It was perfect.

When he felt her clench around him, he had to force himself not to move for fear that he would take her hard, right up against the side of the house with no more finesse than a dog humping a person's leg.

"Ah, Jessie, you feel so amazing," he said. "I'm trying to slow it down."

She pressed back against him, sinking him even deeper into her heat as she whispered, "Why? Take me hard, Zach, make me yours."

Fuck. All reason was lost. Zach grabbed her hips and pounded into her. Harder, faster, hotter, in and out, again

and again. The exquisite tightening of her muscles con-
tracting around him when she released ratcheted his entire
body into one scorching pulse point of possession, but as
he heard her moan and felt her buck against him, her body
clenching him so hard he wanted to shout, he wasn't sure
who was possessing whom.

All he knew as he felt himself pour into her welcoming
warmth with one fierce thrust was that she was his and he
was hers and nothing was going to change that. Not now,
not ever, no matter how this played out.

He hated leaving her but the winter air made the sweat
on their skin icy cold. Zach tied off the condom and dumped
it in his pocket to throw out at home, then he zipped and
fastened Jessie back into her clothes and pulled up his own
pants.

She still had her hands braced on the wall and her head
was hanging down in between her arms as if she'd forgotten how to move. Zach hugged her back against him and
turned her toward the house.

"It's cold," he said. "You need to get inside."

She turned in his arms and hugged him close. Zach
opened his coat and pulled her into his warmth. She fit so
perfectly against him. He could have stayed there all night,
except the temperature was supposed to drop into the teens
and even with the heat they produced, he didn't think
they'd survive it. Pity.

He loosened his hold and spun her toward the door. He
needed to get her inside where she was safe and warm.
Where he could kiss her again and look into her pretty
blue eyes to try and figure out what she was thinking or
feeling.

They stepped quietly into the house. Only one lamp
was on downstairs, its soft light bleeding into the foyer
where they stood. Zach wasn't sure what to do. He didn't
know what Jessie was looking for from him and he didn't
want to scare her off or let her mistakenly think he was
retreating. Maybe Gavin was right. Maybe he should tell
her how he felt.

Jessie took his hand and started to lead him into the

house. He took this as a good sign. She paused in the living room, to turn in his arms and kiss him. As erotic as making love in the freezing cold had been, Zach was just as happy to make out with her in the warm, cozy house. At least here he didn't have to worry about any body parts freezing off.

"I wasn't sure how you felt about us after this afternoon," she said. "I hope I didn't hurt you when I said I couldn't marry you."

"Nah," Zach said. Really, her refusal hadn't been much worse than a hard shot to the man junk. "I'm good."

Jessie leaned back and studied his face. She narrowed her eyes at him. "Is that the equivalent of a woman saying, 'I'm fine'?"

"I have no idea what you mean," he said. Yeah, a guy saying he was "good" was totally the equivalent of a woman saying she was "fine," but he was not about to admit it. Not when he'd just gotten her back in his arms.

"I really do appreciate that you want to help me," she said. "More than you know."

She ran her fingers through his hair, combing it back from his forehead while scoring his scalp and making him want to thump his foot on the ground like Rufus when Zach found his tickle spot.

"It's more than that," Zach said.

He shook his head, shaking off the spell she was putting him under and sending his hair every which way. He needed to tell her this. He needed her to know. "I care about—"

"Momma!" Maddie cried from upstairs. "Momma!"

Jessie gave him a rueful look. She turned her head and called, "I'll be right there, baby." Then she turned back to Zach. "Go ahead, what were you going to say?"

"Momma, I'm thirsty," Maddie cried. She sounded as desperate as if she were stranded in the Sahara and her camel had just died.

"Coming," Jessie called back.

"You'd better go before she wakes up Gracie," Zach said. He leaned forward and kissed her swiftly but with meaning. "Tomorrow after work, let's talk, yes?"

"Yes." Jessie nodded. "I'd like that."

Her eyes moved over him and Zach felt his blood run thick again. How it was possible after they'd just banged each other stupid, he had no idea, but there it was.

On the off chance she was just using him for his body, he said, "Clothed."

Jessie's grin burst across her face like the sun burning away a cloud and she said, "For starters."

Then she scampered away from him, up the stairs with a giggle, and it took everything he had not to run her to the ground.

"Momma!" Maddie now sounded on the brink of expiring.

Well, that helped. He blew Jessie a kiss and headed out the door, locking it behind him.

In the average nine-to-five workday, there were four hundred and eighty minutes, or twenty-eight thousand eight hundred seconds, every one of which felt like eternity. E-T-E-R-N-I-T-Y. At about two in the afternoon, Zach was sure the clock had started moving backwards. Never had he felt this way about seeing someone.

All day long he took out his phone to text her, but he didn't. He even debated taking Rufus into the animal clinic for a checkup just because he really didn't think he could take it anymore. At fifteen minutes to five, he cracked.

He shut off his computer, forwarded his phone to voice mail, grabbed his coat, and headed for the door. The brewery was less than a mile from Zach's house. In an old factory building that they had bought cheap and renovated, it was surrounded by the small industrial houses that had been built for the original factory workers, which was one of the reasons Zach had bought into the neighborhood; he couldn't beat the commute to work.

Now it would get him to his girl. Would it be bad form to be sitting on her porch when she got home? He didn't care. He jogged down the hallway of offices toward the exit.

"Hold up there, Flash." Sam stepped out of his office, blocking Zach's way. "Where are you rushing off to?"

"I have to see a man about a dog," he said, hoping Sam would take the hint.

"You're going to see Jessie, am I right?" Sam asked. He pretended to stretch, effectively blocking the hall with his extended arms.

"Maybe," Zach said. God, did his face just get hot?

"Oh, my god, you're blushing," Sam said. He said it like an accusation, as if a crime had been committed.

"Sorry," Zach said. He made a shooing motion with his hand. Sam didn't budge.

"Hey, Brad, Zach's blushing!" Sam called over his shoulder. Zach's shoulders slumped. He was never going to get out of here.

Brad's head popped out of his office door. He looked like a gopher. He squinted at Zach. "If you have the flu, keep it to yourself."

"It's not the flu, he's in lo-o-o-ove," Sam said. "So, did you tell her?"

"Not yet," he said. "I'm working up to it."

"After the proposal?" Brad asked. "I'm kind of thinking you're working backwards here."

"Wouldn't be the first time," Zach said. He glanced at Brad. "How did you know with Emma? How did you know she was the one?"

Brad shrugged. "I don't know. I liked the look of her, her personality was a plus, I enjoyed being with her, and then one day, I realized that I never wanted to be with anyone else."

"So, unlike this sloppy rush job Zach is doing it took you what, a couple of months, a year, to know this about Emma?"

"Yeah, no, I figured it out pretty much by the end of our first date," Brad said. "Which I told her that very night."

He grinned at Zach, who laughed in relief. Thank god it wasn't just him suffering from this all-consuming-ass-over-ears-crazy-which-way-is-up-dizzy sort of madness called love.

When Sam glanced between them, shaking his head as if they were pitiful, Brad leapt on him, pinning his arms behind his back.

"Run, Zach, run! Don't let this sad single boy stop you," Brad yelled.

Zach laughed at his two idiot best friends and raced from the building. He drove straight to his house where he collected Rufus, knowing that the dog was happiest when he was with the girls and the kitten, much like Zach.

Then he and the dog hiked through the snow to Jessie's. Last night had been beyond a doubt the most singular sexual experience of his life, but tonight they needed to talk. He needed to tell her how he felt. For real.

Chapter 30

He noticed a small white van parked in Jessie's driveway. He glanced at the emblem on the side. It looked like it belonged to the local animal control office. He felt his stomach drop. Had the judge really sent someone to take Chaos away? That prick. This would destroy Maddie and Gracie.

He hurried to the front door. He knocked. No one answered. He tried the door. It was unlocked so he strode into the house. The girls were seated at the kitchen table, working on some sort of craft that involved gobs of yarn and toilet paper tubes.

They both glanced up at him with grins and he felt his heart turn over. They were okay. Man, he had missed them today.

"Hello, my favorite girls," he said. "What are you making?"

"Penguins," Maddie said. She put down her bottle of glue and did her fancy high-five greeting with him. She had recently added a very Michael Jackson bent knee kick. Zach did his best to keep up.

"Marsupials," Gracie said. They exchanged their high five and he realized he was relying on muscle memory now; he didn't even have to think about the moves anymore.

Both girls sat down and Zach looked at the gluey, crusty yarn mess in front of them. "Penguins, marsupials, of course they are. They're incredible." Not a total lie. "Where's your mom?"

"Upstairs with Miranda," Gracie said. "She wanted to meet Chaos."

"Cool. I'll be right back." He kissed them both on the tops of their heads and strode toward the stairs. "Hello? Jessie?"

"Up here," she answered.

Zach took the stairs two at a time. He banged into the girls' room to find Jessie and another woman sitting on the floor of the bedroom with Chaos sprawled on the throw rug between them. He was on his back with his overly large kitten feet in the air, swiping at a cat toy that consisted of a feather on a string that Jessie was teasing him with. The woman sitting with Jessie was laughing at the kitten.

"Oh, look at you," the woman spoke to Chaos. "Who's a warrior? Who is the king of his castle?"

She was wearing a navy blue uniform that consisted of baggy coveralls with the same animal control logo that was on the van on the pocket of the shirt. Her long, tightly curled hair was in a ponytail that fit through the opening in the back of the ball cap that was on her head. The cap had the logo, too. Zach took it to mean the department really wanted people to know their employees were with animal control.

"Hey," he said as he strode into the room. "What's happening?"

"Hi," Jessie greeted him. If she felt weird about last night's shenanigans, it didn't show. "Zachary Caine, this is Miranda Reinhart, she works for animal control. Apparently, they got a call about the ferocious beast I am fostering who is a danger to my girls."

"Your father-in-law," Zach said.

Jessie nodded, looking pained. "I can't believe he did that. I mean, yes, Chaos has been a little challenging as a foster, but it's just because he's so young. I am sure he'll mellow out."

"He only jumped on the judge's pant leg because he was trying to protect you and the girls," Zach said. "I'm sure of it."

"That could be," Miranda agreed. "If he felt the judge was a hostile presence, he might have attacked. Can't really fault him for defending his family, now can we?"

"So, you don't feel you have to take him?" Jessie asked.

"Nah, he's fine," Miranda said. "But if you want me to take him to find him a forever home, I can do it tonight. He's old enough now."

"No!" Zach cried. Both women looked at him and he said, "I mean he's still so little, shouldn't you wait until he's bulked up a little before sending him out into the cold, cruel world?"

Jessie laughed. "You have your own foster animal to worry about but yes, I think I'll wait a few more weeks."

Zach resisted the urge to do a fist pump. He wasn't sure why he felt like his fate and Chaos's were entwined, but he did and if he bought the kitty some time then maybe he was doing the same thing for himself, especially after last night.

"Well, it won't hurt him to get a bit bigger," Miranda said. She glanced at Zach and then tipped her head to the side. "Wait, did Jessie say your name was Zachary Caine?"

For a brief second, Zach thought about denying it. It was never a good thing when a woman looked at him the way Miranda was, like she should know him from somewhere but she couldn't remember where. Usually, it meant Zach had hooked up with her friend, sister, cousin, and one time that he tried to forget about, her mom.

If this was the situation, it would not be setting the tone for the evening that he was hoping for; he decided to go for vague and said, "Maybe."

"Zach!" Jessie gave him an exasperated look.

"Yes, sorry, it's me," he said. He offered his hand and they shook. "I live next door."

"Are you the same Zach who gave Judge Connelly the what-for at the ice-skating rink yesterday?" Miranda asked.

Zach felt Jessie's gaze drill him from where she sat on the floor. Oh, this was not going to go well.

"Uh, we had a chat, yes, we did," he said.

He didn't look at Jessie. He didn't have to. He could feel the hot weight of her stare on his face and he knew without looking that she was significantly not happy about this bit of news.

"A chat?" Miranda laughed. "That's not the way I heard it. Rich, the Zamboni driver, said he heard you tell the judge to go to hell—"

"No!" Zach interrupted. He glanced at Jessie—her eyes were huge—and he shook his head. "I did not say that exactly."

"That's not how I heard it. Good for you," Miranda said. She rose to her feet and slugged Zach on the shoulder with her fist. He staggered back a few steps.

"Yow! Do they have you wrestling bears as part of animal control?" he asked.

She grinned at him as if this was high praise. Well, okay, then.

"I'll walk you out, Miranda," Jessie said. Zach went to follow but she turned on him and snapped, "Don't move."

Zach froze. He let out a slow breath. Just like that, he had a feeling tonight wasn't going to go like he planned. Damn it. He needed to do some damage control and he needed to do it fast.

He debated texting the Maine crew. That wouldn't work. He wondered if he could have flowers delivered to Jessie before she got back up here. Unlikely. He could try and distract her with sex. Well, that thought made him warm all over but if he tried it on her and she wasn't in the mood, it could have dire—as in he'd never get to see her naked again—consequences.

He felt something tug on his shoelace. He glanced down to find Chaos on the prowl. He moved his foot; Chaos froze, wiggled his behind, and then pounced on the shoelace. The lace put up a valiant fight but Chaos flopped onto his back, with the thick string caught between his paws while he chomped on the plastic end with his tiny cat fangs.

"You know this whole thing is your fault," Zach said. "If you hadn't climbed up onto my roof and dragged your people over to my house, we likely never would have met. I would be home alone with your buddy Rufus right now, trying to figure out how to fill my night so I didn't feel so damn lonely."

He bent over and scooped up the cat. Scrawny and as light as marshmallow, the cat draped himself on Zach's hand. His chin rested on Zach's wrist and he was purring. Zach held him up so they were nose to nose.

"I owe you an awful lot, little guy," he said. "You changed everything for me."

Chaos tipped his head to the side in an *Aw, shucks* sort of pose and Zach smiled. He scratched the little fella under the chin and behind the ears until the cat sounded like he had a V8 engine inside his chest.

"Don't you worry, Chaos. I promise I won't let the judge have you taken from the girls," he said.

"Ah!" a gasp sounded from the door and Zach turned to find Maddie and Gracie standing there with Jessie right behind them. From the looks on their faces, he suspected they'd heard him. Uh-oh.

"Chaos!" Maddie rushed forward. She held up her little hands and Zach gently set Chaos into them.

Gracie wrapped an arm around her sister and put her hand on her cat. "Why? Why would Grandpa want to take our cat away?"

"Because he's a me—"

"He means well," Jessie interrupted Zach. "It's because he means well. But, of course, we won't let anyone take our boy. He's our foster and it's our job to find him a good home."

"But why can't he stay with us?" Gracie asked. "He loves us and we love him, doesn't that make us family?"

"Well, we don't know what's going to happen and it

might not be fair to keep Chaos unless we can be sure that we can provide a good forever home for him."

"I'll give him my bed," Maddie said. "That's good, right?"

"And he can have my food," Gracie added. "I won't miss it."

Zach felt his heart crack wide open into two pieces. These girls were killing him.

"Your grandpa isn't going to take Chaos," he said. "I won't let him. I promise."

"Thank you, Zach," the girls said together and they both hugged him.

"Zach, can I have a word?" Jessie was looking at him like she wanted to strangle him.

Zach hugged the girls and kissed each of their heads. He wasn't stalling, he needed the courage.

"Girls, supper will be ready at five thirty," Jessie said. "Why don't you stay up here and wash up? I'll call you down in a few minutes."

"Yes, Momma," they answered. They never took their eyes off Chaos, however, and Zach would have been surprised if they had a clue as to what their mother had just said.

Jessie turned and led the way downstairs to the kitchen. Zach figured she had been making dinner when Miranda showed up, as all of the ingredients for a salad were on the kitchen counter just waiting to be put together. A glance at the oven and Zach saw a baking dish that was emitting a truly fantastic smell. His stomach rumbled.

He watched as Jessie picked up the biggest knife in the block and began chopping the head of lettuce. *Whack. Whack. Whack.*

He tried not to flinch. Then she put the cucumber on the chopping block. This time he did flinch, repeatedly. When she put the tomato on the board, he reached forward and grabbed her hand.

"Were we going to talk?" he asked. She glared at him and he released her.

"I'm trying to figure out what I want to say, you know,

without a lot of swear words," she said. She waved the knife at him and he leaned back. "I just can't believe you."

"At all, in general, or at the moment?" he asked. "Can you give me a little more to go on here?"

"How could you have spoken to the judge and not told me?" she asked. "It's even become local gossip, everyone in town knows except for me."

"Not ev—"

"And how could you argue with him?" she cried. "He's already trying to take the girls. You can't antagonize him."

"Listen, my girl—" he began but she cut him off.

"No! I'm not your girl," she said. "I'm Maddie's and Gracie's mother and that is it. Don't you see? I'm it. I'm the only person they can rely on, the only person who will be there for them no matter what, who loves them unconditionally. And I can't let my feelings for anyone else interfere with that."

Zach studied her. She was mad, no question, but she'd also just admitted she had feelings for him. He felt his heart lift in his chest.

"So, you admit you feel something for me," he said.

She looked at him. She opened her mouth to protest and then she shook her head.

"What?" he asked.

"After all that I just said, your takeaway is that I have feelings for you," she said. She shook her head as if she couldn't believe she was having this conversation. "Of course I have feelings for you, otherwise the things that have happened between us . . ."

Her voice trailed off as if she didn't know how to say it, so Zach helped out, and said, "Orgasms multiple."

Jessie's cheeks turned a hot shade of pink and her gaze darted around the kitchen as if the dishwasher or the oven might have overheard him. Then her blue eyes met his but she didn't look happy.

"Yes, that," she said. "That couldn't have happened if there wasn't some level of trust and caring between us, but it doesn't matter."

Zach raised his eyebrows. "I don't want to be argumentative, but I think it matters a lot."

"No, it doesn't, because this thing"—she paused and gestured between them with the knife—"can't go on."

"What?" Zach asked. "What are you saying?"

"I'm saying that this was fun but I have to protect my girls, and I can't do that if you lie to me," she said.

"I didn't lie," Zach protested. "I just didn't mention a conversation I had with that miserable—"

"It's a lie by omission," she snapped. "Which is the same thing."

"It's not the same thing," he argued. "I was trying to protect you."

"Lying to me is not protecting me," Jessie argued. "The only way I can anticipate how to deal with the judge is if I know what's going on at all times. If you lie to me—"

"Again, it wasn't a lie," he insisted. "I planned on talking to you about it."

"When?"

"I don't know. I hadn't figured that part out yet," he said.

Zach seldom lost his temper. He had discovered early on that it gained him nothing, and life was much more fun if he found the humor in every situation. Right now, he was struggling to do so.

"Sure you were. You can call it whatever you want, but I call it a lie," she snapped. "Which makes you no better than my ex-husband."

Zach felt as if she'd taken her big knife and stabbed him in the chest with it. He stared at her in shock. Had she actually just told him he was no better than the man who had abandoned her and her girls after being a drunken, cheating, emotionally abusive asshole for years?

He stepped away from the counter. He knew she was upset and, yes, he probably should have told her about his convo with the judge right away, but he didn't think anything he had done justified the comparison she had just made.

When he glanced at her blue eyes, they were fierce. Her lips compressed into a thin line. She wasn't rushing to apologize; in fact, she looked like she was going to hold her ground. That wasn't going to work for him.

"You know, I think I'll get going," he said. "I need to take Rufus for a walk, and I think you and I could use some space."

Jessie nodded. She lowered her gaze to the hacked-up vegetables in front of her. She didn't even look him in the eye. Zach felt like his insides had been twisted up like a cloth to let out all of the moisture or in his case all of the feelings. It didn't work. The feelings were still there and they hurt like a bitch.

He turned on his heel and whistled to Rufus, who leapt off the couch and followed him to the door. It wasn't that Zach was stalling, but he took his time putting on his coat and hat and gloves. Jessie didn't come after him. When he peeked around the door frame into the kitchen she was tossing her salad with a large spoon and fork, looking as miserable as Zach felt.

He wanted to go to her and hug her, whisper in her ear that he was sorry and that they'd figure it out. But he didn't think a hug would be welcome right now, if ever. It took everything he had to walk out the door with Rufus and not look back.

Chapter 31

The girls wanted to know where Zach was. Jessie didn't want to tell them she had driven him away with her harsh words. Ugh, how could she have been so cold and so cruel as to compare him to Seth? She was an idiot.

The hurt in his warm brown gaze had been like plunging her knife into her own chest. Zach, who had been nothing but kind and loving, not just to her but to the girls and Chaos, too, hadn't deserved such harsh treatment. And she couldn't even excuse herself by saying she was just so freaked out about the judge trying to take away her girls. Well, she could say that but it didn't justify how she had treated him.

Not wanting to lie to her daughters, Jessie told them the truth. As she dished out the baked ziti, she said that she had been unfair to Zach and had hurt his feelings. She explained that she was concerned that Zach hadn't told her about running into their grandfather at the ice rink and that she had reacted badly when learning about it.

"That's okay, Momma," Maddie said. She gave her a somber look. "All you have to do is say you're sorry. Zach will forgive you."

"Sometimes saying you're sorry isn't good enough," Jessie said. She figured she'd better prepare the girls in case Zach decided he'd had enough of her, what with her rejecting his adorably crazy idea to get married and now comparing him to her ex. Gah, even the thought of it made her a bit ill.

"But you always say that telling the person you're sorry makes it better," Gracie said. "Won't it make it better if you say you're sorry to Zach?"

Jessie let out a small sigh and pushed her pasta around her plate. "It gets more complicated when you're a grown-up."

"Will we ever see him again?" Maddie asked.

Honesty. That was what Jessie had demanded of Zach. Could she offer her girls any less?

"I don't know," she said. "Maybe not as much as we used to."

"But why?" Gracie sobbed. "Why?"

Jessie reached out to put her hand on Gracie's arm, but Gracie flinched away.

"No! I want Zach. He's my friend and I don't want to lose him and if I can't have him then I don't want you either!"

"Gracie!" Jessie stared at her daughter in shock. Gracie was her quiet one, her pleaser, the one who always tried to make everything okay.

"I want Zach!" Gracie repeated.

She shoved back her chair and turned away but not before Jessie saw a tear drip down her cheek. Gracie scrubbed it away with her fist and ran for the stairs.

"Gracie!" Jessie called again.

A door slam was Gracie's only response.

Jessie leaned back in her seat. Maddie was eating her ziti, seemingly unaffected by her sister's revolt.

"Why aren't you mad at me?" she asked.

Maddie swallowed her bite of food and shrugged. "Because Zach will come back."

"How do you know?"

"Because he's one of the good guys," she said. She forked more pasta into her mouth, chewed, and swallowed.

The simple truth of the statement made Jessie's heart hurt. Zach was one of the good guys and she had done him wrong. She had treated him badly because she was so worried about her father-in-law. Okay, that was a lie to herself.

Jessie wasn't worried because Zach and the judge had a tiff. She wasn't thrilled about it but she wasn't that freaked out. She didn't like that he hadn't told her, but it wasn't an unforgivable offense.

No, the truth was she was terrified because she cared about Zach a lot more than she wanted to. Last night when she had jumped on him, it was because she just couldn't bear to be apart from him for one more second.

She missed him all day long and thought about him constantly. He made her laugh so hard she cramped, and when she was with him, she truly felt as if everything was going to be okay, not because he was going to rescue her, but because he was by her side. Just like he had stepped up during the blizzard. He didn't save her but he sure did help her from dealing with it all on her own.

He was the first man in her life who had proven to be dependable, and how had she treated him? By telling him he was like the one man in her life who had consistently let her down. Zach hadn't deserved that. She owed him an apology, a big one.

"I hope you're right," Jessie said. "I hope he comes back."

"I am, Momma, don't worry."

Jessie debated bringing Gracie's food up to her but then she didn't want to start a habit of letting her eat in her room when she was upset. That would not go well during the teen years. No, if Gracie was hungry, she could come back downstairs and get her food.

Jessie couldn't eat. She'd been looking forward to seeing Zach all day. Visions of their rendezvous on her porch last night had kept her distracted at work. Gavin had even laughed at her when she went to make coffee and had forgotten how to work the machine.

Zach, damn him, had come to mean so much to her. He

was great with the girls, he paid attention to them and laughed with them, helped them but also taught them to help themselves. It was more than she had ever hoped for when entertaining thoughts about meeting a man.

And then there was how he made her feel about herself. After years of being made to feel fat, ugly, and sexually repugnant, Zach made her feel beautiful and attractive and sexy as hell. He had helped her find her self-esteem again and she was so desperately grateful to him. Of course, there were also the orgasms multiple. She wasn't sure how she'd lived so long without them and she was pretty sure only Zach could make that happen for her; well, he was the only one she wanted to make that happen. She couldn't imagine letting anyone but him that close to her. Ever.

The hard press of his body against hers, the feel of his fingertips running a path across her skin, the way he watched her with so much affection and awe, and, yes, the way he called her "my girl." A small hiccup that was really a sob slipped out of Jessie's throat. Had she just thrown it all away?

Anger surged inside of her, not at Zach but at herself. The Connelly men had done enough damage to her and the girls. How could she let the judge damage the first good thing that had happened to her in years? She was so thick. She didn't deserve Zach, and she needed to tell him the first chance she got. *If* she got the chance.

When Maddie was finished eating, she left the table to go to her room and play with her sister. Jessie cleaned the kitchen and the dining room table before settling down on the couch and debating what to do.

She held her phone in her hand and considered texting the Maine crew but she didn't want to have to explain what a jerk she had been. The crew belonged more to Zach than to her and she didn't want to lose the tenuous group of friends that she had by showing what a butthead she was. She supposed that was selfish but she couldn't help it.

She wrote a message to Zach, apologizing, and then deleted it. She wrote another message trying to explain and then deleted that one, too. She didn't know what to say. She didn't know what to do. She felt as if she'd had happiness in hand and let it slip through her fingers.

She tipped her head back on the couch and felt one hot tear slip out of her eye and down her cheek. Just like Gracie, she scrubbed it away with her fist. She tried to give herself a pep talk. She tried to convince herself that everything would be okay but she was so very tired.

She tried to fight it but the sweet oblivion of sleep was too tempting a lure to ignore. She gave in and let it crash over her like a big wave pulling her out to sea.

Jessie awoke with a start and found herself staring at the ceiling of her living room. Her mouth was dry and her brain was fuzzy. When she'd fallen asleep, she'd fallen hard. She pushed up to a seated position on the couch and stretched. She wondered how much time had passed and realized she hadn't heard any noise coming from the girls during her unscheduled nap.

She paused in the kitchen to get a quick glass of water and glanced at the clock on the oven. It was almost seven. Good grief, she had been zonked out for about a half hour. She blamed the emotional toll of the past few days and the exercise she'd gotten with Zach last night out in the cold.

Just thinking about it made her warm all over and she was consumed by a sudden longing for Zach that had her reaching for her phone. She stared at the display screen for a few seconds and then put her phone away. She still didn't know what to say to him. Darn it.

It was just as well; she really needed to be wearing her mom hat at the moment. She tipped her head to the side and listened for any noise from upstairs but heard nothing. She didn't think the girls had the wherewithal to put themselves to bed but was pleased that they were playing quietly.

She walked up the stairs, knowing that she had to make things right with Gracie. She knew her girl would likely have calmed down by now and together they could make a plan about how Jessie could handle her apology to Zach. Maybe this was exactly what the girls needed to see. She could show by example how to apologize to Zach for being hurtful and wrong.

Jessie's own parents had never apologized for hurting each other or anyone else. Invariably, if something went wrong, they found a way to make it Jessie's fault. When her mother caught a cold right before a conference where she was scheduled to be the keynote speaker, Jessie was blamed for bringing home germs from school even though Jessie hadn't been sick at all that winter. That was where her life of apologizing for her existence had begun. It was a habit she hadn't broken until Zach.

Zach never seemed to expect her to apologize for the weather, the bad roads, other people's rudeness, the temperature of the hot water in the shower, or just for walking across the room too loudly. It was like having a blindfold ripped off, seeing what a good man he was. Why hadn't she seen this before she chased him away? But then, she probably had and it had probably scared her to death because Zach was exactly the sort of man she could love forever and if he didn't feel the same way about her then forever was going to be a very long time.

When she reached the girls' room, she was surprised to find the door was closed. She rapped on the wood three times before grabbing the doorknob and turning it to push the door open.

"Gracie, Maddie, it's time to get ready for bed," she said. "I'm sorry I—"

Jessie stopped talking. The room was empty.

"Girls!" Jessie cried. There was no answer.

Unease began to beat in her chest in a steady cadence. Jessie scanned the room, moving around the small space and checking under the beds and in the closet in case the girls were playing hide-and-seek with her.

They weren't here. She darted down the hall, looking in the bathroom, the other bedroom, and her room. There was no sign of them. Now the cadence of unease was beating harder and a bit more randomly in a stutter stop that was making it hard to breathe. She hurried down the stairs, calling their names. They didn't answer.

"Gracie and Maddie, you come out here right now!" she cried. "This is not funny! I mean it."

There was no answer and panic began to close up her throat. She hurried to the front door. She went right to the coatrack and looked where the girls usually hung their coats. The hooks were empty. The girls were gone!

Chapter 32

Jessie grabbed her jacket and dashed outside, flicking on the outside light as she went. It was dark with only a streetlight three houses down, illuminating the road. The temperature had dropped and the wind was bitterly cold. She scanned the darkness, looking for the familiar blue and purple coats of her girls.

She cupped her hands around her mouth and yelled, "Maddie!" She listened. Nothing. She did it again, shouting, "Gracie!"

She glanced at Zach's house. They'd been upset that they wouldn't be seeing him as much. Probably they had just gone over there. She ignored the fact that no lights were on in his house. There was nowhere else they could be.

She stomped through the snow. The remnants from the blizzard hadn't melted but the top had gotten crunchy so she dropped into the soft snow beneath with each step, having to haul her foot out of each hole. The going was slow and exhausting.

She kept calling for the girls. There was no answer. She soldiered on, refusing to flip out. Her girls were good. They wouldn't run away, they wouldn't take off, clearly they had just gone outside, maybe to see Zach, and had lost track of the time.

It was going to be okay. It was going to be fine.

Her throat clenched on a sob she refused to let loose, knowing that if she started to cry, she wouldn't be able to stop. It burned like a lump of fiery coal in her throat and she sucked in a frigid gulp of air, trying to ease the pain. It didn't work.

Where were her girls? Where could they have gone? If anything had happened to them . . . she couldn't think it.

She reached Zach's porch, finally, and dashed up the steps to his front door. His porch light wasn't on and she couldn't find the doorbell so she banged on the wooden door with her fist.

She waited. There was no answer. She banged again. Nothing. She moved to the side to peer into his living room window. It, too, was dark.

"Zach!" she cried. "Gracie! Maddie! Anyone! I'm not mad. I won't yell at you. I promise, just answer me . . ." Her throat closed up again, but she cried, "Please!"

There was no answer. Jessie felt herself begin to wilt as the crushing weight of terror pressed down on her. She couldn't live if anything happened to her girls. Her heart would cease to beat, there wouldn't be a reason to breathe, nothing would matter to her. Nothing.

Now the sobs were beginning to punch their way up out of her chest. She refused to give up. She refused to surrender. She ran down Zach's walkway to the road. She would ask all of the neighbors. She would search every yard, every house, every garage on the street if she had to, but she would find her girls.

What if they're lost out there in the cold night? a taunting voice whispered in her ear and she fired back. *And what if they aren't?*

What if they've been kidnapped? What if they hate you for sending Zach away? Jessie shook her head. She didn't want to hear it. She refused to be bullied by her fears. *What if they haven't been? And what if they don't?*

She hurried down the street, calling the girls' names and looking in each yard. The sidewalks had been cleared so she couldn't tell if the girls had walked that way recently. The Lewises, who lived across from Zach's house, heard her calling and came out to ask her if she was okay. She told them she couldn't find the girls and they both went to grab their jackets to help look. Jessie could have hugged them but she was too busy, hurrying to the next house.

A bark brought her attention back toward her house. She knew that bark. Rufus! She turned and started to run. Ahead on the sidewalk were Rufus and Zach. Rufus had his yellow Frisbee in his mouth and Zach was walking beside him.

"Zach! Are they with you?" she cried. Zach glanced up from his phone, looking surprised to see her.

"Jessie, what are you doing out here, without a hat and you're unzipped. Are you trying to freeze to death?" he asked.

Jessie didn't answer but grabbed his arms in a desperate hold. "The girls! I can't find them. Are they with you?"

"What? I haven't seen them since I left," he said. "What do you mean you can't find them?"

"After you left, Gracie got mad and stormed up to her room," she said. The sobs she'd been denying broke through her defenses and Jessie started to cry. "I fell asleep on the couch and when I woke up I went upstairs to talk to them, but they weren't in their room. I checked the whole house and couldn't find them and then I noticed that their coats were missing. Zach, they're gone. If they left right after I fell asleep at six thirty, then they've been out here for forty-five minutes."

Through her tears, Jessie saw Zach's face go a pasty shade of white. He pulled her close and hugged her hard. Then he grabbed her by the shoulders and looked her in the eye, and said, "We'll find them. We'll call everyone we know and we'll find them."

He took out his phone and made a call, "Coop, I need you. Jessie's girls are missing."

Jessie could hear Coop's voice on the other end. Zach told him everything Jessie had told him and then Zach ended the call. He dialed another number.

"Sam, we have a situation, I need you to get everyone to Jessie's house right now," he said. Jessie heard Sam on the other end. Zach's face was grim when he added, "The girls are missing."

Tears and snot were streaming down Jessie's face. Never had she been this afraid. Not when her parents died and she was left suddenly alone, not when her ex wiped out her entire inheritance and she had no idea how she would provide, not when she'd had her daughters, alone for both births because Seth was too drunk to be there. Never had she felt this powerless terror.

"Come on." Zach grabbed her hand and together they raced back to her house.

Jessie hadn't locked the door and Zach walked right in, leading her and Rufus. He shouted the girls' names. They didn't answer.

Jessie was shivering and crying and Zach tenderly cleaned up her face with a tissue and hugged her. "We're going to find them, don't you worry."

"I thought they might have gone to your house," she said.

"I wasn't at my house," he said. "Rufus and I were playing Frisbee at the park. I was trying to clear my head. God, if I'd just gone home maybe they would have come to me and everything would be okay."

"No, don't go there," Jessie said. She squeezed his shoulder. "This is my fault. I overreacted about your talk with the judge—" She stopped talking and stared at him. "The judge!"

Jessie grabbed her phone out of her pocket. She opened the display screen and thumbed through her contacts until she found her in-laws. She hit the dial button and held the phone to her ear.

"What are you thinking?" he asked.

"Maybe the judge took them," she said.

"And you're calling him?" Zach asked. "Do you think he'll admit it? Shouldn't we go over there?"

"No, I'm calling his wife," she said. "She's a good woman and she would never do anything like this to me."

"Hello?" Audrey Connelly answered.

"Hi, Audrey, it's Jessie."

"Jessie, what is it? You sound upset. Is everything all right?"

"No, it's not," she said. "Audrey, the girls are missing."

Audrey Connelly's shriek about split Jessie's eardrum. So there went her theory that her former father-in-law had taken them. After a hurried conversation, Audrey said that she and the judge were on their way.

Cooper arrived first. He called in backup and the police started to work the neighborhood. Officers Polson and Morgan went in two different directions, using the search-lights on top of their squad cars to search the area. According to Coop, they would fan out in slow-moving circles trying to see into every nook and cranny.

The Maine crew arrived next and the group spilt up into pairs, Carly and James, Gavin and Mac, Emma and Brad, and one threesome, Jillian and Sam and Gina. It was evident how scared they all were by the fact that no one joked about a ménage.

Much to Jessie's humbled surprise, Zach's field market-ers showed up to help with the search as well. Savannah, Marla, and Desiree, along with two other girls that Jessie had never met. They were all dressed in heavy winter gear and just like the Maine crew, they trotted out into the cold to search for the girls.

Jessie was ready to go back out and join the search. Surely, with this many people searching, they would be able to find the girls. She grabbed her hat and gloves and was headed for the door when Audrey and Judge Connelly arrived.

"Jessie, what happened?" Audrey cried as she rushed into the house and hugged Jessie close. "How can we help?"

Jessie returned the hug, reserving her fury for the man

who deserved it. If the judge hadn't threatened Jessie, none of this would have happened. She was sure of it.

"The girls are out in the cold somewhere, and do you want to know why?" Jessie asked the judge.

He met her stare but didn't say a word. Smart man.

"Because they heard me arguing with Zach about your altercation at the ice rink. I told Zach not to antagonize you because you threatened to take my girls away," Jessie said. "The girls were upset that they wouldn't be seeing him anymore so when I fell asleep, they left. I don't know where they are, I don't know if they're safe, and I don't know how to find them. This is your fault!"

"I hardly think—" the judge began to bluster but Jessie cut him off.

"Why? Why can't you just leave us be?"

Audrey's face paled with every word and then it flashed a bright hot red as she turned on her husband. "Did you do this? Did you threaten to take her children?"

"It's for their own goo—" Judge Connelly protested.

"Don't you dare!" Audrey interrupted him. "I watched while you spoiled our only son, giving him everything he ever wanted, so that he had no sense of respect or consequences, until he became a miserable, spoiled, angry, useless—"

"He's not—"

"Yes, he is!" Audrey yelled. "And the responsibility for that lies on you and me, because I didn't speak up when I should have. I didn't stop you when you coddled him, never holding him accountable for his actions. Well, I won't make the same mistake now. I will not stand silently by while you harm Jessie and the girls.

"Jessie is a wonderful mother who has given us two beautiful granddaughters. How dare you treat her with anything less than the utmost respect and gratitude? I swear to god, if anything happens to those two sweet angels, I will never, ever, forgive you."

Much to Jessie's shock, Judge Connelly broke down and wept. It was the most emotion she had seen out of him in all the years she had known him. She didn't know what to think, and she glanced at Audrey, who was nodding. And it occurred to her that the judge was just joining the party of people who'd had their hearts broken by his son.

"I just loved him so much, I only wanted him to be happy, and he turned out so wrong—" Judge Connelly broke down completely.

"It's about time," Audrey said to her husband. "Now you have to make it right."

"I'm sorry," Judge Connelly said to Jessie. His eyes were watery and his chin quivered. "I'm sorry for everything my son put you through and I'm sorry I didn't let go of him sooner. I promise I'll make it right. I'll never interfere with you and the girls again."

Jessie studied his face for a few moments. She believed him. She reached out and took his hand in hers. She squeezed his fingers and said, "All right, let's find our girls."

Chapter 33

Jessie and Zach ran back to his house, with Rufus bringing up the rear, to check and make sure the girls hadn't found an unlocked window or door and were even now hunkered down in his house, waiting for him to show up. Jessie silently prayed that this was the case but as they searched it became clear that the girls hadn't been there.

The judge and Audrey stayed at Jessie's house on the chance that the girls might arrive home on their own. Jessie marveled at how the crisis had brought the two families together and she desperately hoped that it lasted, especially when they found the girls, because they would find the girls. She refused to believe anything else.

Standing in Zach's living room, she saw the pictures of Zach and Rufus on the wall and then it hit her. The brewery. The girls knew that Zach worked at the brewery. Would they have gone there if they didn't find him at home? It was a hunch but it was all she had.

"Zach, I have an idea," she said.

He turned to look at her and the desperate hope in his gaze made her heart hurt. He was just as terrified for her girls as she was. It hit her then like a punch to the chest. Oh, how she loved this man.

"What is it?" he asked. "Because I'll do anything to find them. I'm three seconds shy of seeing if I can hire the National Guard and a search helicopter."

"The brewery," she said. "They know you work there, do you think—?"

"Let's go!" Zach grabbed her hand and his keys and dashed outside to his truck. Not to be left out of the search, Rufus followed and tried to jump into the truck when Zach opened the door.

"Okay, Ruf," he said. He lifted the older dog into the backseat. "Maybe you can help us find them."

Jessie climbed into the passenger's seat and Zach turned on the ignition and shot out of his driveway. The brewery was on the outskirts of the neighborhood and Zach drove slowly enough that they could scan the street for any sign of the girls.

There were glimpses of the Maine crew as they knocked on doors and searched. Jessie felt her heart swell up with gratitude. If she hadn't taken the opportunity when Mac offered it to work for Gavin, to make better choices for her family, then she wouldn't have all of these people in her life, including Zach. And if something like this had happened to the girls then, she would have been alone and terrified with no help, no support, and no one who cared.

Zach stopped at a stop sign; he took a moment to scan the street, looking for the girls. His face was tight with worry and he looked like he was on the razor's edge of losing it.

For some reason, this calmed Jessie. Having someone else who cared as much as she did, well, it meant the world to her. He meant the world to her. Jessie reached across the seat and took his hand in hers.

"Zach, I'm so sorry about what I said before," she said.

"It doesn't matter," he said. "Nothing matters but finding the girls."

Jessie let go of his hand and cupped his face. She held his gaze and said, "I love you."

He stared at her, clearly unprepared for declarations of love right now. That was okay. Jessie just needed to say it.

"It's okay if you don't feel—" she began but he interrupted.

"I love you, too," he said. He cupped the back of her head and kissed her forehead.

Jessie's throat got tight with emotion. She forced it back. Now was not the time. There was too much at stake. She forced a smile and said, "I think I've loved you since you rescued Chaos from your roof."

"Yeah?" he asked. A flicker of a smile passed over his lips. "Well, I think I've been in love with you ever since you yelled at me for calling you 'sweetheart' last October at the animal clinic."

Jessie remembered that day. Lord, she had been so wrong about this man. "I'm sorry about that."

"Don't be," he said. "It's a great beginning to our story, which is nowhere near over."

Unable to speak, Jessie nodded and Zach drove on to the brewery. They parked in the empty lot and Zach grabbed a flashlight out of the glove box. He climbed out and opened the back door so Rufus could jump out of the truck.

"Find our girls, Rufus, find Maddie and Gracie," he said.

The dog hurried off with his nose to the snow. Zach switched on his flashlight and took Jessie's hand. He shone the light on the outside of the brewery's building. Jessie held her breath hoping for a glimpse of her girls. There was nothing but large drifts of snow left over from the storm.

Rufus pawed at the wrought-iron gate that led into the brewery courtyard. It was a large space, available for rent, where they held events like Brad and Emma's wedding reception. The gate was closed but not locked and Zach turned the knob and pulled the door open.

Rufus bounded ahead. The old dog seemed to be on a mission and Jessie held her breath, wondering if he could really find the girls. The courtyard was large and dark and

Zach worked his beam of light over the ground like a searchlight.

"The light for the courtyard is in the building," he said. "I'm going to switch it on."

He let go of Jessie's hand and began to stride across the cobblestone patio when Rufus started to bark. He dashed out of the shadows, barked at Jessie, and then disappeared again.

Jessie's heart slammed up into her throat. Had he found them? Zach turned his flashlight onto the area where Rufus had disappeared and Jessie caught a glimpse of purple and blue. The girls' coats!

"Gracie! Maddie!" she cried.

Rufus barked some more and as one, Jessie and Zach made for the spot where the dog stood, wagging. Jessie had almost reached the dog when she heard a quiet voice, shaking with shivers, cry out, "Momma!"

She and Zach ran, dodging the wrought-iron tables and chairs scattered about the patio. They approached a small nook built into the courtyard as a bench seat in the summer. Zach's light bounced but in that dancing light, Jessie saw the sleepy faces of her two little girls. Oh, god, they had been asleep out in the cold. If Rufus hadn't sniffed them out they might never have heard them calling their names.

Rufus was shoving his nose up against them and wagging his tail. Jessie didn't slow down but reached out and snatched up both girls, hugging them to her as if she could absorb them right back inside of her where she knew they would always be safe and never come to harm.

"Oh, my god, oh, my god, oh, my god, I was so scared," she cried. "Are you okay? Are you freezing? Are you hurt? What were you thinking? How could you have wandered off like this?"

"Yeoooow!" A howl sounded from one of the girls' jackets and Jessie loosened her hold.

"Momma, you're crushing Chaos," Gracie said.

Tears were coursing down Jessie's cheeks but somehow this made her laugh. Zach reached around her to hug both of the girls and Jessie. She heard him draw a shaky breath and then he let them go.

"Good boy, Rufus," he said, his voice gruff, as he patted the dog. "You found them, buddy."

Zach stepped back and hurried over to the door that led inside to the brewery. He unlocked it, reached inside, and flicked on the lights that illuminated the courtyard.

Jessie turned back to the girls and saw them blink against the sudden burst of bright light. Their cheeks were pink and they looked frozen. Judging by their spiky lashes, Jessie guessed there had been some crying involved.

Zach came back over and knelt beside Jessie. He studied the girls' faces and then looked at Jessie. "Cold but okay."

She nodded and leaned against him, feeling weak with relief. She closed her eyes for just a second and embraced her gratitude. Then she turned back to the girls. Her face must have reflected her unhappiness because both girls looked wary.

Maddie, in a preemptive strike, threw her arms about Jessie's neck and put her head on her shoulder and said, "We are so sorry, Momma. We just wanted to find Zach. We didn't want him to leave us like Dad did."

Ouch! Jessie clutched her close. "I know. But you know you are never ever to leave the house without telling me, especially at night."

"Are you mad at us, Zach?" Gracie asked. She looked at him as if afraid they'd lost him for good over this.

Zach opened his arms to her. She moved in sideways, so that Chaos, whose head was poking out of her collar, didn't get crushed.

"I'm not mad," he said. He glanced at Jessie as if to see if this was okay. She gave him a slight nod. "But I don't think I have ever been so scared in my life. Please don't ever do this to me again."

"We won't," Gracie promised.

"Is it because you love us?" Maddie asked. "Is that why you were scared?"

Jessie felt her stomach clench. She and Zach had only

just admitted their feelings to each other and kids could be a game changer. Maybe he didn't feel that way, but then again he seemed as upset as she was. Oh, lord, what would she do if he didn't love the girls the way they clearly loved him?

"Yes," Zach said. His voice was definitive. "I love you all very much. If something were to happen to any of my girls, well, I can't even think about it."

"So, we're like family?" Gracie asked. She was staring at Zach wide-eyed as if willing him to answer her the way she wanted.

Zach gave Jessie a quick glance but then answered without her input. "No, not *like* family," he said. Gracie slumped a little but Zach tipped her little chin up until she was looking at him again. "We *are* family."

Then he glanced at Jessie and she knew that since they'd admitted their feelings to each other, everything had changed between them. Zach had been just as frantic to find the girls as she had. It was the first time as a parent she'd had someone who shared her worry and fear. If she hadn't been desperately in love with Zach before, she would be now. Zach held her gaze and said, "And you never have to worry, because I am *never* going to leave you."

Zach meant it, all the way to his squishy middle. He couldn't love these girls any more if they were his own and he would protect them with everything that he had.

"Come on, let's get you home," he said.

Zach and Jessie bundled the two girls into the backseat of the truck with Rufus. He wedged himself between them as if to watch over them and Chaos. Zach paused to rub the dog's ears. This old man had certainly proven that every dog has his day and Zach would be forever grateful to him for helping find the girls.

It was a short ride to Jessie's house and the rest of the Maine crew and Chief O'Rourke trickled in as they were called back since the girls had been found. Gavin checked both girls over while Maddie and Gracie told their story.

Worried that their grandfather was going to take Chaos away and that they'd never see Zach again, they had packed up Chaos and crept over to Zach's house to ask him if he'd take Chaos if they had to give him up.

When they discovered Zach wasn't home, they decided to see if he went to the brewery where he worked because they'd heard their mom say he worked nights. Jessie exchanged a shrug with Zach. She clearly had no recollection of saying that but it just proved that kids were always listening even when adults weren't listening to themselves.

Zach saw Judge Connelly and his wife across the room but he was so angry he hadn't been able to make himself greet them. He noticed the girls didn't run over to the old man either. As far as he was concerned they never needed to see him again.

"Are they okay?" Zach asked Gavin. "No signs of frostbite or hypothermia?"

"No, they're cold but there's no sign of permanent damage," Gavin said. He had examined the girls' fingers and toes, their heart rates, breathing, the pupils of their eyes, all of it. "They'll be just fine."

He took Chaos out of Grace's arms and gave him a once-over as well. Chaos had been in Gracie's coat the whole time so he had fared the best out of them all.

Gina made herself at home in Jessie's kitchen and the feisty redheaded barista gave each of the girls a steaming mug of cocoa. For the adults, it was coffee with a healthy shot of Bailey's in it.

Zach poured his down his throat, hoping for it to calm down the frantic pulse that still pounded through his veins. It warmed him up but it didn't help his nerves. He was pretty sure he was suffering from post-traumatic stress disorder. If anything had happened to the girls . . . he couldn't even think it. He felt as if his world would have ceased to have meaning.

He stepped back when he felt his eyes get damp. Everything was going to be all right. He didn't need to make a scene now. He saw the Connellys move forward.

He felt his hackles rise. He didn't want the judge anywhere near the girls.

Sam, who was standing beside him, put his hand on Zach's arm, holding him back.

"Like it or not, they are the girls' grandparents," he said.

"Not," Zach said. "I like it not." He moved so he was hovering nearby, ready to mitigate any damage the old man might do.

"Girls," Judge Connelly said as he knelt down in front of them. "I owe you an apology."

Audrey stood behind him, her gaze on her precious granddaughters as if holding her breath that all would be well.

"I was wrong about your cat and your friend Zach," he said. "I promise I won't take away your cat or your . . . friend." His wife squeezed his shoulder and he took a breath and asked, "Can you forgive me?"

The girls exchanged a look and then they both stepped forward and hugged the old man. Zach tried not to be moved by the sight of it, but as the old guy wept, it was hard if not impossible to hold on to his anger.

The girls let him go with gentle pats on his bald head and some advice.

"It's okay, Grandpa, but don't do it again," Maddie said. She wagged her finger at him and Zach had to squash the urge to laugh. She was so like her mother.

"And you owe Mom an apology, too," Gracie said.

"You're right, absolutely," Judge Connelly agreed.

The girls moved into their grandmother's arms as the judge turned to face Jessie. Zach glanced over his shoulder. The Maine crew, never the sort to miss a dramatic moment, were all sipping their mugs of coffee and Bailey's watching Jessie and the judge as if it was the final episode of a Netflix series they'd been binge watching.

Zach turned toward them and waved his arms, and said, "They're having a moment. A little privacy please?"

There were grunts and groans but the entire crew

backed away. Jillian was putting together some snacks on the counter and they all went to graze while they awaited the outcome of the judge and Jessie's talk. Zach knew the boys were staying on hand to toss the old man if need be.

Zach watched from a distance, knowing this was for the best. He didn't want to end up doing prison time for assaulting a judge. But even from where he stood, he could hear the judge apologize for how his son had mistreated Jessie and for not stepping up and helping her out earlier in their marriage.

He was not surprised when he saw Jessie take the judge's hands in hers and tell him he was forgiven. Jessie had a big heart. He'd known that from the moment she'd peered down at him in a drift of snow to see if he was okay.

Zach rocked on his feet. Now he knew what was making him crazy. He hadn't touched her since they'd found the girls. He wanted to hug her, hold her, kiss her, and squeeze her. Even more than that he wanted everyone to go away, so they could tuck the girls in where they were safe and sound, under his watch and his protection, and then he wanted to be with his woman, because, yes, Jessie was his. She'd told him she loved him; there was no going back now.

He watched as Jessie and the judge moved to the far corner of the room. The had a whispered conversation with Jessie looking rather intense. The judge nodded, reluctantly at first, but then with more enthusiasm. He took a paper from Jessie, frowning at it through the reading glasses he perched on the end of his nose. Then he took his phone out of his pocket and placed a call. Jessie grinned and then called over the girls.

Zach took a step forward to join her and find out what was going on, but Jessie saw him and she shook her head. She held up her hand indicating he should stay where he was. Zach wanted to protest. Being left out made him feel as if everything they'd just been through was a lie and, damn it, it hurt.

He watched as Jessie knelt down before the girls. She whispered something to them and they both nodded eagerly. Maddie glanced from her mother to Zach and gave him a mischievous wink. Gracie did the same but instead of winking she smiled a bright, beautiful smile. Zach felt his hurt ease.

The judge ended his call and leaned close to Jessie to whisper something in her ear before handing her the paper she'd given him. Jessie turned toward Zach. Before he could figure out what to do or how to feel, the three women who were the most precious beings in his world stopped in front of him and Jessie handed him the paper. It was the marriage license form that Zach had given her the other day.

Zach didn't get a chance to examine it as both girls latched onto his hands with Maddie holding the hand that held the paper. Jessie took her daughters' other hands and the four of them stood in a small circle, shutting out the rest of the world.

Jessie's eyes were bright and her breath was coming in nervous gasps. She cleared her throat and swung her daughters' hands and then she looked at Zach, her blue eyes full of nervous excitement as they latched onto his, and she said, "Zach, the girls and I have talked it over and if your offer to marry us still stands, we'd like to say yes."

Chapter 34

It was a rare thing for Zach to be speechless. Right now, he couldn't remember how to make sound, never mind speak. Luckily, Maddie was there with a nudge.

She hopped up and down and pulled on his arm. "Well, what do you say? Don't you want to be my dad for reals?"

"Mine, too," Gracie added, looking at him with her shy smile and all the hope in the world shining in her eyes.

Zach dropped to his knees on a choking noise that he was pretty sure was a sob and pulled the girls into a hug so he could bury his face in their soft honey blonde curls. Then he glanced up at Jessie, who was biting her lip, looking nervous and overwrought. He let go of the girls and tugged Jessie down to her knees, too.

When she was kneeling in front of him, he cupped her face in his hands and kissed her with all of the love in his heart. When he pulled back, he realized it wasn't just Jessie's tears dampening his face. He wiped the moisture off her face and then his own.

"We seem to be leaking," he said. Jessie chuckled in that throaty way she had that drove him crazy.

"So, is that a yes?" she asked.

"Yes," he said. "Yes, I'll marry you." He opened his arms wide and pulled the girls and Jessie into a group hug. "All three of you."

His three ladies hugged him tight, and Zach thought his heart might explode right out of his chest. In that moment, he knew that he wasn't going to wait a day, a week, or a month to marry this woman and her daughters, oh, no, this wedding was happening right now.

He pulled out of the hug, looked at his women, and said, "Give me one hour."

"What?" Jessie asked.

Zach pulled her to her feet and kissed her forehead. "One hour."

"For what?" Jessie asked.

"To make you my wife," he said. Then he turned toward his Maine crew and announced, "People, we have a mission."

Technically, it was an hour and fifteen minutes, almost nine o'clock, before the Maine crew arrived back at the house. This had given Jessie time to bathe both girls and take a quick shower herself. She had no idea what Zach was planning, shocker, but she figured she'd better be prepared for anything.

Mac arrived first with her aunts in tow. They had a garment bag and they took Jessie by the hand and dragged her upstairs.

More of the girls arrived and Jessie soon found herself in her bedroom surrounded by Carly, Jillian, Gina, Emma, Mac, the aunts, and her girls.

"Okay, let's show her and see what she says," Aunt Charlotte said.

"She's going to say yes, why wouldn't she?" Aunt Sarah asked.

"Because a bridal gown is a very particular thing," Aunt Charlotte said.

"I know," Aunt Sarah said. "But it should never be more important than the vows two people make to each other."

"Agreed," Aunt Charlotte said. "Maybe you should tell her about the dress."

Jessie watched the two silver-haired ladies talking and found herself more than a little curious about what was happening. Judging by the faces of the rest of the women in the room, she wasn't alone.

"I was almost married once," Aunt Sarah said. She glanced at Jessie. Her usual stern demeanor softened as her eyes misted with memories. "He was so handsome and charming. I about fainted every time I saw him in uniform. His name was Captain Stuart Stovall. He was a big, blonde hunk of a man with solid pecs, a lot like your Zach, actually."

Jessie felt her heart beat hard and she held her breath. This sounded like lost love. She didn't like where this story was going, not at all.

"I've never heard of him," Mac said. She looked at her aunt in surprise tinged with a bit of hurt. "Why didn't you ever mention him to me?"

"Because when you've had true love and lost it, it hurts just as much fifty-five years later as it did the day you were told he had died in combat," Aunt Sarah said.

Aunt Sarah glanced down at the garment bag in her hands. Jessie watched as a tear splashed onto the bag and she felt her throat tighten into a hard knot. Poor Aunt Sarah; she couldn't imagine how she would feel if she lost Zach, but she suspected she would mourn him just as much as Aunt Sarah did her Captain Stovall.

Aunt Charlotte helped her sister sit on the edge of the bed and she sat beside her and put an arm around her shoulders. Since Aunt Sarah was not very touchy-feely, allowing her sister to comfort her showed how upset she actually was. Aunt Sarah glanced up at Jessie.

"He asked me to elope with him the night before he shipped out to Vietnam in nineteen sixty-two, but I said I wanted to wait until he came back. The war wasn't underway as yet, and I was sure he'd be back. I wanted a big wedding, a grand to-do, a day where I got to be a princess, so even though he was the love of my life, I chose to wait, spending my time planning our giant wedding so I could marry him the minute he returned to Bluff Point."

She stared out the window, her gaze cloudy with memories. When she turned back to Jessie, her face was a stark picture of ultimate loss.

"But Stuart never came home. He was killed in an ambush while training South Vietnamese soldiers."

Jessie knew what Aunt Sarah was trying to tell her. When the chance to be with the one you love arrives, do not hesitate. She nodded to let her know the message was received.

"I am so sorry, Aunt Sarah," Mac said. She stepped close to her aunt and hugged her tight.

Aunt Sarah permitted it for a moment but not being a hugger by nature, she waved her off pretty quickly.

"Thank you, now stand back or you'll wrinkle the dress," Aunt Sarah said. She rose from where she'd been sitting and unzipped the garment bag. "You can wear whatever you like, Jessie, but since we seem to be about the same size, and have the same taste in men, I thought you might want to wear the dress I would have worn if my Stuart had made it home to me."

Jessie's eyes went wide. She didn't know what to say. The white froth of tulle and satin that Aunt Sarah pulled from the bag was stunning. Three inches of handmade lace decorated the hem of the tea-length gown that poofed out at the waist from the fitted bodice with the sweetheart neckline with cap sleeves made of the same lace as the hem. It looked very Jackie Kennedy and Jessie loved it.

"Oh, Aunt Sarah, it's beautiful," Jessie gasped. She ran a hand over the satin. It was in perfect condition. "I don't know what to say."

"Well, it's quite simple, isn't it?" Aunt Sarah asked. "Yes or no, although if you say no, you should say no thank you, as it's politer that way."

"I don't want to say no," Jessie said. She turned to look at Mac. "But shouldn't you offer this dress to Mac for her wedding? I mean, it's a family heirloom."

Mac looked at her with wide eyes and a mischievous smile, "Am I getting married?"

"Well, I just assumed . . . you and Gavin . . . uh," Jessie stammered, suddenly aware of all the inquisitive stares in the room. Clearly, she had just asked what everyone was thinking.

"Yes, do tell us, Mac, are you and Gavin going to tie the knot?" Carly asked.

"If you're asking me if he's asked me to marry him, the answer is no," Mac said. "As far as I know, you and James are the only engaged couple—well, except for Zach and Jessie but they seem to be skipping over the engagement part."

Everyone was quiet for a moment and then Maddie looked at her older sister and whispered, not in her indoor voice, "Being a grown-up is complicated."

Gracie nodded, causing the women to laugh. The tense moment was broken and Mac looped her arm through Jessie's.

"I would be happy to have you wear my aunt's dress," Mac said. "And I know she would be, too. That being said, if you have something else you'd rather—"

"No!" Jessie said. She glanced at Aunt Sarah and gave her a shy smile. "I would be honored to wear your dress."

Aunt Sarah gave her a nod and the next thing she knew Jessie was being primped, plucked, and polished within an inch of her life while the women fluttered around her doing their own hair and makeup, chatting and laughing and complimenting each other.

Jessie marveled at the warm teasing affection that filled the room. Never in all her life had she been a part of something like this, and she loved it, oh, she really loved it.

Emma did her makeup, Jillian styled her hair, and Carly dressed her while Gina went on shoe recon, looking through Jessie's closet for something to match her dress. Audrey and the aunts took over dressing the girls in their room. Audrey had bought them special dresses for Valentine's Day, which she had rushed home to get, happy to give them to the girls for the wedding. The judge had used all of his influence and connections to rouse the municipal clerk, Kelly Constantine, to file the marriage license application and produce a license for Zach and Jessie. This wedding was turning into quite the family affair.

When the girls returned to Jessie's room, their honey blonde hair was styled in ringlets with sparkly bows fastened on the crowns of their heads. Their matching dresses were in the palest shade of blue velvet with a darker blue satin ribbon along the hem.

"Momma, look!" the girls cried and they twirled in their dresses, watching the skirts billow around them as they giggled. "You try it, Momma!"

Jessie rose from her seat and twirled on the low-heeled white shoes Gina had found, causing her girls to laugh and clap. She had to admit, Aunt Sarah knew what she was about. Jessie felt like a princess in this dress. She ran a hand over the satin skirt and offered up a promise to Captain Stovall that she would always keep an eye on Aunt Sarah for him, and she would love Zach as much as Sarah had loved her Stuart.

A knock sounded on her bedroom door, and Gavin called through the door, "What is going on in there? Are you ladies ready or what?"

"Almost," Mac cried.

She crossed the room and opened the door a crack. Gavin took advantage and pushed the door open a bit wider and made a grab for her. Mac was in a pretty copper-colored dress and she'd done her hair up in a twist.

Gavin growled when he saw her and then pulled her close and kissed her, seeming to forget there were several women in the room watching him. When they finally came up for air, Mac looked a bit dizzy and her hair was mussed.

"Just so you know," he said. "All this mad wedding prep has given me a great idea."

"Oh, really?" Mac asked. "And what is that?"

"I can't tell you right now," he said. He straightened the dark gray necktie that he wore with a white dress shirt under a black suit. "It would ruin the surprise, but FYI, you should practice saying the word 'yes' often."

The grin Mac sent him was blinding. "I think I can handle that."

Gavin looked elated and went to kiss her again, but Emma stepped in between them and put her hand over his puckered lips.

"Easy there, baby brother," she said. "Was there a reason you're here other than to paw at my friend?"

"Yes, there was," he said. He glanced around the room until his gaze found Jessie. Then he gave a low whistle and said, "Zach is going to have a heart attack." He saw Maddie and Gracie and grinned and added, "A triple heart attack. You three are beautiful."

The girls blushed and giggled and Jessie said, "Thank you."

"Just speaking the truth," he said. Then he opened the door wide and gestured behind him. "Jessie, if you're ready, Zach is waiting for you."

The nerves, when they hit, were like being blindsided by a train. Suddenly, her hands were sweaty, her legs felt like jelly, and she couldn't breathe. This was it. Jessie was about to marry Zachary Caine. This was crazy, right?

Aunt Sarah walked past her and paused to squeeze Jessie's hand in hers. It was exactly what Jessie needed to be reminded to live in the moment.

"Okay," Jessie said to Gavin. "I'm ready."

He gave her a nod and stepped out of the room to the hallway. The women filed out, looking like a flock of pretty feathered birds, from Emma's sweet maternity dress in aqua to Jillian's sleek purple number, with Carly's bright red dress—she always wore red for James—and Gina's emerald green curve-hugging chemise.

The aunts wore dresses as well but they were in muted shades of pewter for Aunt Sarah and burgundy for Aunt Charlotte. Mac was the last to go and Jessie watched Gavin extend his arm to help her down the stairs. Mac sent her a wide warm smile, as she took Gavin's arm and they started down.

Who would have thought, Jessie marveled, that Mackenzie Harris and all of her friends would be Jessie's friends one day? That Jessie would, in fact, be marrying one of Mac's friends. It was so unexpected and so wonderful and so lovely, she felt her throat get tight with emotion. She tried to swallow it down but it hurt.

"Are you okay, Momma?" Gracie asked.

Jessie reached out and hugged her girls close. "Never better, and you?"

"Never better," both girls echoed her.

Maddie hurried to the top of the steps and grabbed a big bunch of flowers out of a white wicker basket. It was a ribbon-wrapped bouquet of blue hydrangea and crème roses.

"Zach told us to give you this when you came downstairs," Maddie said. "And he got us each one, too."

She hurried back to the basket and took out two smaller bouquets of the same flowers, one of which she handed to her sister. Jessie looked at her girls in their matching dresses and hairstyles, holding their flowers in their small hands, and felt her tears well up to surface again. Never had she loved anyone as much as she loved these two . . . until Zach.

He had shown her that true love was not only possible, it was hers for the taking if she was brave enough to grab it. Glancing at her two girls with their bright blue eyes sparkling with happiness, she knew this was the best decision she had ever made.

"Are you ready, Momma?" Gracie asked.

"Yes," Jessie said. She looked them both in the eye and asked, "How about you? Are you sure about this?"

"Yes!" they both cried.

"Then let's go," Jessie said.

They walked to the top of the stairs. Maddie raised one finger and gestured for Jessie to wait. Then she hurried halfway down the steps and put her thumb up in the air before dashing back up the steps. Softly the sound of music drifted up from below. It was the traditional wedding march and Jessie felt herself gasp. Truly, was there nothing Zach hadn't thought of?

Maddie looked at her sister. "Remember, you follow

when I'm halfway down, and Momma, you follow when Gracie is halfway down, okay?"

"I know," Gracie said, looking impatient.

"Got it," Jessie said.

Gracie turned her sister to face the stairs and said, "Go."

"Love you, Momma," Maddie said. She began down the steps, clutching her bouquet in one hand and the railing in the other, without acknowledging Jessie's "I love you, too."

"Love you, Momma," Gracie said as she followed her sister, although she did glance back and smile when Jessie said, "I love you, too."

As her girls disappeared down the steps, Jessie smoothed a hand over her skirt. She was nervous but it was a good nervous, an excited life-is-going-to-be-amazing-as-in-orgasms-multiple-from-now-on nervous.

When Gracie was halfway down the steps, Jessie held her bouquet in front of her and started down toward the man of her dreams, Zach, and her new life with him. The joy that filled her up was a beautiful feeling and she planned to remember it and cherish it forever.

Chapter 35

What was taking her so long? Had she changed her mind? Zach couldn't blame her if she had. He wouldn't marry him if he was her, and he couldn't fathom what she saw in him that convinced her this was a good idea. Any woman with a brain in her head would run the other way and never look back. Could he blame her if she did?

And then a tiny white Mary Jane appeared, followed by another. He glanced up and there was Maddie. She was holding the railing in one hand and her bouquet in the other, looking as cute as any five-year-old possibly could. When she grinned at him, he felt his heart do a somersault in his chest. Then she winked and he laughed.

At the bottom of the steps, they exchanged their special high-five greeting but this time he ended it with a kiss on the top of her head. She ran to stand beside Sam who, as a justice of the peace, was waiting to officiate at the makeshift space they had created in front of the fireplace.

Next down was Gracie. She was dressed exactly like her sister, and her big blue eyes looked enormous, as if her two years of maturity over Maddie caused her to understand the seriousness of the evening's event and how life-changing it would be for them all.

When her gaze met Zach's her shy smile snuck out and clobbered him in what was left of his poor old heart. He smiled at her and she let out a breath as if she'd been holding it, afraid he wouldn't be there waiting for her at the bottom of the steps.

Zach knew it was going to take him a lifetime to convince Gracie that she could count on him. It was a commitment he willingly accepted. She paused in front of him and they exchanged their funky handshake and he kissed her on top of the head, too, before he sent her to stand with her sister.

It had been short notice but the men had done their best to transform the downstairs into a wide open space, covered in ribbons and flowers and with enough folding chairs to accommodate everyone in attendance, which included the Maine crew, the aunts, and Judge and Mrs. Connelly, because like it or not they were family now.

For as much as Zach despised Seth Connelly for being a lousy husband and father, he could never begrudge him his marriage to Jessie because without their union, there would be no Gracie and no Maddie and Zach couldn't accept a world without those two imps in it.

That being said, he planned to be the father they hadn't had up to now just as he planned to be the husband Jessie hadn't had. He knew he had a lot to learn about both roles, but he was eager to try and he figured that his enthusiasm made up for his lack of experience.

When he saw the pointy toe of one white shoe appear on the steps above, Zach stopped breathing. A sleek length of leg, another shoe, more leg, followed by the lacy hem of a poufy skirt appeared, and Zach started to feel woozy from the lack of oxygen. A nipped-in waist and two hands, clutching the bouquet he'd had to beg, plead, and pay an exorbitant amount of money to have specially made in a rush job, came into view.

He forced himself to breathe, but his gaze was riveted on his bride. As Jessie came down the stairs, he savored the sight of her. His eyes moved from the swell of female curves he had come to know so well and up to the delicate heart-shaped face he had spent so many hours studying while waiting for the blizzard to pass. Jessie's pretty blue eyes met his and he felt everything in his world shift and lock into place. She was his and he was hers.

She wore no veil, just a pretty hair comb that kept her big bouncy curls in place in her half-up half-down hairdo. His fingers itched to bury themselves in her hair and kiss her senseless, but he resisted. Instead, he extended his hand to her and she shifted her bouquet to one hand and put her fingers in his with the ultimate trust.

Then Zach got down on one knee. He fumbled with his free hand in the pocket of his tuxedo jacket looking for the ring box he had shoved in there. This was important. He had to get this just right. His fingers closed around the velvet box and he pulled it out while never taking his gaze off of her face.

"Jessie, I know we didn't have a conventional start to this relationship," he said. "A few months ago, you thought I was a womanizing player."

Jessie nodded. "And then you rescued my cat."

"And then you and the girls rescued me," he said. He glanced beside him where Rufus sat, in a tuxedo collar and bow tie that matched Zach's. "Well, me and Rufus."

Jessie looked at him with questioning eyes and Zach realized she didn't get it. She didn't know that she had rescued them. So, he told her.

"You and the girls and Chaos rescued us sad boys from loneliness and despair," he said. "From not feeling fully alive."

That made her tip her head to the side and study him. She looked doubtful and he nodded.

"It's true," he said. "I don't think I was really living until the day I looked up out of a drift of snow to see you staring back down at me. You and the girls gave me a reason to wake up every day and you have come to mean everything to me. I don't ever want to go back to those lonely bachelor days ever again."

Zach could hear the *aw*'s behind him. It was nice but it wasn't what he wanted to hear, so he forged on and flipped up the top of the velvet box and looked Jessie in the eye, and said, "Jessie, I love you with all that I have and all that I am, will you marry me?"

Jessie looked completely undone. She didn't even look at the ring, which was a one-carat cushion-cut Harry Winston sparkler, but rather she focused on him.

"Zach," she said his name, drawing it out as if she was drawing out the moment and savoring every nanosecond. "The girls and I were doing all right, getting by, and we would have been fine, but then you showed up in our lives and you changed everything."

Zach couldn't tell if this was the beginning of a rejection or not. He started to sweat. He glanced at Rufus to see how the dog was taking her words. He seemed calm so Zach tried to remain calm, too. It was an effort.

"You brought laughter, joy, music, and shenanigans, lots of shenanigans, into our lives. We hadn't even known what we'd been missing but now, well, I just can't imagine spending my life without you. I love you, too, with all that I have and all that I am and I always will."

Jessie leaned down and kissed him. It was swift and sweet but it gave Zach the courage to stand up and slide the diamond ring onto her finger. He swallowed down the knot of emotion in his throat. Then he hugged her close while surreptitiously patting his other pocket for their wedding rings. They were there. All systems go.

He held out his arm to Jessie and she placed her hand on his elbow. Together they made their way to Sam, who was standing there grinning, obviously delighted to be the officiant at one of his oldest friend's weddings.

The vows were simple and straightforward but Sam managed to work the girls in, too, asking them to vow to watch over the union of these two people and to help them be a loving family all the days of their lives. Zach had to bite his cheek twice to keep from bawling. Although, when he glanced around the room, there wasn't a dry eye in the house and he wondered why he'd bothered. Even Cooper, who had come back for the ceremony and was still wearing his chief of police uniform, looked choked up.

When Sam pronounced them man and wife, Zach let out a whoop and a fist pump that made everyone laugh. Then he pulled Jessie into his arms and kissed her—thoroughly.

The spread, because it had been left up to the men, consisted of a case of champagne, a keg of beer from the brewery, and what looked like all of the appetizers offered at Marty's Pub during happy hour: chicken wings, potato skins, nachos, the works. The cake was a tower of whoopie pies from Jillian's bakery, Making Whoopie, naturally, and it didn't stand a chance under the assault of the Maine crew.

Jessie loved it, all of it, which she told him repeatedly and made Zach love her all the more, which was impressive mostly because he was pretty sure he couldn't love her any more than he already did. Clearly, he'd been wrong.

When Maddie was found asleep in a chair, the party naturally wound down. Zach scooped her up in his arms and let her rest her head on his shoulder, while Jessie tucked Gracie into her side as they waved good night to all of their guests. Together, with Chaos and Rufus underfoot, Zach and Jessie led the girls up to their room.

Zach helped Maddie into her jammies while Jessie assisted Gracie. It was a ridiculously domestic scene and Zach felt his throat get tight yet again as he made a mental promise to love and protect every being in this room. As if reading his mind, Rufus took a flying leap onto Maddie's bed while Chaos curled up on Gracie's.

Zach exchanged a look with Jessie as if to say *Look at how our pack has merged*, and she nodded in understanding, and Zach knew. He knew in that moment what it was like to have his every wish granted. For the first time in his life he belonged, and it was with this family, the family he had made his own.

"Mom, Zach, we need to talk," Maddie said. She ran a hand over her sleepy eyes and sat up in her bed, holding her bespectacled penguin under one arm. Her voice was very serious.

"What is it, honey?" Jessie asked.

Maddie looked at her sister and Gracie ducked her head as she lifted Chaos in one arm and moved to stand beside Maddie's bed. They held hands as if they were putting forth a united front. Zach had a moment of sheer panic that they were going to say they'd changed their minds, that they didn't want Zach and Jessie to be married. They didn't want Zach to be their dad.

The sisters exchanged a glance and he held his breath. When Gracie spoke, her voice was soft but firm. Clearly, this was important to her. "We want to give both Chaos and Rufus a forever home."

"Oh," Jessie said. Her eyebrows lifted in surprise. Zach knew how he felt about it but since they were partners now, he didn't want to weigh in without talking it over.

"They saved our lives," Maddie said. She flopped down on her bed, yanking her sister down beside her. "We were so cold." The two of them feigned shivering, right down to clacking their teeth together. "We cried." They fake sobbed. "We tried to keep warm." They hugged each other close, squishing Chaos in between them.

Zach had to look away to keep from laughing. He felt Jessie's shoulder shake next to his and suspected she was about to lose it, too.

"We would have died!" Gracie proclaimed. Both girls went stiff, with heads lolling and tongues hanging out, all very dramatic. "But Chaos kept us warm."

"And Rufus found us," Maddie said. "We need to give them a home."

Zach looked at Jessie and she gave him a small nod. Zach grinned. They were agreed.

He put one hand on Rufus's head and one under Chaos's chin, and asked, "What do you say, boys? Do you want to stay with us—forever?"

Rufus barked and wagged and Chaos let out a tongue-curling yawn.

Maddie looked from the pets to Zach and Jessie and said, "That means yes."

Jessie laughed and said, "Of course it does."

Zach enfolded the entire crew in a group hug and kissed all of their heads: Rufus, Maddie, Gracie, Jessie, and even Chaos, who did not appreciate the affection at all and bopped him on the nose with his paw, which made Maddie belly laugh.

Gracie gave Zach and Jessie her shy smile and then she said what Zach had been thinking all along. "*Now* we're a family."

"Forever and ever," Maddie agreed.

Zach and Jessie tucked the girls and the pets into bed. Jessie took Zach's hand and led him out into the hallway, closing the girls' door so it was open just enough to allow a sliver of the hallway night-light.

Then she turned toward him, sliding into his arms as she continued to walk backwards toward her room. Zach knew he would never forget the sight of her just like this. Dressed in her fine white dress, leading him to their room after tucking their kids and pets into bed. His life had never been more perfect than it was at this moment.

He lowered his mouth to hers and kissed her, softly and sweetly, and then he said, "I love you, Jessie Caine."

She sighed and her eyes glimmered with happy tears when she said, "I love you, too, forever and ever . . ."

". . . and ever and ever," he finished for her. He used his foot to close the door behind them, because he didn't want to let go of her, Jessie, his wife, his other half, his soul mate, the woman who had against all odds fallen in love with him, and given him everything he'd ever wanted, a family of his own.

Zach was going to spend the rest of his life being worthy of her and the girls and as he hugged her close, he knew just how he wanted to get started. Orgasms multiple.

"Here comes the bride," Melanie Cooper sang as she held a bouquet of multicolored snapdragons in front of her as if she were walking down the aisle.

"Practicing for your own wedding?" Angie DeLaura asked her.

"No, just yours," Mel said, then she smiled. "For now."

They'd been best friends since they were twelve years old, so it was no surprise that Mel would be Angie's maid of honor when Angie and their other childhood friend Tate Harper tied the knot in just one week.

Today, Mel and Angie had left Fairy Tale Cupcakes, the bakery they co-owned, in the capable hands of their employees while they ran around town, finalizing payments to vendors and making sure everything was a go for Angie and Tate's big day. At the moment, they were paying for Angie's flowers, calla lilies with their stems wrapped in aqua and pewter ribbons.

"Annabelle? Hello!" Angie called. She rang the bell on the counter and peered at the back room. "What do you suppose is keeping her?"

"No idea," Mel said. She admired the brilliant yellow petals on a huge sunflower. So pretty.

"Okay, so after we pay the florist, who's next?" Angie asked.

Mel put the snapdragons back in their display bucket and checked her smartphone, where she kept her to-do list updated.

"We need to pay the photographer and the caterer." She glanced at Angie. "Are you really having them make Jell-O? Because 'crème brûlée can never be Jell-O.'"

"'I *have* to be Jell-O,'" Angie said. For emphasis, she tossed her long, curly brown hair over her shoulder.

"*My Best Friend's Wedding*," they said, identifying the movie quotes together, and then laughed.

Since middle school, the three friends, Mel, Angie, and Tate, had shared a love of sweets and movies. Now as adults they tried to stump one another with random movie quotes, and in the case of serving Jell-O at their wedding, Angie had chosen it deliberately. She wanted Tate to know she was his comfort food, his Jell-O, which he had always loved, much to Mel's cordon bleu dismay.

"Do you think we should leave and come back?" Angie asked Mel. "Maybe she's on her coffee break and forgot to lock the door."

"Maybe." Mel frowned. She didn't want to admit she was starting to get a hinky feeling in the pit of her stomach.

Annabelle Martin's flower shop sat in the heart of Old Town Scottsdale. Despite the small size of the space, it was full to bursting with blooms, both real and silk, as Annabelle's talent with flowers was legendary. In Scottsdale, Arizona, a wedding was just not a wedding unless Annabelle did the flowers.

"But even if Annabelle stepped out, why isn't anyone else here? Doesn't she have four assistants?" Mel asked.

Angie nodded and Mel saw her big brown eyes get wide. Mel knew Angie was thinking the same thing that she was. Angie swallowed, and in a soft voice, she said, "Maybe something happened to her?"

They stared at each other for a moment. Over the past

few years, they had suffered the misfortune of stumbling upon several dead bodies. Given that Angie was one week from saying "I do," it would just figure that they would find a body now.

"This can't be happening," Angie said. "Not now."

"Don't panic," Mel said. She blew her blonde bangs off of her forehead. Being a chef, she kept her hair nice and short to keep it out of the food, because nothing said "*Ew*" like finding a hair in your frosting.

"'Don't panic'?" Angie cried, her voice rising up a decibel with each syllable. "Why would I panic? It's only a week until my wedding, you know, the most important day of my life to date."

"Breathe." Mel squeezed Angie's arm as she scooted past her and around the counter. "I'll just check in back and make sure everything is okay."

A curtain was hanging in the doorway to the back room. She knew from being here before that the back room housed all of Annabelle's supplies as well as a kitchenette and her office. It was a tiny space and she had to turn sideways to maneuver through the packed shelves.

Vases of glass, steel, and copper; baskets; ribbons; glass marbles; florist wire in all sizes and colors—all of it was stuffed onto the shelves until they looked as if they'd regurgitate the goods right onto the floor.

Mel squeezed her way past until she cleared the shelves and reached the worktable in back. A couple dozen purple irises were scattered across a sheaf of floral paper, as if someone had just left them out of water and gasping for air.

Annabelle loved flowers; they were her passion. Mel couldn't imagine that she'd have just left these here to rot. Mel felt the short-cropped hair on the back of her neck prickle with unease.

Where was Annabelle? What could have happened to her? Mel closed her eyes for a moment, trying to dredge up the courage to circle the table and see if Annabelle was there, lying on the floor—unconscious, bludgeoned, bloody, bleeding out even as Mel stood there shaking like a fraidy-cat.

"Hello? Annabelle? Are you here?" Mel called.

There was no answer. She opened her eyes. She was just going to have to see for herself. She took a steadying breath and stepped around the worktable. She glanced at the floor. It was bare. The breath she'd been holding burst out of her lungs just as the sound of a toilet flushing broke through the quiet.

Mel whipped around to face the back hallway just as Angie came barreling through the curtain into the back room.

"Any sign of her?" Angie asked.

"Maybe," Mel said. She stared down the hallway, listening to the water running in the bathroom. *Please, please, please, let it be . . .*

"Well, doesn't that just figure?" Annabelle asked as she strode toward them. "It's quiet all morning, and then the second you go to the bathroom, someone shows up."

"You're okay!" Mel cried. Impulsively, she threw herself at Annabelle's big-boned frame and hugged her tight. "You're not dead."

"Oh, honey." Annabelle hugged her back. "You need to calm down, maybe take a vacation or something."

Mel let her go with a nervous laugh. "Ha, you're right. I must be working too hard."

Annabelle fluffed her close-cropped curls and then turned to Angie with a hug and a smile. "And how is our bride? Seven days to go! Are you ready?"

"More than," Angie said. "I'm excited for the wedding, but I'm even more excited to have it over and be Mrs. Tate Harper."

Annabelle clasped her hands over her heart and sighed. "Of all the events I arrange, flowers for weddings are my favorite. Yours aren't here yet, but come on, I'll show you what I just got in."

Annabelle scooped up the irises and put them in water and then led them to the front of the shop. While she and Angie oohed and aahed over some of the fresh flowers, Mel took a moment to get herself together. Clearly, she had some issues if her first thought when Annabelle hadn't been available was that she was dead. Seriously, what was wrong with her?

She had been around an inordinate amount of death over the past few years. She wondered if perhaps it was her own fault. Maybe she found all of these bodies, maybe bad things happened all around her, because she went looking for them. The thought disturbed Mel on a lot of levels.

"Did that daisy do something to offend you?" Annabelle asked.

Mel looked at her questioningly, and Annabelle pointed to Mel's hands, where just the stem and one petal were left of an orange gerbera daisy Mel had been systematically stripping the petals off of without realizing.

Snatching off the last petal, Mel said, "He loves me. Phew!"

Angie looked at her as if she thought Mel was drunk or crazy, or drunk *and* crazy. Mel shrugged. Annabelle gave her a concerned look and took the stem out of her hands and threw it in the trash.

While Angie paid Annabelle for her flowers, Mel picked up the petals and then paced up by the front of the shop. She didn't trust herself not to destroy any of the lovely arrangements and kept her hands in her pockets just in case.

With a wave, they left Annabelle and her flowers to head to the photographer's studio. It was across Scottsdale Road, on a small side street, nestled in among the trendy restaurants and art galleries.

"Okay, what gives?" Angie asked as soon as the door shut behind them.

"What?" Mel asked.

Angie widened her eyes and said, "Come on, you know what. You started shredding flowers in there. What was that all about?"

"Nothing. I just had this random thought," Mel said. "It was silly."

"Good, then you won't mind sharing."

Mel pursed her lips. Angie was a badger. There was no way she was getting out of this.

"Fine, if you must know—"

"I must."

They paused at the corner to wait for the crossing light.

"I just thought it was weird that my first instinct when Annabelle wasn't readily available was that she'd been murdered. I mean, that's weird, right?"

Angie squinted at her. "There's more, isn't there?"

Mel blew out a breath. "Okay, it also occurred to me that maybe, just maybe, the fact that I am always looking for something bad to have happened is what makes it happen."

The light turned and the walk signal lit up. Angie opened her mouth to speak, closed it, then took Mel's arm and pulled her across the street.

Once they stepped onto the curb, she looked at Mel and said, "Now, that is nuts."

"Is it?" Mel asked. "I mean, isn't there a whole philosophy that says whatever you put out there comes back to you?"

"So you think that by putting out thoughts of dead bodies or worst-case scenarios, that's what makes them happen?"

"Yeah . . . maybe . . . no . . . I don't know."

"Listen, we've definitely had some crazy stuff happen to us since we opened the bakery, but don't you think it's because we work in a service industry with a whole lot of different people with all sorts of bad and good things happening in their lives?" Angie asked. "I mean, how many weddings, birthdays, retirement parties, etcetera, have we baked cupcakes for and nothing bad has happened? Quite the opposite, in fact—the person has had the greatest day ever."

She began walking and Mel fell into step beside her.

"You're right," Mel said. "Maybe I just have a little post-traumatic stress going because the bad—when it's bad—is so very bad."

Angie nodded. "I'm sure that's it, but since my wedding is coming up in a matter of days, why don't we just hedge our bets, and you just keep picturing happy things in that head of yours?"

"Like puppies and kittens?"

"Yeah, or go big with unicorns and glitter bombs," Angie suggested.

Mel laughed. Angie was right. She needed to chillax. Probably she was just nervous about the wedding. She was maid of honor, after all, which carried a lot of responsibility. Not that she thought Angie would pull a runner, but it was Mel's job to get her to the church on time, dressed appropriately, and to be prepared to crack some skulls if anyone interfered with her best friend's wedding.

"Okay, glittery unicorns it is," Mel said.

"That's my girl." Angie paused in front of the photographer's studio, pulling out her phone to check the time. Mel glanced over her shoulder and noted that they were right on schedule. Excellent.

Blaise Ione, the photographer, was a friend of Tate's from his days in high school marching band. After graduation, Blaise had gone to art school and lived in New York City for several years, but when his aging mother needed him, he'd come home to Scottsdale to be nearby.

Blaise was a hard-core hipster and wore his short hair bleached white and paired it with his large Andy Warhol glasses, striped skinny pants, and pointy-toed shoes. He was exuberant, enthusiastic, and always made Mel laugh. She knew the wedding was safe in Blaise's hands.

Although it was a small space, Blaise made the most of it with huge portraits decorating the black walls, and midcentury modern furniture that made a statement as well as provided a place to sit. Through the window, Mel studied one of the chairs, which looked to be molded out of cement. The statement she got was, *This is uncomfortable, so move along*, which, knowing Blaise, was exactly what he wanted it to say.

Angie pulled open the door, and a gong sounded somewhere in the back of the space. Leave it to Blaise to have an unconventional door chime.

"Blaise? Hello?" Angie called out.

Mel moved toward the wall to study the portraits. Blaise had done Tate and Angie's engagement pictures and they were spectacular, managing to capture the longtime friendship that had morphed into romantic love between the couple.

Mel's favorite shot had been taken in black-and-white in an old movie theater. In it, Tate and Angie were sharing a bucket of popcorn, the red and white stripes on the bucket the only pop of color in the photo, as they gazed at each other with all the love in their hearts. It made Mel water up every time she saw it.

Oh, and there it was on the wall! Blaise had added it to his display. Mel felt her throat get tight.

"Hey, I didn't know he was going to put that up," Angie said as she joined her. "That's my favorite."

"Mine, too," Mel said. "Wow, it keeps hitting me that in a few days you'll be married to Tate."

"I know, right?" Angie grinned. "Say it again, it makes me dizzy."

"In a few days you'll be married to Tate." Mel laughed and hugged her friend close. "I am so happy for you both."

"Thanks," Angie said. "Man, I can't believe I spent all those years thinking he was in love with you."

"Idiot."

Mel's voice was teasing when she said it, and Angie laughed and said, "Yep."

They sighed and then looked around the studio. There was no sign of Blaise. They glanced at each other and Mel shrugged.

"Blaise, hello," Angie cried out. "It's Angie, your favorite bride."

Silence greeted them. Mel felt the hair on the back of her neck begin to prickle. No, no, no! She wasn't doing that again. She pictured a unicorn prancing through the studio. It didn't really help.

"Probably he's in the bathroom," she said.

"Yeah," Angie agreed. "I'll just poke my head in the back."

"Okay," Mel said. Under her breath, she began to chant, "Unicorns and glitter, unicorns and glitter, come on, unicorns and glitter."

Angie got halfway to the back and turned around. "Come with me."

Mel nodded. She followed Angie to Blaise's office in the back corner. It had no windows into the studio, just a door painted with black chalkboard paint, where people could scrawl messages for him. Several messages in different-colored chalk were there now, including one in bright blue that listed Angie's name and the time. So he had been expecting them.

Angie knocked on the door. There was no answer. She rapped again. Still nothing. She reached down and grasped the handle, turning it and pushing in the door.

The office was a cluttered mess with papers and proof sheets and pop-art tchotchkes littering every surface. A life-size self-portrait of Blaise was on the wall opposite, and Mel almost greeted the picture instead of the man.

"Blaise, hey, are you napping on the job or what?" Angie asked.

Blaise was in his office chair, with his back to them as he faced his very large computer screen. The screen saver was on and the pattern was undulating all over the display. Mel followed it for a second, but then realized that Blaise sitting in front of the computer while the screen saver was on was wrong. So wrong!

"Blaise!" she cried.

She stepped around Angie and into the room to get a look at the photographer. He was sitting upright, staring at the computer with vacant eyes, his lips tinged a faint shade of blue. Mel reached out to touch his hand. It was icy cold. There was no pulse. No rise and fall to his chest.

Blaise Ione was dead.

Ready to find
your next great read?

Let us help.

Visit prh.com/nextread

Penguin
Random
House